THE HUNT

PROJECT PAPER DOLL

THE HUNT

STACEY KADE

HYPERION
NEW YORK

First Edition
1 3 5 7 9 10 8 6 4 2
G475-5664-5-14046

Printed in the United States of America

Library of Congress Cataloging-in-Publication Data
Kade, Stacey.
The hunt/Stacey Kade.—First edition.
    p. cm.—(Project Paper Doll; [2])
Summary: "Sixteen-year-old Ariane Tucker has finally escaped GTX,
the research facility that created her from human and extraterrestrial DNA.
But life on the run is complicated"—Provided by publisher.
ISBN 978-1-4231-5329-0
[1. Genetic engineering—Fiction. 2. Extraterrestrial beings—Fiction.
3. Science fiction.] I. Title.
PZ7.K116463Hu   20143
[Fic]—dc23   2013023993

Reinforced binding

Visit www.hyperionteens.com

To Greg:

Thank you for buying me more chocolate than any writer could ever dream of, for making me smile (usually when I least want to), and for understanding when I forget to bring your pants because the people in my head were talking.

CHAPTER 1

Ariane Tucker

U<small>NTIL</small> I <small>CRAWLED BENEATH THE DESIGNATED</small> D<small>UMPSTER</small> behind the abandoned Linens-N-Things and felt the brush of rough canvas against my fingertips, I really wasn't sure that the emergency bag would be there, as my father had promised.

My first Christmas, I'd been six. It had also been the first time Outside matched the color and sparkle of what I'd seen on television and in my "cultural training" videos in the lab at GTX. The houses in our neighborhood had been decked out with flashing Santas, red-nosed reindeer, and molded plastic Nativity scenes. And through cracks in the blinds, I'd watched people carry in plastic bags full of presents, brightly colored wrapping paper tubes poking through the top.

This strange but wonderful event—so much preparation and fuss over it—called to me in the worst way. I longed to be a part of it. But our living room remained dark and undecorated, the carpeting empty of pine needles and shiny wrapped packages alike, even on Christmas Day. In our house, it was just another day. Worse, even, as my father retreated to his room and didn't come out until the following morning. I was alone. And confused. According to lore, only "naughty" children were punished by an absence of gifts. But I'd done everything I knew to do, followed precisely the Rules my father had given me.

Much later, I understood that it was because my father's true daughter, the original Ariane, had died, and the traditions of the holiday reminded him too much of her. My presence only further highlighted her absence, inflaming a wound that would never quite heal.

Still, it had been the first of many occasions that taught me to understand that my expectations, my hopes, were better kept in check. My father had done his best to be a parent for me (or so I'd believed until recently), but there'd been limits, ones I was usually unaware of until I bumped into them.

This time, though, unlike all those years of dark Christmases, my father had come through. This gift, an emergency bag of supplies, cash, and who knew what else, was exactly where he'd said it would be.

Feeling some measure of tension leave my body, I let out a breath I hadn't realized I'd been holding and promptly choked on the cloud of dirt that rose up in response.

"You okay?" Zane asked quietly. He was pacing nearby, waiting for me. I couldn't see him, but I could hear the scrape of his shoes on the concrete as he moved back and forth, watching for anyone approaching.

It had taken us a little more than two hours to make

our way here from GTX. We'd cut through backyards and taken side streets, doubling back when necessary and keeping to the shadows. But before any of that, we'd had to fight through the overgrown forest preserve that surrounded the GTX campus. Nothing like taking a branch to the face when running full-speed. I'd ended up keeping an arm up to shield myself, and consequently the skin between my wrist and elbow felt shredded, burning as if it were on fire. Zane hadn't fared much better, new cuts and bruises on his face and arms joining those he'd already acquired in the last few days.

I'd expected him to protest or even quit, turning around to head home. Which was, quite frankly, probably the safest place for him. But he'd soldiered on in determined silence. Well, he hadn't said much. He had, however, crashed through the woods like a herd of drunken deer. Stealth training was not something taught in your average school system. But lucky, lucky me, I'd been enrolled in some "special" extracurriculars during my time with my father.

Other parents taught their children how to ride bikes, fish, or bake cookies from the family recipe, but my father had spent countless hours passing along much of the training he'd acquired during his years in Special Forces. It had been, I guess, our thing, our shared interest. Maybe he would have taught his biological daughter, the first Ariane, the same stuff. Maybe not. All I knew was that the day I'd managed to sneak up behind him in the patch of woods near our house where we practiced, I'd never seen him more proud of me.

Until last night.

I shoved that thought away. I wouldn't, couldn't think

about that now. "Yeah, I'm fine," I said to Zane. "One second." I bit my lip, tasting sweat and unpleasant grit, and contemplated my next move. Unfortunately, just because the bag was there didn't mean I could actually get to it. I was already halfway under the Dumpster, trapped between the bottom of the trash receptacle and the concrete beneath it, which meant I had about zero leverage. And I was about ten seconds away from a major freak-out. Dark, confined spaces and I are not friends.

Sweating and keenly aware of the metal ceiling above my head, I strained at the shoulder and managed to grasp a corner of the fabric. But it slipped away before I could get a good-enough grip.

"Damn it," I panted. Though the logical part of my brain knew there was plenty of air, my emotional side was panicking and sucking in oxygen at a far too rapid rate. I could feel dizziness beginning to build.

This would have been so much easier if we could have just moved the stupid Dumpster to reach the bag from the other side. But that meant the shrill squeak of wheels and the rumbling thunder of the empty receptacle moving over the pockmarked and uneven concrete. Not an option on an otherwise quiet night when GTX security was out in force looking for us.

I squirmed closer, a hiss of pain escaping against my will when a particularly sharp bit of rock from the degraded parking lot dug into the abrasions on my forearm.

Zane knelt next to me and tugged at the hem of my lab-issued tunic. "I can get it," he whispered. "Let me."

"What?" I asked, distracted. If I could just release whatever was securing the bag, I wouldn't even have to be under here. I had the ability to move objects without touching them—one of the few perks of my extraterrestrial heritage. The scientists at GTX had played God with a scrap of preserved DNA from the alien entity found at the site of the Roswell incident in 1947, isolating the stem cells and splicing them into a fertilized human egg from a (presumably) willing human donor/surrogate.

I was the result. But it wasn't exactly ideal.

Theoretically, I could lift the whole Dumpster into the air simply by concentrating on it, but my telekinetic abilities were a little unpredictable lately, due to lack of use. So stepping under a heavy metal object that might fall on your head at any second probably wasn't a great idea.

But if I couldn't see what was holding the bag, I couldn't undo it. And just yanking at it would only pull the Dumpster along.

"I can get it," Zane repeated patiently. "My arms are longer than yours."

"No, I can—"

He bent down, his knees suddenly visible at the edge of my vision. "You know, it's okay to accept help every once in a while."

Easy for him to say. I swallowed a frustrated noise. He didn't understand. I'd spent years relying only on myself, trusting only my father (and look at how well that had turned out). I couldn't just stop doing that. I didn't know how. And with Zane, much as I wanted to trust him, much as he'd done nothing to make me doubt him, I could feel the other shoe—an ass-kicking combat boot with a steel toe and a thick tread—hanging above my head, waiting to stomp on me.

Still, retrieving the bag was taking far longer than I wanted. And if Zane thought he could do it faster, all the better.

"Fine," I said, wiggling out. "Be my guest."

I stood up and folded my arms across my chest, watching in the moonlight as Zane stretched his six-foot-four frame out on the concrete and reached under the Dumpster.

It was an ugly but appropriate bit of symmetry that the fate of my future life was tied so closely to an oversize trash can. That's what the last ten years of my life had been—a big load of garbage. Lies told to keep me quiet and compliant.

"Got it," Zane said after an annoyingly short amount of time. That eighteen inches of additional height made a difference, I guess. He'd barely had to stick his head beneath.

He dragged a small but full black duffel out from under the Dumpster until it lay next to him. Shiny metallic strips of duct tape, now twisted and tangled from Zane's efforts, hung off the edges of the bag, like legs of an upside-down spider. From space.

Zane inched out and pushed himself to his feet easily, biceps temporarily straining the sleeves of his green Ashe High lacrosse team T-shirt.

"Thanks," I said grudgingly.

"I told you. Long arms," he said with a shrug, and dusted off his hands. "My superpower." He gave me a tentative smile.

He was . . . joking. Almost like normal.

I blinked, surprised. Well, it was what had passed for normal between us before everything went to hell and he learned I wasn't who—or what—he thought I was. A few hours ago, I wouldn't have thought that anything resembling that state would be possible again.

Relief crashed into me, a heady sensation. "I guess they were out of Sasquatch DNA the day they made me," I shot back. If he could joke, I could joke, right? Humor was a human coping mechanism. I'd used it before, but never about myself to someone else. It was a strange feeling, like stripping naked and waiting to see if people would notice.

But in this case, laughing was a good thing, and I was rewarded by the bright flash of his grin. "Ouch." He rocked back on his heels, clutching at his chest, pretending to be wounded.

Then he stopped abruptly, his hands dropping to his sides.

He was remembering what I'd done to Rachel Jacobs, one of his friends, the other night. I could see the images in quick flashes: Rachel coughing and choking at the pool party, grabbing at her chest as her heart fought against my control.

I hadn't killed her, but I'd come awfully close. And the shock and fear he'd felt at what I'd done was still close to the surface. And tied to his thoughts of me.

I stiffened.

"Sorry," he murmured, looking away.

I shook my head. "It's not your fault," I made myself say over the sudden lump in my throat. And it wasn't. He hadn't invented that scenario. I'd done it. For the right reasons, maybe, but it had gotten swiftly out of hand. Never mind that I hadn't killed her or permanently injured her, even when her own grandfather, Dr. Jacobs, had later pushed me to do so.

I couldn't—wouldn't—hold Zane's reactions against him. How could anyone be expected to respond to this messed-up situation with equanimity?

So, yeah. I guess we had a ways to go yet before "normal."

I knelt next to the bag and tugged at the zipper with shaking hands. But it was stuck.

Without a word, Zane bent down and held the canvas sides steady. And this time when I tried, the zipper slid along the track smoothly.

Before I could thank him, a tight roll of cash, bound with a rubber band, slipped out of the opening and bounced to a stop near Zane's shoe.

A quick glimpse in the bag showed there were a half-dozen identical bundles, right at the top.

Whoa.

Zane gave a low whistle. "I've got to start checking under more trash bins." He picked up the bundle that had rolled free, looking at it more closely. "These are hundreds, Ariane. That means—"

"Thousands," I managed through my shock. When my adoptive father had told me he'd been adding to the emergency cash, I'd never dreamed he'd meant this much. "It's probably his life savings," I said, fighting the rise of conflicting emotions: a bitter sadness and fury.

Mark Tucker had raised me as his daughter for the last decade. But he'd been working for GTX, the corporation that had created me, the whole time. I thought I'd escaped years ago. In reality, they'd just given me a bigger cage, so to speak, and put Mark in charge of monitoring my reactions to the world Outside. It had all been part of a larger plan, wrapped up in lies and deceit.

Beneath the cash, a flash of white caught my eye. I shifted the money carefully to one side, revealing a thin, square envelope.

My father's bold but neat print was on the front: IF I AM NOT WITH YOU.

My stomach gave an uncomfortable lurch as I plucked the envelope out, pinching it between my fingertips. A letter from Mark? I didn't want to read it. He'd first told me about the emergency bag a few years ago. That meant the contents of this letter would likely be an excruciating rehash of everything I'd learned in the last twenty-four hours, a detailed play-by-play of the worst betrayal I could have possibly imagined. No, thank you.

"Hey, Ariane? There are U.S. and Canadian passports in here. And one of those reloadable credit cards." Zane held them up and squinted. "For a Talia Torv."

He flipped to the photo page in the U.S. passport. "She looks an awful lot like you," he said, holding it up so I could see.

It was, in fact, a picture of me. Last year's school photo.

"Except," he said, frowning, "Talia's eighteen, almost nineteen."

Of course she was. I laughed in a moment of near giddiness.

"No one will believe that," Zane said, his handsome face troubled. "You barely look your age."

He was right. My less-than-average height and preternatural thinness made me look younger than sixteen. My A-cup chest wasn't doing me any favors either.

I shook my head. "It won't matter. If the documents are good"—and knowing my father's relentless attention to detail, they were—"no one will question them." Which meant, I could live on my own. Eighteen was the magic number. And with all that cash . . .

For the first time, I felt a rush of hope, lifting the weight of despair and panic I'd been carrying around. Maybe, just maybe, this would work. Maybe I could leave Wingate and start a life, a real life somewhere.

I glanced at Zane on the other side of the bag, where he was busily cataloging the rest of its contents. And maybe I wouldn't have to be alone. We were supposed to be heading to his mother's house in the Chicago suburbs, assuming we could get out of town. I couldn't stay there with him, obviously; it would be the first place GTX would look. But maybe I wouldn't have to go too far. The idea brought an unfamiliar fluttering warmth to my chest. I could make a home for myself, a life. And he could perhaps be a part of it. After all, he was still with me, a miracle if I'd ever seen one. He'd come for me at GTX and stuck by my side, even after everything I'd done.

"There are, uh, clothes in here," Zane said, restacking the items with a haste that suggested he'd discovered something personal.

Great. My face heated. Bra? Underwear? New ones or, oh God, tattered ones I hadn't even noticed were missing from the laundry? I didn't even want to think about it. It was silly to be embarrassed about something like that, I guess, considering. But I was still human. At least partially.

Zane cleared his throat. "And keys. This one looks like an old car key." He held it up, a bright orange plastic tag attached.

"Let me see." I took the key ring for a closer inspection. The plastic tag advertised U-Store-It. The first key was just a plain silver, but it was clearly too big to be for a house or a building. A smaller gold key hung below it on the ring. "Yeah, I think you're right." My father really had prepared for every contingency. Getting out of Wingate undetected would be impossible without a clean vehicle—one unassociated with me or my father.

"So, then, where's the car?" Zane asked.

That was an excellent question. The parking lot in front of the building was completely empty. I'd checked it before sliding under the Dumpster. And there certainly weren't any vehicles back here. An anemic patch of forest with massively overgrown weeds ran up to—and now over—the edge of the concrete behind the abandoned building. "I don't know." I took a closer look at the key ring. "Possibly in a storage locker."

But at which facility? There were probably a half dozen in and around Wingate, and at least a couple of them had to be U-Store-Its. At least from what I could recall. Not that I'd ever paid that much attention. Who pays attention to storage lockers?

The trouble was, we didn't have time to waste checking them out, especially without a car to get us there.

"Maybe there's something in there?" He nodded at the envelope that I was clutching.

I glanced down at the letter, having almost forgotten it was in my hand. "Maybe." But I still didn't want to open it.

He hesitated, then asked, "Do you want me to—"

I shook my head. "No, I'll do it." He was right. If there was something in here about the car, we needed to know. With GTX nipping at our heels, getting a vehicle had to be our top priority. Besides, avoiding the letter was foolish, emotional—my human side holding sway over the rest of me. Because the fact was, even if the letter was years old, it might yet contain useful information mixed in among all the eviscerating details I'd learned in the last day.

I handed Zane the keys and then, steeling myself, I slipped my finger beneath the flap on the envelope and tore it open, the ripping noise sounding absurdly loud in the post-midnight air.

"Your dad is kind of a badass. You know that, right?" Zane said, repacking the bag carefully.

I didn't respond, my attention caught by my name in my father's painfully familiar handwriting.

Ariane—

I have to assume that, if you're reading this, our situation has been compromised and I'm either dead or unable to help you. I don't know how much I had a chance to tell you, and I'm sorry for the abruptness of what you're about to read.

I was surprised to find tears stinging my eyes. His weariness and regret permeated the page.

First, you are not free. You never were. GTX and Dr. Jacobs have known where you were the entire time. You'll never know how sorry I am for my role in this deception. Please know that I did it for reasons that seemed honorable at the time.

His daughter. The original Ariane. Jacobs had promised the latest experimental treatment for her cancer in exchange for my father taking on the job of looking after me. She'd died anyway, but Mark had stayed on, hoping the research they were doing with my "amazing" immune system would save other children from the same fate.

I wanted to hate my father for it. He'd loved his daughter

more than he'd loved me. But then again, he wasn't supposed to care about me at all. I was a job. And yet, this bag was full of proof that I was more than that to him. I was caught between gratitude and the bitter pinch of self-pity. It's hard to know you'll never be enough just because you're not someone else.

"You okay?" Zane asked.

"Yeah." I wiped under my eyes. "I just—" I stopped, my attention caught by a chilling phrase that leapt out from the next paragraph.

Second, there's a tracking chip embedded on the right side of your T4 vertebrae.

My head whirled, trying to rearrange the squiggles into other words with a different meaning. But the sentence remained.

It's an older model, with very short range. But don't take the risk; disable it. According to my research, demagnetizing it should work. You'll find what you need in the bag.

"Ariane?" Zane sounded alarmed. "What's wrong? You look—"

"Is there a magnet in there?" I asked in a strangled voice. A tracking chip. It made a sort of sick and horrible sense— if my father had lost control over me during my years of "freedom" and I'd bolted, GTX and Dr. Jacobs would have needed a way to find me and bring me in. I hadn't even attempted to run, though. I'd believed their ruse.

"A what?" Zane frowned up at me.

I swallowed hard, trying to keep my panic under control. "A magnet, probably a big one." My father had never mentioned, never even hinted at such a thing, not even during our good-bye, which would have seemed like an opportune time to mention something like GTX spyware in my spine. Had it been active this whole time? Or was it something they could turn on and off at will? Were they on their way here right now?

I felt ill.

Zane rummaged deeper in the bag, beneath the clothes. "This?" He produced a flat metal circle about the size my palm.

I nodded, feeling my neck creak with tension.

"What's going on?" Zane asked warily.

"I have . . . there's a tracking device," I said.

He dropped the magnet and yanked his hands away from the bag.

"No." I gave a harsh, humorless laugh. "Not in the bag. In me."

His eyes widened, but he nodded. "What do we do?"

We. What had I done to deserve him? He should have been home right now, reviewing lacrosse plays and studying for chemistry.

"I can do it myself," I said, though I wasn't quite sure how without some significant contortions or lying on the ground, neither of which seemed like a good idea when time was of the essence.

But Zane rallied, standing up with a determined expression and the magnet in hand.

I turned away so he wouldn't see the deeply pathetic amount of gratitude I was feeling.

"Here." I shed my father's jacket and reached up to the back of my neck to point to where the last cervical vertebrae jutted out slightly. "Start here and count down about four. T4 should be between my shoulder blades."

The air shifted slightly as Zane moved closer, and I shivered.

"How do you know that?" he asked. "About T4. I wouldn't have the faintest clue."

I smiled tightly. "Years of studying human anatomy, remember?" He was already getting a front-row seat to my freak show, why not remind him once again that I was created to be a killer?

His fingertip lightly touched my neck at the point I'd showed him and moved down my spine, tripping over the fabric of my tunic.

"Ariane," he began. "I'm not sure which—"

I understood his hesitation and—well, at this point, was it really a good idea to let modesty stand in my way?—grabbed the back of my shirt and yanked it up past my shoulders, exposing my skin to the night air. That would make counting vertebrae a lot easier.

Zane sucked in a breath.

"What, can you see it?" I twisted around, trying to look, cursing my years of naiveté. I should have known GTX—Jacobs, specifically—would do something like this. If I'd searched myself, maybe I would have seen the chip before. A little bubble under the skin near my spine, like a malignant tumor just waiting to cause chaos later.

"They did this to you." It was a statement, but I could hear the question in it.

I thought he was talking about the tracker, until his finger touched my shoulder blade, tracing the letters and numbers emblazoned on my skin. The GTX logo and my project designation: GTX-F-107.

I flinched, humiliation setting my face afire. This was getting better and better by the second. In my panic about the chip, I'd forgotten about the tattoo. Normally it was covered by a bandage, but I'd taken that off before the party a couple nights ago and never had a chance to put another one on.

Now Zane knew I was marked like cattle. I was a possession. A thing.

"Yeah. They did." I bit the words off and waited, my shoulders tense. Any second now, I'd hear his uncomfortable laugh, echoing against the building, and the sound of his retreating footsteps. This would be the final straw, the piece that pushed him over the edge into seeing me for what I was instead of who.

But, somehow, miraculously, it wasn't. "This is probably going to be cold," he warned a second before applying the magnet to my back between my shoulder blades.

He was right. The sudden shock of metal against my skin made me gasp.

I started to shiver for real, then, and Zane stepped closer, looping his free arm around my shoulders in the front, a backward sort of hug, while his other hand kept the magnet pressed in place between us.

"Better?" he asked.

I could feel the rise and fall of his chest against me, the softness of his shirt on my skin, and, faintly, the solid and reassuring beat of his heart.

I wanted to cry, to turn around and bury my head against him. To cling to him, to crawl inside. Instead, I cleared my throat and said, "Yes."

"Is it supposed to beep or something?" Zane asked a moment later.

"I don't know." I looked again to the letter, now crumpled in my hand. There were only a couple paragraphs remaining.

Third, and this is the most important part: you know about Arthur Jacobs, but he is the least of your concerns. He wants you alive so you can win the trials for him. But David Laughlin (Laughlin Integrated Enterprises, Chicago, IL) and Emerson St. John (Emerson Technology, Incorporated, Rochester, NY) would rather you were dead. One less competitor for the trials they have planned.

The trials. That's what they were calling a fight to the death between the various "products" created by the three companies vying for a lucrative government contract to make supersoldiers/assassins/spies. ("Products" was the sanitized word for beings like me, lab-created hybrids of human and alien DNA.)

So now, as if the possibility of death in a formal competitive setting weren't enough, I apparently had to worry about plain old murder. That was new.

A full body shudder ran through me, and Zane pulled me closer against him.

They've had informants keeping tabs on one another's progress for years. Your escape won't go unnoticed for long. And once you leave the state—GTX's "territory" as designated by the rules they established to prevent sabotage—you'll have all of them after you. Laughlin, in particular, will not hesitate at the thought of collateral damage if it means eliminating a threat to his success.

Dizzy suddenly, I felt myself swaying. I knew where this was going even before I read my father's final words.

Cut ties to Wingate and anyone you care about, immediately. You'll want to protect those who've been kind to you, but you're a

danger to anyone in your presence. Find somewhere isolated, prefer-
ably outside the country (the U.S. government is complicit in all of
this, remember). Stay there.

Be good; follow the Rules I gave you. Take care of yourself.
Again, I am sorry for my role in all of this.

Mark

"Are we good?" Zane whispered near my ear, his breath
tickling my cheek. "Is it off?"

It took me a second to process what he was asking about.
The chip. Was the chip deactivated?

I nodded numbly, even though I had no way of knowing
if that was the case. Surely my father had not intended for
me to walk around with a magnet permanently affixed to my
back. And even if he had, there were now larger concerns.

With a quick exhale of relief, Zane removed the magnet
and bent to tuck it inside the bag.

I tugged my tunic into place and put my jacket on, my
head spinning with too many thoughts.

Cut ties to Wingate and anyone you care about, immediately.
When my father had written that, he'd probably been thinking of my former friend Jenna or maybe even himself. But
Zane . . . Oh God, he was most definitely included in that
category, which meant I knew what my father would have
wanted me to do.

My stomach ached. Here, at last, was the boot I'd been
expecting, dropping to clobber me from a totally unantici-
pated angle.

The selfish part of me was shrieking "No!" at the top of
her lungs. I couldn't just abandon Zane, especially not here.
GTX would snap him up in a second. Not to mention, I
didn't *want* to leave him at all.

I blinked back tears. But logically, reasonably, his safety had to come first. If I cared so much about him, I couldn't be a party to his death or endangerment. Which left me with what?

Take him with you, my emotional side pleaded. He's come this far. He'll go.

Maybe. Maybe not. Going to his mother's was one thing; going on the run for the rest of his life? I shook my head. I couldn't ask that of him.

Walk away now, the cooler, calmer voice in my head advised. It's the best choice for both of you. Jacobs will find him, but Jacobs is the lesser evil compared to the others. He will want to keep Zane alive to use as incentive.

I rocked back and forth on my heels, caught on twin prongs of misery and indecision. It was impossible to know what parts of my personality came from which side. What was human? What was *other*? All I knew was that when it came to big choices like this one, I was torn between emotions that raged inside and the logic that tried to snuff them out—to the point where it felt like the fight between them might spill out into the physical world. Me arguing with myself, with no peace in sight. It felt like more proof that maybe someone like me wasn't meant to exist.

"Are you all right?" Zane asked, startling me.

I turned to see him frowning at me. Then he grimaced. "I mean, I know you're not, not after everything . . . but was the letter . . ." He trailed off awkwardly.

The absolute end of everything I was hoping for? "It's fine." I forced the lie out, hearing it thud in the space between us.

Zane squinted at me, reading something on my face that I didn't want him to see. "Ariane—"

Tires crunched over loose pebbles on concrete on the other side of the building.

We froze.

Zane stood, lifting the bag with him. "Is that GTX?" he asked, barely audible.

At this point, I had to hope so. The alternative, that Laughlin or St. John had found me already, was even worse. It was laughable—a crazy person's hysterical cackle—that GTX had become the best of all possible options.

"Probably," I said, adrenaline kicking into overdrive, bringing details into hyperfocus. "Only one car, though, so far, by the sound of it. A scout, checking out the situation." Like someone who'd caught the blip of my tracking chip's signal before we'd disabled it. Or maybe it was simply someone making a U-turn in a convenient parking lot, but I couldn't take that chance. My luck was just not that good.

"Then I guess we better run like hell, 'Talia,'" Zane said. He tipped his head toward the trees and held out his free hand with a grin that hurt my heart.

I faltered, unable to move. How was I supposed to do this? How was I supposed to say good-bye to the one person in the world who knew the real me and had stuck around anyway?

"Ariane?" he asked, his smile slipping a little.

I couldn't. Not yet.

So I did the only thing I could do—selfish and human as it was.

I took his hand, and we ran like hell.

CHAPTER 2

‖‖▮▮ ‖‖ ‖‖‖▮▮‖ ‖▮‖‖ ‖▮‖▮▮

Zane Bradshaw

SOMETHING WAS WRONG. ARIANE WAS TOO QUIET.

She'd never been particularly chatty—and I certainly didn't expect her to be talking up a storm after what she'd been through in the last day or so—but this was different.

In between paranoid checks of the rearview mirror for vehicles following us (none yet), I kept glancing over to make sure she was still there, curled up in the passenger seat, her knees tucked to her chest beneath the oversize black GTX jacket.

Ariane hadn't really spoken since we'd found the bag. Actually, not since she'd read the letter that was inside. She was clutching it, as if she couldn't bear to let it go. But she hadn't said what was in it, and I didn't want to push her.

It had to be harder than hell to learn your whole life is a lie. I was pretty sure the letter had been more of the same stilted apologies and explanations Mark Tucker had given her in person. I was willing to bet that it sucked as much in replay on paper as it had hearing it live. Plus, the whole tracking device thing. That was messed up.

Still, I wished she'd talk about something, anything. It was almost three thirty in the morning, and the silence was starting to get to me. Nothing but the thoughts circling endlessly in my head and the hum of the tires on the road.

Obviously, we'd found the vehicle that went with the key. Actually, it had sort of found us. Doing our best to keep to the shadows, we'd run from the old Linens-N-Things building and whoever was in the parking lot out front. We hadn't gone far when Ariane had stopped suddenly and pointed up.

A big, glowing orange sign—U-Store-It—hovered above the treeline in the distance, like a welcome beacon.

Ariane gave a strangled laugh and led me across the street and onto the storage facility grounds, right to Unit 107—the same number tattooed on her back. The lock opened with the smaller key on the ring, and inside the storage locker we found a tarp-draped van. The outside was beat to hell, but the engine started right up with a smoothness that suggested a new engine, or at least one that had been well maintained.

The interior of the van contained only two seats, driver and passenger, leaving the entire cargo area echoey and empty, except for a scrap of carpet covering the metal floor.

Or so I thought, until Ariane climbed back there and started poking around. After just a few minutes, she found a hidden compartment in the floor that was the size of a person.

"A smuggling compartment?" I asked, stunned.

"'I use them for smuggling. I never thought I'd be smuggling myself in them,'" she murmured, knowing I'd catch the *Star Wars* reference.

It was more than appropriate for the situation. GTX was an evil empire of sorts, I supposed.

Inside the compartment we discovered more rolls of cash, sleeping bags, baby wipes, a first-aid kit, bottles of water, and protein bars. Mark Tucker really was a badass. He'd thought of everything.

"How did you know to look for that?" I asked Ariane.

She shrugged. "Why else would the back be empty?"

Kind of a good point, just not the way I was used to thinking. For as familiar as Ariane had become to me in the last few days, there were still moments when the differences between us seemed vast and uncrossable. As if we were from two different planets. Which, I guess, we were.

Alien. The word echoed loudly in my head, and I struggled to shut it out before Ariane could hear. I wasn't freaked out by it so much as shell-shocked. It was one thing to learn that life on other planets existed; I'd kind of suspected as much when I'd bothered to think about it, which wasn't often. But it was entirely something else to discover that that distant and ambiguous "life" wasn't a collection of molecules or bacteria visible only beneath a special microscope but was part of the girl who'd sat in front of me in math class. And the things she could do, the things they'd taught her, were both terrifying and amazing.

That queued up a strange sense of panic in me. Not because of what she was but who. I mean, who was I in comparison? How was this going to work with us, whatever we were? People had spent millions of dollars and years of their time just to make sure she'd exist. My own father thought I was a waste of space. Ariane was special—maybe not the kind of special she would choose, but still. I was just a garden-variety human, not even the best one in my family. (That would be Quinn, my older and perfect brother.)

The question was, how long before she realized it and dumped my ass on the side of the road? I grimaced. Or, worse, maybe she'd already put that together and her silence was just her trying to figure out how to tell me.

I shook my head, trying to push down those thoughts. "Almost there," I said into the quiet, to distract myself and just for something to say. I tapped my thumb against the steering wheel in a nervous fidget. We were well on the Illinois side of the Wisconsin border in a small town. Fox Lake, according to the signs.

Ariane stirred reluctantly in her seat. "We should stop."

I stared at her. "You're kidding, right? We're only forty-five minutes away." Give or take, according to the map we'd picked up about twenty miles outside of Wingate at an all-night gas station. Without our phones—Ariane had abandoned hers somewhere along the way and she'd removed the battery from mine to prevent them from tracking us—we had to go the low-tech route. No GPS or turn-by-turn directions for us. But considering that we were trying to avoid the most obvious routes into the Chicago area, the map had been more help than I'd expected.

"I don't think this is the best way to make a first impression," Ariane said, plucking at the dirt- and blood-smeared front of her formerly white tunic.

"My mom won't care." At least, I was pretty sure she wouldn't, but I hadn't seen her in more than a year. And in that time, she hadn't once attempted to contact me, not even over e-mail, where my dad wouldn't have known about it. I understood why she might feel she couldn't take me with her—my dad was the chief of police and a local hero. My mom was one of the trailer-trash McDonoughs. If he'd decided to fight her on custody, there would be no question who'd win.

But to not even call? Or send a text?

I felt another sudden flash of anxiety. Maybe this was a mistake. I didn't know exactly why she'd left. I mean, why that particular night, literally hours before my birthday? My dad claimed that she'd wanted to take me with her, but there really wasn't much evidence to back that up.

So, we were about to knock on the door of someone who maybe didn't even want us—well, me—there.

"Besides, it'd be better if this looked more like a surprise visit instead of us fleeing town," Ariane was saying. "Too many questions otherwise." She glanced over at me, her unusually dark eyes serious. I was getting used to her natural eye color. There were colored contact lenses in the emergency bag—the same type, presumably, that she'd worn every day to school—but she hadn't bothered to put them in. I liked that. Made me feel as though she trusted me, as though I was on the inside of this secret and she wanted me there.

I realized she was looking over at me, waiting for a response.

I nodded hastily. She had a point. Explaining everything to my mom would involve either some major eye-opening revelations about the existence of life on other planets that I wasn't sure Ariane was ready to get into or some quick talking around the facts. Either way, we hadn't prepped for that. And my mom, no matter how much she may have changed in the last year, was not stupid.

Stopping for a few hours to get some rest and our stories straight seemed like a pretty good idea. Assuming we could find somewhere.

"You, uh, have any particular place in mind?" I asked. We appeared to be on what passed for the main drag in this town, tiny even by Wingate standards. Most everything was closed. And I had no idea what Ariane was thinking. An empty parking lot? A motel?

My mind shied away from the latter option. It had implications that I didn't want to put out there. She might think I was angling for more than the chance to sleep with my legs stretched out.

Never mind the fact that the idea of hooking up while GTX was kicking down doors and burning up the highway hunting for us was kind of ridiculous.

The mental image of just that—the two of us together—flashed into my head with crystal clarity, and I shifted uncomfortably in my seat. Okay, it was ridiculous and maybe a little hot. We were alive, we'd made it this far. And all that life-and-death adrenaline was apparently still flowing through my system.

Remembering the few times we'd made out in my truck, my heart stuttered with anticipation. Of course, that was before I'd known the truth about her, about where she came from.

Would it be different now? I didn't think so. She'd stood in front of me, protecting me at her own expense. Nobody had ever done that for me.

My fingers itched suddenly to feel the smoothness of her skin again, a chance to see for myself that she was actually unharmed.

A quiet sniffle came from the other side of van. "I was thinking more about a hot shower."

I looked over to see Ariane trying to smile at me even as she wiped under her eyes. She was crying.

"Ariane, what's wrong?" I asked, bewildered. Was she reading the letter again? No, it was still folded in her hand. "What happened—"

I clamped my mouth shut, the realization clicking in a second too late. She'd "heard" me. The motel, me wanting to touch her, the memories of us kissing.

My face burned. "Oh my God, I'm sorry," I said quickly. "I was just thinking about it. I would never have—"

She gave a choked laugh. "Stop apologizing. It was nice."

"Nice enough to make you cry," I said.

"I'm just tired, that's all. Kind of a long day." But her gaze didn't quite meet mine, and I felt like an asshole. Ariane was dealing with her whole life falling apart, and I was the jerk fixated on being in a motel.

I wanted to apologize again, but her focus had shifted to the street. She leaned forward in her seat, watching.

"There," she said, after a minute. She pointed to a neon blue VACANCY sign flashing in front of a stubby two-story building on the left side of the street. Definitely not a five-star establishment but, judging from the sheer number of minivans in the parking lot with pool floaties strapped to the roofs, safe.

I pulled in and found a space near the glass door marked OFFICE with another neon sign.

"No," Ariane said quickly. "Somewhere closer to the back of the lot, in the shadows. I don't want the desk manager to see us."

I hesitated, then drove farther to a spot that matched her description. "Uh, you're not planning on breaking in, are you?" I asked, putting the van in park. Kind of a stupid question, I guess, but I had to ask. I knew she could do it. I'd seen her unlock an elevator in a secure facility; I was pretty sure a motel door wouldn't even be a challenge. But there were other issues, ones I was betting she'd never think of.

She looked at me, surprised. "The fewer people who witness—"

I sighed. "Some of these places, they have a system that alerts them if the door on an unoccupied room is opened without a key."

She raised her eyebrows in question.

"Homecoming after-party last year at the Fairfield. The lock on the door to the adjoining room was broken, and Jonas decided to expand the party." I shrugged. "Which was fine, until someone went out through the main room door. The key card system notified the manager, and she called the cops." Which had included my father. I grimaced at the memory.

Ariane nodded thoughtfully. "Okay."

"Are you sure this is a good idea?" I asked. What Ariane had said about getting cleaned up and making this look more like a normal visit made sense, but I still felt like I was missing something.

"As much as I'm sure about anything," she murmured with a strained smile that somehow spoke of sadness and set off an alarm in the back of my brain, though I didn't know why.

Before I could ask her, she was digging into the duffel bag

at her feet, pulling out the baby wipes she'd added from the secret compartment and the package of contact lenses.

With an economy of motion, she wiped off her face and hands, using the mirror on the sun visor as a guide. Even in the dim light, I could see dozens of scrapes and cuts on her face, neck, and hands. And I noticed, for the first time, how careful she was with her left arm. The light was dim in here, but I could see blood, a lot of it, crusted on the edge of her sleeve, turning the small portion sticking out from the cuff of her black jacket from white to a dark brownish red.

"Ariane . . . your arm," I said, horrified.

"It stopped bleeding a while ago," she said, tucking her sleeve under her jacket with a wince. "It's fine."

I wasn't so sure about that—and I didn't know how she could be either, since I hadn't seen her so much as look at the wound—but her tone brooked no argument.

She pulled the top off a set of contacts and slid the lenses in, her eyes watering as she blinked.

"Be right back," she said, zipping her jacket up and brushing off the front of it.

I stared at her like she was crazy, belatedly realizing her intentions. "You can't go in there."

"I'm the only one with a name that won't attract attention," she said, waving her new U.S. passport at me.

"Yeah, but he's not going to rent a room to you."

"Why not?" she demanded.

I paused, trying to figure out how to say this without hurting her feelings. Oh hell. "You look about twelve, particularly in that." I nodded toward the oversize jacket that covered her from shoulders to knees, hiding her lab-issued clothing.

She frowned. "If my identification says I'm eighteen, he can't deny—"

"He's not going to care about anything but covering his ass, and you scream teenage runaway or worse." I unbuckled my seat belt. "Let me do it." People always thought I was older than I was just because of my height. And this, at least, was a way I could help.

She shook her head. "Your dad may have already reported you missing. We can't risk it."

I made a face. "Doubt it. That would mean admitting something was wrong at our house." I held my hand out. "Just give me the cash, and I'll take care of it." I had an emergency credit card, but absolutely nothing would bring my dad down on us faster than using that.

She wavered, and then dug into the bag and pulled out a roll of money. "Stay calm, be confident, and ask for more than you want," she said. "Basic rules of negotiation."

"Got it." I pulled a few bills off and stuffed them in my pocket—pulling out a wad of hundreds would only raise more questions and possibly the amount of whatever bribe I might have to give to get us a room—and reached for the door handle.

"Wait, come here." Ariane gestured at me to come closer, producing another baby wipe from the package.

She leaned in, dabbing carefully at my face, her forehead pinched with concern. "You're so scratched up." She sounded as though she felt responsible.

"Had to make the other side match," I joked, making a vague gesture to the stitched cut on my left cheek, courtesy of a flying beer bottle the other night. At least, I hoped it was still stitched. Honestly, until now, I hadn't really stopped to think about what hurt, and now that I did, everything ached and burned. "I'll survive."

That didn't seem to reassure her. Frowning, Ariane ran her hands through my hair, plucking out a few leaves and dropping them to the floor.

Under her touch, I wanted nothing more than to stay right here.

She lowered her hands slowly, her gaze searching my face, looking for what I wasn't sure. But her eyes seemed brighter, shinier, closer to tears than they'd been.

"All better?" I asked, my voice thick.

"Yes." She reached out as if she might caress my cheek, not for the purpose of cleaning me up but just to do it, but then she seemed to catch herself and turned to stare out the window instead. "Be careful, okay?" she said.

A little baffled by the quick change in her mood, I nodded slowly. "Yeah. I'll be right back."

I climbed out of the van, my legs protesting the sudden movement after hours in the cramped space behind the wheel, and headed for the office door.

As soon as I got about ten feet away, the strangest feeling came over me, the insistent intuition that Ariane would be gone by the time I returned.

No. She wouldn't do that. Would she?

I looked over my shoulder at the van and waved, but I couldn't see whether she waved back.

Better just to hurry up and not chance it.

An old-fashioned bell rang as soon as I pushed open the door. After a long moment, a big dude in a flannel shirt appeared behind the registration desk.

"Help you?" he asked, rubbing his eyes with a meaty fist.

"Yeah, man, road trip gone wrong, you know?" I shook my head. "Got lost, flat tire, the whole deal." I gestured at my banged-up face. "Gotta get some rest before I keep going." I could hear myself rambling and yet couldn't seem to stop. What the hell. I used to be good at this kind of stuff.

He eyed me carefully, and I worked to meet his gaze and not fidget.

Then he gave a yawn, one that made his jaw crack. "Credit card." He made a give-it-to-me gesture.

"Cash. But I've got ID." I slid two bills across the counter and pulled my driver's license from my wallet.

He looked at the money and my license and then back at me. "No trouble from you, though. Got it?"

"No, not at all," I said. "Just need a quiet place to sleep for a few hours."

He grunted. "All I got is a double. And checkout's at eleven."

He tapped at the computer halfheartedly for a few seconds, then the money disappeared into his pocket without any mention of change, even though there was no way this place cost two hundred bucks a night. Good enough.

"Room 205." He shoved key cards across the scarred Formica counter to me. "Second floor, on the end."

That had been easier than I'd thought it would be. Then again, the guy was half-asleep. And/or completely apathetic. I wasn't sure which, but either way it worked to our advantage.

I nodded my thanks, took the cards, and headed back out into the parking lot, trying not to look as if I was rushing.

The van was where I'd left it. The relief almost made me dizzy.

Once the manager could no longer see me, I picked up my pace and trotted directly for the passenger-side door.

Ariane, watching for me, opened it as I approached.

"Room 205. Second floor, on the end," I said.

"Any problems?" she asked, her gaze flicking between me and the parking lot, staying alert for someone approaching, no doubt.

"Nope."

She nodded and swung down from the van, the duffel bag over her shoulder.

I led the way up a creaky set of wooden stairs that bent beneath my weight to the last door on that level. After a momentary struggle with the key card, we were in.

The room was small and seriously fugly with carpet in a shade between aqua and green that hurt my eyes. It smelled damp and mildewy, like laundry left in the washer for a few days—thanks, most likely, to the actively dripping AC unit on the far wall. Still, the second the door shut behind me, I felt better, safer. It was probably a false sense of security, but I found it reassuring all the same.

Ahead of me, Ariane carefully placed the duffel bag on a battered-looking armchair near the foot of the queen-size bed. The lone bed in the room. A dresser with a TV bolted to the top of it and a bedside table with a grimy-looking phone were the only other pieces of furniture.

"They didn't have a room with two beds, sorry," I said, my words sounding absurdly loud in the small room.

Without looking at me, Ariane shook her head. "It's all right."

Trying not to crowd her, I took an extra step to the right

33

to turn on the lights in the bathroom and look around. "Not too much worse than the locker room at school," I said, attempting to keep the mood light. "But—"

Ariane was in front of me when I turned toward the main room.

"Sorry," I said, and tried to get out of the way, feeling as ungainly and awkward as I had when I'd first shot up over six feet.

She moved with me, her gaze meeting mine directly, and it took me a second to realize she'd done it deliberately.

Rising up on her tiptoes to examine me more closely, Ariane sucked a breath in through her teeth.

"Sit," she said, pointing at the toilet.

When I frowned at her, she held up the first-aid kit. I hadn't even noticed it in her hand. "I can't reach you unless you're sitting," she said.

She was still worried about my face. I shook my head. "No way, your arm—"

"Looks much worse than it is," she said calmly.

Oh no, I'd accepted that answer before because I'd been caught off guard. But now?

I folded my arms across my chest. "You first." I could be stubborn too.

Ariane glared at me. "I can take care of it myself." But she pulled her arm closer to her body, protectively, as if I might try to grab it. Which told me that she was hurt worse than she wanted to let on.

"One-handed?" I asked, doing my best to keep my voice flat, even. She seemed to respond better to logic than emotional pleas when it came to her own well-being. I could play

34

that game. Part of me wondered if she just wasn't used to it, used to someone caring about her.

"It's my left arm. I'm right-handed," she argued.

I rolled my eyes. "Yeah, I'm sure that'll be no problem."

Her mouth tightened. "I said I'm—"

"The longer you argue with me, the longer we're going to stand here," I said, leaning against the counter.

Her fingers tightened on the first-aid kit as if she were contemplating throwing it at my head.

"And the longer my injuries go untreated." I gave her a pitiful look.

She heaved an irritated sigh. "You're making this much more difficult than it needs to be," she snapped, thrusting the first-aid kit at my chest as she pushed past me to sit on the closed lid of the toilet.

"I'm really, really good at that," I said, unperturbed. "Or so I hear, anyway."

"You don't have to look so smug," she grumbled as I set the kit down and washed my hands.

"Are you kidding? I think that's the only argument I've ever won with you. I'm going to put it on my college applications in the Special Accomplishments section," I said.

"Funny," she said. "Besides, you didn't win. I quit. There's a difference."

"Uh-huh. Whatever lets you sleep at night." I dried my hands on one of the threadbare white towels on the counter.

"How are you with blood?" she challenged, unzipping her jacket and shrugging it off her shoulders.

"I play lacrosse. I think I'll be fine," I said dryly. "Plus, my dad comes from the school of 'rub a little dirt on it and get back out there,' so I'm not going to faint on you, if that's what you're worried about."

That, for some reason, seemed to convince her, though she didn't seem happy about it. "Deliberately rubbing dirt in a wound seems foolish."

"It's a saying. A sports thing," I amended, since people did more than say it. They actually did it.

She raised her eyebrows and shook her head, dismissing it, no doubt, as one of the many things we did that made no sense.

Gingerly, she pulled her arm out of the jacket sleeve, and though I'd been expecting signs of injury, this was far worse than I'd imagined. Her shredded left sleeve was plastered to her skin with dried and drying blood.

I inhaled sharply. "Shit, Ariane." I knelt in front of her for a better look, the uneven floor tiles digging into my knees.

The tattered fabric had adhered to the entire underside of her arm, wrist to elbow. I couldn't even tell where her injury was. But I knew there'd be no pulling her sleeve up without breaking open the wound that had caused all this bleeding.

"Are you, uh, wearing something under that?" I gestured awkwardly to her shirt.

"Are you trying to talk me out of my clothes?" she asked, her jaw tight and her gaze fixed solidly at a point over my head.

"No! I just . . ." I paused, looking at her tense expression and the way she was very deliberately avoiding looking down at her arm. "Do *you* have a problem with blood?" I asked, amazed.

"In this quantity? Just my own," she said in that cool,

detached tone that reminded me, of course, she likely wouldn't have a problem with anyone else's blood. She'd been trained to—

I pushed that thought away before I could finish it. "The problem is, I don't want to make it worse by just yanking your sleeve up."

She flinched.

"So I want to try to wet it and then peel it away from your arm. But I think that would be easier from the other direction. Like this." I mimed the action of pulling my shirt over my head and down my arm.

She nodded reluctantly, her tangled hair sliding in front of her pale face.

"But if you're not wearing—"

"It's fine." She wiggled her right arm into the inside of her shirt and hitched that side up to her shoulder.

Realizing belatedly that I probably didn't need to be six inches away for this part of the process, I stood and turned my back. I could give her some privacy, at least.

I grabbed a couple of the small towels from the counter and soaked them in warm water, working very hard to concentrate on that, blocking my worst impulses that were urging me to watch her undress in the mirror.

"Okay," she said a few moments later, and I faced her.

Her injured arm was carefully balanced on her leg, her discarded shirt piled on top of it. A white sports bra covered her breasts. Her hair was more tangled and mussed than before, and her shoulders were curved inward, her free arm wrapped around her waist protectively.

The tattoo on her right shoulder—I had been right about

that all along, though also very, very wrong—was just visible.

I'd seen cheerleaders wearing little more than what she had on. But somehow it mattered more now that it was Ariane wearing it. I snagged one of the bath towels from the rack above her head and draped it over her shoulders.

"Thanks."

"Yeah."

I cracked open the first-aid kit and pulled out antibacterial cream, packages of gauze bandages, and tape.

"Gloves," she said sharply.

I froze. "Is that necessary?" Even with the evidence right in front of me, I kept forgetting that she was more—and less—than just the girl who'd sat in front of me in Algebra II last year.

"I don't know. They always wore gloves in the lab." She lifted her chin, meeting my eyes defiantly. She was going to fight me on this, I could tell.

So I dug out the gloves and put them on before grabbing one of the wet towels from the sink and kneeling in front of her once again.

Slowly, inch by painstaking inch, I soaked the fabric and gently pulled it away from her skin.

She held very still, preternaturally silent. I didn't want to think about what had happened in her early life at the lab to teach her that kind of stoicism.

Several angry slashes and ugly bruises decorated her wrist at intervals, but the worst was a thick gash across the meat of her arm, just up from her elbow. Her jacket should have protected her, but it was about ten sizes too big and had obviously fallen down or been pulled away by stray branches.

"I really think you should have stitches, Ari," I said, carefully tilting her arm toward the light.

"And somehow I think going to a hospital right now would be more dangerous," she said, sounding slightly strained.

"They can't have someone at every hospital and urgent care clinic," I pointed out.

She shook her head. "It's not worth the risk. Just patch me up. I'll be fine."

I disagreed, but short of bodily removing her from the room, which I doubted she'd allow, there wasn't much I could do. I wiped away as much of the blood as I could, smeared the antibacterial cream on gauze pads, and applied them carefully, taping the edges to keep them in place.

"It'll heal fast," she said softly. "I promise. I'll be better before you are." She reached out and touched my face, her fingertip lightly tracing my stitches from the other night. "Not such a pretty boy anymore." She gave me a sad but teasing smile.

I started to protest that that label had never applied to me, but then her thumb brushed the corner of my mouth and the air went electric. I turned my cheek into her caress, pursuing it. And when I pressed a kiss against the center of her palm, she caught her breath.

Her eyes were dark behind the blue-tinted lenses and seemed to be growing darker. Her gaze dropped to my mouth, and she bit her lip.

I swallowed a groan, and with my heart pounding too hard, I leaned in.

But then she dropped her hand and turned away.

Confused, I pulled back. "What's—"

"I should . . . I want to shower. Get the GTX off of me," she said with a forced smile, not quite looking at me.

My face flushed. "Sure, yeah, okay." I stood up hastily. "Sorry." I peeled off the gloves and tossed them in the garbage can beneath the sink.

"Nothing to be sorry for," she said, pulling the towel tighter around her shoulders.

Except, clearly, there was. I backed out of the room, tugging the door shut after me.

Had I pushed too far? I didn't think so. She'd been right there with me up until the end, when she'd withdrawn.

I shook my head, and walked the few short steps to the bed and flopped down on my back.

It would make perfect sense that she would want to clean up, after GTX, after the woods, after the Dumpster.

I made a face. I probably didn't smell so great either.

But it was more than that. I was missing something; I could feel it. I just didn't know what it was.

That was maybe the most frustrating thing about all of this. Ariane could hear what I was thinking at any time, if she wanted to. But I was stuck trying to puzzle her out with only the barest clues. I'd thought I'd had her figured out before, and I just kept discovering new facets and shadowed corners, previously hidden to me.

Though, honestly, if pushed, I'd have to admit that I actually kind of liked it, moments of complete and utter bewilderment aside.

Or maybe it was just that I really liked *her*, enigmas and all.

CHAPTER 3

Ariane

THE SHOWER HAD GONE COLD A FEW MINUTES EARLIER, but I couldn't convince myself to move. Hunched at the far end of the tub, with the spray hitting between my shoulder blades, I had my injured arm stuck out from behind the curtain to keep the bandages dry.

I should have been crying. Sobbing, even. But instead, my eyes were burning dry. I felt numb, empty. As if a protective shell had formed over all my wounded feelings and now there was nothing.

I wanted to be relieved, but I knew it was only temporary. Eventually, days from now or maybe just hours, that shell would break and everything would flood in, throbbing and angry, inescapable.

Zane wanted to kiss me. I closed my eyes. Oh God, even after everything, even after what he'd learned, he still wanted me. Me. The freak made in a lab. The science experiment. The nonhuman. Or, the not-completely-human, anyway.

But none of that seemed to matter to him.

I opened my eyes and looked at my arm, his careful work on my wounds, the straight lines of the white tape against the indistinct edges of the dark bruises.

He was protecting me, taking care of me the best way he knew how. And I was endangering him. Every second I stayed with him brought him closer to death.

And yet protecting him in return would mean leaving him, the only person I had left in my world.

I felt the first crack in the shell.

I stared up at the black-mold-speckled ceiling, shouting in my head at the supposedly benevolent force that controlled the universe. *How am I supposed to do this? Why do I have to? How is this fair?* I hadn't done anything to deserve this— nothing except survive in the twisted and messed-up world that had created me.

And maybe that right there was proof that the supposedly benevolent force didn't exist at all. I was on my own, truly alone for the first time in my life. Yet somehow it was not the blissful freedom I'd always imagined.

My teeth were clacking together now in a steady but uneven rhythm. I had to move, get out of the shower at least. Eventually, Zane would come knocking, wondering if I was okay. Not to mention there was also the distinct possibility of hypothermia if I kept this up for too much longer.

I knew what I was doing—hiding. In here, I could hold on to the illusion that the world had stopped, that I could avoid making decisions.

But it was just an illusion. While I shivered in here, Dr. Jacobs had teams out there looking for us. And once Laughlin and St. John heard about my escape, there would be three times as many people looking for us, if there weren't already.

I had a mental image of black vans pulling silently into the motel parking lot, vomiting out retrieval teams, while I sat in the bathroom, too focused on my feelings to hear them approach.

That was enough to motivate me to get out of the tub and shut the water off.

Shaking with the cold, I wrapped one of the thin bath towels around myself, struggling a little with securing it, thanks to my injuries.

Zane had been right; it would have been tough to bandage my own arm. I could have done it, but not nearly as easily or well as he had.

I opened the bathroom door. "Sorry it took me so long," I said, my throat dry and tight. "I just—"

I stopped short at the sight of a pile of clothes, neatly folded, at my feet.

Zane. He'd pulled them out of the bag for me so I wouldn't have to cross the room in a towel and dig through the bag for them.

Taking care of me again.

Looking to the left, I noticed something else. A ragged but thick phone book wedged under the room door. It wouldn't keep someone out forever, but maybe long enough for us to get away through the window, assuming we could manage the drop to the ground.

Smart. I wasn't sure where Zane had learned that trick. Maybe something he'd discovered to keep his brother out of his room? It hadn't been a technique that I'd been taught, but it would be effective.

He wanted me to feel safe.

My lower lip started to shake, despite my best efforts. The initial fracture in my shell spiderwebbed out, weakening the entire structure.

I stepped out into the room, to find him and say thank you. If I could speak without breaking into tears, that is.

But Zane was asleep on the bed, his breathing slow and even. His feet would have hung off the end, so he'd curled up on his side, facing me. His hands were tucked under his arms, as if for warmth. He'd taken off his shoes, one white-socked foot resting on top of the other. The cuts and remaining smudges of dirt on his face showed up even more clearly against the white of the pillowcase.

He seemed so much smaller. So vulnerable.

So human.

The sight of him like that hit like a punch, and the protective shell around my heart shattered, breaking my heart along with it.

Tears welled hot and fast, pouring down my cheeks and dripping off my chin. I wanted to crawl in behind him and curl up as tightly as possible, like maybe if I could get close enough we'd disappear into each other and the rest of the world would just fall away.

The ache in my chest radiated outward, taking over my whole body. But I made myself scoop up the clothes from the floor and retreat into the bathroom.

I scrubbed my hand over my face, pushing away the tears even as they kept flowing. How could I live with myself if something happened to Zane because of me? Because I'd been too selfish and kept him with me? Because I'd stayed when I should have gotten as far away from him as possible?

I already knew the answer to those questions: I couldn't. It would kill some part of me if he were hurt, or worse, because of my choices.

Which meant only one thing—I couldn't stay.

Something inside me wailed at the idea, but that didn't change the facts.

It's safer for him without you. And you'll be able to move faster on your own, said the cool, logical inner voice. My alien heritage speaking.

I hated that part of myself more than ever right then. But I couldn't deny the truth it espoused. I might have been willing to take on more risk for myself, but not for Zane.

Besides, what were mere feelings compared to his living or dying?

Everything! My emotional—human?—side insisted. *They make life worth living; they give you something to fight for. And it's not your choice; it's his.*

But that voice. . . . It sounded too good to be true. I couldn't trust it.

With trembling hands, I pulled on my clothes—a plain, long-sleeved T-shirt and nondescript jeans that I hadn't noticed missing from the dozens just like them in my room—before bending down on wobbly legs to put on my shoes, a blue pair of imitation Chucks that I thought my father had thrown away months ago for being "too ratty-looking." He'd been relentless about anything that might draw attention to me. All part of an act, it turned out.

And yet seeing those shoes, being reminded of my old life and the lies, brought on a sharp stab of longing. Made me wish I could somehow step back into the last moment I'd worn them, before all of this had happened, when everything was still a possibility. When I'd still have a chance to make this end differently.

But I couldn't.

So, I had to go. Now. Before they caught up with us. Before Zane woke up and my resolve faltered. Before I threw caution to the wind and did what I wanted instead of what I knew was right.

CHAPTER 4
IIIIII II I I IIIIIII I IIII III III
Zane

I WOKE ABRUPTLY, WITH A STARTLED JUMP INTO ALERT-
ness. Like I'd been dreaming about falling off a cliff and
something snapped me out of it right before I hit the ground.

It took me a second to orient myself, to remember that I
wasn't in my room at home. I hadn't intended to fall asleep.
I'd just kicked off my shoes and closed my eyes to wait for
Ariane.

Ariane.

I sat up. Light slanted out of the partially closed bathroom door, and though the shower was now off, the smell of
it—a flowery, soapy humidity—still filled the room.

So I hadn't been asleep for that long.

The clothes I'd put on the floor were gone. She was probably getting dressed.

I lay back against the lumpy pillows and relaxed.

Or tried to.

I frowned. Something wasn't right.

Eventually it dawned on me that there was a strange,

empty quality to the silence in the room. At first, I thought it was just the absence of the water thundering through the pipes and pounding into the tub. No pressure issues here.

Then I realized that it was both more and less than that.

I could hear a dog barking in the distance. Cars passed with a quiet *whush-whush* on the road in front of the motel. But nothing closer, nothing in the room. No rustle of fabric, no bare feet slapping against the tile floor.

Ariane was quiet, definitely. She'd moved through the forest preserve tonight like a ninja, with me blundering on behind her.

But even she couldn't be completely silent.

Unless . . .

I bolted upright. "Ariane?"

No response.

. . . unless she wasn't here.

I looked immediately to the chair in the corner where she'd put her emergency bag. It was gone.

Maybe that didn't mean anything. She hadn't let it out of her sight since we'd recovered it. I could easily see her deciding to haul it with her if she went to get ice or hit a vending machine or something.

I was still rationalizing when I saw the note on the dresser, a small square of white pinned down by a lone roll of cash like the world's most expensive paperweight.

My heart fell. I knew what this was without even reading the note.

And yet that didn't keep me from scrambling, half falling off the bed to get to it.

Zane, I'm sorry.

The words crushed something hopeful and fragile in me, something I hadn't even known still existed until it was gone. My mind immediately flashed back to a very similar note I'd found on the kitchen counter the morning after my mom left. Clearly I was doing something wrong, to keep getting these things.

With an effort, I forced my attention back to Ariane's words.

Things have changed, and this is more dangerous than I realized. I can't put you in any further risk.

It had to be the letter. The one in the emergency duffel. Not that she'd told me what that letter had said. But that was the only thing I could think of that could have changed her understanding of the situation this dramatically.

I'm leaving money for a cab to take you to your mom's house. I wish I could go with you. I wish

Whatever she'd wished, or nearly wished, she'd crossed it out so thoroughly, the paper had ripped beneath the point of the pen.

—When you call for a cab, DON'T give them the room number.

—Wait until you see the cab in the parking lot before you leave the room.

—Don't leave the room if you see any other vehicles waiting.

—If you feel unsafe . . .

I crumpled up the note without reading the rest, frustration and hurt warring inside me. She was trying to protect me. I understood that. But it wasn't *her* decision.

I wasn't as skilled as she was—no big leap there—but I'd known the choice I was making when I'd left with her. Didn't that count for something?

I snagged the ball of cash off the dresser. Thousands of dollars for a cab ride that *might* cost fifty bucks. She was looking out for me, again, at the expense of herself.

I shook my head, my jaw so tight my teeth ached.

I'd been expecting this, sort of. The moment she realized that she didn't need someone like me hanging around. *Slowing her down*, a voice in my head added. It sounded suspiciously like my dad, which only made me angry.

But I'd thought there'd be a chance to try to talk her out of it. Or, at least, to say good-bye.

The lump in my throat made it hard to swallow. I just wanted . . . I didn't know what I wanted. But it wasn't for this to end now, to never see Ariane again.

In the too-loud silence of the room, I heard an engine turn over in the parking lot below, cough, and then catch.

Electricity shot through my veins. Had I just missed her? Had I woken up just seconds after she left? It seemed impossible, the odds completely against me. If she wanted to sneak out and disappear without being caught, she could do it. And yet . . .

I jammed the cash in my pocket and bolted for the door, jerking it open without bothering to check through the peephole first (even as Ariane's instructions from the note nagged at me from the back of my head).

In the parking lot, our van was backing slowly out of the spot where I'd left it.

I threw myself down the stairs, taking multiple steps at once until I reached the bottom.

By the time I got there, she was already shifting into drive—I could hear the change in the engine noise. If I tried to run toward the van, she'd easily accelerate past me, leaving me behind for good.

That pretty much left only one option, one that banked on Ariane being more concerned with my safety than her own need for escape. In other words, an option that I wasn't entirely confident in.

I took a deep breath, and with the bitter metal taste of fear in my mouth, I darted directly into the path of the van, little rocks biting through my socks and into the vulnerable bottoms of my feet.

The headlights blinded me instantly, tires squealing on the asphalt a second later as she hit the brakes.

The van stopped about three feet in front of me, and I let out the breath I'd been holding.

"What are you doing, Zane?" Ariane asked, cold and distant but clear enough. She must have unrolled the window.

"I think that's my line," I said, somehow angrier now that she was talking to me. "What the hell, Ariane?"

"Get out of the way," she said flatly.

"No."

She heaved a sigh. "I'm trying to protect you."

"By leaving me in the dark?" I gestured to the sky. "Literally."

"This . . ." She paused as if trying to find the right words. "This isn't your problem," she said finally. "I can't ask you to take any more risks."

"Here's the thing: you didn't actually ask me anything. You just left." I could hear my hurt and anger, and I didn't bother to hide it. She'd sense it in my thoughts anyway, so what was the point.

"You have no idea what you're dealing with," she said, that edge returning to her voice.

"You're right. Because you didn't tell me!" I was shouting now and found I didn't care.

"Hey, is everything okay out here? Do I need to call someone?" I looked over to find the burly manager standing in the doorway of the office. With my vision temporarily impaired from the headlights, he appeared more like a human-shaped blob. But he was apparently a human-shaped blob with a phone and an itchy 911 finger.

I faced Ariane, holding my arm to partially block the headlights. "I don't know. Is it?"

The tension of the moment spread out, a taut line between Ariane and me and a fainter tentacle stretching out toward the motel manager.

I decided to push. *I know you can hear me, Ariane, so let me put this in a way you'll understand: If you don't let me into this van and tell me what's going on, I swear to God, when GTX finds me, and you know they will, I'll happily tell them everything I know about Talia Torv and her Canadian citizenship.*

I sensed more than saw her shock. It was an ugly threat and not one I would have willingly followed through with, but it was the only one I had to make. If she was playing dirty, so was I.

"Get in," she said.

I waited until I heard the engine shift into idle and the thump of her unlocking the passenger door before I moved.

"No worries," I said to the manager, who was watching suspiciously, as I climbed in. "We're fine. No trouble here."

He grunted at me, indicating his disbelief in those statements. I wasn't sure I could blame him.

CHAPTER 5

Ariane

ZANE WAS BLUFFING WITH THAT THREAT. I WAS PRETTY sure. But all the emotion radiating off him made it hard to be certain. And determination ranked right at the top of that list. He wasn't going to give up, and with that manager standing right there, ready to call the police, I couldn't afford to waste any more time arguing with him.

Damn it. I shoved the gearshift into park and then reached over to unlock the door for Zane.

What might have been relief flickered over Zane's face as he registered the sounds. Then, his mouth tight, he headed to the passenger side.

I shook my head. It was like just getting the bleeding to stop and then reopening the wound.

You never should have shut the room door. It woke him up.

All I'd had to do was walk out and leave the door slightly ajar. Just enough to keep the lock from engaging—a sudden and loud click that might be disruptive—but not so much that it would be noticed by a casual observer outside.

Easy, in theory.

And yet, in reality, not so much.

As I'd shut the door, I'd glanced at Zane one last time, sleeping and vulnerable, his limbs slack with exhaustion. His dark hair was a tousled mess, making him look younger and more at risk for harm.

Leaving the door unlatched—and therefore, unlocked— meant leaving Zane open to attack. Not just by GTX or the others who might be searching for me, but regular, disreputable humans who might not hesitate to take advantage of him. Or the money I'd left for him.

And wasn't the whole point of this exercise to keep him safe?

I'd imagined Zane waking up with a stranger looming over him, his fear and confusion, and my hand had jerked, as if an electrical shock had passed through the metal handle. The door had snapped shut, the lock engaging with a declarative click.

And that had decided that.

Who, exactly, are you attempting to fool? You knew the risks of that action and took it anyway. You wanted this.

I winced. Great. The part of me that I counted on to be unemotional and logical—my "alien" side, as I thought of it—had apparently discovered the joy of sarcasm. Not that it was inaccurate.

Zane climbed in the van, saying something to the motel manager who was staring at us, a cell phone clutched in his thick hand.

"Thanks for getting him involved," I said to Zane, as he closed the door.

"Never would have happened if you'd just talked to me instead of skulking out in the middle of the night," he pointed out sharply, surprising me a little.

"I wasn't skulking. Skulking implies shame or wrongdoing," I said, stung. Stupid. It was a ridiculous response, but seeing him like this had thrown me. Struggling with my own mixed emotions, I hadn't fully considered his feelings. Yes, I'd expected him to be upset when he woke and found me gone, maybe even feel a little betrayed, but I'd figured relief would outweigh both of those emotions. I mean, who wouldn't want a free pass out of this nightmare that was my life?

Not, of course, that I'd planned to be here when he was running that particular emotional gamut.

You might not have planned it, but you certainly made it possible. Oh, shut up.

Back in the world outside my head, Zane raised his eyebrows. "Really? That's your defense? Arguing word choice?"

By now, I was feeling slightly provoked and attacked from multiple sides. "I told you, I was trying to protect—"

"Protect me, yeah. From what? What is so different now from a few hours ago?" he demanded.

"It's complicated," I hedged, putting the van in gear and pulling out of the parking lot onto the road. The last thing we needed was the manager calling the police anyway, because we weren't leaving.

Zane narrowed his eyes at me. "This is about that letter, isn't it? What does it say?"

I hesitated. If there was the possibility I could get him to leave without dragging him deeper into this mess, all the better.

He made a frustrated noise. "We've been over this already. If you don't tell me—"

"You want to know so badly? Fine," I snapped. "Good luck trying to ever sleep again. I won't be."

He waved his hand in a "give it to me" gesture.

"According to my father's letter, GTX shouldn't be my primary concern. Dr. Jacobs wants me alive. His competitors— David Laughlin and Emerson St. John—do not," I said flatly. "One less hybrid to beat in the trials."

Zane flinched.

"And apparently, they aren't particularly worried about taking out innocent bystanders if it means getting rid of me," I said. "Anyone near me is in danger of being killed. Not captured, not tortured, not used for motivation. Dead. Do you get that?" I could hear the hard edge growing in my voice and forced myself to breathe.

Zane let out a slow breath and slumped in his seat, rubbing his hands over his face.

Disappointment crept over me, but I shoved it away. This was good. He should know the stakes, the odds against his survival.

I pulled over into the mostly empty parking lot of a Dunkin' Donuts and dug into my pocket for the key card to the room, which I'd kept for reasons I didn't want to examine too closely. "Here," I said softly.

His gaze flicked between the card and my face. "Do you not want me here? Am I . . ." He paused, as if searching for what to say, and then he exhaled sharply, frustrated with himself or me, I couldn't tell.

"Am I slowing you down?" he asked finally, the words coming out rapidly, as if he was afraid of the answer.

I gaped at him, too shocked to respond at first. "No, of course not," I managed. "I mean, yes, I want you here, but it's too dangerous."

At that, he gave me a bitter smile, his white, even teeth flashing in the dim light. "Has it ever occurred to you that, even without crazy government people chasing me, I don't have much to go back to?"

"They're not government. At least not yet. For now, it's just the corporate." I didn't know why I felt the need to correct him, to pick at minute points of his argument rather than the main one. Maybe it was because I was having trouble finding fault with it; maybe it was because I didn't want to.

Zane rolled his eyes. "Whatever." He shifted in his seat, turning more toward me. "Ariane, do you think I can go home again? Do you really think I can live with my dad after all of that?"

I remembered the shade of reddish purple his father's face had turned when Zane defied him. There was no love lost between them now, if there ever had been. That much was clear.

I shook my head. "But you have everything. You have a future. You've got . . . prom and graduation and college." All the things I wanted and could never have.

"Your reasons for keeping me away are so that I can attend lame school functions?" he asked.

"You're being deliberately obtuse," I said, exasperated. If he could throw around "skulking" . . .

He smirked. "My favorite color."

"Funny," I said dryly. Then I shook my head. I wouldn't let him distract me. "Okay, so going back to Wingate isn't an option. We already figured that anyway. But your mom—"

"Vanished in the middle of the night more than a year ago and hasn't made contact since. Left a note full of apologies." He gave me a piercing look.

Ah, that explained why he'd reacted so badly to what I'd done. I grimaced.

"Is it so hard to believe I want to be here? With you?" he asked quietly.

I froze. God, how was I supposed to respond to that?

I took a deep breath and worked through my choices. Could I force him out of the van? Yes. Would he be safer without me? Probably. Maybe. I wouldn't be there if someone came after him, which was its own trouble. And he did, through my own foolishness, know my new identity. Which was a vulnerability that could be exploited, even against his will.

I had only the truth to give at this point. "I can't . . . I couldn't live with myself if something happened to you because of me," I admitted.

He turned toward me. "Yeah? How are you going to stop it? Especially if you're not around?" His tone was gentler than his words.

"You'd be safer without me," I blurted out in an approximation of my worst fear. *Better off. He'd be better off without you.*

Zane seemed undisturbed. "Maybe. Maybe not. I don't think you can know that," he said. "I don't think anyone can. Besides, even if that's true, even if it's more dangerous for me to stick it out with you, don't I get to choose?" He leaned closer, bracing one hand on the dashboard, forcing me to meet his gaze. "Isn't that why you hate GTX? Because they took away your choices? You want the opportunity to make decisions for yourself. Why do you get that freedom and I don't?"

I opened my mouth and closed it again without saying a word. I didn't have an argument for that.

You don't need one. Just remove him from the vehicle.

No. I tried the other way. Maybe he's right.

I sighed and shoved the arguing parts of myself to the back of my mind. There would never be agreement on this matter, I knew that much already. "What do you want to do?" I asked Zane.

To Zane's credit, he didn't react as though this was the capitulation he'd been seeking. He just sat back in his seat. "I want to go to my mom's and make sure she's okay."

I opened my mouth to protest.

He shot me a look. "If they're willing to kill people to get to you, she might be in danger because of me. And I need to warn her at least. You owe me that much."

He was right. I'd wreaked enough havoc on his life. I could do this one thing for him to try to set things right.

"Okay, but then what?" I asked. "I need to get out of the country and—"

"Run for the rest of your life? Find an abandoned cabin in the woods somewhere and hope for the best?"

"Yeah, maybe," I said.

"You're willing to fight for everybody else but not yourself," he said, more to himself than me.

"What's that supposed to mean?" I demanded, bristling.

"I mean, all of this started because you couldn't stand to see Jenna suffering and then you were willing to do whatever it took to keep them from hurting me. You saved Rachel even after everything she did to you." He shook his head in wonder. "But you won't give yourself the same consideration."

I didn't like the direction of this conversation. Hearing the names of my former best friend, my *only* friend, and my high school nemesis only reminded me of the wreckage trailing behind me, a past I couldn't escape. "Do you have any better options?" I asked tightly.

Zane shrugged. "I don't know. What about going public?"

My jaw dropped. "Oh, yeah, that'll end well," I said. "Zane, in case it's escaped your notice, there's just one of me. Up against three very powerful companies with unlimited resources and, I don't know, eventually the United States government maybe. I'm not human. I may not even have rights. They could classify me as an enemy of the state or a terrorist or something."

"I think an argument could be that you're as much human as anything else," he said.

I tried not to wince. Is that how he thought of me? Is that the only reason he was okay with me? Because I was "as much human as anything else"? It was and was not true. Part of me was human, most definitely, but I would never be human "enough." There would always be something *other* about me. It was just part of who I was, who I would be forever, the struggle between human and not.

"But fine," Zane continued, completely unaware of my inner turmoil. "Even if that's not the right answer, my point is that there are other possibilities. You just haven't given yourself a chance to figure them out." He paused. "You deserve more, Ariane. You deserve a life of your own." His fierceness was unmistakable. He *meant* it.

Hope flared in me and stubbornly refused to go out. Was Zane right? I wanted so badly to believe him. Wanted to believe in the idea that there might be something to my future other than hiding. But I'd had this same feeling twenty-four hours ago, when fleeing GTX, and trusting in that little bit of hope again was more than I could do right now.

Through the window, I watched the employees moving around in the doughnut shop, giving myself time to think. "I'll go with you to your mom's house to make sure she's okay," I said finally. Beyond that, I couldn't—wouldn't—commit to anything. And if I could find a way to convince him to go back to some semblance of a regular life in the process, I'd take it. This kind of half-life, always running or hiding, wouldn't be good for him, even if he couldn't see that right now.

Zane gave me a curt nod and pulled his seat belt into place.

The difference between us now and an hour or so ago was marked and chilly. I tried not to let that hurt. It's not as if I expected him to want to kiss me again. He'd fought to stay with me. That was enough, wasn't it? I guess that didn't keep me from wanting him to want to kiss me, foolish as it was.

"One more thing," he said as I turned out of the Dunkin' Donuts parking lot onto the street.

"Yeah?" I asked cautiously.

"I get that you were leaving me to protect me," he said. "But what you're missing is that it's too late. I'm already in, with both feet. I don't need you to shelter me like I'm too weak to handle it. So stop it."

The thing was, I wasn't sure I could. Especially when

I looked down and realized that those feet he'd referenced metaphorically were literally bare—well, socks only.

He'd left his shoes in the room when he'd chased after me, leaving himself vulnerable. And I had to wonder if that was the real metaphor to be worried about.

"Is that it?" Zane asked.

The sun was slowly coming up behind us, painting the street and the plain brick duplex ahead of us in pale blue light.

"Yeah," I said. "1701B." I put the van in park and checked the back of the grease-spotted receipt where I'd scrawled the address, just to be sure. We'd gotten lucky that his mother was listed in the phone book. I hadn't realized how dependent I'd become on my phone until I didn't have it. The third gas station I'd tried in Gurnee had had both breakfast sandwiches and a relatively recent phone book.

"It doesn't look like much," Zane said, which brought the total words he'd spoken in the last half hour up to about twenty. And six of those had been his breakfast order.

He'd gotten progressively quieter the closer we got to his mother's house. But his leg was jouncing up and down with an excess of nervous energy.

He might still be a mad at me for trying to protect him instead of including him. He thought I counted him as someone lesser just because he wasn't like me. That was, I suspected, thanks to his dad drilling that concept into his head for years. But now that we were here, any residual anger with me was taking a backseat to a growing uncertainty about seeing his mom.

I didn't know what to say. I wasn't sure what he'd been expecting at her home. Signs of a better life, the one his mother had felt it necessary to leave him for, maybe?

If that was the case, he was out of luck. The two-story duplex had all the depressing charm of a brick box. Square, dumpy, with black metal bars on the lower windows. The grass was dried out and crispy yellow, a sharp contrast to the miles of green lawn we'd left behind in Wingate.

The only sign of life was a small planter near the front door on her side. Red flowers of some kind flourished and spilled over the edge of the faux-cement plastic container.

I couldn't help but think about how that must look from Zane's perspective. She'd taken the time to plant flowers and care for them but not to make contact with her youngest son? The one she'd left the night before his fifteenth birthday?

I kind of hated her on principle for that.

"Do you feel anything?" he asked. "Is someone . . . waiting for us?" He meant GTX or one of the other companies.

I closed my eyes to focus. Zane, next to me, was the loudest source, due to proximity and his tangled-up emotions. I did my best to tune him out, pushing past to "hear" the others nearby.

Most of the time, I did my best to ignore the constant low-level buzz of thoughts in the back of my brain. I was a radio picking up dozens of stations at once, all of them chattering over one another. It gave me a headache if I paid attention to it for too long.

Fortunately, at just after six in the morning on a Sunday, almost everyone in the immediate vicinity was sleeping. The muted feelings and thoughts of dreaming humans had a distinctly hazy feel to them, making them pretty easy to distinguish.

A few people were up and moving already.

. . . out of coffee.

If I don't wake Julie now, we'll never make Mass. . . .

. . . just one more. If I can get one more, I'll be okay. Just one more . . .

I grimaced at that last one, someone jonesing for another hit of something. This might not be the best neighborhood.

But I didn't pick up any of the sustained tension and adrenaline that would inevitably accompany a GTX retrieval team lying in wait for me.

Which was a little weird.

I frowned. Surely someone had reported the encounter we'd had with Zane's dad by now. I'd pulled the city name out of his thoughts. That's how we'd known to head here. And surely GTX, with far more resources than a tattered phone book, would have easily been able to locate Zane's mom's address.

Then again, maybe that was why GTX wasn't here. They knew I'd be on my guard, listening for them. So Dr. Jacobs would be forced to find another, sneakier option, something I wouldn't see coming.

My stomach ached at the thought. I'd have to be so, so careful from now on, trying to outthink them outthinking me. And that sounded exhausting, impossible, and filled with pitfalls.

"No retrieval teams here," I told Zane.

"What about my mom? Is she in there?" he asked, tilting his head toward the duplex.

"Someone's in there. Just one person, I think." My ability didn't make distinctions between buildings.

"You don't know if it's her?"

I shook my head. "Most people don't walk around thinking their names. Especially not when they're asleep," I said.

He made a noncommittal noise in response.

"What time does she normally get up?" I asked, trying to keep the conversation up and running.

His jaw tightened and he kept his gaze focused on the building. "I don't know."

Surprised, I looked at over at him before I could stop myself.

He dropped his gaze down to his hands in his lap. "She was always up before I was."

The waves of guilt coming off him now were almost overwhelming. It broke my heart.

"Zane—" I said.

"Look, I know you didn't have anything resembling normal when you lived in the lab," he began.

I braced myself for whatever was coming next.

"But was there someone who took care of you, someone you didn't want to let down?" He fidgeted with the cap from his orange juice bottle. "Besides your dad."

Who had, after all, betrayed me, therefore nullifying any disappointment I might have caused him, I suppose.

I thought of the parade of technicians, scientists, and doctors, some of them far worse than others, traipsing through my little cell and the observation room above it. When I was very young, I'd had caregivers, all of them affectionate and loving and just the tiniest bit distant. With good reason, they were traded out on a weekly or monthly basis, depending on my level of attachment. Apparently, Dr. Jacobs had wanted to make sure I was *capable* of forming emotional bonds—a sociopath with my abilities was a frightening thought, even for me—but not to the point of actually enjoying the warmth and security of said bonds.

"No, not really," I said quietly. The only exception might have been Mara, my favorite lab tech. She'd been kind to me, treating me like a person instead of an inanimate object, as the other doctors and technicians did. She'd even tried once to stand up for me against Dr. Jacobs, when he'd wanted me to kill Jerry, a lab mouse, and I'd refused.

But in the end, Jacobs had won that round. I'd killed Jerry, and Mara had disappeared. I'd always hoped it was because she quit and went on to some happier life, rather than a more drastic alternative deemed necessary for maintaining project security. Just another day in my childhood as a science experiment—worrying about murders committed simply because of my existence.

Zane sagged in his seat, flicking his OJ cap into the bag of garbage at his feet. He now had shoes, at least. Knock-off Adidas. Another of my purchases, that one at an all-night Walmart.

I leaned over closer to him, careful to keep my hands to myself. I wasn't sure how receptive he'd be to my touching him right now. "No matter what life experiences I have or haven't had, I can guarantee you one thing. It's not your fault she left."

"You can't even tell me if that's her in there, but *that* you're sure of?" He snorted. "Right."

"I am," I said. "Because nothing you could have done or not done would justify cutting contact with you."

"You don't know that. I was pretty awful to her." He paused, as if he couldn't quite make himself say the words. "My dad thought I was too much like her, so I did everything I could to keep her away."

I straightened up. "Yeah, okay, so you're oblivious sometimes and prone to choosing the path of least resistance—"

"Thanks." He glared at me.

I ignored him. "My point is, you're human. You may have made mistakes, but those aren't who you are in here." I risked reaching across the gap between us to tap his chest. "You fought for me when no one else would, not even the man who raised me. As far as I'm concerned, that makes you a pretty spectacular person. My very favorite full-blooded human, in fact," I said with a wobbly smile.

He exhaled slowly, and his blue-gray gaze fixed on my face, as if searching for answers he desperately needed.

I wanted to reach out to touch him, to reassure him, to impart my certainty that he was worth so much more than he thought, more than he'd ever been shown.

But then the moment broke, and he looked away.

"Let's just go," he said unbuckling his seat belt. "Get this over with. If she wonders why we're here so early, we can tell her we're on our way somewhere else and just stopped by to say hi."

I wasn't sure anyone ever stopped by this early in the morning just to say hello, but whatever. Sitting here on the street for another hour or two, like a couple of easy targets, didn't seem a particularly great option either.

"Okay," I said slowly, freeing myself from my seat belt.

He shoved open the door and climbed out, not waiting for me.

But when I rounded the front of the van, he was there, and to my surprise he took my hand, his fingers slipping in against my palm.

He kept his gaze fixed firmly ahead, and I knew better than to react to it, even though my heart was dancing an overjoyed and relieved jig.

I clenched my teeth. If this woman hurt him again, I would have a hard time not hurting her back. I didn't care how bad her marriage was, how much of a jerk Zane's dad had been (and I could believe he'd reached epic jerk proportions), there was no excuse for what she'd done. Leaving? Okay. Completely abandoning her son? No way.

Never knowing either of my biological parents—genetic material donors, really, one human, one alien—was difficult enough, at times. I couldn't imagine what it would feel like to have them reject me.

Next to me, Zane took a deep breath. "We'll just ring the doorbell and see if she answers. If she does . . ." His grip tightened on my hand.

I hated seeing Zane, normally so confident, knocked back on his heels like this. "You'll say hello," I said firmly. "Then she'll take it from there, I'm sure."

And she'd better freaking smile and welcome him with open arms.

At the base of the concrete steps leading to her door, Zane hesitated.

I pulled free of his hand and gave him gentle push.

"Go. I'll wait here." The porch wasn't really big enough for both of us to stand side by side, and besides, I didn't want anything—like, who is this strange girl you've brought with you?—to interrupt the potential reunion.

He went up the steps, rang the doorbell, and stuffed his hands in pockets to wait, rocking back on his heels. I could feel the nervousness flowing through him.

"No one's home," he said over his shoulder. "We should go."

I rolled my eyes. "Just give it a second." I paused, then added, "Chicken."

He glared at me, but he stayed on the porch, just as I'd figured he would. He was stubborn if pushed on something that mattered to him, a quality I was incredibly grateful for.

The sounds of locks disengaging on the other side snapped his attention away from me and to the door.

Please be happy to see him, please, please, please. I tensed, ready to . . . I don't know, pull Zane back, to protect him from his mother's indifference, if necessary.

"Zane?" Her voice, thick with sleep, held uncertainty and surprise.

"Hi," he said, the word escaping in a quick rush of air, as if he'd planned more but that was all that came out.

She gave an inarticulate cry of joy. "What are you doing here?" Her hands appeared on his shoulders, pulling him closer.

That was a good sign. I tried to relax but found myself fighting against a small and surprising surge of envy. I was alone, but Zane wasn't. He had someone to welcome him, to know and love him unconditionally, as family was supposed to. It only amplified the feeling of being alone in a much larger world than I'd ever anticipated.

This is a good thing, I told myself. He needed this after everything that had gone down with his dad. And it might mean that I had an ally in convincing Zane that his life was better spent not on the run with me, no matter how much I wanted him to come with me.

But then Zane bent down to hug his mom, and I saw her face over his shoulder, her eyes squeezed shut.

I'd half expected to recognize her in a vague way, a face glimpsed at a distance in the hallways at school or behind the wheel of a passing car on the street. Even though I hadn't been allowed out often, Wingate was a relatively small town, and Zane and I were in the same grade.

But it was more than that, so much more. I *knew* her.

My breath caught in my throat. It had been ten years since I'd last seen this woman, and she had gray in her hair now and deep wrinkles, near her eyes and on either side of her mouth. But it was clearly, unmistakably her. It was almost as if thinking about this woman had summoned her into reality. Mara. Lab tech. GTX employee. Most definitely not dead.

I must have made some choked noise, because Mara's eyes snapped open suddenly and focused on me.

The color drained from her face. She released Zane from the hug only to yank him toward the door to the duplex, putting herself between us as if she thought I might charge forward. "You're supposed to stay away," she hissed at me. "I've done everything he asked me to."

Behind her, Zane frowned, confused. "Mom?"

I retreated automatically, my hands up in defense. I had no idea what she was talking about. *He who? Dr. Jacobs?* She was afraid and angry, both of which were pulsing so loudly through her mind I couldn't track her thoughts.

"You have no right to be here, threatening my son!" she shouted at me.

I cringed, all too aware of the scene we were making—well, she was making it and I was in the middle of it. Did she think I was here to hurt her? Had Dr. Jacobs threatened to send me after her at some point?

I backed up, off the sidewalk, checking all sides, expecting the flash of black retrieval team uniforms across the sun-baked yard. But there was nothing. The street remained empty. No one sprang out from behind the desiccated bushes.

"Mom, what are you talking about?" Zane asked from behind her, his voice strained with worry. "No one's threatening anybody." He tried to push past her, but she was determined, throwing an arm across the doorway to bar him.

"Where are the others, Ford?" she demanded, her gaze searching the yard and street behind me.

I gaped at her. The others? Which others? Her fellow GTX employees? And who or what was Ford?

I looked to Zane, but he seemed as baffled as I was. And a lot more freaked out. Of course he was; it was his mother who was behaving so strangely.

"Nixon, Carter, I know you're out there somewhere," Mara snarled. "Stay the hell away."

And with that nonsensical statement, she pushed Zane into the house with enough force to send him stumbling and slammed the door after herself.

I stood there, the crash echoing in my head, and blinked in the sunshine as it crested over the roofs, and birds in the surrounding trees resettled themselves and began a frenzied fit of chirping. Otherwise, nothing moved, and it was quiet, except for the hum of traffic in the distance.

If this was an attempt to recapture me, it was possibly the weirdest, least-effective snare ever.

Ford, Nixon, and Carter. They were all former presidents. What that had to do with anything, I had no idea.

Was Mara crazy? Had she become mentally unstable in the years since I'd seen her? Her thoughts had been so corrupted with the bright clanging of fear, it was hard to tell. But that might explain her behavior today as well as her decision to abandon Zane without further contact.

But what about—

Ariane! A sudden spike of panic broke through the silence and into my head. Zane. Something inside the house had him freaking out.

I abandoned any further examination of the situation and raced up the sidewalk to the door.

CHAPTER 6

Zane

"THIS WON'T STOP THEM, BUT IT'LL SLOW THEM DOWN some," my mom assured me, locking the door. It was far from a simple process. Seven locks decorated the wood: three dead bolts—two of which were so new they were shiny—three security chains, and the little tab lock on the doorknob itself.

I watched in stunned silence, not sure what the hell was going on. "Are you okay?" I asked cautiously. Her hands were shaking as she set the last chain; it took her two tries to get the little hook into the slider bar.

"Don't worry about me. Did they hurt you?" she asked breathlessly, turning to scan me for obvious injury.

"Who are *they*?" I asked. You could hear the emphasis when she said it, communicating a single malicious entity made up of multiple parts. But it had been just Ariane and me out there.

She shook her head. "This must be really confusing for

you right now, and I'm sorry that I can't explain everything. But right now, I really need you to go to the basement."

I gaped at her. Was it even possible for someone to lose their shit so completely in eighteen months?

Her eyes were too bright, and her cheeks were flushed with the exertion and anxiety. She appeared too thin, bony almost, and older, as if she'd aged decades in the time she'd been gone. The wrinkles on her forehead were deep grooves now, and the gray near her temples had spread through the rest of her dark hair, like silvery spider threads. Even though I'd surpassed her in height a couple years ago, she wasn't short—five feet ten, the same as my dad. But now she seemed shrunken and frail.

It was as if something had been eating away at her, taking little pieces of the person I knew with every bite.

"Okay," I said slowly, eyeing her as a stranger with my mother's face. "Why the basement?"

"Because they've probably got the back covered," she said, tugging at my arm. "But they don't know about the other exit. Leads to the unit next door." She gave me a grim smile that looked more like a baring of teeth.

Crap. Making tinfoil hats couldn't be far behind. What had happened to the calm, stable person who'd weathered my dad's shifting moods and short temper with the relatively serene disposition of someone confronted with a raging storm? Nothing to be done except endure. Just make it through.

"Mom—" I began.

Her hand tightened around my wrist like a claw. "Move." She yanked on my arm with surprising strength, pulling me through the bare-walled entryway, past a staircase leading up, and over the threshold into a small kitchen. With her free hand, she pulled a cell phone from her bathrobe pocket and pressed a button.

"Whoa, Mom. There's no need to call anybody." I envisioned police officers, angry after weeks of paranoid calls from this address, showing up at the door. I doubted that GTX or my dad had filed any kind of report on either Ariane or me, but it wasn't worth taking the chance.

I lurched for the phone, but my mom twisted out of my reach.

Shit. Ariane! A little help!

"Get him for me," my mom said into the phone. Oh God, was there even a person on the other end of that call? Was she that far gone?

"Mom," I begged. "Please listen to me." Her nails were digging into my wrist, and she didn't seem to notice. She was still pulling.

In the hallway, I heard the locks disengaging, one at a time, and felt a rush of relief. Ariane was coming.

I probably should have been worrying about what my mom would say when she realized Ariane had gotten in. But then again, if my mom thought the mysterious "they" could penetrate locked doors, maybe Ariane's sudden appearance inside wouldn't strike her as too odd.

"I don't care if he's busy. You get Dr. Laughlin on the phone now. It's Mara."

Laughlin. I froze. That was one of the names mentioned in Ariane's letter from her father. "David Laughlin?" I asked. "How do you know that name?"

My mom frowned at me, moving the phone away from

her mouth. "Where did you hear it? Did they mention him to you?"

Again with the "they."

Before I could respond, the front door opened, the undone chains clacking against the back of it.

"Run!" My mom, wide-eyed with panic, let go of my arm and tried to shove me toward a closed door on the opposite side of the room, but I planted my feet and refused to move.

Ariane appeared a moment later at the threshold to the hall. She spared my mother a quick glance and then focused her attention on me, assessing me with those too-dark eyes hidden behind blue lenses. "Are you all right?"

She could have left, but she didn't. That was the only thought echoing in my head, and the sudden swell of gratitude made my throat feel tight. "I'm okay."

She nodded, a strand of her pale hair falling across her face.

I turned to my mom, who was watching us with a strange expression on her face, the phone in her hand seemingly forgotten. "Mom, this is my—"

"107?" my mom asked faintly.

My heart stopped beating for a second. 107. That was Ariane's GTX designation, the number on the tattoo on her shoulder. I'd never heard anyone but Dr. Jacobs refer to her that way.

Ariane, though, seemed completely unsurprised by this development. She gave my mother a nod.

My mom sagged back against the counter in relief and started laughing, albeit with a hysterical edge. Then she lifted her phone up and ended the call with a definitive press of the button.

I looked back and forth between the two of them, but no answers appeared forthcoming. "All right," I said, frustrated. "I guess I'll be the stupid one and ask. What the hell is going on?"

Ariane spoke up with obvious reluctance. "Mara was a lab tech at GTX for a while. As for the rest . . . I don't know."

Hearing her use my mom's name sent a jolt through me. I was pretty sure I'd never mentioned it to Ariane before.

A sick feeling grew in my gut. "Is that true?" I asked my mom. "Did you work in the lab at GTX? Did you do that . . . stuff to Ariane? Tests and experiments?" As far as I'd known, my mom had been an office assistant during her few years at GTX.

When she wouldn't meet my gaze, my heart fell. I looked to Ariane.

Ariane hesitated. "No. It wasn't like that. She tried to help. She—"

"Yes," my mother said flatly. "I did."

I stared at her, seeing not just an altered version of the person I'd known but maybe someone I hadn't known at all.

"I'm so, so sorry," she said to Ariane, her voice cracking.

Ariane nodded and glanced away, clearly uncomfortable.

"But I don't understand," my mom said with a frown. "How are you here? Where's Mark?"

Mark Tucker, Ariane's adoptive father. So my mom had known about that too?

I waved my arms, signaling a time-out before Ariane could answer. "Wait, let's go back to the part where you worked on a secret project involving extraterrestrial DNA and human experimentation."

My mom flinched as if I'd hit her, but I ignored it.

"When was this?" I asked. "And if you know her, then why were you acting all crazy? Talking about 'them' and—"

The phone rang in my mom's hand, startling all of us. She stared down at it as if she'd completely forgotten she held it, and I remembered what we'd been talking about before Ariane had walked in.

"It's Laughlin," I said to Ariane quickly. "She knows Laughlin somehow."

"I thought you were one of his," my mom said to Ariane. "They're not supposed to come here anymore but—"

"One of his what?" I asked, baffled.

Ariane cocked her head to one side, a posture I recognized as her listening to something the rest of us couldn't hear. "Mara thought I was one of his hybrids. Ford," Ariane said suddenly with the air of someone solving a mystery that had troubled her. "It's a name."

I frowned. Ford was a weird name for a girl. Unless . . . wait, Nixon and Carter, that's what my mom had shouted out the door earlier. Three sequential president names. Nixon, Ford, and Carter. Some kind of naming scheme Laughlin had used instead of numbers? If so, that would mean there were *three* hybrids.

My mom nodded. "You look just like her, but Ford is . . ." A faint sheen of sweat appeared on her face. "She's different."

"I don't understand," I said. "If she's a hybrid, how can she just be wandering around like—"

"If I don't answer, they'll know something is wrong," my mom said as the phone entered its third ring. "They may send someone." She spoke to the room at large, but then she looked to Ariane, with deference and perhaps a hint of fear, for permission.

Ariane nodded. "Answer it. But be careful, please."

I wasn't sure if that was a threat or a warning. And I had no idea how to feel about it either way. This was my *mom*, after all. Then again, I wasn't sure the person I'd thought of as my mom actually existed. I'd felt guilty about the way I'd behaved toward her before she left—and I still did—but I couldn't make all that compute with these new secrets revealed, with this new side of her. What she'd done to Ariane was horrible. So, was it wrong to still feel bad for not being better to her?

I shook my head. It was so messed up and confusing.

But my mom just nodded at Ariane, as though she'd expected nothing less, and lifted the phone to her ear. "Hello?" she said. "Dr. Laughlin?" Her panicked breathing was loud enough to be just as audible to him as it was to us.

She was going to give us away without saying another word. He'd have to be an idiot not to realize something was wrong.

I must not have been the only one thinking along those lines, because Ariane started toward my mom with her hand out.

But my mom backed away, setting her chin in determination. "I just wanted to tell you that it's not necessary for you to send your little drones to spy on me while I'm shopping," she said in a steadier voice, one threaded with indignation. "I don't think they really need to know whether I prefer frozen broccoli or asparagus."

She paused, listening to him on the other end, her anger

spreading fresh color over her pale and sunken cheeks.

"What difference does it make to you when I go to the store?" she demanded. "Maybe it is early for a grocery run, but it's not as if I'm sleeping much anyway." She gave a bitter laugh.

Another pause, and her mouth tightened at whatever he was saying. I knew that expression. She was getting pissed. I'd seen that face plenty of times when Quinn and I were arguing over toys or the TV remote or who drank the last of the orange juice.

"I don't care if you say they're still at the facility. I know what I saw," she said. "I've kept my end of the agreement, you better keep yours." Then without waiting for a response, she ended the call, dropped the phone on the counter with a clatter, as if she couldn't stand to touch it for a second longer, and covered her face with her hands.

I edged closer to Ariane, giving my mom a wide berth—well, as much as possible in this small kitchen. I felt as if I didn't know what my mom would do, how she would react—a wildly unpredictable variable in an already difficult situation. Weirdly enough, in this room with the woman who gave birth to me, Ariane was my source for familiar.

"Did he believe it?" I asked Ariane quietly, resisting the urge to pull her closer, tuck her under one arm like I needed the stability. But the tension in her shoulders and the tight set of her jaw told me she was on guard. She was in war mode, or whatever she called it, and probably wouldn't appreciate me hampering her ability to respond.

She shook her head. "I don't know. I can't read thoughts over the phone. And unless he's in the neighborhood, his mind is outside my range."

"He believed it," my mom said, looking up, her cheeks damp. "He thinks I'm scared and paranoid, which is exactly what he wants." She smiled, tears overflowing again. "The worst part is, he's right. I was telling the truth. I got so used to looking for them around every corner, I thought I caught a glimpse of Ford at the store last week. Watching me from the end of the frozen-food aisle." She laughed, an awful, choked sound. "It's not possible. Laughlin says he restricted them to the main facility a few months ago, except for when they're in school, so I don't know, maybe I really am going crazy."

Ariane frowned and looked to me.

I shook my head. I had no idea what was going on, how much of it was real and what percentage might be in her head. But there were some coincidences that couldn't be overlooked. Like the fact that she and Ariane knew each other and that the name Laughlin was being tossed around.

"Mom," I began.

"I'm fine," my mom said, straightening up and wiping under her eyes. "But you need to leave. He may have someone check up on me, and he cannot find you here. I won't make it that easy for him." She made a shooing gesture at me. "Go now."

I stared at her. "You must be crazy if you think I'm leaving here without answers."

"Zane," she said in that exaggeratedly patient Mom tone, "I don't have time to explain everything, so you're just going to have to—"

"Fine, forget all of that," I snapped. "How about what you're doing here? Why you lied to me? Why you left in the middle of the night and never came back?"

She squared her shoulders, as if preparing for a fight. "You don't understand. I was trying to—"

"What is your arrangement with Dr. Laughlin and his company?" Ariane spoke up next to me. "Did you seek him out to continue your . . . career?"

Oddly enough, that question—or maybe the fact that it came from Ariane—seemed to break through my mom's resistance.

She slumped back against the counter with a defeated air. "Of course not," she said. "When I took this job and moved here, I swear to you, I thought it was the office job I applied for. Laughlin Integrated has so many subsidiaries and branches, I didn't even know it was his company."

"That doesn't explain GTX," I pointed out. And Ariane. That, to me, was the most difficult part to wrap my brain around—that my mom had bundled me off to kindergarten with a kiss on the forehead and then gone to work where she'd stood on the other side of that glass wall and watched Ariane suffer or, worse, actively participated in the experiments and tests on her. Just the thought made me feel ill.

"I had the best of intentions, I promise you," she said, but she couldn't quite meet my eyes. "I didn't know the extent of the project when I signed on. We needed the money, and your father was thrilled that I was working at GTX."

Of course he was.

"I did the best I could, and I thought it was for a good cause," she said, looking down at her hands, her fingers laced together.

"Yeah, that's what they all say," I muttered. That was pretty much the same excuse Ariane's adoptive father had given for his role in everything. He'd done it to save other human children from cancer. Well, how could you argue with that? Except after seeing Ariane trapped in the small cell, miserable and alone, I couldn't imagine anyone *not* arguing with it. "She's not a freaking lab rat."

Ariane cleared her throat. "It's okay. She was kind to me."

"Compared to what?" I demanded.

"Zane," my mom protested weakly.

"If I am willing to accept her apology for what she did to me, then you need to as well," Ariane said in that calm way of hers.

"That's bull," I said. "There is no apology to cover what they did to you."

"Maybe not, but it's more than any of the others have ever offered," she pointed out. Then in a deliberate effort to change the topic, she turned her attention to my mother. "How does Laughlin come into this?"

I exhaled loudly. Trust Ariane to keep on point.

"He wanted someone who knew what GTX was doing with their . . . with you," she said. "When I started applying for jobs—"

"So you were planning to leave?" I asked stiffly. I'd suspected that, of course, but hearing it was something different. Somehow, if she'd just, I don't know, snapped and left on the spur of the moment, I could have handled that better than the fact that she'd made preparations for weeks or even months in advance. A thousand opportunities to tell me or even hint at it, and she'd said nothing. That made every moment I'd spent in her presence during that time a complete and utter lie.

"Oh, honey." She reached for me.

I stepped back, and Ariane touched my arm, staying my

retreat, her fingers cool, light, and reassuring against my skin, like a washcloth on your forehead when you have a fever.

My mom frowned, and Ariane dropped her hand.

"Things weren't good at home," my mom said. "You know that. We'd agreed to stay together until you were both out of high school, but with Quinn graduating, it was only getting worse."

Much like this conversation. The fact that my parents hadn't had the best relationship was not news to me. Learning that they'd had some kind of cold, factual agreement, with a timeline and everything, was.

"It was as if once he could see the light at the end of the tunnel, it only made him angrier that he was in the tunnel in the first place," she said. "I was going to take you with me, but you were so determined to follow in Quinn's footsteps and your father wasn't going to give up without a fight. . . ."

"So you're saying it was my fault," I said, fighting a swell of fury and hurt, even though I'd suspected that same thing all along.

"No!" she said, shocked. "I didn't want to take you from your home, to make you miserable." She paused. "And I didn't want to make you hate me more than you already did."

She had a point; back then, that was exactly what I would have done: hated her and done my best to make her regret taking me away from my chance to make my dad proud of me. It was only after she'd left that I'd realized the absolute futility of that quest.

"How did Dr. Laughlin find you?" Ariane asked, once more redirecting the conversation. I wasn't sure whether to be grateful or frustrated.

"I had GTX on my resume, but it was just the regular assistant job that I'd been told to use as a cover when I started working there. But Dr. Laughlin . . . he knew somehow. They all spy on each other." She shuddered.

"What about Emerson St. John? The third competitor? You've met him," Ariane said.

My mom shook her head. "No. Laughlin isn't interested in his approach. He's trying to use some kind of viral delivery system to effect changes within a human system."

Huh?

To my surprise, Ariane nodded. "Rewriting the existing human code rather than trying to combine human and alien DNA to create a new entity."

"Something like that. Laughlin doesn't consider him a threat in the trials, so I don't know much about him."

"So, now you work with Laughlin's hybrids?" I asked.

"Sort of."

"What are they like?" Ariane asked softly. And I realized then we were talking about the closest thing she had to family on this world, maybe on any world, which somehow took a lot of the fuel out of my anger. My mom had lied to me, and my dad was a jerk, but I had them. They existed, providing a solid connection.

My mom shuddered. "They are . . . not human."

"Neither am I," Ariane said.

"No, you don't understand," she said. "Before, it was better. The four who survived the start of adolescence—two from each of the last test groups—they were mostly quiet. Submissive, distant. They seemed to live more inside their own heads than out in the world. But that wasn't enough.

Jacobs, Laughlin, they're trying to find the balance between independent thought and obedience, between humanity and all the accelerated benefits of your . . . other people." She shook her head. "They need someone who can take direction and think for herself. Even the best plans can't account for every variable. If a mission doesn't go according to the specifications, they need an operative who can still get the job done."

"And Laughlin's hybrids can do all of that," I said.

"Not exactly. Not all of them." She grimaced. "When Johnson . . . when Ford took over for Johnson, things changed. The bond between them has always been intense. They should have been competitors, but it's something in their genetic makeup from the alien side. They *thrive* in a communal environment. The survival rate increased dramatically once Laughlin realized that." She glanced at Ariane, as if searching for some sign of the same in her. Or perhaps recognizing that it was a miracle she'd survived alone, isolated in her tiny cell. "But the consequence is that they're more like one entity with separate bodies. They're networked through their telepathy. When Johnson was in control, it was all right, but Ford is leading now. They don't blend as well as one-oh . . . as Ariane. They stand out too much. And Ford doesn't care. They make people uncomfortable, and they seem to enjoy it." She lifted her hands helplessly. "I've done my best but—"

"Your role is to help humanize them," Ariane said.

"Technically, I'm a consultant. But yes. They didn't have the upbringing you did. They are lacking in human cultural references and experiences. Laughlin wanted to minimize emotional attachment. They were raised without caregivers, other than for their physical needs. The idea, I guess, was that they would find it easier to follow orders without the complication of feelings. But the trouble is, now they don't relate to humans except as order-givers. Laughlin realized that would put them at a disadvantage during the trials, especially when compared to others who are more conversant in human conventions, more relatable." She dropped her gaze to the floor, avoiding Ariane's eyes. "He wanted to know what GTX had done to promote those qualities." She paused. "I tried. I did. But with Ford . . . they hate us so much."

"Are you surprised?" Ariane asked with an edge. So maybe she wasn't as okay with what had been done to her as she outwardly seemed to be.

"We were only trying to—"

"—completely disregard the ethical considerations of creating a life simply as a means to an end? Or how about the right of another living creature to exist unmolested and free of pain?" Ariane asked.

Yep, definitely not as okay with it as she seemed. I looped an arm over her shoulder, and she stiffened at first and then relaxed into my side.

My mom shook her head. "You're probably right. That's why you need to go. They're clever. Sneaky, even. Unless Dr. Laughlin has given them strict orders, they will pursue their own . . . interests." She lifted her hand to her throat, as if imagining fingers wrapped around it. Or if these other hybrids shared Ariane's telekinesis, they wouldn't even have to use their hands. "As I said, they're not supposed to come here anymore, but—"

"That's why you thought Ariane was Ford," I said, finally getting the last piece of the puzzle. "What does she have against you? Other than being human and one of her captors, I mean?"

My mom winced, but she didn't argue. "Johnson, the one who was in charge before Ford. She was . . . eliminated. She couldn't adjust to the strain of outside life. She'd respond to thoughts instead of what people said. She'd forget to move things with her hands instead of using her abilities. She was too distant, too removed from the outside world." Mara gave a helpless sigh. "She was attracting too much attention to the others at school."

"School?" I asked in disbelief. "You sent them to school?"

"I had to do something," she said defensively. "It's fine. They have a cover story. They've been 'diagnosed' with a genetic condition that affects their appearance and their behavior."

I rolled my eyes. As if *that* was the real issue here.

"And Ford holds you responsible for Johnson's death," Ariane said with the air of someone confirming something she already suspected.

"She does, yes. That's why you need to go home. Please," my mom begged. "Wingate is GTX territory, and that offers you some protection. Dr. Jacobs is a flawed man, but he, at least, let me go when he realized that the work was not for me. Laughlin is not nearly as generous. He's not above . . . extreme methods to induce cooperation. Hurting people." She swallowed hard and looked up to the ceiling, blinking rapidly against tears, making me wonder exactly what she'd seen during her tenure with Laughlin.

"I'm stuck here until the trials, working for him," she said. "In exchange, he's promised to leave my family alone." She stuffed her trembling hands into her bathrobe pockets. "But if he discovers you're here, he'll send Ford and the others after you. You need to go home," she pleaded.

Which meant, much as I hated to admit it, my mom was in some ways as much a hostage as the hybrids she'd been hired to work with.

I glanced at Ariane, who gave me a weary nod.

"Wingate is not an option anymore," I said.

"I understand that your father is not the easiest man to—" my mom began.

"It's not him. Or, not just him." I sighed. "GTX wants us."

"You mean Ariane," my mom said.

"No, both of us," I responded.

"I don't understand," she said slowly.

Apparently, in the confusion and chaos of our arrival here and her misidentification of Ariane, my mom hadn't had time to put it all together. That GTX wouldn't just let Ariane leave town, especially not without her "father" in charge. That I'd been freaked out by my mom's strange behavior, but not at the discussion of alien/human hybrids and experimentation or Ariane getting in through a door with seven locks. That we were comfortable with each other in a way that suggested more than a casual school acquaintance.

I saw it the moment the ball dropped, and she figured it out.

She paled. "Oh no," she whispered, staring at me and then at Ariane. "What did you do?"

I felt Ariane cringe next to me, hearing the inherent accusation in my mom's words.

"It wasn't like that," I said as calmly as I could. "It started out as a stupid prank, something Rachel Jacobs cooked up. Ariane and I were working together against her, and everything just sort of developed from there." In spite of myself and the situation, I felt a sudden lightness inside at the memories of happier days, the activities fair, the *Star Wars* conversation, breakfast in the truck. She was the first person who'd really seemed to like me for who I was, not for who I could be or should have been.

"The Rules," my mom said desperately, as if she could just find the right thing to say, all of this would go away. "Mark Tucker had a list of rules you were supposed to follow to keep this exact thing from happening."

That was the first I'd heard of it, but when Ariane was nodding, her face set in grim lines.

"Don't get involved, don't trust anyone, don't fall in love." My mom shook her head. "I can't remember all of them, but a lot of thought went into them for this reason."

That's what Ariane had been battling inside herself the whole time we'd been playing against Rachel and getting to know each other? No wonder she'd had a panic attack getting into my truck that first time. Warmth and pride filled my chest. She'd had to fight hard to carry through with our plan, defying not only her adoptive father but also rules that had probably been drilled into her head for literally years—and she'd done it. That kind of strength of character only made me admire her more. I wasn't sure I would have been able to do it if I'd been in that situation.

"And you thought chaining her down with those rules was a good idea?" I demanded of my mom. "Who can live like that?"

"The point was to protect everyone else," she said, then turned on Ariane. "I cut off all contact with my son for eighteen months to keep him out of this mess, and you drag him back in? How could you do that?"

"Mom." I held up my hand, angling to keep her from moving closer. "She didn't drag me into anything—"

"I wasn't dealing with a full set of facts, as you well know," Ariane said hotly, finally goaded into defending herself.

"—I am capable of making my own decisions," I said.

"You may not have known everything, but you certainly knew *what* you were," my mom said to Ariane, as if I hadn't spoken.

The air went out of the room.

Ariane stiffened, and I stared at my mom, unable to believe what had come out of her mouth.

"What is wrong with you?" I asked, trying again to see the person I'd once thought her to be in the stranger before me. Where was the mother who'd scolded me for teasing Quinn when he'd gotten that huge zit on his forehead? I'd called it an alien horn. I'd gone on a whole riff with it, called him Xenar, asked him when he was going back to his home planet, when did he expect the horn to make a full appearance. Typical annoying little brother stuff. And if it had been a few years later, he'd have beaten the hell out of me for it, but at that point we were fairly close in size. So when it got out of hand, with Quinn screaming at me and his eyes all shiny with tears, my mom intervened with a lecture about treating people the way I wanted to be treated. I'd rolled my eyes during the entire speech, but it stuck with me. Mainly because I'd never actually expected to upset Quinn.

Granted, that was just a temporary complexion problem (probably the last time Quinn would be less than perfect in anyone's eyes) and this was something far more complicated, but didn't that mean the lesson would be even more applicable in this situation? Unless, of course, my mom had meant to imply limits that I hadn't even known about then by using the word *people*. It gave me an additional shock to realize that at the time of that conversation, my mom had already come and gone as a GTX employee, that she knew about Ariane and had left her to Dr. Jacobs's schemes and devices.

"Sweetie." My mom approached me with her hands out as if she would touch my face, and I backed up, taking Ariane with me. "I'm sure you think this is a grand and romantic gesture, but there is no way this can end well, do you understand that? She doesn't deserve what's happened to her, but she's not human."

I struggled to formulate a response that wasn't just inarticulate yelling, but my mom moved on before I could.

"What was your plan?" she asked Ariane. "Run for Canada and hope for the best?" If it was possible, I could feel Ariane getting smaller by the second, shredded by her words.

"Do you think they won't have thought of that?" my mom continued. "Do you think there's a border crossing out there that doesn't have your picture posted? You have no idea what you're up against." She threw her hands up. "If you're *lucky*, you'll end up back in the lab at GTX."

At the idea of Ariane being trapped in that tiny white room again—and that my mom would think that a best-case scenario—something in me snapped. "Okay, we're done here." I grabbed Ariane's hand and tugged her out of the room with me.

"Where are you going? Zane?" My mom followed us to the front door. "Wingate is your only—"

"No." I led the way out onto the porch, then reached back and slammed the door once Ariane cleared the threshold.

"Come on," I said, pulling her down the steps and across the grass to the van. She didn't protest the pace, even though she had to take two strides for my one. "Keys."

Ariane handed them over without argument, and I knew I was in trouble, then. No questions about where we were going or what we were doing. This wasn't good.

I opened the passenger-side door and made sure she got in, mainly because I wasn't sure she'd speak up if I drove off without her.

I climbed in behind the wheel and pulled away from the curb with a screech of tires on the pavement, generating a reproving look from an old guy across the street out picking up his newspaper.

Blowing out a slow breath, I let my foot off the gas a little as we left my mom's neighborhood. Driving angry wasn't a good idea right now. We couldn't take the chance of getting pulled over.

Turning back onto the main road, I picked left, randomly. It was the opposite direction we'd come from. And it was as good as any for the moment. The lack of a specific destination made me a little edgy, but there was nothing to be done about it for now. I didn't have Ariane's training, but it seemed to me the smartest thing to do was find somewhere we could blend in and hide until we could figure out a next step.

"She's right," Ariane said after a few moments, her tone flat, emotionless. "I was being selfish. I could have left the motel without waking you up. But I shut the door. I wanted you to come after me, even if I couldn't admit it." Then her voice broke over a hiccup. "I wanted you with me."

Oh God, she was killing me here. I couldn't look at her and keep my eyes on the road.

"Listen to me," I said as firmly as I could, "I'm here because I want to be. Until I met you, no one had ever put me first. Do you get that? Even with my mom, leaving my dad was more important than I was." I glanced at her to see if my words were making a difference.

She was shaking her head. "We have nowhere to go, no plan. You can't stay with me. You shouldn't."

This was my mom's fault. Ariane might have left me behind before in an attempt to protect me, but now, it was more than that. My mom had said those horrible things, and Ariane had believed her. About her not being human, about it not ending well. Along with a strong implication that maybe she didn't deserve to hope for anything more. All of it confirming what I suspected Ariane already believed.

If I didn't do something, she'd take the first opportunity to sneak away or, God forbid, offer herself up to Laughlin in exchange for my safety, just as she'd tried to do the other day at GTX.

Ahead on the right, I saw bright and cheery signs for a mall, and beyond them a vast expanse of parking lot. Cars

moved around the outer edge with purpose. Like ants surrounding a dropped sandwich, they were collecting around
several early morning restaurants—McDonald's, IHOP, and
something called Walker Bros. Pancake House—within the
mall complex.

I made a snap decision and jerked into the turn lane,
ignoring the blare of a horn behind us. "Let me ask you
something—how shallow do you think I am?" I demanded,
letting more of my frustration bleed through than I'd
intended.

Ariane looked at me, surprised, her eyes damp.

"Do you really think if you sent me back to Wingate, I'd
just drift into a normal routine?" Assuming, of course, that
Dr. Jacobs would allow it. "Do you think I'd forget all about
this? Do you think I'd just drive by GTX and not wonder
if you were in there, if they were hurting you?" My voice
cracked, and I had to swallow hard to keep the words from
getting stuck with the lump in my throat. "Do you really
think that little of me?"

Her mouth fell open. "Of course not, but—"

"But what?" I challenged.

"I'm trying to do the right thing!" she shouted, frustrated.

"I'm sure that's what they thought too when they gave you
that messed-up list of commandments. Thou shalt not have a
life. Always remember that you're a freak and not deserving
of anything resembling happiness."

She inhaled sharply.

"I'm here, with you, because I want to be," I said, trying
to put my feelings into words, hoping they would convince
her, if nothing else. "It's not your job to save me."

Her silence spoke volumes.

Weary suddenly, I pulled into a parking space, near a clump of cars on the far side of Sears—either employees getting an early start or overflow from Walker Bros. "I can't make you believe that, though, and I can't keep you from leaving. So, if you're going to go, then fine." I shoved the gearshift into park, turned the van off, and got up, staying half stooped to avoid the roof.

"What are you doing?"

I gestured to the parking lot around us. "It looks like it's going to be busy as hell here in an hour or two. So I think this is as safe as it gets. Neither of us has slept in days, and I'm tired. We're going to get some rest and then figure out what to do next, preferably before the van reaches a temperature hot enough to cook us alive."

Without looking at her, I headed to the back of the van. I unrolled one of the sleeping bags that had been hidden in the smuggling compartment and unzipped the edges to create a blanket, some small measure of comfort against the hard metal floor of the van.

Then I lay down, tucked my arm under my head, and turned away from her, my heart beating too fast. It was a gamble to take this approach. I couldn't convince her of anything; she had to reach the conclusion on her own. But would she?

I closed my eyes. I couldn't watch.

After a few seconds, I heard her seat belt unclick, and swallowing the growing lump in my throat, I waited to hear the clunk of the door opening.

Instead, I felt the sleeping bag shift underneath me, and

I opened my eyes to see her kneel down next to me. "I don't know what I'm doing," she whispered to me, the words aching, raw, and full of fear. That must have been hard for her to admit, being someone who relied on strategy, training, and plans.

I rolled over and lifted my arm in welcome, and she curled herself against me, resting her head on my other arm. Her tears dripped on my elbow.

"Welcome to the club," I whispered back. "It's called, we're all just doing the best we can, and it's better if we stick together."

She was quiet for a long moment. "Are there membership cards? Because I don't think that name is going to fit."

Caught off guard, I laughed, surprising myself. "You should try to get some rest while we can. Then we'll figure out what to do," I said, sounding more confident than I felt. "It'll all make more sense later." At least, that's what I was hoping. Because honestly, right now, I had no clue.

CHAPTER 7

Ariane

EVEN WITH THE SOOTHING SOUNDS OF ZANE'S STEADY breathing next to me and cars rushing by on the road in the distance, as rhythmic as waves hitting the beach (not that I'd ever seen either waves or a beach in person—it was at the top of my list, though), I couldn't fall asleep.

My eyes were gritty from being awake for too long and swollen from crying, and the darkness behind my eyelids was a blissful relief. But I couldn't shut down my brain, and my eyes kept snapping open, studying the molded metal roof above us.

We needed a plan, a course of action, a goal. Something. Zane was putting up a good front, but I knew that revelation about his mother had thrown him more than he wanted to admit and he didn't know what to do next. The perils of hearing thoughts even when you didn't want to. And it occurred to me now, a little belatedly, that even as the strategy expert, maybe I was out of my depth. After all, I'd been designed to follow orders, not create them.

Tell me to infiltrate a building. Sure, no problem. Perimeter scan and threat analysis. Determine the position of doors and windows relative to available cover. Am I dealing with locks or live security? Identify and disable exterior surveillance cameras. In case of trouble, what other tools are at my disposal?

I'd seen the inside of almost every building in Wingate that had any form of security. My father had called these little adventures "training missions," taking me out on the few nights a month he had off from work.

"It'll do you no good, even with your abilities, if you don't know the basics," he'd said to me, over and over again. "If you can't beat the alarm or sneak past the cameras, how will you escape if they capture you?"

Just the idea of being caught, helpless and stuck behind a door that I couldn't open, had been more than enough motivation for me. I'd had lessons in the lab, of course, but no real-world experience. That had to change.

We'd started off small. Model homes in an unfinished subdivision on the north side of town. The houses were alarmed to the local police, but no live cams, no security guards. Easy peasy, as the saying goes. Except, of course, I hadn't counted on a dog, belonging to one of the families in one of the finished homes nearby, barking his head off.

I'd almost gotten caught my first time out by a nosy neighbor stepping out to see what might be sending the dog into fits. But I'd learned from it, applied it to future training sessions. One more question to ask each time: is there a dog in the vicinity?

After that, we'd gradually moved on to more difficult targets. The department stores after hours. (I'd bounced on the fake beds in the linen section; they were way harder than they looked.) The houses of the wealthy in town when the occupants weren't home. (I'd snooped in their pantries and refrigerators.) The same houses when they were home. (I'd hit the medicine cabinets that time; you can learn a great deal from those. Lots of acid reflux on that side of town.)

The only place we hadn't ventured anywhere near was, for obvious reasons, GTX.

But it occurred to me now, for the first time, that they'd probably been very well aware of what my father was doing, what he was teaching me. He may have even been acting on orders, continuing my training outside the lab at their request.

I shifted uneasily on the van floor, my heart aching at the idea. It was just one more way in which my father had lied to me.

Then again, he'd also done everything he could to help me escape GTX last night and get out of town cleanly.

I bit my lip. So, wasn't it possible that he'd trained me because he'd wanted to, because he'd truly had my best interests at heart?

Given the choice, that's what I wanted to believe. And since it was unlikely I'd ever see him again to ask, that was all I had.

Either way, though, my father had taught me well. And from his very thorough lessons, I knew what questions to ask; how to break down the larger objective into smaller, more manageable pieces; and how to create an action plan to complete each of those steps with the best chance of success for the overall mission.

I could break, enter, spy, steal, kill . . . any number of relatively complicated things, including figuring out creative ways around problems.

But never in all of my years of training—in the lab or with my father—had there ever been a moment when I set my own objective. Even as recently as last week, it had been Zane who'd approached me with the idea of defeating Rachel at her own game and a rough plan of what needed to happen.

The idea of taking on the responsibility—without the experience of having done it before or any guarantee of success—made me queasy. It wasn't just my life at stake anymore.

I looked up at Zane, his arm slung over me loosely and his handsome face peaceful in repose. The police chief's son. The lacrosse player. The guy that girls, including my former friend Jenna, giggled about. Human.

How had he ended up here? With me?

It felt as if this was some kind of moment clipped from a normal existence and spliced into mine. Like maybe he'd fallen asleep after I'd come over to watch a movie at his house or something, and I'd have to wake him up to take me home in a little while. But not yet.

The thought of such a normal moment—the idea of having it, the fact that we couldn't, not now, maybe ever—made my chest tight with longing and fear. I wanted that for him, for us, and I was terrified to the point of being paralyzed that thinking about it, being foolish enough to hope for it, was asking for more than I deserved. And that would only make fate or God or karma or whatever come down that much harder to make sure the point was clear.

I reached up and touched his chin lightly, feeling a day's worth of stubble against my fingertips, and even in his sleep, he turned in to my touch.

I'd thought he was a coward before I knew him, someone who couldn't or wouldn't think for himself, but now . . . I was beginning to suspect he might be the bravest person I'd ever met to throw his chips in with me. I wasn't sure *I* even trusted me to figure this out.

Blinking back hot tears, I let my hand drop. Zane trusted me, regardless of whether I thought that was the smart choice. He was counting on me.

I couldn't mess this up.

Taking a deep breath, I refocused my efforts on the trouble at hand. I knew what I wanted. I wanted us to be free, to live our lives—whatever they looked like—without the threat of interference from the government or evil megacorporations.

But that was too abstract. There was no step-by-step plan for that. I wasn't even sure if I was looking at it the right way. Maybe freedom wasn't even the right objective; after all, destruction of your enemy would bring freedom as a by-product of success, right? But the steps to accomplish that—as if it was even possible—would be completely different.

I blew out a loud breath in frustration, and Zane stirred next to me.

I froze until his even breathing resumed.

Start with what you know, my logical side spoke up. *Take stock of your strengths, weaknesses, and resources, and then potential courses of action. Evaluate each against your current position and factor in likelihood of success.*

We were alive and free . . . for the moment. Strength.

We were away from Wingate and GTX. That was good.

Zane's mother, a potential vulnerability for us, wasn't hurt, at least not physically, nor did she appear to be in any immediate danger. Not any more than she had been before our arrival, anyway. Also, good.

Zane's mother happened to be Mara, the former GTX lab tech. I put that in the neutral column. I wasn't sure whether that would work to our advantage or not. Mara did not like me, nor did she care for her son's involvement in all of this. But she did seem to have his best interests at heart. Of course, that might mean she'd sacrifice me to accomplish that goal. I just didn't know.

Weaknesses . . . oh God, too many to count. We had multiple enemies—the equivalent of a war on several fronts, never a good idea because it divided your attention and your resources—with near unlimited funds and a burning desire to see me dead or recaptured, with Zane as collateral damage or potential bait.

As for courses of action . . . fleeing the country—our primary plan until an hour or so ago—was probably no longer an option, if Mara was to be trusted. And I didn't. Trust her, that is. But she'd made a good point.

Zane had suggested going to the media, which was, at least, a possibility. Albeit a difficult one. I had no doubt that I could convince someone—a single individual—I was telling the truth, but getting a legitimate news source to run the story without proof beyond the tattoo on my back and my word might be a little tricky. I could use my abilities to read thoughts and float things across the room, which might convince those physically present. But Internet trickery and special effects were too prevalent for anyone to take such a demonstration seriously on TV or the Web. And we didn't exactly have time for a cross-country road show.

The trouble was, I needed to create a stir, but people were kind of immune to "alien" claims.

In any case, I wasn't entirely sure that the idea wasn't fatally flawed—freedom from harm by simply telling the truth. Yes, okay, pulling the curtain off my existence might prevent our enemies from taking action against us because the world would be watching, or whatever.

But that "freedom" also looked a whole lot like exposure.

After all, how easy was it to make one person disappear? It wasn't just GTX and its competitors involved in this, but the government. To what lengths would they go to hide that they'd been lying, not only about human experimentation but also the existence of extraterrestrials? Talk about bad press.

On top of it all, I had no idea which way public opinion would swing. Would they see me as an underdog, someone deserving of their sympathy, or a threat to all of humanity that the government had been trying to contain? I knew which way the Department of Defense would try to spin it. They'd stuck to that ridiculous weather balloon cover story for Roswell for more than half a century. Issuing official bald-faced lies was not new territory.

But if I took going public off the table because of the risks, that left us with what? Pretty much nothing, other than driving around the country in aimless circles until our luck or money ran out.

I held in the scream of frustration building in my throat.

Even out here, GTX and the others were controlling me—limiting my choices and forcing me to react to their moves, like a stupid pawn being chased around the board. Vulnerable and powerless, worthy only as a sacrifice.

I hated this. Hated them. Jacobs. GTX. Even Laughlin and Emerson St. John, neither of whom I'd met.

They hate us so much. Mara's words echoed in my head. She'd been referring to Laughlin's hybrids, but it might as well have been me. She'd sounded wounded, almost surprised, by this, but I could well imagine it, if their experience was anything like mine.

And it seemed as though Ford had been taking action in her own way, playing a cat-and-mouse sort of game in the absence of the ability to really hurt or punish Mara for what she'd done. Laughlin would have likely forbidden that, as he probably considered Mara an asset, but mental games seemed like a potentially gray area. I didn't condone it exactly, but I understood it. I might have even done the same thing, if I'd had the freedom. . . .

I sat up, making Zane's arm fall to my lap. What was it Mara had said about them? That unless Dr. Laughlin had given the hybrids strict orders, they pursued their own interests. She'd also said something about them being in school and/or in public, an attempt to mimic the cultural immersion portion of my training. Either one meant the hybrids were at least sometimes outside of what was likely some pretty formidable security at Laughlin Integrated.

If I could find them, I could try to talk to them.

The idea sent chills skittering over my skin, in both excitement and uncertainty. They were, in all likelihood, the closest thing to blood relatives I had. But I knew from watching full human families, including Zane's, that shared DNA was no guarantee of kindness or even similar perspectives.

And technically, I was a competitor. They might want to kill me. That had to be a consideration. Approaching the other hybrids, assuming I could find them, would mean gambling that they hated Laughlin more than they wanted to beat me.

But to have any hope of winning this game—and freedom for Zane and me—I needed to get on the board as a player instead of a pawn, and that would be a lot easier with allies, some extra hybrid help. If I could, for once, *act* instead of react, and take GTX, Laughlin, and whomever else by surprise, Zane and I might have a chance.

Of course, I wasn't really sure mutual hate was a solid basis for a potential alliance, but it was worth a shot, right?

It wasn't like I had any better options. Or, for that matter, any options at all.

Zane shifted in his sleep, pulling his arm tighter against me, and I lay back down.

Especially not with everything I had to lose.

CHAPTER 8

Zane

I'D NEVER SLEPT WITH A GIRL BEFORE. NOT ACTUAL sleeping, anyway. So I didn't have anything to compare it to, but waking up and finding Ariane still next me was one of the best moments of my life.

The van was hotter than hell. Ariane was curled up against my side, making her seem even smaller than she was, which was a feat.

Her pale cheeks were flushed with heat, and her whitish-blond hair appeared darker, sticking to her skin in funny ringlets and waves. It probably wasn't good for her—for either of us—to be so warm. We needed to get out of here. To where, I wasn't sure. But not here was a start.

I sat up and shook her shoulder gently. "Hey," I whispered to her. "Ari."

She blinked at me, the blue tinted lenses in her eyes slipping a little with the motion.

"Hey," she said, the word raspy with sleep.

"Don't you need to take those out?" I asked, frowning.

Ariane stared up at me befuddled, as if she wasn't quite awake.

"Your contact lenses," I said with a laugh. Evidently she wasn't a morning person either. "Aren't you supposed to—"

She reached up and touched my face, her fingertips tracing the outline of my mouth lightly, and I stopped talking. Stopped breathing.

Then she pulled away, her eyes wide as if her action had taken her by surprise as well. But she didn't retreat completely, her hand hovering between us, as if she wasn't sure what to do.

I didn't move. We were on the edge of something. She hadn't let me kiss her at the motel. I didn't know if she wanted me to now; we hadn't since before GTX, since before that awful party at Rachel's when Ariane had stepped up to help me and revealed herself.

And I wanted her to choose. She was a mind reader. She knew what I wanted, but it was up to her. Things were infinitely more complicated than they'd been before, when we were pretending to date to fool Rachel, and I wouldn't hold the precedent over her head. We were, in effect, starting over.

Ariane sat up slowly, her pale and heavy hair loose and sliding around her shoulders. I could hear my breath rushing in and out as she moved closer, and I could see the pulse throbbing in her throat.

She curled her fingers hesitantly in the collar of my shirt, and keeping her gaze fixed on me, she leaned in.

Her lips brushed lightly over mine. So light, in fact, it felt more like one of those accidental mouth brushes when you go to kiss someone on the cheek and miss.

It was still electrifying, oddly enough, ramping up the tension and anticipation I could feel building between us, but I didn't understand it.

She did it again, watching me carefully, her expression serious, cautious.

And it finally clicked with me. She was afraid. Afraid I'd pull back or run away. Afraid I'd panic. She was giving me an out.

I didn't need one.

I slid my hand to the back of her head, my fingers tangling in her hair, and angled my mouth against hers, tasting her deeply, showing no hesitation, no fear. It was easy. I didn't feel any.

Ariane clutched at my shoulders, her breath escaping in a quiet gasp, sending a gratifying thrill through me.

Then she wrapped her arms around my neck and pulled herself into my lap.

Blood rushing away from my head, I promptly forgot about pretty much everything except for her tongue in my mouth and her body against mine. I'd seen those slight curves before, in the motel, but feeling them pressed up against me was an entirely different sensation.

Framing her face with my free hand, I could feel the delicate bones of her cheeks and jaw under my questing fingertips. When she tipped her head back, I pulled my mouth from hers and pressed my lips against the pulse fluttering frantically at her throat, beneath damp skin.

Then she shifted her legs, moving them to either side of

my hips, which shot the intensity level up from about ten to a thousand, and I swallowed a groan, wrapping my arms around her and pulling her closer.

God, it was so hot. In every sense of the word.

We were wearing too many clothes. But I could fix that.

I slid my hands beneath the hem of her shirt and started inching it up.

"Zane?" she whispered against my throat.

I was having a little trouble focusing on words. The bra that I'd seen earlier was now beneath my fingertips. "Yeah?" I managed.

"I want to find Ford and the other hybrids," she said breathlessly.

"Wait. What?" I stopped, with one hand caught in the fabric of her shirt, the other searching for a fastener of some kind at the back of that undergarment that would probably play a starring role in my future fantasies.

I'd heard that wrong. Had to have. I'd caught the "I want" part, but nothing after that had made any sense.

"I figured out another option when you were sleeping," she said. "Ford and the other hybrids. I want to find them." She pulled away from me slightly, her cheeks flushed pink and her eyes hazy but slowly regaining focus.

Reluctantly, I let go of her shirt and scrubbed my hands over my face, not entirely sure I was awake. If I wasn't, I was kind of disappointed at the left turn this sex dream had taken. "Right now?"

She blushed, color spreading up from her neck. "Not this second, no."

I struggled to focus, when my whole body was screaming

at me to close the distance and kiss her again, to get us both down on the floor of the van. "Why do you want to find *them?*" Avoiding Laughlin's hybrids entirely seemed like a much better goal to me. Healthier.

Ariane frowned, sharp intellect replacing all the softness in her expression. "So far, we've just been reacting to what everyone else does. GTX, my father, your mother. An alliance with Ford and the others could give us leverage, an advantage." She shrugged and, I noted with regret, pulled her shirt into place. "If we all refuse to cooperate, they can't have their competition." Her voice held a note of grim satisfaction.

I sighed, shifting her weight in my lap slightly to make it more comfortable and less distracting. Clearly the make-out portion of this conversation was over. "We've seen how 'persuasive' GTX can be. I doubt Laughlin's any different. These hybrids probably spend half the day throwing knives at your picture on the wall," I pointed out.

She rolled her eyes. "You watch too many movies."

"Really? You're saying that to me?" Based on what she'd told me, most of her early education about the outside world—in other words, anything beyond the ten-by-ten-foot space of GTX cell—had come exclusively from movies and TV they'd shown her. And it seemed, given the number of pop culture references she used, those films and shows had had a lasting effect on how she viewed things, a filter over her real-life experiences.

"Fine," she said with an impatient exhale before pushing herself from my lap and resettling on the van floor across from me, adding distance between us. "You watch too many bad movies. That's a cliché."

"And this isn't?" I asked in disbelief. "You want to approach the bad guys, hoping they'll want to talk when it's far more likely they'll just try to kill you."

Her gaze skittered away from me. "They're not the bad guys," she said, staring at a point somewhere to my left, her shoulders tight suddenly.

Smooth, Zane. Way to insult her. "I'm sorry," I said with a wince. "I didn't mean they were bad because they were hybrids. I just meant—"

"They were raised by Laughlin, just as I was raised by Dr. Jacobs," she said. "That gives us more in common than it divides us."

Hearing her talk about "us" and mean herself and the hybrids instead of the two of us sent a twinge of worry through me.

"How do you know that they haven't spent the last fifteen or twenty years just waiting for the chance to prove themselves?" I argued. "What if he's promised them freedom if they win the trials? What if they don't even want to be free?"

"Then why would they hate the humans so much?"

Her use of the word "humans" and the cool distance in her tone—as if we were some simple inanimate object, like grapefruits or something—made me shiver despite the heat. It was easy to forget sometimes that she was more than just Ariane Tucker, the quiet girl who'd been in my math class. She blended in, just as they'd intended. But other times, like now, she seemed foreign, unknowable. Like all those Earth-like planets you hear about in the news; we can see them but we'll never be able to get there.

Perhaps sensing what I was thinking, she reached out and

touched my knee. "There's a chance that you're right—"

"Just a chance," I muttered.

She ignored me. "But we have to try. It's our best option for getting out of this"—she gestured to the van but, no doubt, meant the entire running-for-our-lives situation— "with a chance for any kind of a real future." She wasn't pleading, but I could feel her intensity pulling at me. She truly believed this was the best choice.

And technically, she could be correct; we didn't have enough information about the hybrids to know one way or another. They might, in fact, welcome her with open arms. Just not me.

I swallowed a sigh and rubbed at the headache beginning to throb behind my forehead, whether from the heat or this conversation. "You're the strategy expert," I said with a shrug that hurt. "How do you plan on finding our new best friends?"

"She said they're in public at times," Ariane said. "In school, even."

I noticed her avoidance of "your mom" or "Mara." My mom had managed to wound her with what she'd said, I realized. Not that that was surprising, because my mom had been awful. But Ariane, most of the time, gave the appearance of being pretty impervious to the stupid shit people said about her. Rachel had only managed to goad her into reacting by attacking others. Jenna. Me.

It made me wonder if Ariane was more vulnerable than she let on and better at hiding it. And that made me want to pull her close again, as if that could shelter her from whatever people had said to or about her.

I cleared my throat. "In case you haven't noticed, there's a lot of public here to go around," I said, gesturing to the mall and the now-busy parking lot, visible through the windshield.

She glanced away from me. "We do have a source."

I gaped at her. "You're kidding. You want to go back to my mom?" There were so many things wrong with that idea, it almost distracted me from the complete insanity of chasing after Laughlin's hybrids. "She's a little off her rocker at the moment. You get that, right?"

"She's not crazy," Ariane said with a certainty I didn't feel. "She's reacting to stress."

"No," I said. "Mainlining Swiss cake rolls while watching junk TV is reacting to stress. Putting six extra locks on your door and imagining that you're being followed is something else entirely. Besides, I don't think she'd be too excited to help us." Us being anyone and anything related to Ariane.

Ariane met my gaze directly, reading through my weak subterfuge. "You're right. She wouldn't . . . what's the phrase? Spit on me if I was on fire."

I winced. True enough, it seemed. My mom's guilt over working for Jacobs at GTX was enough to push her into apologizing, but that was likely the extent of it.

"But she's not going to do it to help me. She's going to do it to help you," Ariane said.

I raised my eyebrows. "I assume you have a plan to convince her of that."

"Of course," she said easily.

I shook my head. "All right," I said, holding up my hands in surrender. "In absence of another, better plan, I guess we can give it a try. But we're going to need to stop for Swiss cake rolls."

She laughed.

I got up, keeping my head down to avoid the roof, and climbed into the driver's seat. She followed and settled herself on the passenger side.

"I also wanted to say that I . . . I'm sorry about earlier," she said quietly, clicking her seat belt into place as I started the van and cranked up the AC.

I frowned. "What are you talking about?" I asked, backing out of the parking place.

She stared down at her hands, folding them and unfolding them in her lap. "I woke up and you were there, looking so worried about me . . . my contacts. It was nice. You caring. And I was just . . . I was just glad." She grimaced.

Oh. She'd had so few people care about her that she felt she had to apologize for responding to affection? She'd kissed me; I'd wanted her to. End of story, as far as I was concerned. But evidently not for Ariane. And I thought my life was messed up.

"Nothing to apologize for," I said, doing my best to keep my tone even. I didn't want to make her self-conscious. "Anytime you want to be glad like that again, just let me know." I grinned at her.

She nodded without looking at me, color creeping into her cheeks again.

I shifted into drive and headed for the parking lot exit.

"Is that, um, something you'd want?" she asked after a few seconds of silence. "I mean, not what we did, but what we could do. . . ."

I glanced over at her sharply. Sex. Was she asking about sex? My mouth worked without words coming out. I didn't know how to answer that.

"I guess what I'm asking is"—she squirmed in her seat—"it doesn't bother you, what I am? Some people wouldn't even want to share a straw with me, if they knew. . . ."

Ah, now I was getting it. But that didn't really help me with an answer. She was worried about being pushed away, now or sometime in the near future, whether there was some invisible line that I wouldn't cross with her because of who or what she was. I could address that, but I didn't want to inadvertently add pressure to an already crazy situation.

"You know I'm not expecting anything like that, right?" I asked carefully.

"That wasn't my question," she said.

"No, it doesn't bother me. Obviously." I jerked my head toward the sleeping bag.

She nodded, but she didn't seem reassured. "But you have. Before, I mean."

I shifted uncomfortably. I hadn't planned on this conversation. If things had gotten this intense and so quickly under normal circumstances, then yeah, I'd have been expecting it. But this was a bizarre moment of reality intruding on a pretty surreal landscape. But then again, Ariane, in addition to being a half-alien soldier/spy/whatever, was just somebody trying to figure out how to navigate the world, just like the rest of us. "Yeah," I admitted.

"Who?"

I sighed. She wasn't going to like this answer. "You wouldn't know her. She was a senior when we were freshman."

Caught by surprise, Ariane actually looked at me. "Really?"

I let out a slow breath, trying to figure out how to word this. "It was complicated. She wanted Quinn, but he was . . . occupied." Not that I'd known that at the time. I was stupid and half drunk at my first high school party; I'd taken Tara's interest at face value. A senior cheerleader asking me if I wanted to go somewhere where we could "talk"? Uh, hell, yeah.

It was only afterward, stumbling out of a darkened bedroom at her stepfather's house, when I heard her taunting Quinn about it, that I'd figured it out. I wasn't sure whether she'd done it to get back at him for choosing someone else or to just make him jealous. Either way, fail.

Quinn had glanced from her to me and back again and got pissed. Just not in the way Tara had intended.

"What the hell is wrong with you?" he demanded of her. "He's not even fifteen. That's messed up."

Before I could protest that I'd participated voluntarily, Tara lost her shit and starting screaming at Quinn and punching his shoulder.

By then, we were attracting a crowd with our little drama: Tara, red-faced and shrieking; my brother looking disgusted, shaking the beer off his hand where Tara had caused it to slop out of his cup; and me, a foot taller but years younger than everyone else, standing there awkwardly, like a complete tool.

Eventually, Tara's friends showed up and dragged her off, holding her arms down and whispering to her in the tone used by sane people coaxing a jumper off a ledge.

Yeah, *that* was the girl who'd slept with me.

And then Quinn, who normally ignored me at parties, at school, hell, even at home when he could, frowned at me, concerned. "You okay?"

Somehow that made it all the worse. Bad enough to be used as a revenge fuck, but to be pitied for it by the emotional target of said revenge fuck, who also happened to be my perfect, universally loved, older brother? God.

Pinned by the stares of those lingering to just gawk, I'd forced myself to nod. "Yeah, whatever." I'd been terrified that my brother was going to keep talking about it when all I wanted to do was die or become invisible.

But he didn't. Quinn had just nodded, almost absentmindedly as the incident was already fading from his mind. "All right." Then he'd turned away from me to face the crowd. "What are all you pussies looking at? Let's get our drink on!"

They'd followed him to the kitchen, leaving me alone. And I'd found the first door out and sneaked away. It was all anybody would talk about at school the next Monday, but among most of my friends, it became about "bagging a senior chick" instead of blinding stupidity and degradation. A small favor, I guess.

Remembering it even now, after almost two years of better experiences, still made my stomach churn and my face hot.

Ariane touched my arm. "It wasn't your fault," she said fiercely. Clearly, she'd picked up on at least some of my thoughts about that night.

I tried to smile. "Thanks." I flipped the signal on to indicate our turn from the mall parking lot onto the main road. "So, in answer to your question, do I want to with you?

Yeah." I made sure to look at her so she knew I wasn't just telling her what she wanted to hear. "But it should mean something, you know?" I shifted a little in my seat, feeling as though I were straying from the agreed-upon code of *sex anytime, anywhere is good*. But she'd asked, so I was answering honestly. I'd learned that lesson the hard way the first time, and I had no desire to revisit it. "And right now, we're a little busy with just trying to stay alive," I said.

Ariane nodded, a hint of a frown crossing her face.

"So there's no rush," I said firmly, as much to myself as to her. I wasn't the type to push. Not my style. But I already felt more for her than I had for anyone else. Ever. That made it a lot harder to keep moments like the one a few minutes ago from spinning out of control.

"So, as long as you're comfortable with everything so far . . ." I paused, a new thought occurring to me. I tapped my fingers nervously on the steering wheel. "Uh, I mean, assuming everything works the same way."

She laughed, a bright, unexpected sound. "As far as I know, yeah."

I let out an exaggerated sigh of relief. "Okay, good. Because if there's something special about your elbow or whatever, you need to tell me."

She cocked her head to one side with a frown. "Wait, so the elbow *isn't* special? What's third base, then?"

My face burst into flames just hearing her saying the words *third base*. Because apparently I hadn't progressed past the age of twelve. "I, um . . ." I said, fumbling for words.

But then I caught the faint upturn at the corner of her mouth. She was teasing.

I shook my head. "You're hilarious, you know that?"

"I'm sorry. I couldn't resist. An elbow, really?" She raised her eyebrows at me.

"It was the weirdest body part I could think of off the top of my head, okay?" I said, exasperated. "I was trying to be sensitive."

"Like my elbow."

"Yes. No! Damn it, Ariane. . . ." I sighed.

Shaking with laughter, she held her hands up. "I'm sorry. I'm sorry." Her eyes were shining with tears of mirth, something I'd never seen from her before. I loved it.

I held my hand out and with only split second of hesitation—nothing like when we'd first started talking, just days ago—she took it, intertwining her fingers with mine.

A few moments passed in silence, just the rumble of the van engine and the echoes of her laughter in my head. "I wish all of this was easier, safer," she said quietly. "More normal."

I shrugged. "If it were any of those things, we probably wouldn't be here together." Extreme circumstances had pushed us toward each other to begin with; it seemed unlikely that would change anytime soon. Plus, what was so great about normal? If we'd stuck with that, she might have still been trapped inside the cell at GTX.

"This will work," she said with renewed determination. "We'll find Ford and the others, and we'll get a chance to turn things around. Then *we'll* get to decide our future."

I nodded. "Yeah, absolutely," I said, and hoped she couldn't hear my false certainty. She was worried about failing, which I understood, but a part of me was equally worried about what would happen if she succeeded. We were in this together for now, but would that be true if she managed to convince the other hybrids to come to our side? Her side, actually.

I was only human. And all too aware of it.

The trip to my mom's went much faster than the first time. We were closer, of course, but it was also probably because all the anticipation and anxiety was gone, replaced solidly with dread. We knew what we were walking into this time.

Then as I started to make the last turn, Ariane sat up sharply. "Wait. Stop."

Or, not.

I braked immediately, stopping halfway through an intersection. "What's wrong?"

She had the alert posture—back ramrod straight, gaze sharp, concentration almost palpable—that I recognized as belonging to Ariane the soldier. Something had triggered her instincts and/or her training.

"Something's wrong. Different," she said, her fingers turning white where she clutched the armrest.

I fought against a pulse of panic. "My mom?" I asked. I still didn't know how I felt about what she'd done—really, who she was—but the worry about her safety was instinctive and unstoppable.

"I don't know. It's . . . there's a new thread." Ariane cocked her head to one side, listening.

I opened my mouth and then shut it again. "What does that mean?" I asked finally.

She made a frustrated noise. "It's hard to explain. It's as if . . . something has changed. There was a certain feel to the area before, and now it's altered." She looked over at me. "Have you ever walked into a room right after an argument?"

Uh, yeah. I'd lived with *my* parents for years, after all.

"You can tell that something is wrong, that something's happened even if no one is saying anything, right?" she continued.

She seemed to actually be asking—maybe she wasn't sure what I could sense as a regular, nonspecial human—so I nodded.

"It's like that. The tension is up. But I can't hear anything specific. We're too far away." She frowned, her mouth tight. "And it's not safe to go closer without knowing what's going on."

A car pulled up short behind me with an impatient squawk of tires. "Uh, Ariane? We're about two seconds from getting honked at."

"Keep going," she said distantly, her attention focused once more on nothing I could see.

I straightened out of the turn and continued on slowly.

"Left here," she directed, a block later. Not that she was even looking at the road. She'd moved to the edge of her seat and twisted to stare in the direction of my mom's house. It was as if she'd tapped into something near my mom's house and she was still connected, a cord stretching out between her and some distant point.

I took the turn as instructed and found we were on a large cul-de-sac of small houses and utilitarian brick duplexes just like my mom's. A half dozen of them had real estate signs in front—for sale or rent—or they appeared dilapidated enough to perhaps be abandoned.

This was definitely not the best neighborhood. The good news, though, was that even at noon, not many people seemed to be out and about to notice us. Or, maybe that wasn't so good—nobody watching meant that anything could happen. Lack of credible eyewitnesses was never something I'd thought much about before this week, and now it seemed an essential variable to consider in every situation.

Ariane was frowning out the window, her gaze searching the sky, first one direction and then another, as if she was calculating something.

"That one," she said, pointing to a house with a REDUCED PRICE banner slapped across the real estate sign planted in the front yard. It was a two-story house, not particularly large, but taller than the others surrounding it.

"Okay, what about it?" I asked slowly.

She blinked, breaking her trance of concentration. "Park in the driveway. And then act like we belong."

Oh. That sounded ominous. And possibly illegal.

I pulled in and put the van in park. Before I'd even shut the engine off, though, Ariane had pushed open her door and slid out.

I followed her hurriedly, taking an extra second to lock the van. Nothing like leaving thousands of dollars lying around, unattended.

"What are you doing?" I whispered when I caught up to Ariane on the front walk. She was heading to the door like she owned the place.

Ariane smiled at me, big and false, and then looped her arm through mine. "We're very excited to see this house. Now smile at me in case the neighbors are watching."

What? "We're going in?" I asked through my own version of a fake smile, but I could feel the tension pulling at the corners of my mouth. I wasn't as good at it as she was.

"Yes." She tugged me forward and onto the sagging wooden porch. Then she pretended to fumble with the metal keybox hanging from the handle for a moment, as if she had to open it to get at the key.

Then she angled herself so that her body blocked the view of anyone who might be watching and lifted her hand. Inside, the dead bolt slid back with a solid thunk, and I watched as the doorknob, inches away from her outstretched fingertips, twisted slowly, as if it was being operated by an unseen presence.

The door popped free and swung open, revealing a dim and empty entryway. Cool air rushed out to greet us. The air-conditioning was on. I struggled momentarily between conflicting feelings: relief that it wasn't sweltering inside and fear about what that might mean in terms of the occupants.

"You sure no one is home?" I asked.

She waved my words away. "Not here." Then she stepped inside.

"As in, they're not here right now or as in, people live in this area but not in this particular house?" I asked, shifting my weight uneasily at the threshold. Or, as in, *Don't ask me that here.* There were any number of ways her statement could be interpreted, some of which might not exclude the possibility of some dude in his boxers, rounding the corner unexpectedly and catching us.

Ariane paused and glanced over her shoulder at me.

"You're nervous," she said with a curious lilt.

"Breaking and entering is kind of a new experience for me," I said tightly. And yeah, okay, given the scope of everything we'd gone through in the last few days, it was nothing, but it was the first actual crime we'd committed. And I guess, after years of my dad lecturing me on all the dumbass things I could do that would jeopardize his good name and my future, some of it had actually sunk in, despite my best efforts.

Ariane crossed back to the door. "No one is here, I promise. It's safe." She paused, considering. "As safe as it is anywhere for us," she added. "For now."

Wow. That was reassuring.

She held out her hand, but I stepped inside of my own free will. If I was going to do it, then I would do it.

The dark interior left me half blind after the brightness outside; it took my eyes a few seconds to adjust. The door swung shut as soon as I cleared it, courtesy of Ariane's power, snapping closed with a loud click that echoed and made me jump.

"Come on, this way," she said, heading deeper into the house.

The entryway, with its battered wooden floor, was empty except for a few dust bunnies. To the left, it opened up to a room with dingy carpeting—and cleaner spaces where the furniture had been—and nothing else.

No one was living here. I let out a breath of relief. Ariane could have told me that.

"I didn't know for sure," she said. "Not until now."

"Stop making me feel better," I muttered.

Following the sound of her voice, I turned the corner out

of the entryway and into an actual hall with stairs on the right, leading up. Ariane was already halfway to the next floor.

She moved without hesitation to the second floor and then straight to a partially closed door on the landing, as if she were on the trail of something I couldn't see.

The door led to a bathroom, small and kind of rank, but that didn't seem to bother her. She went immediately for the window, which was set high up in the rear wall. She stepped up on the closed lid of the toilet and pulled at the closed metal blinds, which gave with a twanging sound, to look out.

"There," she said with an air of satisfaction.

Moving to stand next to her—I didn't need the assistance of the toilet to see out—I peered out to find a view of the dead backyard with a rusted swing set and the rear side of an equally despondent-looking house. "What . . ."

Ariane reached up and gently turned my chin to the right slightly, and I realized if I looked between the neighboring houses at an angle, I could see my mom's place.

And the large black SUVs parked on the street out front.

I pulled back instinctively, as though they could see us up here. "Laughlin?" I asked.

"Probably," Ariane said.

"Did she call him on us?" I struggled with a rush of anger at the idea.

"I don't think so," Ariane said thoughtfully, her tone one of someone contemplating an academic problem. "If they were here for us, it would look different."

I shook my head. "Meaning?"

"Either there would be a lot more of them, or we wouldn't see them at all," she said.

Great. I really needed to stop asking questions. The answers only made things worse. Problem was, I didn't have anything *but* questions.

"And that wouldn't explain him," she added.

"Who?" I leaned closer, and she pointed to the house directly behind us. In an upstairs window, bare of curtains or blinds, I could see a silhouette of a man standing at the front of the house. He held what appeared to be binoculars, watching the goings-on at my mom's house. Or maybe even inside her house, depending on how powerful those binoculars were.

"One of Laughlin's guys?" I asked.

She shook her head. "Why would he be hiding?"

Good point. But he definitely wasn't just a neighbor, not with the binoculars and what appeared to be a complete lack of furniture inside the house. It was evidently another empty one for sale.

"Then who?"

She shrugged. "Someone from GTX maybe? Or Emerson St. John? Just because Laughlin and Jacobs aren't interested in what he's doing doesn't mean he's not interested in them."

God, when did these people have time to actually accomplish scientific breakthroughs with all the time they allotted for espionage? Or maybe that's how they accomplished those scientific breakthroughs. I wasn't sure.

"Okay, so now what?" I backed away from the window to lean against the sink. The sight of the dude spying and the SUVs had shaken me. Ariane had sounded casual, unconcerned, during our discussion, but I was beginning to think that flat, unaffected tone was how she reacted to unexpected stress.

She hesitated. "I don't know. Mara is our best lead on the hybrids."

But we couldn't wait here forever. Our van was parked in the driveway. The owners of this house might not live here, but that didn't mean they wouldn't come by and check on the place. Plus, the neighbors would eventually get curious, wouldn't they? In Wingate, someone would have already been knocking at the door.

"We could come back later," I offered, though oddly that idea made me uneasy. We couldn't do anything from here, but it felt, somehow, like everything would escalate even further out of control if we weren't watching.

She shook her head, her gaze fixed on the view outside. "That'll just attract more attention."

She was the expert at being just this side of invisible, I suppose.

"We could try to track down another Laughlin employee," I said, but even before the words were out, the sheer impossibility of that idea washed over me. Because it wasn't just finding any employee that would do; we needed one who had knowledge of a top secret project and access to details. We, at the moment, didn't even have a connection to the Internet. The basic Laughlin Integrated Web site was out of our reach, let alone a confidential employee directory of some kind, assuming one existed.

"Do you think they're hurting her?" The question popped out before I could stop it. I grimaced. "Sorry . . . I'm sorry."

Ariane looked away from the window to me, startled. "Why are you apologizing?"

I couldn't meet her eyes. "She worked in the lab. She . . . hurt you." And she lied to me about it. It wasn't that I felt she should have told me, as a kid, about her work on a secret project, but more that her work on that project irrevocably changed who I thought she was. And I didn't like this new version of my mom.

"It was her job. And I told you she was kinder to me than any of the others," Ariane said evenly.

"Yeah, but that's not saying much," I pointed out. I paused, trying to figure out how to say what was churning inside me. "My dad spent years telling me I was just like my mom, and I hated him for that."

"And now you're afraid he's right?"

I scrubbed my hands over my face. "Yeah," I admitted, more of an exhale than a word. I mean, I'd always thought he was right, but about stuff like lacking in ambition, being soft, or lazy (by his definition). Not like this, though. Nothing like this. When my understanding of my mom changed, so did my view of myself. And yeah, now I was scared as hell that my dad was still right. Would I do what she'd done? Would I somehow find myself in a situation where I'd ignore my conscience because I thought I had no choice or because it somehow felt like the right thing to do, the tiny space between the proverbial rock and a hard place?

Ariane stepped down from her perch on the toilet and grabbed my hands. "First of all, no. I don't think they're hurting her. I'm not sensing anything like that." She nodded in the direction of my mom's house. "Fear, anxiety, yes, but not pain. If anything, she's angry. And that's a good thing." Her mouth twitched. "Most likely someone was dispatched to follow up on her call this morning. She's not making it easy for them, and she definitely hasn't said anything to them about us."

Yet. But I nodded, feeling something tight in my chest easing slightly at Ariane's words, even as I hated myself for it.

"Second, consider my background. One of my parents was an alien. Maybe he or she was simply the envoy of a curious race. But given the advanced technology and abilities he or she evidently possessed, the more likely scenario is that of an advance scout from a superior species, which likely would not have ended well for the humans. Domination, at best. At worst, a careless disregard for life here, like a child stepping on an anthill," she said calmly. "On the other side, my human mother was probably bribed or blackmailed into allowing my existence, which doesn't say a whole lot for her character." She rolled her eyes with a sad smile. "And one has to assume a petri dish played a healthy role in all of it."

I choked on an unexpected laugh.

"So, generally speaking, when it comes to predicting future dysfunction, I think we ought to leave the 'you are where you come from' theory off the table, or else I so have you beat." She stepped up on her tiptoes to kiss my cheek, her skin smooth against mine. "We make our own choices," she whispered.

Tears stung my eyes unexpectedly, and I wrapped my arms around her, warmth and gratitude filling my chest. "I love you." The words came out before I could stop them, riding that wave of emotion. I wasn't even sure how I meant them, like "I love you for saying that" or "I *love* you." Both, maybe. But it was too late to think more about it; the words were already out.

Ariane stiffened immediately, her whole body going tense as if under attack.

I froze. "I'm sorry. . . . I didn't . . ." I didn't know how to finish that sentence.

"It's fine," she said, and pulled away so quickly I might as well have been on fire. So, clearly it wasn't fine.

Stupid, Zane.

"If we're going to stay here, we should take shifts watching," she said, carefully avoiding my gaze. "That way we can get some rest. As soon as they leave, we'll need to be ready to get over there to talk to Mara." She sounded almost normal but for the faint strain in her voice, as though it took effort to maintain that front.

"Right, okay, sure," I said, my face hot. "I've got first watch."

"Are you sure?" she asked, but it was perfunctory, as if she were already itching to get away.

"Yep," I said too brightly. It was as if we were following some entirely different script than a few moments ago. In this one we were pretending to be cordial strangers.

"Okay," she said, and then she moved to the left at the same time I moved to my right, and we did that awkward back-and-forth dance while we tried to get out of each other's way.

"Sorry," we said at the same time.

Then I pulled myself against the far wall, and she took off as if all the oxygen had been sucked out of the room.

Great. I leaned my head against the yellowed wallpaper, the peeling strands rough against my forehead. *Because things weren't complicated enough already. You had to go and drop an ambiguous "I love you" into the mix. Nice, man. Very smooth.*

It wasn't that I expected her to say it back—hell, I hadn't even expected to say it all. I mean, the last few days had been intense, and that made a big difference, but still, we'd only known each other, really known each other, for a week? Less? And maybe love wasn't even something she wanted from me. Or from anyone. It was such a loaded and dangerous word, emotion, whatever. After all, the last person who'd claimed to love her, her adoptive father, had betrayed her completely. And with my parents, I wasn't sure I had any better examples to follow.

I sighed, suddenly longing for my earlier worries about being arrested for breaking and entering. That seemed so much simpler.

CHAPTER 9

IIIＩＩＩＩＩＩＩＩＩＩＩＩＩＩＩＩＩＩＩＩ

Ariane

TWO-HOUR SHIFTS, I DECIDED ON MY WAY DOWN THE stairs, my hand clinging to the railing so tightly my knuckles throbbed. That made the most sense. Enough time for the person resting to get some decent sleep but not so much that the one on watch duty would get overwhelmed and too tired.

Yes, two hours. I nodded decisively, even though absolutely no one was around to see me. If I just kept myself focused on the task at hand, everything would be okay. Except . . .

I love you. Zane's voice echoed in my head. Half surprised, half relieved, as if it hadn't been a conscious decision to speak the sentiment aloud.

My heart ached at the instant replay.

Don't do this, Ariane. Don't do this to yourself.

But he said, "I love you." Words I'd never imagined hearing from anyone. Ever.

I should have been elated. I'd never felt anything like the warmth and affection that had accompanied his words.

I wanted to wrap those feelings around me and live in them forever.

He loved me. The mix of exhilaration and adrenaline was like carbonated bubbles in my bloodstream, a physical representation of joy. This is what joy felt like. No wonder people lived and died for this feeling.

I'd known days ago that I loved him. I'd felt it before we'd even left Wingate, before he'd known who and what I was. I'd broken the rule expressly against falling in love, #5, for Zane.

But in all of that, I'd never considered the idea of him loving me in return. That concept was, absurd as it sounded, completely foreign to me.

I wanted him to like me, to care about me, of course. And to want me. That, to me, was the most important idea. As someone who'd been wanted only for what I represented to others, the idea of being wanted for who I was seemed both impossible and impossibly wonderful.

But love?

I swallowed hard. People did crazy things for love. And being responsible for someone else's feelings like that felt powerful and terrifying. As if I'd been given some delicate and fragile object to carry over rocky and uneven terrain with shaky hands.

What if I screwed this up? Or, worse, what if he figured out I wasn't worth everything he'd just given me? My own disappointment, hurt, and brokenness—that I could handle. But seeing all that from Zane? It might kill me, saving everybody else the trouble.

With a sigh, I settled myself at the base of the stairs,

where I could easily hear Zane if he called. I didn't want to rely on hearing his thoughts, not now, when I was trying to give him some privacy.

I covered my face with my hands. Up there, I'd reacted on instinct. Confronted with my own panic, I'd done the only thing I knew how, what I'd been trained to do when confronted with an unknown threat: I'd retreated. (Retreat to reevaluate your strategy and your options.)

You can't allow this to distract you, my logical side argued. You must stay focused on the mission if you want to survive. The cool and implacable portion of my heritage was especially tempting right now, a pool on a blisteringly hot day. I didn't have to care. It could be just as simple as that. Zane's love for me could be nothing more than a resource, a tool to use to my advantage, if the opportunity arose.

No. I shook my head violently, letting my hands drop. I wouldn't do that to him. He'd taken a chance, made himself vulnerable, and I couldn't do any less. I loved him. I'd fought for the chance to feel that for someone, and that he felt it in return was a miracle, one I would not ignore.

Tell him, my humanity urged. You need to tell him how you feel.

It'll make you weaker, my logical side advised. Slow your response time, cloud your thinking, and put you both in more danger.

Maybe. Maybe not. Having something—someone—to fight for could make all the difference in the right situation. There are countless examples in human history.

But you're not human, not entirely.

True. But I wasn't entirely *anything.*

I was a mix, a mutt, an unnatural concoction that probably couldn't draw firm conclusions from (without conclusive
allegiances to) either side of my heritage because of it.

Not that that would stop the internal argument. I rested
my head on my knees. This was going to be a long day.

At midnight, with no change in the situation at Mara's
house, I slipped out to the van and retrieved the duffel bag,
one of the sleeping bags, and the snacks we'd accumulated
at various points on our road trip. Ordering a pizza was a
little out of the question, so we'd have to make do with
what we had.

Not that Zane complained when I handed everything but
the sleeping bag off to him for safekeeping. (It seemed only
logical that the person who was awake should be in charge
of the money and the food.)

He didn't say much at all, actually. To be fair, neither
did I. In our shift changes so far, we'd exchanged a mini-
mum of words. Yes, the SUVs were still present, as was the
mysterious man in the empty house.

God, was it possible that I was going to screw this up simply by trying *not* to screw it up? That thought had haunted
me equally during my two-hour "rest" periods and on-duty
shifts.

The only few minutes of respite I had was when I changed
places with Zane, and then only because I was on alert, my
palms sweaty and my head full of things I wasn't sure I
should say, as we passed each other.

Downstairs again, after my shift at two A.M., I'd finally
managed to doze off when something woke me up.

I blinked, checking the dull green digits on the stove

clock, just visible around the corner in the kitchen. Five forty-one. So just a few minutes before my six A.M. shift was due to start.

"Ariane," Zane whispered urgently from the top of the stairs, the sound echoing through the silent house, off the bare walls and floors.

That's what I'd heard. He'd been calling me.

I shook off the last vestiges of sleep and a dream that involved climbing a never-ending mountain of corn chips— another lesson against eating junk food for meals—and sat up. "What's wrong?" I asked, careful to keep quiet, my heart catapulting inside my chest.

"Something's going on." There was an odd thread of excitement, mixed with tension, in his voice.

I shoved the sleeping bag away and scrambled to my feet.

Upstairs, it was dark, but the bathroom was warm and damp, smelling of fresh soap and shampoo. Zane had taken a shower at some point, using the toiletries I'd snagged from the motel.

"Come here. You've got to see this." He waved me forward to his position by the window.

The room was small, but there was plenty of space for me to pass without bumping into him. And yet I didn't take it. I brushed against his side on my way to the window. He smelled so good and looked even better. In the gray predawn light, he was deliciously rumpled with his dark hair damp and not styled and more stubble on his cheeks and chin.

I wanted to wrap myself around him with an intensity that frightened me. I wanted to feel the scrape of his unshaved skin against mine, taste the mint of the toothpaste in his mouth, and sink my hands into his hair.

"One of the SUVs left," he said, his attention on the view outside.

Huh? I shook my head, my brain somewhere else entirely.

"The other is still there, but with the engine running now." He pointed, and I reluctantly abandoned my fantasies to step up on the closed toilet and peer out.

Sure enough, he was right. The forward-most SUV was gone, leaving the second in place, the dim glow of the interior lights confirming at least one dark silhouette inside.

"And check out our mystery dude," Zane added, near enough to my ear to send a bolt of heat through me.

Get a grip, Ariane. I forced myself to pay attention. In the house directly behind us, with lights blazing in the upstairs window, I could see the unknown man, his hair ruffled and standing on end, frantically shoving things into a bag. He was packing up his stakeout. In plain view of anyone who happened to glance in his direction.

I rolled my eyes. Amateur.

"He's not GTX, that's for sure. I don't even think he's . . ." I paused and shook my head. "I don't know what he is except really, really bad at this."

"What are they doing?" Zane asked, tilting his head toward the remaining SUV.

I focused on his mom's house, where the lights were on now, movement flickering as shadows. From this distance, it wasn't easy to pick up on specific thoughts. General emotional impressions were easier. Dread, resignation, the pinch of uncomfortable clothes, bitterness, anger.

I closed my eyes, concentrating, picturing Mara and attempting to focus in on her mind.

. . . toast is burning! I don't need an escort to work . . . just want an excuse to spy on me some more . . . keys, keys, where are my keys?

Then a strong surge of worry and a very clear image of Zane. *Please, let him be safe.*

Not yet, but I was doing my best.

I opened my eyes to find Zane studying me.

"I think she's going to work," I said, my face warm under his appraisal. "The SUV is going to follow her." Maybe to observe and protect her, a response to her claim of seeing one of the hybrids at the grocery store. Or more likely, given how angry she'd been on the phone earlier when talking to Laughlin, a reminder of who was running her life. She was not a free woman, but a resource owned by Laughlin Integrated Enterprises.

Either way, it meant we wouldn't get the opportunity to talk with her alone.

I frowned. Unless we were willing to take a chance.

I leaned closer to the glass, taking in the angles, the different approaches between our location and the target. We couldn't walk up to the front door and ring the bell again, not with the occupants of the SUV watching, plus our mystery observer. And I was willing to bet that barging in through the back door probably wouldn't get us a better response from Mara.

Our only option might be to take her by surprise without letting any of the others see us. The garage was attached to the house, and if she was taking her own car to work . . .

"What are you doing?" Zane asked.

"Thinking. Working on timing," I said, distracted. "Do

you think your mom locks the door between the house and the garage?"

He gave a strangled laugh. "You saw her," he said. "I think she locks everything. Twice, at least."

Fair enough. That would cost us an extra second or two, but it would also force her to take more time before leaving the garage. Of course, if she'd barricaded the sliding glass door at the back of her house with anything more than a standard security bar, I'd never be able to get it open in time and we'd be out of luck, but, barring any other, better ideas, it was worth a shot.

I turned to Zane. "How do you feel about running?"

"To or from something?" he asked, and I could see the wariness in his expression. He was wondering if I was going to try to force him to leave.

"To." I outlined my plan.

When I finished, he was shaking his head.

"What?" I asked.

He opened his mouth, hesitated, and then said, "Sometimes I forget you've got all this . . . stuff in your head. Plans, schemes, skills. It's like you're two different people sometimes." He didn't seem to be sure if that was a good thing or bad thing, or just weird.

"Tell me about it," I muttered.

I led the way downstairs and out the back door of "our" house. If we stuck close to the walls, the dark blue shadows of the early morning would likely cover us. Plus, we needed to be outside to hear Mara's garage door going up. Our signal to run.

I took a deep breath and shivered in the damp air. The

overgrown grass was slippery and cool with dew that would be burned off as soon as the sun was up, but for now it was soaking into my shoes and the hem of my jeans.

Next to me, Zane raised a questioning eyebrow.

I nodded. I was okay. It was just that this was the second day in a row that I'd been awake to see the sunrise.

Actually, the third. Today was Monday.

Saturday morning, I'd just been stuck underground in the lab and unable to see it.

I felt tired suddenly, worn down. I needed a vacation. Or at least a solid night of uninterrupted sleep. But I wouldn't turn down a hammock and the peace of mind of being on a distant island where no one could find me.

Us. I altered the mental image of the hammock to include Zane and found I liked it even better. Maybe when all of this was done.

A low rumbling noise sounded in the distance, sending my pulse into high gear, and Zane tapped my arm lightly, his whole body tensed and ready.

I nodded, and we ran.

I was fast, but Zane's longer legs gave him equal advantage, matching me stride for stride as we bolted through backyards on a parallel to the street. Once we reached the far side of the third house, we made a hard left, putting us directly in line with the rear side of Mara's duplex.

At least that was the plan. But rounding the corner, I slipped on the grass and started to fall. I flailed, reaching for power to correct my balance, but my concentration was too scattered. My body stiffened, preparing for impact, for pain. We were moving too fast for me to roll through it. There would be broken bones. A wrist, most likely, and those were a bitch.

But Zane grabbed my elbow and yanked me upright before I hit the ground, his quick reflexes honed from years of sports, probably.

I shot him a grateful look but didn't have time for more; the sliding glass door at the back of Mara's duplex was looming large.

My hand up, I focused on the locking mechanism and flipped it up, and then turned my attention to the white security bar, stretched across the glass. One solid yank at the joint with my mind and it was dangling like a broken elbow, clattering against the door. Then, with another mental shove, the sliding glass door retracted so hard it bounced when it hit the end of the track.

Zane and I jostled up the concrete steps and into the kitchen, which reeked of charred toast. Our shoes squeaked on linoleum.

"This way," I said in a rough whisper, broken by my panting. A left took us into a tiny living room with a small TV on a tray table and a tired-looking sofa, stuffing leaking out of one cushion.

On the far wall, a door with three shiny dead bolts. The garage.

Once again I pulled at the locks in advance of our approach. Only this time, I accidentally pulled the locks from the wooden door with a small explosion of splinters and sawdust—oops. But good enough. We burst through into the garage, with Zane ahead of me, as planned, just as Mara was backing up in her little silver Mazda.

She braked with a sudden screech, her face pale even behind the windshield tinting. "Zane." Her mouth formed the word clearly even though the sound didn't reach us over the engine noise. Then her gaze fell on me, and her mouth pinched in displeasure. But she didn't leave.

I pulled Zane back a step, trying to keep him in the shadows as much as possible. I wasn't sure what the SUV guys would see if they looked in the garage, and I didn't want to risk it.

He gave me an unhappy nod—I knew he hated this part of the plan—then I slipped past him, down the steps, and climbed into Mara's backseat.

"What are you doing?" Mara gasped, as I closed the door with a quiet thunk.

I ducked down to hide in the footwell and leaned to one side so I could see her in the gap between the seats. "Just go."

She didn't move.

"If you don't, those guys in the SUV will be up here to check, and they'll find Zane." I didn't like using her drive to protect her son to manipulate her, but it would work, and that was what I needed.

She released her foot from the brake and the car rolled backward again. "If you get him hurt, I will make you sorry," she snarled, glaring at me in the rearview mirror.

"I believe it," I said without hesitation. "Close the garage."

Mara obeyed immediately, pressing a button on the remote clipped to her sun visor, no doubt recognizing the benefit of hiding Zane from view.

From my position on the floor, I couldn't see him, but I imagined him standing there alone, his mouth turned down, watching us leave. I hated leaving him behind, but I figured that bringing Zane along, therefore putting him in further danger, would have made Mara even less cooperative.

"Now just go to work like you normally do," I said.

Mara gave a strained laugh as she put the car in drive. "Because this has so much in common with normal. What do you want, 107?"

Oddly enough, with the adrenaline pumping, I didn't even flinch at the numerical designation.

"If you're looking for a hostage, you picked the wrong person," she continued. "They're not going to do anything to save—"

"I don't want you as a hostage," I said, swallowing my impatience with her. "I just need information."

"I don't know anything," she protested. "They don't tell me—"

I cut her off. "Where are Laughlin's hybrids? Ford and the others."

She inhaled sharply. "What do you want with them?"

"I'm changing the game," I said grimly.

"What does that mean?"

I ignored her. "You said they're in public sometimes, right? At school for training."

"Yes, but—"

"Where?" I persisted.

"What are you planning?" she asked suspiciously.

I stayed quiet. I doubted Mara would turn me into Laughlin right now, not when doing so would jeopardize her son. But I couldn't be sure.

"You don't want anything to do with them, I promise you," she said darkly.

"I don't have a choice," I said. "Where can I find them?" I concentrated on the buzz of her thoughts. Even if she wouldn't say the name, she might think it.

But Mara's mind was an uncoordinated scramble of half-finished thoughts.

I can't—

If I tell her, then Laughlin will . . . Oh God.

Why not? Let them finish each other off and—

A, B, C, D, E, F, G . . .

She was attempting to block the name from surfacing by focusing on something else. The alphabet song. It would work. For a while. But eventually, she'd slip. I just had to wait her out. And she knew that.

Inside, her voice was shaky with panic. But on the outside, she was silent. The only noise came from the tires on the road and the low hum of the engine. It was lulling, particularly in combination with the rhythmic chanting of the song.

So when the melody in her head abruptly cut off and she spoke aloud again, it startled me. "If I tell you where to find them, you have to leave Zane alone. Drop him off somewhere, send him home to Wingate," she said, the words tumbling out as if she'd been barely holding them back.

Ah, that I'd been expecting. She loved Zane, regardless of the crappy ways she'd chosen to show that. "He is free to leave me anytime he wants," I said, though just the thought of him walking away ripped at me with sharp teeth. "But he's made his choice, and I won't abandon him." *Unlike you.*

I didn't say the words, but she picked up on the implication anyway and flinched.

Instead of protesting, though, she nodded stiffly, as if this

145

had decided something for her. "Assuming you can magically resolve this—" she began.

"It's not magic," I interjected. "You should know that better than anyone."

"—by killing Jacobs and Laughlin or negotiating with them, whatever your plan is," she continued as though I hadn't spoken, "do you think you'll be happy with a normal life?"

The question took me by surprise, and I answered honestly before I could stop myself. "It's all I've ever wanted."

"But you've never lived it," she pointed out. "You've been on a mission your whole life. First, in the lab, to learn your abilities, and then to hide them once you were thought you were outside. Will you be able to shut off the part of yourself that enjoys what you are?" she pressed, sounding almost sad. "Will you be satisfied using those same skills to calculate the closest parking space at the store or figure out who keeps letting their dog do his business in your yard?" She shook her head. "I'm sorry, but 107, you are not made for a normal life."

Her words echoed something Dr. Jacobs had said to me the other night in the lab. *You weren't created for high school, dates, and football games.*

It sent a chill through me. At the time, I'd thought he was simply trying to convince me to cooperate. But what if they were both talking about something far more complicated? Like I somehow lacked the capability to live a normal life? Like, I don't know, a dishwasher trying to make toast.

I jerked my head in denial. No, I was being ridiculous. Human or not, I was still a person. I still had choices. "You're wrong," I said firmly.

"I was there. I've studied you, seen your test results," Mara said in that same soft, pseudo-compassionate tone.

"Studying me doesn't mean you know me," I snapped. "Dr. Jacobs made that mistake. Look how that worked out for him."

"All right, all right," she said soothingly, and I felt her nervousness increase. She knew all too well what I could do if I felt threatened. "It's okay."

"No, it's not," I said through gritted teeth. I wanted her to take it back, to admit that she was lying to manipulate me into doing what she wanted.

I could feel my power building up, a tingling in my arms and legs that had nothing to do with my cramped position. I hadn't lost control in days, not since destroying the mental block that had kept me from accessing most of my ability. But now, the car windows were shaking in their frames and the radio was giving off an alarming squeal of interference.

"Okay, fine. Forget what I said. How about a token of good faith? Ford and the others are at Linwood High School in Lake Forest." She lifted her shaking hands from the wheel momentarily, as if to show she held no weapons. "No coercion, no promises."

Strangely enough, that did more to convince me that she truly believed what she'd said about me. The mounting power within me dissipated abruptly, and I felt dizzy, empty. She had to be wrong. *Had* to be.

"Just keep my son safe," she added, her mouth tight.

Until you realize that I'm right.

This time, it was her turn to leave words hanging in the air, unspoken, but I heard them all too clearly, just the same.

CHAPTER 10

Zane

ARIANE BAILED OUT OF MY MOM'S CAR LIKE SHE DID IT every day.

I watched in amazement from the driver's seat of the van as the door popped open and Ariane slipped out. She kept low as she closed the door and crossed to the sidewalk. Then she straightened up and started walking at an easy pace, as though she were just any normal person out for an early-morning stroll.

And it worked, as far as I could tell. The Laughlin surveillance SUV had been forced back a car or two by traffic. So no one noticed a thing, except maybe whoever was in the car directly behind my mom's.

I shook my head in disbelief, then accelerated to meet up with Ariane. Per the plan, I'd left my mom's place and hustled back to the abandoned house where Ariane and I had stayed to gather our belongings and get the van.

"Follow at a discreet distance" had been her direction,

which I'd interpreted as about a block and half. It hadn't been difficult to find them and catch up, thankfully. My mom had been proceeding well under the speed limit, a combination of early-morning rush hour traffic and probably being distracted by the conversation with her stowaway.

Ariane pulled open the passenger-side door of the van and boosted herself inside in a smooth movement. I didn't even have to come to a complete stop.

She was like a female version of freaking Jason Bourne.

"That was unreal," I said, unable to disguise the admiration in my voice, even as it made me cringe a little. I was like some kind of slack-jawed yokel, amazed by electricity or something.

"Thanks," Ariane said, sounding distracted as she yanked the door shut.

"Did she say—"

"Linwood High School," Ariane said abruptly, her gaze fixed on some unknown point in the distance. "Lake Forest, Illinois. If I remember the map correctly, it's about twenty minutes from here, southeast. So head back to the highway."

Okay. I frowned. She sounded almost as mechanical as the GPS we didn't have (and could have used). Something wasn't right here. I could almost feel her pulling into herself, retreating somewhere I couldn't reach.

"Is everything—" I began, and then cut myself off, a hot flush of embarrassment flooding my face. Of course everything wasn't okay. Yesterday, I'd gone and dropped a bomb on the delicate balance that existed between us.

I love you. I winced. *Zane, what were you thinking?* I'd never before said that to a girl, but I knew too well the destructive power of an ill-timed declaration like that. Quinn, my brother, had dumped girls for lesser infractions. Even if I had meant it more as, I love you for saying that, which—let's be honest—wasn't what I'd meant at all, it was still too much, too soon. Obviously.

I never should have said anything. I had to do something to fix this. I might have felt what I felt, but announcing it? Bad idea. I felt sorry suddenly for all the girls who'd opened up to Quinn only to find themselves deleted from his phone. It was humiliating.

"Listen, Ariane, I just wanted to say . . ." I struggled to find the words that would erase the ones from before, words that would bridge the distance I'd stupidly created. "About yesterday. That was dumb. I never should have said that."

"What?" Ariane looked over at me, genuinely confused, as if she'd been somewhere else entirely for the beginning of the conversation.

"The thing I said?" I shied away from repeating it. Once was bad enough. "I'm sorry for laying that on you. Especially right now, in the middle of everything that's going on," I said, forcing a shrug. "So let's just forget it, okay? I take it back." I tried for a casual smile, but it felt more like a grimace.

She stared at me for a long moment, her forehead furrowed, as if trying to decide something.

I shifted uneasily in my seat. "Look, I didn't mean—"

"No," she said finally.

I gaped at her. It wasn't a yes-or-no question. In fact, it wasn't a question at all. "Uh, no what?" I asked.

"No, you can't take it back," she said, a hint of color rising in her pale face and her chin tipped up in defiance. Then she hesitated, vulnerability flashing across her features. "Unless you've changed your mind."

Then it was my turn to hesitate, confused. She didn't *seem* upset about my blurt, but something was clearly wrong. But even bewildered, I knew better than to lie to someone who could hear me doing so. "No," I said cautiously. "It's not that. I just shouldn't have—"

"Then you can't have it back," she said, raising her eyebrows in challenge. "It's mine."

The sheer ferocity in her tone startled a laugh out of me. "Okay, okay." I held my hands up in surrender for a quick second before returning them to the steering wheel. It was flattering, at least, and made me feel a little better. Though I couldn't help noticing that she hadn't said anything about returning those feelings.

Let it go, Zane.

"I do, you know," she said quietly. She drew her knees up to her chest, folding herself in the seat. "I have, since before we left Wingate." She gave me a shy smile. "Pretty much since the activities fair, I think."

"Really?" I had to stop myself from grinning like an idiot. That had been our first night out. It had ended with Rachel Jacobs, Ariane's mortal enemy at the time, screeching in outrage and covered in shaving cream. Never let it be said I don't know how to show a girl a good time, I guess.

"I just . . ." She took a deep breath. "You have to understand this is all new to me, and I've been working my whole life to avoid giving up control to someone else."

"I don't want to control you," I said.

She shook her head violently, sending her hair, already a chaotic mess, flying around her face. "No, I know that, but the feelings are huge and they make things so complicated. . . ." She blew out a frustrated breath. And I thought about the miracle that we were able to understand each other, coming from such ridiculously disparate backgrounds.

She took a deep breath and tried again. "You know how you said sometimes it seems as if I'm two different people?"

I nodded.

"Sometimes, it feels that way to me, too." She lifted her thin shoulders in a shrug. "I have years of training and instincts that come from this place deep inside me. And then I have these feelings and needs." Her gaze flicked to me, and she blushed. I guessed she was thinking about our hookup in the van yesterday.

"I don't know what to trust. I mean, I'm human and other," she said carefully. "So, I'm both, but neither one. And that was hard enough before, but now . . . I don't know how to do *this*." She gestured to the space between us. "Or if I even should do this." She bit her lip, as if there was more she would say but had stopped herself.

I had no idea what that was like for her, but I knew what it felt like to be caught between conflicting loyalties. "All right," I said, thinking furiously. "How about this? We'll just keep talking about it, when, you know, we're not breaking into houses or sneaking out of cars. Do our best to make sure *all* of us are on the same page."

She flashed me a weak smile, uncertainty flickering in her eyes. "Yeah, I guess."

I smirked. "Awesome. A threesome."

And when she rolled her eyes and shoved at my shoulder, I felt better, lighter than I had in days. I wondered how long that would last.

"*That's* their school?" I stared at the sight before us.

"Apparently, Mara left out a few details," Ariane said, sounding less than pleased.

Like it wasn't Linwood High School, but Linwood *Academy* High School. The difference being one word and probably $25,000 a year.

Above us on a slight hill, the expansive building was situated on a sprawling green lawn, an oasis in the otherwise drought-ravaged suburbs. The walls angled out with unnecessary metal flourishes at the roofline, in that modern we-hired-an-expensive-architect kind of way. I could just make out a secondary building behind and to the right that, from the size, was probably a gym or a natatorium. It was also probably a safe bet that there were tennis courts up there somewhere too. Maybe even a putting green or two for the golf team.

I rolled my eyes.

Students in perfectly pressed school uniforms were all over the place: swarming toward a covered entrance at the side of the building (which was supported by three columns that appeared to be oversize statues of men, their raised hands supporting the roof), lounging under the perfectly coiffed weeping willow tree near what had to be a man-made pond, or hanging out on benches on white patches of gravel in the pristine grass.

Evidently, we'd arrived just before the first bell.

I shook my head. "It looks like—"

"—a museum," Ariane said, with the smallest note of envy.

I shrugged. "I was going to go with fancy rehab facility. But that works too."

She eyed me questioningly.

"Everyone's dressed the same, they have white blobby meditation sculptures, and the grass is so green and even it looks like a rug." I ticked each item off on my fingers. "This place practically screams, 'No sharp objects allowed.'"

She frowned at me. "How do you know that?"

"Rachel once showed me the Web site of the place where her mom stays. It looked a lot like this." I frowned. "Fewer people in plaid, though."

"Plaid is probably déclassé in California," Ariane said with a small smile. "All the cool recovering addicts are wearing white."

I snorted. "Yeah."

Someone honked behind us, just a polite tap on the horn. No one here was ill-bred enough to really lay into it. I found myself wanting to hold our position, blocking traffic, just to see how long it would take them to break form.

But keeping a low profile—well, relatively low—was more important. "Our van is not nearly expensive enough to be parking in this neighborhood," I pointed out as I let up on the brake and turned the corner, heading up the incline toward the school. "We're not going to have much time before someone is out here trying to get us to water the grass or reporting us to the police as creepers."

"I know." Ariane kept her gaze trained out the window, watching for what, I wasn't sure. We didn't even really know what Laughlin's hybrids looked like, except one of them must resemble Ariane at least a little. Enough for my mom's paranoid brain to confuse them, anyway.

But there were a lot of blue-blazer, plaid-skirt, and khaki-pants people wandering around out there. It was dizzying, like trying to focus on a single grain of sand on a whole beach.

I found a parking spot near the rear of the smooth, blemish-free asphalt lot that still gave us a decent view of what appeared to be the main entrance—the one with the three dudes raising the roof—and parked nose out.

"So what, exactly, is the plan?" I asked, cutting the engine.

"Find them, talk to them," she said, her words terse with her attention focused elsewhere.

"I think you forgot: 'and hope they don't kill us on sight,'" I muttered.

She tore her gaze away from the Linwood elite to regard me with something like amusement, which I didn't particularly care for. "Even if they're not hiding, as I was, they will still be under orders to be discreet. Laughlin will not be any more inclined toward a public spectacle than Dr. Jacobs was. They can't afford the exposure. That's why tracking them down at school, in front of witnesses, is our safest option."

I'd kind of thought it was our *only* option, but whatever. "I thought the whole point was they might not be into following orders so much."

"I think it's more that they follow orders very specifically. They weren't ordered *not* to stalk your mother, so they took advantage of that gap. Small rebellions. They didn't actually hurt her. They're limited."

I wasn't sure my mother's condition qualified as unhurt, but that was neither here nor there at the moment.

"If they hate the humans and had the capacity to change their situation, they would have already. So there must be some limit to what they can do with their orders, boundaries that they know they cannot cross," Ariane said.

It was a good point, but I had to wonder how in the hell this Laughlin guy managed to keep them walking such a fine line. There must be something big hanging over their heads. "Yeah, but you have no idea what their standing orders are in regard to you," I said.

For the first time, she hesitated. "I'm kind of banking on the fact that nobody's ever thought a meeting would occur outside the trials."

My mouth fell open. "You're kidding."

She shook her head.

So, this truly was a desperate, go-all-in-and-gamble-with-your-life moment. Well, shit.

"Okay," I said slowly. "But what's your plan if—"

But before I could finish, two black SUVs with heavily tinted windows pulled past us and wound their way to the covered drop-off area.

Ariane sat up in her seat, her hands clutching at the arm-rest so tightly that her knuckles blanched.

Of course. They *would* have an entourage. Ariane had been forced to blend in and be average, but these hybrids seemed to be doing the exact opposite. This school, their freedom (albeit limited) to come and go from their home at the facility, their look-at-me arrival on campus.

Assuming this was actually them and not some washed-up rock star's offspring.

I leaned forward to watch, barely breathing.

They, whoever they were, exited on the opposite side of the vehicle. I could see the motion, the SUV swaying slightly as its occupants climbed out.

"There," I pointed, my heart thundering in my chest. It wasn't much, a brief glimpse of the same white-blond hair Ariane possessed, as the first SUV pulled away and the second moved into its place, but it was enough.

Ariane nodded. "It's them."

We were both scrambling to release our seat belts when the second SUV pulled away, revealing two big, black-clad security guys tagging along after the presumed hybrids. I couldn't really see them with the guards in the way, just flashes of that pale hair here and there. But watching how the other students scrambled out of the way and then stared after them removed any doubt I might have had.

"Crap." Ariane bit her lip. "What are the odds that they're just escorting them to the door?"

"Uh, guarding them from all the perils that could spring up in that extra ten feet or so?" I asked. "Doubtful."

Which meant the guards were going into school with them, possibly even into their classes, an idea that was almost immediately confirmed when the guards disappeared inside the school seconds later, following their charges.

Ariane slumped in her seat.

"At least we know we're in the right place," I offered.

"Yes, but if their security protocol is the same after school, we won't have a chance to speak with them then either. And the longer this takes, the more likely it is that word will spread that I've escaped. Laughlin might then start looking for me. . . ."

And whatever orders his hybrids might or might not be under now would change, probably to decidedly more specific ones when it came to Ariane. And we'd be back to no plan, no hope.

She was quiet, but I could sense the wheels turning in her brain.

I closed my eyes and sighed. "You want to go in, don't you?" It was the only logical conclusion. And after the last few days with her, I was finally starting to get a grasp on how she thought.

"I'll go by myself," she said. "It's safer for you to stay out here."

I felt a quick pinch of frustration. "No, I said I was in. So I'm in. But . . ." I gestured to the students wearing the Ralph-Lauren-on-crack collection. "We don't exactly blend in." Preppy was one thing. These people looked as if they were seconds away from sailing away on a private yacht or playing polo. Or both.

"No, we don't." She frowned. "Not yet, anyway."

Oh, I bet I was going to regret this. "What does that mean?" I asked warily.

She smiled. "How do you feel about khakis?" she asked.

I groaned. She was going to dress us up like pod people, and I bet that would include one of those stupid ties. I hated anything pressed against my neck. "Better than I do about plaid skirts?" I offered grudgingly.

"Good. Then we need to find a place to do a little shopping."

And here I thought confronting potentially homicidal hybrids was going to be the worst part of my day.

CHAPTER 11

IIIIBB II IIIIBBI IBII IBIBB

Ariane

DR. DAVID LAUGHLIN WAS A HANDSOME MAN WITH A cruel mouth.

I'd learned to study faces early on in the lab at GTX. So often the larger expressions didn't match the thoughts and feelings I heard. That was confusing at first, a dissonance that was hard to manage until I learned which to rely on. People could make their faces say anything with enough practice, I discovered, but they rarely bothered with their thoughts.

Still, even the most skilled deceivers often gave themselves away with the tiniest hints of their true nature. A curled lip. Eyes narrowed ever so fractionally. Shaking their heads no even as their mouths said, "Yes."

In the photos I'd found, Laughlin was smiling, but his lips were tight and narrow across his too-white teeth, like a predator signaling an impending attack.

He wasn't particularly camera shy, either. A single Google search on our newly purchased disposable phone had provided dozens of pages of results. Articles, yes, about the man himself and his company, Laughlin Integrated Enterprises, but also pictures of Dr. Laughlin attending various events. He seemed to have some social standing in the Chicago area. There were multiple photos of him at black-tie and red-carpet events. The opening of a new play. A party at the Lyric Opera house. Shaking hands with the new mayor.

All with that thin, bloodless grin.

Zane emerged from the dressing room, tugging unhappily at the tie knotted loosely around his neck. He stopped dead when he saw me waiting.

"You're ready." He sounded surprised.

"Yes." I glanced down at myself. Had I missed something? Blue skirt, white blouse (with a white T-shirt underneath to make sure my tattoo didn't show through), patterned scarf, navy ballet flats. I looked just like the girl on the Linwood Academy Web site. Well, to the best of my ability to replicate.

After our stop at Best Buy for the disposable phone with Internet access—I hadn't realized how much I'd missed it until I didn't have it anymore—I'd found a department store that carried a section of items intended for school uniforms. They didn't have the Linwood crests—those apparently came from the school—but everything else was basically what we'd seen this morning. Well, a cheaper version, I was guessing.

"I just . . . I thought you'd want to shop more," Zane said with a frown.

"Here?" I raised my eyebrows. "Their denim selection is kind of pathetic."

He stared at me. "What?"

I shook my head. Of course he had no knowledge of my

"hobby," the result of which was the impressive jeans collection I'd been forced to leave behind at my house. Not that it really mattered. Except it did, in the sense that it was part of who I was, part of who'd I *chosen* to be, and there were so few of those pieces, I really hated to lose any of them.

"Never mind," I said.

"Hey, nice scarf." He tugged at it lightly. "You look like an accountant."

I thought about that and then gave him the finger, much to the displeasure of the eagle-eyed store employee watching us.

Zane laughed. At times, it was so easy to surprise and amuse him. I liked that. It made me feel as if I was doing something right, as if I had some value to him and I wasn't the only one getting something out of this.

"What do you have there?" He nodded at the phone in my hand, which was still displaying Laughlin's picture.

In answer, I turned the screen toward him so he could see the caption beneath the photo with Laughlin's name.

Zane's forehead creased with worry. "You think he's going to be at the school?"

"No. But I want to be able to recognize him if he is." I had no idea how often Dr. Laughlin checked on his progeny. Perhaps he was there to pick them up after school every day.

Zane nodded. "Okay." But he still appeared concerned.

"It'll be fine," I said briskly. I hoped. "Got your tags?" I was betting we had only a few more seconds before that clerk was over here to hassle us about buying or leaving. I'd be tempted to wave a fistful of hundreds in front of her face, but we were trying to be discreet.

Zane handed me the mangled bits of paper, the bar codes barely legible.

"I didn't have scissors in there," he protested when I gave him a questioning look.

"I could have helped," I said with a sigh.

"Maybe next time," he said lightly but with a heated gaze that sent a jolt through me. No one had ever looked at me that way.

My face flushed. "I meant with the tags."

"Oh. That too." He grinned.

Yeah, I was possibly in a little over my head.

Our spot in the Linwood Academy parking lot was still open, but all the students who'd been wandering around before had vanished.

Staring up at the monstrosity of the main building—it really was ugly and just weird looking—and imagining all the strangers within, I felt a fresh wave of uncertainty.

The first rule of a successful operation was adequate preparation, and I didn't know this school or these people.

After taking the keys out of the ignition, Zane unbuckled his seat belt, but I made no move to do the same.

"What's wrong?" he asked.

I stared down at the phone in my hand and squeezed it so tight my knuckles ached. "The Web site didn't list a bell schedule, so I'm just guessing at the timing for lunch."

Sneaking in during mealtime would give us the best shot at blending in unnoticed. Lots of students moving around all at once and for more than three or four minutes at a time, as they would between classes. That was the theory, anyway.

The trouble was, it didn't give us a lot of time, and I had no idea where the hybrids might be. And while Linwood was small—"An elite student body, made up of the best and brightest," according to their About Web page—a thousand kids in four grades meant a lot of rooms to search.

"I'm assuming fifty-minute class periods from the listed start time, which would give us three overlapping lunch periods of half an hour each, but I don't have anything to confirm that." I let out a shaky exhale. "And I don't have a building layout or a breakdown on the organizational system they use for assigning classrooms." If the hybrids were juniors, as I was supposed to be, theoretically, they'd be in junior-level classes. But that was assuming that (a) these hybrids were supposed to be my same age and (b) that Linwood's curriculum was in some way similar to ours. "I just don't have enough information."

Zane was staring at me. "I think we'll be fine," he said slowly, as if I were crazy.

"I'd feel better if we were more prepared," I said. The plastic casing on the phone squeaked against the pressure of my hand. I released it.

He shook his head. "You've done the best you can do with what you have. Isn't that something you learned in all your training?"

No, because I'd never had any real-world experience with missions. Not where I set my own objective, anyway. And in lab-created scenarios, I'd always had access to everything I needed to succeed, even if I had to work hard to get it. No Kobayashi Maru tests at GTX. Maybe Dr. Jacobs had been saving that for my return. Or maybe, he, like Captain

Kirk, didn't want to contemplate the possibility of a no-win situation.

"Besides," Zane continued, "rich people, hybrids, or whatever, this is still a high school." He shrugged. "It can't be that different from ours."

"Yes, and my experience at Ashe High was certainly a model for success," I said flatly.

"Hey, look at me," he said.

I glanced up from the phone and yet another utterly useless Web search for information about Linwood.

"We'll find them, okay?" he said, his gaze steady and calm. "Without getting caught."

I nodded, feeling a great surge of love for him. This wasn't his idea, not something he even wanted to do, but he was working hard to reassure me anyway.

He tapped his fingers against the steering wheel, thinking. "These hybrids, they're, uh, different, right?"

I nodded. "Mara said they don't blend in well." I hesitated, then added, "Dr. Jacobs once said something strange to me, that they couldn't talk. But that can't be right." If it were, there'd be no point in trying to "humanize" them, would there? Not talking would make so-called normal interactions with full-blooded humans pretty difficult.

"Then all we have to do is get in. Someone will know who they are and probably even where we can find them," Zane said with a shrug. "Everyone always knows who the . . ."

He stopped himself before the word *freaks* exited his mouth, but I heard it just the same and it struck like a slap.

He grimaced. "I didn't mean—"

"No," I said quietly. "You're right. They are. *We* are."

"Ariane," he began with chagrined expression.

I shook my head. "Don't. Let's go," I said. I didn't want an apology. Can't apologize for the truth.

I pushed open my door, climbed down from the van, and started for the entrance.

Zane followed, taking long strides to catch up with me. "So, do you have a plan?" he asked.

Actually, I did. And what Zane had said a moment ago had only confirmed my idea. "Yeah," I said. "We're going to ask someone."

"That's . . . direct," he said, startled.

It was, which was the beauty of it. I'd considered other alternatives—eavesdropping on thoughts, searching likely rooms or wings, simply waiting in a central location (like the cafeteria) for them to walk by—but considering our time constraints and our paper-thin cover as Linwood students, it seemed best to move, and move quickly.

"What you said before was right," I said, ignoring the wailing of my all-too human feelings. "High school generally functions on a caste system. For that to work, participants must know who the untouchables are."

Zane flinched.

"We'll find someone likely to have a good grasp on the social workings, a student, not a teacher, and just ask where we can find Ford, Carter, or Nixon." Assuming, of course, that the hybrids hadn't adopted new names upon entering school. If they had, well, then this would be that much harder. But not impossible. Ford, Carter, and Nixon's . . . unusualness wasn't limited to what they were called. Someone would know who we meant, even if we had to describe them based on our vague details.

"Okay," Zane said reluctantly. "What the hell." He tried

to smile. "Can't be any worse than wandering the halls aimlessly."

The closer we got to the doors, the more my nerves grew. The strange pillars—men in loincloths holding the roof up over their heads with strained expressions—seemed to be glaring down on me as we passed. The bright white concrete leading up to the building looked as if it was power-washed on a weekly basis. No black spots of gum or chalk messages for Linwood students.

Never in my life would I have ever imagined feeling a fondness or longing for Ashe High, but that was exactly what I wanted right then—to be back on familiar ground.

I should be in Brit Lit right now. The realization almost made me stumble; the idea that my "normal" existence was continuing on without me felt like a shock somehow. That there'd be an empty desk that would still be "mine" even though I wasn't there to claim it anymore.

I wondered if Rachel was back in school. If she'd noticed that Zane and I were both missing. Was Jenna still angry with me? Was it a Tater Tot day in the cafeteria? Or french fries?

My chest ached with a confusing mix of sorrow and relief. For all its flaws and imperfections, my life in Wingate had been . . . well, my life. And Ashe High, along with the rest of it, was gone for good.

Except for Zane.

Without letting myself stop to think about it, I reached over and slid my hand into Zane's.

I felt his surprise, but he didn't hesitate, closing his fingers tightly over mine and giving a gentle squeeze.

"Thank you," I said, fighting the tears that suddenly welled up.

"For what?" he asked.

"For this," I said. "For going through with this even though you think it's a bad idea. For being here." With me.

He glanced at the doors before pulling me off to the side. He caressed the line of my cheek with his thumb, his eyes serious, and then he leaned in and kissed me.

And this was not just any "hey, good luck" brush of the lips. His hand was buried in my hair at the back of my neck, pulling me close, and I could feel his breath against my skin, his tongue sweeping over mine.

I wrapped my hands in his shirt, likely making wrinkles in the otherwise smooth fabric, but I couldn't bring myself to care even a little bit.

The way he made the world fall away so I couldn't hear anything, couldn't feel anything but this? It was magic. And I wanted more. I wanted everything.

"Just . . . be careful, okay?" he asked when he finally pulled away.

I blinked, struggling to process both the kiss and the emotions I could now sense pouring off him. He was worried that I'd find Laughlin's hybrids and they'd hurt me. I could hear that from him plainly. But he was equally worried about what might happen if they *didn't* attack, if they greeted me with open arms.

"I promise," I said, still reeling.

The bell rang, then, a fancy mellow-sounding tone that sounded more like a call to meditation.

He grinned at me. "Told you we'd be fine."

Guessing the bell schedule correctly was only part of the equation, but I had to smile back. It was hard to resist his confidence.

Zane pulled the door open, holding it for me and then following me in.

I crossed the threshold, stepping onto a pristine and polished blond wood floor of another world. No trophy cases or state championship banners hanging here. The air, though, smelled familiar. A combination of cleaning products, too much body spray, and angst.

In the distance, where the entryway turned into a hall and met with another corridor, I could see blue-and-khaki-clad students flowing through, like deoxygenated blood returning to the heart.

But thankfully, the entryway where we stood was empty, for the moment, so no one had witnessed our arrival. Four sleek, metal benches lined the walls, a tiny sculpted tree in a matching pot between each set of benches. A doorway on the left side of the hall, between the benches (and trees) buzzed with the sounds of voices, laughter, and a phone ringing. Adult voices. Teachers. The office, most likely.

Great. I'd expected it to be near the entrance, of course, but I hadn't anticipated that it would be quite so isolated here. No crowds of students to blend into.

"Where to first?" Zane asked under his breath.

"Away from here." I bobbed my head toward the door, where a man in a gray uniform was now visible, his arm looping over the door frame as he finished talking to someone inside.

Zane stiffened, and I felt a spike of dread from him.

"Keep your head up, and walk quickly, but not like we're rushing," I whispered.

He nodded.

I led the way, flinching at every squeak of our shoes on the polished floors. It felt as if it took hours to cross those ten feet or so. Long enough for me to seriously reconsider this plan. I had no idea what the consequences would be for trespassing on private school property and imitating Linwood Academy students. But I was betting it involved the police, which was the last thing we needed right now.

When we passed the office door without anyone sounding the alarm, Zane flashed me a grin, as if to say, mission accomplished.

Well, sort of. More like "not-immediate-mission-failure." Which was, I suppose, something.

"Let's see if we can find the cafeteria," I said quietly, nodding to a point ahead of us where the hall branched to the left and right. "More people in one room raises our chances of—"

"What do you think you're doing?" someone demanded from behind us.

Well, that couldn't be good.

CHAPTER 12

|||██ || | || |██| | ██|| |█ |██| |

Zane

I STIFFENED, THEN TURNED, MOVING TO STEP IN FRONT of Ariane, only to find a thin, weedy guy scowling at us a few feet from the doorway of the office, a stack of papers in hand. His white button-down shirt had a Florida-shaped coffee stain on the left side, and his ratio of hair to bald spot was definitely heading in the wrong direction.

"I'm waiting for an answer," the teacher prompted, his expression distinctly sour.

I opened my mouth to say something—I didn't know what, some kind of excuse—but then I realized he wasn't even looking at me.

"Were you outside? You know you're not supposed to leave the building during school hours," he scolded Ariane. "Especially unescorted."

I frowned. Okay, that was weird.

Ariane froze under his glare, and I remembered belatedly that she'd spent years trying to fly beneath the radar.

Getting called out by an authority figure was probably new to her; I, however, had had years of practice in the fake obeisance department, thanks to my dad.

"It was my fault," I began. "I had to get—"

"Sorry," Ariane said. "I just needed some air."

He jerked as though she'd poked at him with a stick. "You were with *him?*" he asked Ariane, pointing at me, his eyes wide with surprise.

Ariane's pale cheeks colored slightly. "We were only outside for a few minutes," she said, her tone stiff. I didn't need to be a mind reader to get that she was taking his shock as a personal insult.

He frowned at her. "That's no excuse," he said, but his anger was muted now under something more like confusion.

Then he shifted his attention to me, scanning me from head to toe. "Where's your jacket?"

The Linwood blazer that we couldn't reasonably replicate, thanks to the oversize and douche-y crest on the breast of it? Yeah, we'd skipped those, thinking that no one would actually wear that once they got inside the building. But apparently we were playing by private school rules now.

"Probably left it in my locker," I offered.

His mouth screwed up in distaste. "Funny." He narrowed his eyes at me. "Being out of uniform will cost you both a demerit." His gaze skated to Ariane again. "I don't care who your father is."

Huh. Okay, that was kind of random.

I looked to Ariane, but she gave a tiny shake of her head. She didn't know what he was talking about either.

The teacher reached into his shirt pocket and produced a pad of green slips.

On which he'd want to write names (or student ID numbers, possibly) that we couldn't give him. *Crap.*

"That's why we're going to get them right now," Ariane said, and then, before the teacher could protest, she turned and walked off down the hall.

I followed hastily. A quick backward glance showed him standing there with a scowl, but he wasn't, thank God, chasing after us.

"What was that all about?" I asked when we were safely around the corner and out of sight.

"No idea," Ariane said, sounding a little breathless. "He just kept thinking, 'I never thought I'd see the day' and 'I deserve better than these damn kids.'"

Fantastic. This was getting better and better.

"Let's find someone to ask so we can hurry up and get out of here," I said grimly. At this point, I was beyond caring whether we succeeded or not.

Ariane cast an evaluating gaze around the teeming hall. Shining metal doors, some closed and some open, punctuated the polished wood walls. Evidently, we'd walked in during class change, or maybe Ariane was as good as I suspected she was and we'd landed right in the lunch hour.

Although the hall was full of people, it seemed eerily quiet. It took me a second to identify the missing noise. No lockers slamming. In fact, I didn't even see any lockers. Or even books. Only students with iPads in hand.

It took everything I had not to gape. Seriously? No lockers, no books. Did they fly them to France for French class too? No wonder the cranky bald dude had gotten pissed when I said I'd left my jacket in my locker. He'd probably thought I was mocking him.

"Her." Ariane pointed to a cluster of three or four girls who'd just emerged from a bathroom.

But I knew immediately which one she meant. Tall, blond, beautiful, her uniform skirt about four inches shorter than everyone else's, revealing a lot more leg. But the key clue to her identity came from the adoring throng around her, girls leaning forward to catch her every word, their skirts rolled up to imitate hers.

I groaned. "Oh, come on, Ariane."

Ariane raised her eyebrows. "She'll know."

"Yeah, but that doesn't mean she'll tell us," I pointed out. At least not without something in it for her. I knew that girl's type. So did Ariane. Every school had a Rachel Jacobs—maybe more than one. And Ariane had unerringly zeroed in on Linwood Academy's version.

"She'll talk," Ariane spoke with a grim certainty that was kind of alarming and reminded me what she could do if she put her mind to it. Literally.

"All right," I said quickly. "How about if I try?" If this girl decided to cop an attitude with Ariane, I wasn't entirely sure we'd make it out of this without lights exploding and windows breaking. Ariane wouldn't hurt anyone intentionally, but I bet she wasn't above scaring someone a little, if necessary. And we were already on thin ice. I doubted we'd get out of here unscathed if she went that route.

Ariane frowned but shrugged her assent.

I took a deep breath and crossed the hall against the flow

of traffic, feeling as if a spotlight shone on my white shirt in the sea of blue blazers.

"Hey," I said to the blond girl, eliciting a chorus of giggles from her flunkies.

She looked up from the tablet in her hand—it was flashing through a slide show of party pictures, in which she was featured prominently—and gave me a long, appraising glance.

"Hey," she said in a warm tone, before closing the cover on her tablet with a definitive slap.

Oh, damn. Weeks ago I'd have been flattered and maybe a little tempted. Now this was just awkward. "Um, so listen, I was wondering if you could help me with something."

"I would love to help you," she purred. "I'm Lara, by the way."

God, how did she manage to make that sound like she was offering much more than I was asking for? I was all too aware of Ariane behind me, silent as a ghost, across the hall, where she probably couldn't hear what this girl was saying, but she could probably still "hear."

"Great." I resisted the urge to pull at my tie, which was feeling much too tight at the moment. "Thanks, Lara."

Lara paused. "You're new here, right?" She squinted at me with disapproval. "You're not, like, a freshman?"

"No," I said. A freshman, really? I would have been insulted, but I was too busy trying to keep up with the conversation so I'd have some hope of directing it. I probably should have known better.

"Okay, good." She smiled, obviously relieved.

"I'm supposed to find someone," I began.

Lara smiled and leaned close, obviously expecting this was the lead in to some kind of pickup line. Like, "I'm supposed to find *someone*, but now that I've met you, not just *anyone* will do" or some other crap. I don't know. I'd never been particularly good at stuff like that even when I was *trying* to make it work.

"This girl, I think her name is Ford?" I said, blundering on. She stiffened. "What?"

"Ford," I repeated. Was she not going by that name here? That would be a problem. "It's kind of a strange . . ."

Lara's expression shifted from confused/annoyed to straight-up pissed in a fraction of a second. "Is this a joke?" she demanded, her gaze flicking between my face and some point behind me.

"No," I said, confused. I turned to see who she was looking at, half expecting the cranky teacher who'd confronted us. But he wasn't there. It was just Ariane and more Linwood students, a large majority of which now seemed to be heading in a single direction, probably to the cafeteria.

"Fuck you," Lara snarled. "Help yourself." Then she pushed past me to stomp off down the hall, in the opposite direction as everyone else. Her gaggle trotted after her, all wide-eyed and whispering.

What the hell? I shook my head and crossed the hall to Ariane, yanking at my tie to loosen it. Clearly looking the part was *not* helping as much as we'd hoped.

"She thought you were making fun of her." Ariane's voice held the lilt of curiosity.

"Yeah, I got that," I said, my mouth tight. "But why?"

"I don't know. She wasn't thinking about that part of it.

More just shocked that you'd dared to do it." Ariane sounded both bewildered and amused.

Well, that was helpful. I raked my hands through my hair. "We need to get out of here and figure out another way. This is not working." It felt as if there were a giant timer somewhere counting down the seconds until this blew up in our faces, and we were dangerously close to zeroing out.

I was watching Ariane, expecting her to protest, so the look on her face was my first clue that something was off. Her gaze moved from me to a point off to my left, her eyes widening a fraction of an inch and her lips parting slightly.

And for Ariane, that was as close to an expression of shock as you were ever going to get. It was roughly the equivalent of a normal person shrieking in surprise and clapping a hand over her mouth.

My stomach tightening with dread, I turned to see what had caught her attention. I thought I knew what to expect— that we'd found Laughlin's hybrids. Or rather, that they'd found us.

But I was so, so wrong.

I mean, the hybrids were there. That much I got right away. They drifted down the hallway against the flow of traffic in a perfect triangle formation, two guys in the back and a girl in the front. Ford, accompanied by Carter and Nixon, though I had no idea which was which.

They were all blond, that shade of pale white that I suspected Ariane would also have if she stopped dying in the darker streaks to look more "normal."

These three, though, didn't seem to give a rat's ass about normal. They moved in a creepy unison, as if they were one entity with six legs. It wasn't human. At all. Neither were their flat expressions and utter silence.

If anyone had had any idea that it was even possible for there to be aliens—or half aliens—among us, they would have picked these guys out immediately.

As it was, the other students gave them subtle but perceptible distance, moving around them like water around rocks. It was as if some part of their brains registered a threat that they didn't understand.

But none of that was what had me reaching for Ariane, fumbling for her arm and locking my fingers on her wrist just to make sure she was still there.

I'd known that Ford would resemble Ariane. I'd been prepared for that, a girl who looked like Ariane in a vague, smeared way, like siblings or first cousins. Like if you squinted your eyes—or were half-crazy from stress and pressure—you might think they were the same person.

But Ford didn't just look like Ariane. They were freaking identical. Not just the same out-of-control white-blond hair, pale skin, thin limbs, and small nose—we're talking mirror image. Except Ford hadn't bothered with blue-tinted contact lenses to hide the true color of her eyes. None of them had. Of course, no one here would theoretically be searching for them as escaped lab projects, so maybe they could get away with that. They were just weird-looking kids, as far as anyone else knew. Exotic, from another country, albinos. Or suffering from a rare genetic condition, as my mom had suggested.

Still, it was creepy.

I shuddered. Ariane and Ford's shared features were a

huge, screaming reminder that they'd both been deliberately and precisely created. Manufactured, for lack of a better term. It went beyond eerie, venturing into downright freaky and unnatural. Was this girl simply Laughlin's version of the GTX "Ariane" model?

Suddenly all the strange behavior we'd witnessed since walking through the door at Linwood made sense. The teacher had thought Ariane was Ford. So had Lara. No wonder she'd been angry; she'd seen Ariane and thought we were making fun of her with my search for Ford.

Laughlin's hybrids drew closer, and I saw the girl—Ford—notice us. Rather, notice Ariane.

She cocked her head to one side in that curious bird mannerism that I'd seen from Ariane countless times.

It sent a weird jolt through me. Some part of me responded as if it were Ariane, even knowing logically that it wasn't, and the urge to reach out and pull her away from the others rose up before I quickly squelched it. Because an equally powerful urge was screaming at me to *run*.

Something about Ford was wrong. Her eyes were too hard, too empty, something. I couldn't even say what it was for sure, or how I knew, except that maybe it was in how they moved. They were predators in a field full of prey. I'd never, ever felt that from Ariane. It was like seeing a version of Ariane with all the humanity and personality drained out.

I stood my ground but found myself blinking rapidly, as if that might help, as if this was simply a matter of double vision.

It didn't; it wasn't.

Ariane and Ford locked gazes, and I braced myself, not

sure what to expect. Would we be slammed against the wall by invisible hands? Or, worse, would Ford summon Ariane forward and welcome her with, what, a hug or a handshake or some kind of secret alien greeting?

I envisioned them silently making room for Ariane in their midst, a quartet instead of trio, and the four of them floating off down the hall.

Just the thought of it made me feel vaguely ill, and I wanted to step between them to prevent even the possibility of that happening.

Instead, after a long moment, Ford's gaze moved on from Ariane, returning her attention to the hallway in front of her.

As if nothing had happened. Which, I guess, technically, it hadn't. But it was more as if she'd simply decided Ariane didn't exist.

"That was . . . weird," I whispered to Ariane, staring after them. None of them even glanced back; they just kept moving, in step with each other. "Wasn't it?"

Of all the potential scenarios I'd imagined, that was not one of them. And the rush of relief that followed made me feel disloyal to Ariane, but I couldn't help it. If they were going to ignore us—her—I could only see that as a good thing compared to everything else that *might* have happened.

When Ariane didn't respond, I turned to glance at her, expecting to find her frowning at their backs.

But instead she was watching, transfixed, her body angled in their direction, as if they were magnets drawing her in.

Damn.

CHAPTER 13

Ariane

IT WAS LIKE LOOKING IN A MIRROR. I'D HEARD FULL-blooded humans use that expression before, marveling at the resemblance of their offspring or horrified at seeing their own worst characteristics reflected in someone else.

But I'd never experienced it. Until now.

In all three of Laughlin's hybrids, I could see pieces of myself. The pale skin, the dark eyes, the minimal nose and disproportionately small ears. It was disconcerting and also somehow a relief. *Family. Connection.* Proof that I wasn't alone.

Looking at Ford, the female, though, it went beyond all of that. She was . . . me.

It made my breath catch in my throat, and I felt the ridiculous urge to wave to see if she would mimic the motion, just as a dutiful reflection would.

Or maybe I was the reflection.

I shook my head. How was this even possible? The obvious answer, under normal (a.k.a. human) circumstances would be twins. But we'd been made, not conceived. And even if someone had created two identical "samples"—I hated that term—I doubted that either Laughlin or Jacobs would have been much in a sharing mood with a competitor.

Next to me, I could feel the prickling of Zane's discomfort. He thought it was unnatural. And it was. *We* were. Humiliation churned inside me. This was just one more explicit reminder that I was not of his kind. That he and I were not the same.

I told you, Mara's voice drifted across my memory.

Mara. Both she and my father alluded to GTX and Laughlin Integrated regularly spying on one another. So, perhaps, then, our shared looks were simply a sign of successful corporate espionage. I could easily imagine Laughlin or Jacobs driven to act on the information gathered or materials stolen. Out of scientific curiosity, maybe. Or, more likely, a case of thumbing his nose at the other guy. Anything you can do, I can improve upon.

I wondered which I was—the chicken or the egg. It didn't matter, really. But it felt like it did. Was I, on top of everything else, just an imitation of someone else's creation?

Upon closer inspection, we weren't completely identical. Ford might have been an inch or two taller. Her hair was paler than mine, but I was pretty sure that was only because she had not dyed it. Her eyes were the same penetrating darkness that I saw before I put my contact lenses in. She was more me than me, in that respect.

As they passed, Ford turned her head to look at me. Meeting her gaze sent a shockwave through me. It felt like falling forward into open space with no way to catch myself and only a vague idea of where the ground might be.

From this angle, I could now see that she bore a small,

dark line on her right cheekbone, like a single hash mark. It appeared almost as though someone had written on her face, but it was too precise and permanent-looking to be someone's carelessness with a pen.

Before I could figure out what to say or do, if anything, she broke eye contact, and they continued down the hall without any further sign that they'd noticed my existence.

I automatically took a step after them and did what I would have done under any other circumstances—tried to hear what they were thinking. My ability was erratic, at best. I lived in a world of constant noise, usually a dull static at the back of my mind that I worked to ignore, but occasionally, when I focused—or when someone was a particularly loud thinker—I'd get something useful.

This time, though, I got nothing. Literally nothing. No static, no indistinct mumbles.

I frowned. It had to be a fluke, a momentary gap. They were well within my range.

I listened harder, focusing specifically on them as they walked away.

But no, nothing. And the texture of silence surrounding them was different; it wasn't a temporary quiet, a lull in mental acrobatics, but a complete absence of sound.

In an overpopulated hall, teeming with the emotions and thoughts of the humans surrounding us, they were a blessed blank space on an ink-blackened page. A void of peaceful silence amid all the screaming.

The quiet curled up in my ears and lured me forward, like the pie aroma in one of the old cartoons I'd watched in the lab. I wanted to follow. I wanted to plunge inside that bubble of emptiness and roll around in the delicious lack of sound. It felt right in a way that I'd never experienced before.

I moved on reflex, chasing that sensation of quiet. But after a step or two, someone moved in front of me to block my path, barring me with his body.

Get rid of him, instinct ordered.

Annoyed, I prepared to shove at this obstacle that tried to stand in the way of—

"Ariane, stop! Please!" Zane's urgent whisper broke through, his hand tight on my arm.

I started at the sound of his voice, blinking rapidly, and looked up to find him staring at me, fear and frustration etched on his features.

His mouth tightened, the corners turned down, creating harsh lines on his face. I'd done that. I'd made him look so frightened and severe. "The guards." He jerked his head in the direction the hybrids had taken.

I leaned out cautiously to peer around him. Sure enough, two large men in dark suits were trailing Laughlin's hybrids at a discreet distance. Likely the same men we'd seen following them into the school. Obviously, whatever cover story Laughlin had provided for them allowed for guards to be an expected presence. Maybe they were supposed to be the children of a high-profile exec or something. That would make sense with what the teacher had said to me about "my father" when he thought I was Ford. No doubt the guards reported to Laughlin on a regular basis, keeping tabs on the hybrids and their exploits.

And I hadn't even noticed them. I'd come this close to exposing us to more danger. I might have been able to talk

Ford and the others into an alliance, but Laughlin's paid security detail—goons was the colloquial term, I believe—wasn't likely to be as amenable.

My heart beating in a panic, I retreated behind Zane again, just on the off chance that one of them would turn around. Zane might be mistaken for a normal human Linwood student. I would not, especially given the look of their charges.

"Are you okay?" Zane asked, his breathing uneven and too quick. I'd really scared him. Scared myself, too.

Folding my shaking arms over myself, I nodded rapidly, trying to clear my head. "Yeah, yes."

"What happened?" he asked.

I took a deep breath and let it out slowly. "I couldn't hear them."

He frowned, not understanding. "What?"

Of course not. He'd have no idea what it was like to live with an incessant rolling murmur in the back of his mind, an ocean of voices swelling to drown out your own thoughts.

"You know I can hear thoughts."

He nodded.

"Some people I can hear better than others, but I can get something from everyone." I shook my head. "It's a constant noise." I paused, trying to think of how to explain it in a relatable way. "My father once threw a television away." Actually, he'd smashed it to the floor first in a rare fit of anger. "He'd tried to fix it, but something in it was just broken. It emitted a high-pitched buzz whenever text appeared on the screen." Which, given his news-watching tendencies, was pretty often. "It drove him crazy." I gave a tight shrug. "It's like that. All the time."

Zane winced.

"I've learned to live with it, but I never imagined . . ." I heard the wonder in my voice and hated it, the weakness.

The smooth tone that indicated a class change sounded overhead, startling me. The students remaining in the hall scrambled in all directions.

Zane took my hand, his palm warm and reassuring against mine. "We need to get out of here," he said grimly, and started down the hall, back toward the main entrance, pulling me along with him.

It took me a second to shake off the last vestiges of shock and twist free. "No, we can't."

He stiffened. "Look, I don't know if you're aware of what almost happened . . ."

I flinched at the censure in his voice but forced myself to ignore the emotion and focus on the salient strategic point. "Nothing has changed. Gaining their cooperation is still our best option."

He narrowed his eyes at me. "They completely ignored us. I think we should take that as the first bit of luck we've had in forever and get the hell out of here."

"And do what? Go where?" I argued. "Besides, we're here. They know we're here. Retreating would send the wrong message."

"And what message is that?" he asked, his mouth tight. "That we're smart enough to leave while the leaving is good?"

I shook my head. "That we're vulnerable, weak. Open to attack. It's a basic principle of predator and prey. Running only confirms that you don't believe you have the strength to win."

"How about the 'sitting duck principle'?" he hissed, tipping his head at a point behind me in the hall. I glanced over my shoulder and found a pair of teachers watching us with suspicion.

Zane was right; we couldn't stand here, obvious targets, in the hallway. We'd be caught by the humans for sure. We needed a chance to regroup, rethink. Some place out of sight where no one would notice that we weren't quite up to snuff as Linwood Academy students or that there seemed to be two Fords running around today.

"Come on." I caught at his hand and tugged him deeper into school, away from the teachers.

He came along with me, not quite dragging his feet but making it clear that he was going against his better judgment.

I concentrated on the rooms beyond the hall, hidden behind heavy and polished wooden doors, listening to try to find an empty one. But with so many minds nearby, it was easier said than done.

"Here." Across from a glass-enclosed courtyard filled with more of the brightly colored flowers and grass that appeared too green to be real, I found a "quiet" room and shoved the heavy wooden door open.

I stopped dead on the threshold, Zane bumping into my back and grabbing carefully at my arms to keep me from stumbling forward.

The room wasn't like anything I'd seen at our school. First, the entire left wall was mirrored. Second, the space was virtually empty. Unlike almost every square inch of Ashe High, which had been occupied to beyond capacity, this room held only a few rows of chairs and a baby grand piano.

And a startled kid—young, swimming in his school-required blazer—seated on the piano bench.

So much for empty. But it was probably the best we were going to get.

I stepped inside and Zane followed, letting the door swing shut behind.

The kid at the piano saw us in the mirror. He froze, and then spun around to stare at us, his face pale and his throat working, as if he were trying to find words.

"Do you mind—" I began.

He nodded hastily, as if his head was loose, and gathered up his music, spilling half of it on the floor as he bolted out the door. I was beginning to think that Ford might have a reputation equal to or greater than that of Rachel Jacobs when it came to evoking fear and dislike among the populace.

"Now what?" Zane asked. He jerked at the knot in his tie until the slippery fabric pulled free from his collar.

"I don't know," I admitted. "I'm working on it. The guards seem to follow them to classes, but surely they don't sit in the actual classroom with them. If we could just find a way to get a message to Ford or one of the others—"

Zane sighed and sank into one of the plastic chairs across from the piano, dropping his tie onto the seat next to him. "Ariane . . ." He shook his head. "You're assuming that they're even capable of that kind of functionality."

I frowned. "What are you talking about?"

"You saw how they were." He leaned forward, as if pleading for me to understand. "The way they moved." He shuddered. "It wasn't normal."

"It wasn't human," I said carefully. "But that's not the same thing, is it?"

His mouth tightened. "What if you didn't hear their thoughts when they walked by because there wasn't anything to hear?" he asked. "She didn't even react to seeing you."

"She looked at me," I argued, realizing even as I did how weak that sounded. "Beyond that, their choices were limited if they are under orders to be discreet," I said. "Besides, not reacting causes confusion in the enemy and—"

"But, see, you're assuming all kinds of things about their orders and nothing about them," he said. "My mom said Laughlin controls them. If he's in control, there's not much for them to think about, right?"

"You think they're just . . . shells." Empty living bodies, responding only to programmed stimuli. Just the idea made me feel queasy.

"It's possible, isn't it?" Zane persisted.

I nodded reluctantly. "Anything is possible." GTX and Laughlin Integrated had made that more than clear. But that theory—living robots, operating only on command—didn't mesh with Mara's experience as she'd relayed it to us. She'd seemed convinced that they hated her. Empty vessels don't hate. And they don't stalk, either. So either Mara was mistaken about what she'd experienced (one more vote for her being perhaps less than the best source for reliable information) or these hybrids had very, very good game faces.

My initial inclination had been toward the latter, but now, after Zane had raised the question, I couldn't completely dismiss it, much as I would have liked to.

I bit my lip. "It was a strategic response." Or nonresponse, rather. "It *had* to be." And I could prove it. All I had to do was figure out how to engage them in a situation where they would be free to speak or otherwise communicate.

"Are you sure?" Zane asked quietly. He held my gaze, those familiar blue-gray eyes warm with sympathy.

Frustrated, I could feel the ache in my jaw from clenching my teeth too hard. What did he want me to say? No, I'm really not sure, but this is the last hope I have, so I'm clinging to it for all I'm worth? I opened my mouth. "I—"

The lights flickered suddenly overhead and then went out, the only illumination now coming from the windows set high in the back wall. Zane leapt to his feet, as though his chair had shocked him. He glanced up at the lights instinctively and then over at me.

I shook my head, adrenaline lighting me up on the inside. I wasn't doing it. Which meant, unless the school was suffering from an unexpected power loss, they were coming. Guess they'd decided to take matters into their own hands.

"Yeah, pretty sure," I murmured in answer to his earlier—and now likely forgotten—question.

I turned to check the door—still closed—my chest thundering with a heady mix of anticipation and dread, which felt oddly familiar, almost comforting.

Facing Zane, I said, "Get to the corner. It's more defensible."

"And origin of the phrase 'backed into a corner,' in case you've forgotten," he muttered. "This is so not a good idea." But he did it anyway. He trusted me. God, I hoped I was worthy of it.

I moved to the center of the room, putting myself between Zane and the entrance. "Keep your eyes on me," I said to him. "Don't watch the mirror." In the dim light, the mirror could easily be used as a source of confusion or distraction. And with two of us who looked alike already, adding reflections to the mix could make this go downhill quickly.

"Got it," Zane said grimly.

I should have been feeling the same—determined, resigned, frightened—but I couldn't help the strange thrumming of excitement in my bones. *You are not made for a normal life.* Mara's words echoed in my head.

I ignored them and tightened the scarf around my neck, double-knotting it so it wouldn't come loose. If nothing else, I needed Zane to know and trust that I was me and not Ford.

I'd just lowered my hands when the door opened, startling me even though I'd been expecting it.

Ford entered in the lead, the two boys behind her. As soon as they cleared the doorway, though, they spread into the same formation they'd held in the hall: Ford in the front, the other two on either side and slightly behind her.

Facing them, I now had a better view of all three. Ford resembled me as much as I remembered; there'd been no mistake about that. The line on her face looked somehow embedded—a tattoo? Could it be a number one, something to do with her model or version number? But to put it on her face . . . I shuddered. Neither of the others had a similar mark that I could see.

The guy to her right was considerably taller. His thin frame topped out at close to six feet, still shorter than Zane but surprising for one of us. Ha. Like I knew anything about "us." But based the Internet research I'd done at home in Wingate, the "grays," our alien forebears, were usually understood to be quite diminutive. More like the other boy, the one on Ford's left.

He was the smallest of the three, but he appeared young as well. Perhaps he was the newest hybrid iteration? That would make him Carter, if they'd been named in succession. That left the tall one as Nixon. Carter appeared almost cherubic. His hair had a rebel curliness to it, nothing like the uneven chaos that Ford and I shared or the straight, fine hair that Nixon had. Carter also looked like he might have dimples. If he, you know, ever smiled. He was also the only one carrying an iPad, like the rest of the human students.

"Your human thinks too loudly," Ford said bluntly, startling me with the suddenness of her voice in the otherwise silent room.

The squeeze of power surrounded me, thicker and heavier than I'd imagined. It was like being encased from the elbow down in thick but mildly pliable plastic. There was also a faint and disconcerting sensation of movement, warm and fluid against my skin, as if it were alive. I could flex my muscles but not move any of my major limbs. Which, of course, was the point.

"Don't struggle," I said to Zane, who gave a strangled laugh. He'd probably figured that out before me, having witnessed me doing the same thing to others. I was the one new to it.

"That would be for the best," the boy—I couldn't think of him as anything but that due to his size—advised in an apologetic tone. "It will be easier for everybody if you remain still. We don't want to hurt anyone unnecessarily."

"Speak for yourself, Carter," Ford said without even

glancing at him. The cold flatness in her voice sent a chill through me, as did Carter's immediate submission. He dropped his gaze to the floor and closed his mouth firmly, as if making sure no further words would escape by accident.

Crap. "You can't kill us," I said. "Discretion has to be part of your mission standards."

Ford raised her eyebrows. "True. But that's only a problem if we are *caught* killing you."

A good point that I hadn't thought of. Very literal and logical.

Zane muttered something under his breath about ducks, and I could feel sweat gathering at the back of my knees.

"Oh, I'll make sure you're caught," I said with a shrug that I hoped conveyed ease, confidence, instead of the horrible, creaking tension in my shoulders. It was like balancing on the edge of a cliff, not sure which way the wind was going to push you—toward solid ground or into stomach-dropping, life-ending nothingness. Not that, of course, any kind of wind was going to move us anywhere with them holding us down.

It was taking every ounce of self-will I had not to struggle against the power binding me. I didn't need my hands to fire back at them. Knock them over, throw them together in a heap, find and stop their hearts. The power buzzed eagerly in my head and under my skin, building in an automatic response to the threat.

But fighting back would (a) confirm that this was indeed a fight, which I was trying to avoid, and (b) give them an idea of my strength.

My logical side was whispering that that would be a very

bad idea. The fact they didn't know how strong I was—
or wasn't—might be the only thing holding them from an
all-out attack. They didn't want to take the chance of a mission failure. In this case, it was better to let them wonder
whether I could beat them rather than to try and prove that
I couldn't. As hybrids, we knew nothing about one another's
capabilities, and that same ignorance that had put Zane and
me in danger walking into the school might now save our
necks.

"Yes, you are the GTX superior specimen. So we have
heard." Ford's dark eyes were fixed on me, her gaze boring
through my head.

I frowned. "I—"

"But there are three of us against you and a *human*." The
sneer in her voice, if not actually showing on in her expression, was quite obvious.

I sensed Zane bristling behind me and prayed he would
stay quiet.

"You are still so confident?" Ford said.

"Yes," I said, even though it had sounded more like a
statement than a question. But no sense leaving any doubt
on the table.

Ford cocked her head to one side, like a bird examining
an unknown object.

With a jolt, I recognized the movement as one I used as
well. But viewing it from the outside, the foreignness of it
sent a chill through me. It screamed NOT HUMAN. No
wonder Zane had noticed something off about me, despite
my best efforts. Had we inherited that gesture from the alien
species from which we'd been made, something buried in

the DNA that survived even after it was comingled with the human cells?

I wondered what, if anything, the three of them knew about our genetic donor. My father had always said that a body—alive or dead, he'd never been clear—from the Roswell crash in 1947 had been the source. But I had no way of knowing if that was true. They likely didn't have any more information than I did, but I felt a pull toward them, a tug of kinship. We were, essentially, four orphans from the same family. If we could compare notes . . .

"Perhaps we should turn you over to our creator instead for examination and analysis," Ford said. "He would welcome the opportunity to deconstruct a superior specimen."

So, no family gabfest, then. Ford's tone had gone flat again, but I suspected she'd used the word *superior* in sarcasm. She was really hung up on that whole idea—someone had gone to a great deal of trouble to convince her that I was the real deal. I guess that answered my earlier question of who came first.

"Perhaps our creator would reward us," she added with enough of a speculative lilt to make my stomach cramp with dread.

I hadn't given much consideration to the idea that she would sic Laughlin on me; I'd been counting on her hatred of him to rise above everything else. But her desire for advancement and/or preservation of her unit might be stronger. I had no way of knowing what her "home life" at the lab was like.

"Or maybe he'll just decide he likes her better," Zane spoke up for the first time, his voice ringing out clear and with a hint of a sneer. "I mean, one of you is clearly the original and the other just an imitation. Which do you think he'd rather have?" Zane continued.

His words stole my breath. "Zane," I whispered through gritted teeth.

But when I turned to glare at him in warning, he wasn't looking at me; he was staring defiantly at Ford instead, as if challenging her to deny his words.

I tensed, waiting for the first sign of her attack, prepared to break free and intervene if necessary.

TRUST ME. Zane's words echoed loudly in my head, his attempt to make sure I heard him.

I winced.

SORRY . . .

And to my surprise, he seemed to have picked up on something I'd missed. Because Ford didn't attack. She simply watched him for a moment longer, as if he were a monkey who'd managed to hoot something that sounded like Shakespeare before lapsing into nonsense again, and then she returned her attention to me. "Why are you here?" she asked. "It is an automatic disqualification from the trials to attempt sabotage."

"I'm not here to sabotage." Well, not technically. "I just want to talk," I said.

"There is nothing to discuss. We will meet in the trials and we . . . I will kill you, proving our . . . my superiority."

That had been an odd little hiccup. Perhaps the interconnectedness went deeper than I'd realized. That was the first time she'd referred to herself as an individual entity rather than "we," and she'd seemed to struggle with it.

Huh. I didn't know what to make of that, exactly, but

I bet I could use it. Surely, all three of them wouldn't be allowed to compete as a single unit. That meant two of them would be left behind. Carter and the as-yet-silent one, Nixon, most likely.

"Is that what you want?" I asked. "The *humans* dividing you up, using you for whatever they want, however they want?"

Behind me, I sensed Zane's spike of alarm at my words. But getting them on our side was vital, and if that meant drawing a firmer line between human and not for the moment, so be it.

And it seemed to be working. The three hybrids inched closer together, as though I was the one threatening to separate them. "Our fate is none of your concern," Ford said.

And yet, she . . . they weren't leaving.

"If we refuse to participate in the trials, then they lose control," I offered, the words tumbling out as if speed would keep her from rejecting the proposal. "We could leave, do anything we want."

A faint furrow appeared on Ford's forehead, as if I'd said something that truly mystified her. "How are you here?" she asked. "What kind of supply did you obtain?"

What? I struggled to keep my expression blank, praying that the silence I heard from them went both ways. They'd done and said nothing to indicate otherwise.

Ford tipped her head to the side slightly, an inquisitive posture that reminded me of the raptors in *Jurassic Park* seconds before they moved in for the kill. "Did you wean yourself?" she asked rapidly, the speed of her words lending intensity where her expression did not. Whatever she was talking about, it was *important*. That much was obvious.

But before I could begin to work out how to respond, the door to the room opened, sending a wave of surprise through everyone. The power holding tight around me immediately disappeared, and it was a struggle not to stumble backward.

The teacher who'd confronted Zane and me at the school entrance—I'd dubbed him Mr. Coffee after the stain on his shirt—stuck his head in and scowled at Ford and the others. "What's going on in here? Did you kick Kyle Wagner out of his practice time?"

Crap. If Mr. Coffee saw me, he'd realize there was one more strange-looking student than there should have been. That'd set off some alarms, I bet.

I turned my back to him swiftly, only to be confronted with my image in the huge mirror. Damn it.

Zane, figuring out my dilemma, took two long strides toward me, his arms out in preparation to pull me against him. Evidently, they'd freed him also.

I could almost feel the embrace already: his arms reassuringly tight around me, the warmth of his chest beneath his scratchy white shirt pressing against my cheek, and the steady thump of his heartbeat in my ear. I wanted it—all of it—badly.

But I made myself shake my head, and he stopped in midstep, hurt flashing across his face. My chest ached in response, and I longed to close the distance the remaining between us. But if this got ugly, I wanted him to be clear of the danger. Well, as clear of it as he could be when we were all in the same room.

So, instead, I lowered my chin, letting my hair fall forward to hide my face, and waited to see what would happen.

"Leave," Ford said to the teacher. She sounded bored.

"Now, listen here, young lady, I told you I don't care if your father is the CEO of . . ." He faltered, and I watched through the veil of my hair as the three of them turned as one. They stared him down with eyes so cold and dark, there was no humanity in them. I knew that for a fact. I'd seen (and consequently avoided) my own reflection often enough.

The teacher held his hands up, responding instinctively to a threat he couldn't understand but sensed nonetheless. "I'll report this to your father," he blustered, a last-ditch attempt to save face.

I wonder who was playing the role of their "father," whether Laughlin had cast himself or enlisted an underling. Either way, the hybrids didn't seem particularly concerned.

They just kept watching Mr. Coffee until he caved and left the room.

When the door clicked shut after him, the hybrids swiveled as one to face me again, and Ford raised an eyebrow, as if to say, *You were saying?*

Turning to face her again, I fought the absurd urge to laugh even as chills raced up my arms. That facial expression was a particularly human one, something she must have absorbed unintentionally along the way, but seeing it on her only amplified her otherness.

I took a breath before responding, trying to think through my options quickly. Clearly, Ford thought I knew something or had something she wanted. But I didn't. She'd mentioned supply and weaning off of it, whatever it was. A drug? One that had been given to them, and she assumed I'd been dosed as well? I could try lying, but I wasn't sure how long I could pull that off, and that might cause more damage in the long run.

"I don't have any on me," I said, settling on something ambiguous but true.

The crinkle in Ford's forehead returned, her version of a frown. "Then how are you here? How did you escape?" she persisted.

Wait, wait. I shook my head, trying to fit all the pieces into place. Laughlin kept them in line by dosing them, it sounded like. "I broke out," I said bluntly, opting for over-simplification over losing them in details.

The three of them stiffened as one, as though an electrical charge had passed through them.

"What's going on?" Zane whispered behind me.

"I don't know," I whispered back.

"You are not being treated with the enzyme," Ford said in another of her statement/questions.

Once more, I hesitated before answering. I had a feeling this was, as the saying went, the $64,000 question (which had never made sense to me as a metaphor—it's a relatively paltry sum to indicate great significance). "No," I admitted.

Carter's mouth fell open in surprise and stayed open as if he desperately wanted to say something, but at a signal I didn't see or hear, he snapped it shut. Nixon's distant expression remained unchanged. I wasn't even sure if aware he was of what was going on.

But Ford just bobbed her head in that strange birdlike nod again. "We will see you at the trials when we . . . when I kill you," she said, and turned to leave.

"No, wait!" I lurched after her. "Listen, we could go public. Force them to give you the . . . whatever you need." I didn't particularly relish the thought of using the media as a defense when there was just one of me, but with four of us, we might actually have a chance.

"We have no interest in explaining ourselves to the humans," she said dismissively. "By the time they have finished arguing among themselves as to our intentions, we will be dead. And that is only if they don't decide to execute us immediately."

I shook my head. "I don't understand. What do you mean?"

But Ford was done talking. She started for the door, followed by Nixon, only for both of them to rock to a stop, as if yanked by an invisible rope. Only Carter remained where he stood, as if locked in place.

Slowly, Ford and Nixon turned, focusing their attention on the lone member of their party who hadn't moved. A long, uncomfortable silence held for several seconds, the tension in the room building, as they stared at one another.

Huh. Apparently, they weren't quite as "one unit" as Mara had seemed to believe.

Behind me, I heard Zane shifting his feet uneasily and had to fight the urge to do the same. The air was filled with expectancy. Something was about to happen. Bad or good, I wasn't sure.

"You desire our cooperation in your endeavor for freedom?" Carter asked, his chin set stubbornly.

"*Our* endeavor for freedom," I corrected cautiously. "And yes."

"Good!" Carter said.

I blinked.

"Hi," he whispered with a shy smile that transformed his narrow face. He did have dimples.

Whoa. He seemed almost normal by human standards.

I smiled back reflexively. They must have seriously recalibrated Carter's human/alien percentages. Nixon had yet to even indicate that he was aware of our existence in the room, his blank stare focused somewhere over my head.

"We can't live without an artificial enzyme, Quorosene," Carter began.

"Carter," Ford said sharply.

He ignored her, but at his sides his hands balled into fists, as if he were steeling himself against her displeasure. "It is how we were created. If we go for more than twelve hours without a dose, our internal organs start shutting down. Death follows. Painfully. It's how they control us."

"And how they eliminate us when we are no longer useful," Ford added, her flat monotone a sharp contrast to Carter's expressiveness. "You would do well to remember that, Carter. It's a lesson Johnson never quite mastered, and they made her pay." Her hand drifted toward her cheek and the line marked there.

It *was* a hash mark, I realized suddenly, my stomach lurching. Johnson. That was the name of the hybrid who'd been killed when she couldn't fit in. So . . . Ford was keeping score? Tracking Laughlin's sins, perhaps, and in a manner that must have infuriated him. I couldn't imagine that someone so interested in making them blend in had been thrilled to see that she'd marred her face in that way.

Had they all been connected at the time Johnson died? It seemed likely. Had they felt the life slowly drain out of one of their own? What torture that must have been. I felt like throwing up, just imagining the helplessness they'd felt. No wonder they'd hunted Mara.

"We've been trying to break our dependence, or at least reduce our need so that we can build up a supply. But . . ." Carter's narrow shoulders moved up and down helplessly in a shrug. "It has been difficult. If we had the opportunity to experiment with our limits more often, it might be possible, but we are monitored too closely."

"She cannot help you," Ford said, moving closer to Carter until he turned to face her.

"You don't know that," he said. "You've done your best for us, but that is a temporary solution at best."

"It has worked so far," Ford said. "I've done all that I can to—"

"What has?" I asked.

"If Ford cooperates, behaves herself, and wins the trial, Nixon and I stay alive," Carter said, his mouth twisting in a bitter smile. "And I get to keep coming to school. But that's only if Dr. Laughlin keeps his word. Do you trust him, Ford? I don't."

The two of them stared at each other, a silent standoff that dragged on for far longer than was comfortable. Clearly, telepathy was their primary method of communication.

I glanced at Nixon, who had shifted just slightly in the direction of Ford and Carter. Participating in the conversation, perhaps? I wondered if he was the cause for the rumors that Dr. Jacobs had heard and passed along to me, that

Laughlin's "products" weren't able to speak. Ford and Carter didn't have issues with speech, when they chose to use it, but either Nixon was the ultimate in "strong but silent" or he just didn't talk. Whether through lack of ability or desire, I didn't know.

"Fine," Ford said abruptly, breaking off whatever discussion had been going on inside their minds. "If that is what you both wish." She didn't sound happy. "But we will not be foolish about it."

"What you're suggesting is too difficult, Ford," Carter protested.

"That is the point," she said, before shifting her attention to me. "You want our help? We need a supply of Quorosene or information on how to eliminate our dependence," Ford said bluntly. "That is the price for our aid."

My mouth fell open. "How am I supposed to do that?"

"From what we've been able to learn, it's manufactured elsewhere. But Dr. Laughlin seems to keep a small amount in his office at Laughlin Integrated, just in case of an interruption in the supply," Carter offered apologetically. Clearly, even though he disagreed with Ford, he wasn't going to take a stand against her.

"Isn't that where you are? Why don't you just get it yourself?" Zane asked suspiciously.

For the first time, Carter seemed to hesitate, looking at the other two. "The price for disobedience is not worth the risk. As you have likely already deduced, only one of us will be allowed to compete in the trials, per the agreed-upon terms."

Which meant Dr. Laughlin had two lives to hang over Ford's head.

I grimaced. If their bond was as deep as it seemed to be, I understood Ford's motivation, but I couldn't help thinking that if Laughlin was anything like Dr. Jacobs, she'd just given him two opportunities to further control her.

"So, you expect Ariane to, what, break in and start nosing around?" Zane demanded.

"I don't expect anything. How you accomplish the task is not our concern," Ford said, talking to me as though I was the one who'd spoken. "You asked for our assistance. We are merely defining the parameters under which we'd be willing to provide it." She sounded both annoyed and amused.

"That's crazy," Zane insisted.

No, it was a test (one that Ford obviously thought I would fail). I didn't like it, but I understood her reasoning. Why should they trust me when they didn't know me? I could just as easily be here trying to find a way to disqualify or discredit her. But if I could do as they asked, I would prove myself. And they'd have what they needed to rebel with me.

Or, quite simply, it could be a trap. One less competitor for the trials, plus some bonus points for being the ones to arrange my capture.

Either way, though, the bottom line was the same—they wanted me to walk into Laughlin Integrated and try to steal something that was most likely locked up tighter than they were now or I'd ever been.

Right.

CHAPTER 14

Zane

THE SILENCE THAT FOLLOWED FORD THE HYBRID'S ultimatum (Ford hybrid—it was testimony to how frightening she was that I didn't laugh at that) was the longest of my life. With Ariane's back to me, I couldn't see her expression—not that I always had a lot of luck reading her anyway. But the thoughtful quiet in the room gave me chills.

Ariane wasn't seriously considering their "offer," was she? She couldn't be.

"This is bullshit," I blurted, panic lighting the fuse on the words. "You want her to take all the risk."

Ford turned her attention to me again, and once more I couldn't help comparing her to Ariane. They were eerily similar, but Ford's gaze lacked Ariane's warmth and emotion. It was like staring into twin abysses. A whole lot of nothing. Ariane, as much as I knew she hated it, felt things deeply. With Ford, I wasn't sure whether she was better at hiding her feelings or whether she just lacked them completely.

No, wait, that wasn't true. She'd certainly demonstrated jealousy earlier. In some way she seemed to think of Ariane as an older sibling, one with whom she was forced to compete. I definitely recognized that emotion, even if she hadn't shown it in a traditional manner. Ariane, an only child, both in her home and at the lab, hadn't picked up on it.

So, maybe Ford was a broken toy, able to feel only the negative stuff. The bad things. That might make her even more effective as a soldier. Hate, fear, envy—those were pretty powerful motivators, weren't they? Probably the source of most every war.

"We risk much simply by not reporting this contact to our creator," Ford said, her expression flat, dead. "Would you rather we opted for that choice instead?"

So she'd moved on to threatening already? I stepped forward, fury and adrenaline pumping, prepared to move between Ariane and Ford, if necessary. I wasn't stupid. Ford could stop me dead, literally, but it wasn't right that she was taking advantage of Ariane being on her own. Someone had to call her on it.

"Your human is very valiant," Ford said to Ariane, and somehow made it sound like an insult. "Is that an acceptable compromise? Being less than what you could be just to make him comfortable?" She sounded genuinely curious.

I couldn't breathe for a second. It was like Ford had dug around in my head and found my worst fear, the very last thing I'd ever want Ariane to hear. And hell, who knows, maybe she had. "*We* are none of your business," I snapped, trying to rally. But the heat burning in my face betrayed me, I knew.

"Zane," Ariane said quietly, giving me a warning look in the mirror, one that said, *Please shut the hell up before you make things worse.*

That I could read just fine.

Whatever. I moved back into my corner, folding my arms over my chest. I hated this useless feeling, like a fist squeezing my heart. Ariane was on her own, and I couldn't do anything to help.

"I will take your proposal under consideration," Ariane said to her evil twin. "I will let you know what I decide."

"We will be here," Ford said without even a hint of humor twisting her mouth, as it would have if Ariane had said the same. But then again, maybe Ford didn't recognize the irony of declaring that she'd be here after explaining in (albeit limited) detail why she couldn't go anywhere.

Then the three of them turned to leave without so much as another word.

That was it? "You've got to be kidding me," I muttered. But I clamped my mouth shut when I saw Ariane stiffen in response.

Carter, the last out of the room, paused at the doorway. He gave Ariane a small, pathetic smile and a little wave.

I rolled my eyes.

My God, it was practically the Oliver Twist "Please, sir, I want some more" moment. The only thing missing was the perfect single tear from one of those dark, creepy eyes. They were manipulating in every way possible: threats, bribery, and now an attempted tug at the heartstrings. Like I said. Bullshit.

But I kept quiet until the door closed after him.

"It's a trap," I said flatly as soon as it clicked shut. "Please tell me you see that." Bastards. Ariane had risked everything to find them, and they wanted to use her in a win–win for themselves.

"Not here," she said, her voice taut with tension.

I gaped at her. Was she pissed at me for speaking up?

She kept her gaze fixed on the door. Was she expecting them to come back? Or afraid they would? I wasn't sure. When another moment or two passed without incident, she nodded seemingly to herself. "We need to go. Now," she said.

That I wholeheartedly agreed with. "Finally." I grabbed my tie off the chair.

Ariane pulled open the door, leaning out slightly to confirm that the hybrids were gone before waving me forward to follow her.

We wended our way back through the hallway, hustling past closed classroom doors toward the main entrance without actually running. It seemed to take longer this time, even though we knew where were going. But maybe that was because we were the only ones in the hall, our isolation a spotlight shining down on us.

With every second that ticked away, the tension in me wound tighter. My shoulders ached with it. I kept expecting that angry shout of "Hey!" and the sound of rushing of footsteps in pursuit.

But the main doors came into view, glowing white with the brighter light outside, without so much as a whisper behind us, and the tight knot in my stomach started to ease.

We still had to get past the office, though. At our school, the door would have been shut to preserve the precious air-conditioning for the administration, reducing our chances of getting caught to someone looking up and out the window at the right time. But here, where AC flowed freely and abundantly to the whole building (as it should if everyone was supposed to wear those stupid blazers all the time), the door stood open.

One more reason to hate this place.

Ariane took the lead, moving swiftly past the door, her shoulders straight and head held high, giving off no air of sneaking around or fear of getting caught. Which probably was the best bet for passing unnoticed.

But, unfortunately, with the placement of the office so near the front doors of the school, the only place we could be going was outside. So if anyone was paying even the least amount of attention . . .

"Hey!" A startled female voice called as soon as we passed.

I cringed. I knew we couldn't get that lucky.

But Ariane only glanced over her shoulder and with a twitch of her hand, the office door slammed shut. A muffled thud sounded as someone slammed into it, expecting the door to give. Oops.

"We need to hurry. I don't want them to panic," Ariane said quietly.

In other words, she didn't want to hold the door shut for so long they started to freak and called the cops or the fire department or something. And yet we needed to be gone before someone caught up with us.

She didn't need to tell me twice. I broke into a run and pushed through the doors out onto the concrete driveway, breathing deeply of the fresh air and the smell of new asphalt. Ariane was a step behind me.

We cleared the covered drop-off area, passing through the

weird pillar/statue guys, and headed into the parking lot. The sudden heat against my skin was a relief. I hadn't realized until this exact second how unsure I'd been that we'd make it out.

The van was where we'd left it. Thank God. Not like I'd expected otherwise, but these days I'd learned not to take the normal function of the universe as I knew it for granted. There was always something, usually pretty messed up, going on just outside your realm of knowledge.

Just as I was berating Mark Tucker for not springing for automatic locks on the van to save us those precious extra seconds, Ari lifted her hand toward the van, and I heard the doors unlock. Guess a fancy key fob wasn't necessary with Ariane around. That was handy. Especially with the security guard and a couple teacher types who'd just shoved through the front doors of the school after us.

I got in, slammed my door, and cranked the engine.

We peeled out of the parking space, leaving, I hoped, ugly tracks across several of the bright yellow lines. It wasn't so much the school that I had a problem with but the privilege it represented—Ford and the others fit in here perfectly, making demands they had no right to make.

"In the future, if someone makes an offer that we don't intend to participate in, can we agree not to announce that in front of them, when they can still call for backup?" Ariane asked tightly, her hand locked on the grab bar above her window as I jerked the wheel around, our tires squealing. "Their guards probably have direct contact with Laughlin, and I think we can agree that's a complication we don't need."

Something tight in my chest eased. *That's* what she was angry about. "Sure. Yeah. No problem."

She nodded, her expression distant.

"So, what now? Where to?" I asked. Lacking any specific directions, I'd just started in the direction from which we'd come, back toward my mom's house.

When Ariane didn't respond, a tiny seed of doubt began to grow in my gut. She wouldn't. She *couldn't*. "I've been thinking about it," I said, a little too loudly, as if that would stop her, blockade her thoughts and her words. "Chicago is a major news city. They've got what, at least two or three TV stations here. I know you didn't want to go public alone, but you wouldn't be. I mean, I would be there. And if we went to more than one, that might improve our odds."

She was too quiet.

"What?" I asked with a growing sense of dread.

"I think it's worth talking to Mara to confirm their story," she said eventually. "Find out what she knows."

Her words struck like a series of heavy blows. "I . . . You're kidding. Please tell me you're kidding."

"Having more information can only help us," she said.

"Only if you intend to do something about it!"

She looked at me, her expression unreadable. "You do know this is what I was made for: deception, infiltration, recovery."

I fought to keep a handle on my temper. "It's a setup." An elaborate one maybe, but a setup just the same.

"You can't know that," she said simply.

I gaped at her. "How can you—"

"If their goal was simply to eliminate me, there are much easier ways. They could have called their guards down on us. Or report us to Laughlin."

"How do you know they didn't?" I demanded.

"Because we got out of there without the guards chasing after us," she said. "Plus, it's only reasonable that Ford would want to test my motivations in some way. They don't know whom to trust. I could have easily been sent to spy on them, setting them up to take—"

I shook my head, my jaw tight. "Okay, fine. Let's say that you're right. Maybe they're telling the truth. Maybe *she* just wants to see if you can do it. Which I think is complete crap, but whatever. My point is, they're using you. They've got nothing to lose. If it works, great. If not, then they have one less competitor. You're the one taking all the risks. How is that fair?"

"Because I'm the one asking them for a favor," she said. "Isn't that how the system usually works?"

I gritted my teeth. I hated the way she could turn everything into a logical argument. Wasn't there anything to be said for a gut feeling, any value on instinct? Mine was screaming that they were trouble. I didn't trust them at all, let alone in a sketchy situation like the one they wanted Ariane to enter.

"Besides, they can't help me unless I help them first," she said.

"So she says," I muttered.

"You think she's lying about that?" Ariane asked, her eyebrows raised.

"Well, if not, why not help you more?" I threw my hands up. "Why not give you more details on how to get into the building or suggestions on how to get the pills or medicine or whatever?" They hadn't even specified what form their precious Quorosene took, which was more than a little suspicious. Wasn't it?

"And you'd trust that information?" she asked.

"Probably not," I admitted reluctantly. "But—"

"Are you sure you're not reacting to more than just their proposal?" she asked. But she wasn't looking at me. She stared out the side window, as if fascinated by something out there or, perhaps, worried about something in here and not willing to face it. Or me.

"Like what?" I asked warily.

Ariane straightened the scarf around her neck in a long moment of silence. "They made you uncomfortable," she said.

I should have been expecting this—the stuff my mom had said was probably wearing a track in Ariane's brain—but it still made me angry. I pulled over into a gas station parking lot, cutting off a bread truck, whose driver apparently loved the sound of his horn, and turned to face her. "No. Absolutely not. You don't get to do that." I jabbed a finger in her direction. "I was uncomfortable because they threatened us, and because they want to put you in danger. It had nothing to do with their . . . heritage."

But how much of one was indistinguishable from the other? Was it a little freaky that Ford had to talk through someone else? Yeah. But what I hated more was the cold way Ford had looked at Ariane as if she were a tool to be used, how she called me "human" like that was a synonym for dog shit, as if Ariane deserved better. So I guess the question really was, was Ford just a jerk or was she an alien jerk? Either way, no thanks.

"Besides, if anyone's acting differently because of where they're from, it's you, not me," I continued.

She whipped her head around to face me. "What?"

"It took me how long to even get you to talk to me, let

alone trust me, but one conversation with them and their magical 'silence,' you're ready to drink the Klingon Kool-Aid or whatever." I wanted to scream in frustration. How could she not see this?

She stiffened. "That was a totally different situation."

I snorted. "Yeah, one where you risked being caught, but at least that evil scientist wanted you alive."

She didn't say anything, but she seemed to retreat into herself, as if I'd lashed out at her physically.

I sighed. "I didn't mean that. Nothing would ever make what Jacobs wanted okay. I'm sorry." I put the van in park and waited for her to decide if she was ever going to talk to me again.

Several long moments passed before she spoke. "I am who I am because Dr. Jacobs put me out into the world," Ariane said.

My mouth went dry. "Don't tell me you're grateful for what that asshole—"

"No," she said, "just that I've been shaped by my experiences. It's the same with them. They are behaving the only way they know how. If I hadn't been raised by my father, taught to blend in with the humans, I might have been just like them." Was there the tiniest hint of longing in her words or was that just my worried imagination? Were we, an entire planet of people, not enough to combat her loneliness? Was I not enough?

"No, you wouldn't," I said vehemently.

"Are you sure? Or is it more that you don't want to think about that possibility?" she asked quietly. "I'm not human. Not the way you are." She held up a hand, cutting off my protest preemptively. "I'm not saying that I trust them. Just that I see this differently than you do."

My mouth worked, no words emerging at first. I was losing this argument, I could feel it—and her—slipping from my grasp, even as she sat right next to me. "I've never wanted you to be anything but who you are," I said. Lame but true.

"How about now?" she asked, tilting her head at me.

Wait, so now she was positioning this choice as some kind of representative decision about her as a person? Like, if I cared about her, regardless of her genetic makeup, I'd let her do whatever she wanted? But if I thought going on Ford's quest was stupid and reckless, then it was because she was too alien for me? No. No way. "That's crap reasoning and you know it," I said. "This is not about you. This is about them, and—"

"This is about all of us," she said. "The three of them, me, whomever Emerson St. John has hidden away. We have to work together if we're even going to have a chance to survive. *They've* made it that way." Disgust colored her tone, and I knew then that she meant Jacobs, Laughlin, and the others. Humans.

"So, it's the four of you against the world?" I asked, my jaw tight. No full-blooded humans allowed in that clubhouse, I guess.

"I didn't say that," she said a little too quickly.

"That's exactly what you're saying, just not in so many words." My hands ached from gripping the steering wheel too hard.

"Zane," she said. She touched my shoulder, her hand light, tentative. "I need to at least check into it. Please."

I looked over at her, the glow of sunlight turning her white-blond hair into a halo around her head. It reminded me of that first night, on our way to the activities fair. We'd come so far, so fast. This girl had stood up for me when no one else would. Maybe this was my chance to do the same for her.

I blinked hard against the stinging in my eyes. "We'll talk to my mom," I said finally. "Find out what she knows." I put the van in gear and pulled onto the road.

Ariane sagged with relief in her seat. "Thank you."

I should have stopped then, just shut my mouth. I had one last card to play, and I should have held on to it until we found out what my mom had to say once she got home tonight. But I couldn't.

"If you go through with this, I won't be there," I said conversationally, even as that sensation of jumping off the cliff spiraled through me. Whatever was between us would not be the same after this—it wasn't an ultimatum, simply a statement of truth, but I knew she wouldn't see it that way. "I'll go to my mom's with you tonight and then make my way back to Wingate. I don't care if she tells you which cabinet their meds are in and draws you a freaking map."

Her eyes went wide. "Are you . . . are you threatening me?" She didn't sound angry, more hurt.

"I'm not trying to threaten or blackmail," I said, hearing the deadness of my tone. "I can't stop you from doing what you're going to do. You know that."

She flinched.

"But you have to understand I can't sit by and watch you walk into one of those places." I would be haunted for the rest of my life by the image of her in that tiny room, the monitors, the implements, the tests, the bright red blood splattered on the gleaming white floor. Granted, that time it had been Dr. Jacobs's blood from the head wound that Ariane had inflicted in knocking him out. But I knew that was not the case for all the years previous. And how would I sleep at night imagining her in that room, or one just like it in Laughlin's complex? Or worse, a room full of microscope slides, test tubes, and sample jars, all marked with her name. The only things left of her.

A tear escaped and slid down my cheek, and I wiped it away swiftly, hopefully before she noticed.

"It's my choice," she said. "Isn't that the point of all of this? For me to have the freedom to make my own choices." For the first time, she sounded frustrated. "As someone who claims to love me, I'd think you'd want that."

I stiffened. She wasn't pulling her punches anymore. "It's your choice." I forced a laugh. "And yet, weirdly enough, as someone who loves you, I don't really want to watch you get yourself killed. Or worse. That's *my* choice to make."

She clamped her mouth shut at that, turning to stare out the side window.

And then, thank God, the conversation was apparently over. But somehow getting the last word wasn't nearly as satisfying as it was reported to be.

CHAPTER 15

Ariane

ZANE MEANT WHAT HE'D SAID. THAT IDEA ROCKED ME to the core.

I hadn't detected even a hint of deception from him. Would he really leave and go back to Wingate? Would I let him?

It was all I'd been pushing him to do from the second I'd read the letter from my father and realized that Zane's life would be in further danger. But that was when I'd been prepared to let him go. At that point, I'd steeled myself against my own feelings. Pulled them back, stuffed them down, buried them under concern for his safety. That had to be the top priority, not my own wishes, not the longings that I couldn't allow myself to say aloud.

Now, though, after I'd finally become convinced that Zane meant it, that he really intended to stick with me through the insanity that was my life at the moment, I'd stopped holding back, I'd let go and let myself feel. Only to have him pull away. It was like leaning into the wind, counting on it to support your weight, just as it vanished beneath you, dashing you to the ground, leaving you bloodied and bruised.

I drew my knees up to my chest, tucking my skirt around my legs. I felt skinned, exposed. More so now than I had since that night in the lab when the observation wall had turned to glass, revealing the truth about me to Zane.

I didn't know how to go back. I didn't know how not to feel these things for him, now that I'd opened the door. And worse, admitted it to him. My face burned at the memory. Not with regret, exactly, but more with the realization of how vulnerable I'd made myself.

I dared a glance at him. His hands were tight on the wheel, his knuckles turning white, the only outward sign of his inner turmoil. He was afraid for me. My whole life I'd longed for someone who would care about me, just for being me. Not because of what I could do for him or because I reminded him of someone he'd lost.

But I hadn't considered the repercussions. That once you were no longer isolated, alone, but involved in a larger unit, a relationship or a family, there were additional considerations, obligations. Ties.

Part of me wanted to rage at Zane. How dare he muddle this up with his feelings. His worries. If I was willing to take the risk, wasn't that all that mattered?

Zane hated Ford's approach, but she'd done exactly what I would have done, if she or one of the others had come to me when I was living in Wingate.

She was being careful and putting safety first. After all,

it wasn't just her life at risk. She was in charge of Nixon and Carter as well, which only made sense. Nixon seemed too distant to be involved, though I had no idea what was going on in his head, obviously. And Carter, with his shy smile, desire to stay in school, and eagerness to talk, might not have the edge needed to make the hard decisions. Looking at them collectively, I was pretty sure I was seeing Dr. Laughlin's version of a variety pack. Different genes switched on, resulting in a range of human/alien combinations.

Ford, apparently, had the right mix that made her a natural leader. So she was skeptical of me, expecting a trap. In her position, I would have felt the same.

But someone, somewhere, had to trust. Had to make the first move. They had extended that trust to me by not (a) immediately killing us or (b) signaling their guards to contact Laughlin.

If Ford's intention had been to turn us in to Laughlin, she wouldn't have taken the risk of letting us leave or allowing us to set the time and date of our return, if we returned at all.

That was only logical.

I watched Zane from the corner of my eye. He was concentrating on the road, his mouth tight. He truly thought that they'd manipulated the situation to take advantage of me.

But in reality, Ford had only accepted the situation as it presented itself. Offering to aid me in developing a plan was pointless. If it was so simple to escape, they would have done so already. And the decision to take the chance had to be mine, not based on their limited ability to help.

It made sense to me. She had not spelled it out, but I

understood how she thought, even if I couldn't hear her thinking. I parsed information in a similar way. To me, she'd done nothing objectionable or even truly surprising during the entire encounter.

Zane saw it differently. He couldn't help that. He filtered information through his own background and experiences, which were not at all similar to mine.

Fine. We'd encountered that difficulty before and found common ground.

The trouble was, this time, whether he realized it or not, he'd made it very clear that I'd have to choose—not just whether to help Ford and the others but which "side" I was going to take. Human or other? I would ally myself one way or the other and lose something. Or someone. There was no way around that.

Zane slowed to make the turn onto his mother's street and inhaled sharply. "Shit."

His adrenaline washed over me, bringing the world into sharp focus.

I sat up, putting my feet on the floor. "What's wrong?"

"My dad's here." He nodded toward the end of the street.

Sure enough, a familiar-looking dark blue SUV, emblazoned with WINGATE CHIEF OF POLICE, sat in front of Mara's half of the duplex. And, surprisingly, Mara's little silver Mazda was in the driveway, parked at a dramatic angle, as if she'd pulled in without any care or in a big hurry.

I frowned. She shouldn't have been back from work for hours yet, assuming she put in a regular eight-hour shift.

The ubiquitous dark SUV, Laughlin's spy or spies, was here again as well, though parked at a more discreet distance, closer to the intersection where we were than to Mara's house.

"Something's wrong," I said, as I tried to isolate the anxious vibe that radiated from the area, a weird itchy/tickling sensation at the edge of my brain that wouldn't let up.

Zane tensed. "Is he . . . is my mom okay?"

Did he hurt her? That was the question in his head, the one he wasn't asking.

I bit my lip. Zane had never specifically said that his dad had hurt any of them. But when Zane had been worried that my father was abusing me, he'd had a certain grim familiarity when checking my arms for bruises. He'd known what he was looking for. And regardless of whether that was based on personal experience or simply supposition, the possibility that his dad might hurt his mom existed in his mind, and that was enough. Chief Bradshaw had been beyond furious when my father had him ejected from GTX. And he'd blamed Zane's willingness to defend me—instead of turning me over to Dr. Jacobs—on the influence of Zane's mother. All of that added to a potential volatile situation in Mara's tiny duplex.

I struggled to tune out the surrounding noise—Zane's thoughts and feelings, those of the random people in the neighborhood—and focus on the occupants of the building at the end of the block. "I'm not picking up any physical pain." Pain shouted the loudest of anything, and it was unmistakable, always accompanied by some blend of fear and shock. (Even when people are expecting the hurt, the actual physical sensation is always more intense than anticipated and still comes as a surprise.)

Zane gripped the steering wheel tighter. "If we go in, we might make things worse."

Assuming that his dad had come to see his mom to shout at her for her role—as the chief imagined it, anyway—in our escape, then yeah. I had to agree. We'd be proving his theory correct, that we'd run to her for help. And if he was here because he hoped to track us down and turn me in to Dr. Jacobs, then going in would make our status plummet from "iffy" to "certain doom."

"It's probably best to wait and see what happens," I said. Actually, there was no "probably" about it. When all else fails, gather more intel and wait for an opportunity—no question. But those were his parents in there, and I wasn't sure he'd feel I was qualified to dictate in this instance. If it had been my father in potential danger . . . well, that was complicated, assuming I'd ever even see him again.

"If there's obvious . . . distress, we'll intercede," I added, taking care with my word choice. Zane had been very careful in what he had *not* said. I would do the same.

Without waiting for direction from me, Zane accelerated through the intersection and made the necessary turns to take us back to our house.

I caught myself and shook my head. Not our house. The house. The abandoned home for sale where we'd spent the night last night. Somehow in the last twenty-four hours, I'd begun attaching possessive pronouns to it.

A sudden memory of Zane and me standing shoulder to shoulder (well, with my height aided by the step stool of the toilet), peering out the window. That coziness, familiarity, that comfort of having him near when everything else was uncertain and frighteningly unstable.

I wanted that. Wanted him. Needed him.

A dull ache started in my chest. A crappy abandoned house,

dirty carpeting, no furniture, in a shady neighborhood. It was a twisted and shadowy version of my Dream-Life vision of suburban perfection. But it was real, actually located in this world. If that was as close as I'd get to my dream, I'd take it.

But what would I have to give up? If Zane forced me to choose between him and what I thought was right . . . I shook my head.

"Don't fall in love" had been one of my father's Rules. And I'd broken it before I fully understood why he'd included it. But it was too late; I couldn't—wouldn't—take back the past. The only question now was how it would affect the future, if I let it.

Zane led the way up the sidewalk to the door with more confidence this time, stepping aside only for me to unlock and open the door. Apparently, breaking and entering was growing on him.

Once inside, I closed the door after us. Nothing appeared to have been disturbed since our last visit.

I opened my mouth to say as much to Zane, but he was already bounding up the stairs.

Trying to avoid me? Worried about his mother? Both?

I sighed and followed him. I found him in the bathroom again, staring at his mother's house as if by intense scrutiny he could divine anything that was going on inside.

"Do you hear anything?" he asked without looking at me.

I closed my eyes and concentrated on the gossamer threads of words and feelings emanating from that location. But I couldn't hear anything other than a distant and furious buzz with the occasional out of context phrase.

. . . your fault.

If you hadn't been so concerned with . . .

. . . can't blame me for your inadequacies . . .

"They're arguing," I said. "But other than that . . . there's too much emotion," I said. I could feel waves of fear—lots of it—mixed with anger and suspicion, like water lapping at a distant shore. If we went in closer, I might have a better shot at isolating thoughts or even identifying who was thinking what, but from here, no.

Zane exhaled loudly, leaning against the window frame, tapping his fingers anxiously against the top of it.

I slipped my arm around his back tentatively, attempting in my own less-than-smooth way to offer comfort.

He tensed, surprised enough to glance down at me, but he didn't pull away, which felt like a victory.

I fumbled, alternating between awkwardly patting and just maintaining the contact. It felt unnatural, as if I were trying out some new skill. And to be fair, it wasn't like I'd had a lot of practice. For most of my life, I'd done my very best to avoid being touched, which included touching other people. Zane was pretty much the only exception to that rule, the only person from whom I more than just tolerated physical affection. And that had taken time, patience (his), and a situation that hadn't given me much choice but to challenge the barriers I'd erected for myself. Pretending to be in a relationship, though, hadn't given me much practical experience in actually being in one.

Keeping an eye on what little I could see outside— the windowsill was just below eye level for me—I moved my hand aimlessly over Zane's back, trying for a soothing motion. Rubbing at the knots below his shoulder blades, tracing the hollow at the small of his back and the rise of muscle on either side of his spine through the slightly damp and scratchy fabric of his shirt. I hadn't realized the material was this unpleasant; no wonder he'd been so miserable in this outfit.

Eventually, I realized he wasn't watching out the window anymore, but staring down at me.

I glanced up and caught my breath. His gray-blue gaze was dark with emotion.

"You know I'm just worried about you, right? I would never try to keep you from them for any other reason." The urgency and pleading in his voice was hypnotizing, pulling at me.

Biting my lip, I nodded.

He lifted my hair away from my cheek—any taming I'd done earlier was long gone—tucked it behind my ear, and brushed his thumb over my lower lip until I released it.

I'd heard the phrase "time stood still" but never understood it until that second, when every thud of my heart seemed to expand, taking hours to complete the contraction and move on. All my attention was focused on the feeling of the connection between us, like a live wire completing a circuit—his thumb grazing the lower edge of mouth, my hand clutching at his back. Round and round we went, a circle of sensation that called to me to forget everything except for this feeling.

I inched closer to him, drawn by the almost magnetic urge to fit myself against him. Then, following a bold impulse I barely recognized as my own, I tugged at his shirt with shaking fingers until it came free, giving me access to his warm skin.

My bravery only went so far, though, and my palm just grazed his bare side before I pulled back.

His breath caught in his throat audibly, a funny little sound between a sigh and a groan. Then he leaned down— so fast I barely had time to register the movement—and his mouth closed over mine.

His tongue tangled with mine, and I wrapped my fists in his shirt, trying to pull myself closer still and out of the awkward angle caused by our height difference.

Then he bent down and lifted me up, one arm around my back and the other behind my knees.

I gasped at the feeling as much as the sudden movement. The back of my knee was not a particularly secretive or private place as far as I knew; I mean, it had been exposed all day long while I was in this skirt. And yet his fingers tight against that vulnerable skin sent fire zipping through my veins.

Now, this . . . this is why humans did such stupid things for love. To feel this heady sense of belonging and connection, this temporary abatement of perpetual loneliness.

The new level of intensity probably should have frightened me, but instead it had a strange grounding effect, as if this were what was keeping me here instead of floating away. As if, despite how fuzzy and out-of-focus these feelings made me, they also certified my reality.

Without breaking the kiss, Zane turned to set me on the edge of the bathroom counter. The van keys, which had been balanced on the edge, fell into the sink behind me with a loud clatter. Then he moved to stand between my knees, a sensation that stole my breath.

I slipped my hands beneath his shirt, my courage returning in a hot rush of feeling. It felt so good to touch and be touched. He was the one who'd taught me that. And it seemed like the more I had, the more I craved.

His hands were gentle on my face, at the back of my head under my hair, and then tracing a line from my jaw down my neck, under the collar of my shirt and the T-shirt beneath it.

His fingertips skidded to a stop on the first button of my shirt, and I shivered in anticipation.

"Okay?" he whispered.

"Yes," I whispered back, trying not to sound as breathless and desperate as I felt.

He released the button slowly and then moved to the next, again so slowly. Giving me time to think, to object.

But I didn't want that. Didn't need it.

I pushed his hands out of the way and he froze, an apology written across his face. I got my remaining buttons open in seconds, and I was struggling with my sleeves before he caught on enough to help me pull the cuffs free over my wrists.

I still had a thin T-shirt on—and he'd certainly seen me in less when he'd bandaged my arm—but the heat in his expression told me this was different. More, somehow.

I pulled at the front of his shirt and he needed no further encouragement, releasing the buttons as efficiently as I'd dispensed with my own.

Beneath, he was all lines and muscle where I had curves.

(Okay, not many curves, but enough, evidently.) His skin was darker than mine, but not so much that I couldn't see the faint blue of veins in his chest. The rapid moving of his ribs as he breathed at an increased rate fascinated me almost as much the precise alignment of the muscles beneath.

I knew I was staring, but I couldn't help myself.

Then he touched the hem of my T-shirt, just at my waist, which set off a barrage of conflicting messages to my brain about where I wanted him to touch next.

"Okay?" he asked again, sounding hoarse.

This time, I reached up and pulled his head toward mine, kissing him fiercely as my answer, wrapping my arms around his neck as his hand slid under my T-shirt and up.

His thumb brushed over the front of my breast, and I wanted to curl into the caress like a cat, but my position on the edge of the counter, with the sink directly behind me, was already precarious.

He leaned in farther, bringing us almost chest to chest, and my head sang with the near-skin contact. Without thinking, I pulled him closer. He braced one hand behind me to keep his balance . . . and accidentally turned on the faucet.

I squeaked involuntarily in surprise at the sound of sputtering water and scooted forward directly into him. Which was a whole new sensation.

"Crap. Sorry!" he said, pulling his hand from under my shirt and fumbling for the knob behind me. Once the water was off, he let out a slow breath and rested his head on my shoulder. Then he gave a muffled but chagrined laugh against my neck. I shivered at the vibration of his voice against my skin.

"Can we try that ag—" he began.

The distant sounds of shouting outside caught our attention then. Zane's head swiveled toward the window.

"It's my dad," he said after a second.

Zane stepped away to the window and shoved it open. Part of me wanted to kick my feet against the cabinet in frustration. But he was right. Whatever was happening with Mara—and by association, his father—had to take priority.

With a sigh, I tugged my shirt into place and slipped off the counter to follow Zane.

Ascending onto the toilet once more, I could see Mara's yard fairly clearly, where it wasn't blocked by the house in between us. Chief Bradshaw, out of uniform and looking a little disheveled, was in the middle of the grass, shouting up at his former wife in the doorway.

"You're destroying his life, Mara. I hope you can live with that," he spat at her. "You might as well pull the trigger yourself."

Mara flinched but remained silent, looking a pale and hunched imitation of herself. She was ridiculously shrunken for someone of her height.

"He's really upset," I said, disconcerted to see that level of emotion from the chief, especially in regard to Zane. Chief Bradshaw had made it very clear to Zane on countless occasions that he considered his second son exactly that: secondary. Or worse. At GTX, when Zane had stepped in front of me to protect me from his father, there'd been a moment when I wasn't sure whether his father would consider his presence sufficient enough reason not to shoot me. And yet, right now, the waves of desperation radiating off him had to be obvious even to those who weren't telepathic.

Zane frowned. "Yeah."

Zane's dad gave one last inarticulate shout of disgust and hurtled something thin and flat at Mara. It landed on the small porch, narrowly missing her legs, but she didn't move, either to avoid it or pick it up.

Then he turned and stalked off toward his SUV without looking back. A few seconds later, the engine revved and his tires screeched as he whipped around in an impressive 180-degree turn before accelerating down the street in clear defiance of the posted speed limit.

The chief's car hadn't even reached the corner before the unmarked black SUV, Laughlin's spy vehicle, pulled smoothly away from the curb in pursuit.

Great. Although the absence of surveillance was a benefit for now, I wondered what it meant. I reached over and pulled the window closed. How much of that fight had Laughlin's guy overheard and/or understood? If Laughlin learned we were here and in contact with Mara, that would not be good. Clearly, they were now following the chief for a reason. I didn't know what it was, but I kind of doubted it was general curiosity. Maybe they were hoping he'd lead them to us.

Already buttoning his shirt, Zane looked over at me. "If you're determined to talk to her, this is probably our best chance, right?" he asked, his forehead wrinkled with concern.

He was right about this being our best chance . . . except what we were walking into? I didn't know and couldn't predict it, which made me very uncomfortable. Mara had no way of reaching us, so she didn't know where we were. We could have fled town, gone into hiding, or, heck, been killed by Laughlin's hybrids, for that matter. Would Mara insist on calling the chief once she realized we were here? I had no idea what kind of ties remained between them. They didn't like each other—that much was obvious—but the joint goal of keeping their son safe and/or away from me might yet be a common bond.

I hesitated and then nodded, with a sigh. No matter what else was going on, Mara was our best and only source of information.

Zane reached over and touched the bottom of my lip. "Stop," he said gently.

I knew he was talking about my biting my lip, but it felt like he was talking about everything. The whole situation. Everything from the moment since I'd exposed what I really was by lashing out at Rachel Jacobs at that party. It had been only a few days ago, but it seemed like years. And I really, really wished we could—stop, that is. Just end all of this and find some kind of peaceful space, preferably together, without worrying that someone would find us. But that was just not an option right now.

Maybe ever.

The trip across the backyards for the second time wasn't nearly as perilous or adrenaline filled, but I felt strangely exposed. Watched.

I wasn't picking up on anybody noticing our presence, no lonely older person or bored soccer mom staring out a window, so it was likely my own self-consciousness, but still. I didn't care for it and pushed for a faster pace to reach the back door of Mara's condo as swiftly as possible.

The security bar across the sliding door still dangled loose against the glass. In fact, the little metal lock lever was still up, indicating that the door itself wasn't even locked. So

Mara hadn't been home very long, or else she'd been too distracted to resecure her home after our interruption this morning. Either way, it didn't bode particularly well for us. After all, she shouldn't have been home at all, and if something was big enough to keep her from obsessively locking her doors . . . well, if you asked me to guess, I'd have said that nothing was of the magnitude to cause that kind of disruption in her routine.

Through the glass, I could see that the kitchen was empty. A plate with crumbs was on the counter next to the toaster, and a chair was turned on its side next to the table.

I raised a questioning eyebrow at Zane, and he shook his head. It hadn't been like that when he'd last seen it.

I tugged at the splintery wooden handle on the door, using my ability to keep the security bar from making noise against the glass. I couldn't hear anyone other than Mara inside—her emotional and chaotic thoughts a roaring ocean of noise—but that didn't mean she wasn't drowning out someone else's much quieter thoughts. Plus, given her wobbly mental state, I thought it might not be a good idea to scare her into thinking someone was breaking in. Which, okay, we technically were. Although it was more of a walking in, but still.

Zane crossed the threshold first, before I could stop him. I glared at him, which he ignored, searching the room for signs of his mother's whereabouts.

When he finally looked to me, I gestured toward the doorway that led to the hall. Going to the left would lead us to the front door, but the noise of Mara's thoughts felt more like it was coming from the right.

Zane nodded, his expression grim, and started in that

direction without waiting for me to take the lead.

I followed, gritting my teeth against the urge to call out for him to stop. Hadn't we had enough nasty surprises in the last few days? Did he really need to charge ahead as if he were the one with superpowers, so to speak?

I could have stopped him, against his will, but I suspected that no matter how much that option appealed to me from a practical standpoint, he wouldn't appreciate it.

As I passed the kitchen table, I noticed a tablet computer placed with care in the center, on a dish towel. It gleamed dully under the fluorescent lights. The corners were battered and cracked, and the glass screen bore an ugly set of parallel scratches as if someone had skimmed it across a gravel parking lot. A very expensive Frisbee.

I frowned. Wait, was this what the chief had thrown at Mara? It was about the same size and shape. She must have picked it up before coming inside.

But what the hell had driven him to throw something so pricey at her? The Bradshaws weren't poor, but they weren't the "toss crystal goblets into the fireplace in a toast" type either.

And why had Mara then taken it inside and treated it not just as item to be returned or thrown away, but with a certain respect or reverence? I wasn't familiar with her relationship with her ex, but I had trouble with the idea that she'd take something hurled at her in anger and idolize it simply because it belonged to him. After all, she'd had the courage to leave him in the first place.

I shook my head. Something wasn't making sense.

Acting on an impulse that I didn't completely understand,

I scooped up the tablet from the table and tucked it under my arm before scurrying out to follow Zane around the corner into the hall.

The staircase that I'd noticed earlier curved in a tight right angle, making it impossible to see upstairs or even beyond the first five steps.

But of course that didn't stop Zane. He took the first three steps as one.

I sighed inside. When this was all done . . .

Don't you mean if*? If you survive. If he survives. If he is still speaking to you.* A melancholy voice whispered in my head.

I ignored it.

When this was all over, I was going to have to teach Zane some very basic sneaking-around skills. And not charging ahead into a blind corner would be Lesson 1.

Fortunately, this time, the curve on the staircase was empty of anyone lying in wait. As was the tiny landing at the top.

Peering around Zane's back, I could see four cheap, wooden doors, the flimsy kind that cave in at the slightest pressure. More a suggestion of a barrier than the real thing. Two were closed, and two were open.

Zane paused a second on the landing and then headed for the second door on the right, one of the open ones. Mara was up here somewhere, but in this small of a space, I couldn't pinpoint exactly where. When I stopped to listen with my ears instead of telepathy, then I could hear the rustling movement of quick steps on the carpet coming from that room.

Moving swiftly on his heels, I reached the doorway only a second after him.

Leaning to the side of him—he really made a better door than the actual doors—I could see an open suitcase in the center of a bed with rumpled covers, overflowing with clothing hastily tossed inside.

Clearly Mara had had enough, and she was headed out. But where? To meet someone? Or was she just fleeing town, her resistance worn to the breaking point from the events of the last day?

And where was she now? The room, other than the bed and a tiny TV on a stack of plastic milk crates, was empty.

Then, before I could voice the question or tap Zane on the arm, the *click-clack* noise of hangers being shoved aside came from an open doorway parallel to the one we were standing in. A closet. A second later, Mara bustled in with an armload of clothing.

"What are you doing?" Zane asked in what felt like an outrageously loud voice but was probably only slightly above normal.

I winced.

She spun around, dropping the clothes on the floor and revealing a large butcher's knife clutched in her right hand.

Lesson 2 for Zane: never startle jumpy—and potentially armed—people.

I lunged around him, elbowing him out of the way, and raised my hand to direct the power already tingling in my fingertips. I didn't know if she'd try to throw it or simply lurch at us, but either way I had it covered by clamping down on her wrist and fingers. That knife wasn't getting anywhere near us.

As soon as she saw it was her son, though, Mara released the blade without a fight. With a little direction from me, it landed point down in the thin carpeting, where it promptly listed to one side under its own weight.

"You're okay," she breathed, eyes only for Zane.

Then her gaze fell on me.

"You."

I flinched and then steeled myself for whatever stream of invective would follow.

"You have to come with me," she said.

I blinked. That was not what I'd been expecting. "Go with you where?"

"Back to Wingate." Then she bent down to scoop up the clothes she'd dropped and hastily piled them onto the mound already in her suitcase before slamming the lid closed. Or trying to, anyway. Sleeves in a variety of colors oozed out the edges, like invisible hands raised in protest at their treatment.

Zane gave me a worried frown, and I lifted a shoulder in a shrug, my mouth tight. It was the same song from before. Go back, you don't belong here, you'll never have a normal life, etc., etc. The only thing new was this overwhelming sense of urgency radiating from her. And I had no idea what might have triggered that.

"Mom, listen, I don't know what Dad told you, but I'm fine. We're fine," Zane said, emphasizing the "we" of that statement by gesturing back and forth between us.

Mara paused in her frantic attempts to zip her suitcase. "You saw that? You were that close?"

Zane stiffened at the pain and near accusation in her voice and then nodded slowly. "He's just angry because of Dr. Jacobs. He missed his chance to get in good with GTX." But he didn't sound quite as convinced of that as usual, which was evidenced by his next words. "I'm fine. He doesn't have to worry about me." His voice held a note of wonder, amazement that his father would worry about him. Which made my chest ache for him. Zane deserved so much better than that.

Plus, it wasn't exactly true, what Zane had said. There were still plenty of reasons to worry about him, despite my best efforts. But Mara already knew about those, even if the chief didn't. Which meant we were still missing something.

"Mara," I began, and her eyes focused on me for the first time for more than a second.

Her face paled the second she saw the tablet pinned between my arm and my chest. She darted forward and snatched it away, clutching it to her body as if it were an infant I was somehow threatening.

2 P.M. Tuesday. I can make a trade . . . the information is valuable . . . not enough, not enough . . . has to be enough. She has to come with. MY FAULT. I can't save him . . .

The stream of panicked chatter was accompanied by equally nonsensical images. A castle, a flag with a cartoon representation of an orange cheese wheel, a parking lot, a blond baby sitting up unsteadily on a patchwork blanket.

I shook my head in frustration. Enough already. "What's going on, Mara?" I asked.

"They took him." She turned her back on us and continued trying to zip her suitcase one-handed.

"Who?" Zane asked, bewildered.

Then the pieces clicked. The blond baby, Mara's new determination to return to Wingate, Chief Bradshaw's sudden and unusually intense distress over his son's well-being.

When I lived in the lab and in the years after with my father, I'd suffered through any number of lectures and lessons about questioning your assumptions and how making the wrong leap could cost you the mission or your life.

Although no one would admit it, war was a guessing game, all about trying to know your opponent better than he knew himself.

And sometimes, no matter how hard you tried, one or two of the blanks got filled in incorrectly. You just had to hope it wasn't one of the vital pieces that would alter your entire understanding of the situation.

In this case? It was.

I kicked myself mentally for not catching it sooner: We'd been focused on the wrong son.

"It's your brother," I said to Zane quietly. "They took Quinn."

Zane paled. "What?"

"He goes to school in Wisconsin, right?" I asked.

He shook his head as if trying to wrap his brain around this development. "Madison, yeah. Why?"

This had Dr. Jacobs written all over it. He couldn't get to me or Zane (thereby getting to me through Zane), so he'd gone for the next best thing. Except it was so much worse. Quinn had not elected to get involved in this mess, unlike the rest of us. He'd been drafted. Which probably meant he had no idea what was going on and was likely terrified.

At best.

At worst . . . I remembered the determined, almost fanatic gleam in Dr. Jacobs's gaze when he'd sent his own granddaughter in to me to be killed, all for the sake of this project. So it might very well be much, much worse.

"That's why Dad was so upset," Zane muttered to himself with a bitter smile. "Of course." His shoulders slumped.

After all of this, he still cared what his father thought, and his father never seemed to miss an opportunity to crush him, even when it wasn't intentional.

I wanted to reach out and comfort him, but I was too worried about what we didn't know. "What's on the tablet?" I asked Mara. I could feel the tension building in my arms and my nails digging into my palms. Dr. Jacobs could have hardly chosen better, which almost made it worse. He did know me.

I'd never met Quinn before and felt no great love for him based on all that I'd heard from Zane. But this scenario, an innocent caught up in something much larger than he realized and against someone with all the power, was my weak spot. The injustice of it, the helplessness it created in the victim, the disregard for the individual as anything more than a pawn in a bigger game—it sent this huge, roaring fury through me. One that screamed at me to charge in and *destroy*.

I felt the heat soaring through my veins, warming my face and my hands until I felt I was glowing with it.

At times like this, the cool stir of my alien abilities felt like an entity unto itself. It whispered to be set free, to address the issue, to eliminate the emotional confusion and chaos that upset our normally harmonious system. It wanted to restore the balance in a very logical, efficacious manner. If X is the problem, then we simply eliminate X.

And in the meantime, my human side was screaming with the urge to crush, kill, avenge. If Dr. Jacobs wanted my attention, he would certainly have it. In blood, broken bones, and destruction.

I was the two worst halves of my disparate heritage. Clinical, dispassionate logic—no compassion or sympathy—triggered by overwhelming emotion. A hammer driven by intense strength and feeling.

With an effort, I clamped down against the emotional response, my human side reacting before all the facts were known, and breathed slowly, in and out, until the power quieted to a more manageable tingle rather than the state of near overflow.

"The tablet," I repeated.

"You'll come with me?" Mara asked, turning the computer outward so the screen faced us but making no move to turn it on. She wanted a guarantee first.

This can't be good, a panicked voice inside me cried. "Just show me," I said firmly.

Next to me, Zane closed the distance between us, his hand wrapping around my wrist for reassurance when my fingers wouldn't unclench to take his.

Mara pressed the wake button on the tablet and the screen lit up, revealing a single icon—a movie clapboard—floating in an ocean of serene, and artificial, blue.

She took a deep breath and, with a shaking finger, tapped on the icon.

The screen shifted immediately to a much dimmer image, a view of a much darker room with white walls. In the center, under a spotlight, one person sat alone in a chair, his blond head bent down, hiding his face, and his body a blur of frozen motion.

"Quinn," Zane confirmed in a whisper.

Before he could say more, the video kicked on.

"Oh God, I told you, you have the wrong guy," he screamed from his bent-over position, obviously in agony. The side of his face, visible only as he tried to curl into himself, was red, the tendons in his neck popping out like cords beneath his skin.

Next to me, Zane inhaled sharply, his hand tightening on my wrist.

On the screen, Quinn lifted his head with a struggle, staring at someone or something past the camera, and with a jolt I realized I recognized him. Yes, in that vague way as someone who'd been a senior when I was a freshman.

But it was more than that. It was the way his eyes crinkled at the corners, albeit currently from pain rather than laughter. It was the exact manner in which his mouth turned down, carving those precise lines in his face, the right not as deep as the left. It was how he set his jaw when he was obviously determined.

My heart gave an uneven thump.

He looked like Zane. Not in his lighter coloring or stocky build—he was a younger version of the chief in that way— but in those flashes of expression. That brotherly resemblance tore at me. It wasn't Zane, thank God, but it could have been, and I could see him in Quinn.

Quinn managed to reach an almost upright position, revealing for the first time his arm strapped to his chest in a makeshift sling. "It's not . . . I'm not . . . My parents don't have any money to pay you," he panted through clenched teeth, directing his words to someone off-camera. Even with the awkward angle, you could see something wasn't right with his arm. It was bent in strange places, like he'd developed new joints between his wrist and elbow. One of them appeared to have broken through the skin, leaving a bloody gash and a flash of white bone.

Nausea rose in the back of my throat. I'd had my arm broken. Multiple times. Sometimes by accident, sometimes deliberately. The sharp pain—and the sound, oh God, the sound was the worst, that horrible crack that took you apart at the seams, signaled you were mortal, frail, and broken.

The screen bobbled, Mara crying as she tried to hold the tablet steady, and the image of Quinn froze and then broke apart smoothly into blocks, a fancy fade to black.

I clenched my teeth so hard my jaw ached. Clearly, someone fancied themselves a filmmaker, concerned about effects and appearances in what amounted to a torture video. Oh, I would show them all kinds of effects when I got ahold of whoever had stood by and filmed this.

Words appeared on the screen in a slow scrawl, each line bumping up the next, *Star Wars* style.

> His arm appears to be fractured in two places.
> His ribs may be cracked.
> He resisted.
> That is unfortunate.
> With timely medical care, a full recovery is likely.
> Provided infection doesn't set in.

It was like a horrible (and misguided) attempt at poetry. The video started again immediately, but it was impossible to tell how much time had passed since the previous segment.

Quinn was calmer now, swaying slightly in his seat. "I'm sorry I didn't tell you about school," he mumbled. His eyes were glassy, his skin now an unhealthy shade of grayish green. Either they'd given him something to address the pain or he was moments from passing out. "I was going to . . . Maybe

243

you can send the tuition check to these bastards instead."

Zane sent a questioning look to his mom.

"He was having trouble adjusting, failed a few classes," Mara choked out. "They cut his scholarship last semester. Your dad found out when he called the school after he got this video. Quinn wasn't answering his phone, and his room-mates haven't seen him since Sunday." Her voice dissolved into a barely contained sob.

"That's why he didn't come home this summer," Zane said, more to himself than either his mother or me.

"And tell Zane I'm sorry," Quinn said, his words muzzy with exhaustion.

Next to me, Zane jerked as if he'd been struck. I slipped my hand into his, and he squeezed it tightly.

"I should have been a better brother," Quinn said as his head dipped down to his chest—whether he was succumbing to the drugs or passing out, I wasn't sure. The screen faded to black again—this time by making the image ripple and wobble into nothingness—and my stomach clenched in anticipation. Another message was coming, no doubt. They hadn't yet gotten to the point, but they would. They weren't going to all this effort just because they could.

And sure enough, seconds later, the word scrawl started again.

> Ariane Tucker:
> Exit 340 on Interstate 94
> 2 P.M. Tuesday

Even though I'd been expecting to see my name eventually—what else could this be about? It wasn't like Quinn was a highly desirable ransom target in any other situation—it still sent a shock through me, the familiar letters in such a strange context. And that punctuation after my name, one little colon, made my stomach fall.

It changed everything.

This message was addressed to me. I'd known this was my fault, but seeing it spelled out so clearly made me want to throw up.

They'd sent to this to the chief, counting on him to get Mara involved, which would then, eventually, lead to us.

The worst part was that they couldn't have known I'd get the message or even that I'd be close enough to meet their deadline. There were any number of places where their plan could have fallen apart. But Dr. Jacobs didn't care. He was arrogant—or desperate—enough to take Quinn and hurt him anyway.

Zane's fingers tightened on mine, and I realized I'd already begun backing up, heading for the stairs.

"You aren't going," Zane said, his voice rough. "We'll find another way to get him back."

Before I had a chance to respond, the words vanished from the screen and another image of Quinn appeared.

I froze. I'd thought the video was over. Threat implied, message received.

But Dr. Jacobs wasn't done with me yet. No, that would have been too kind.

On screen, the frozen image blinked into movement and Quinn bent over, retching from the pain and moaning every time his arm and ribs were jostled. But he couldn't stop. It was an awful, vicious, escalating cycle that devolved into hoarse screams and whimpers within seconds.

Even the cameraman seemed affected, the focus on Quinn

slipping momentarily to the wall before fading to black.

But the screaming continued. It was a loop, I was pretty sure, of previous audio, but it was horrible just the same.

The color washed from Mara's face, and tablet slipped in her grip, dangling from her fingers.

Zane grabbed the tablet and thrust it at me before taking his mom's arm and helping her to the edge of the bed.

I fumbled with the device to pause it. The sudden silence in the room made my ears ring.

"It's okay," Zane murmured to his mother, who had her face buried in her hands. "It'll be okay." He gave me a helpless, pleading look. One that begged me to make the words he'd just said true. His family might have been messed up, but it was still his family. His brother suffering and his mother in pain because of it.

But I couldn't respond. Something was gnawing at me. Something wasn't right. Obviously. But beyond Quinn and the message and the entire situation.

I'd missed . . . what? What was it that had triggered this additional unease, the growing sense of dread in the pit of my stomach?

I frowned. It was in those last few seconds of footage; it had to be. Right when the otherwise unflappable auteur had lost his cool and gone to the wall. Something about that didn't sit right with me. Why include it when the rest of the video had been ruthlessly edited? Clearly it wasn't an accident or a lack of skill.

I found the volume buttons on the side of the tablet and turned down the sound all the way before pulling the slide bar back on the video to the final segment.

Somehow it was more gruesome without sound, possibly because there was nothing to distract from the image on screen. But I forced myself to watch.

And . . . there. Flash to the wall. I hit pause.

"Ariane?" Zane asked with a frown.

"Hang on," I said tightly.

The walls were nondescript, but upon closer inspection a very specific kind of nondescript. One I recognized.

And I should. I'd spent enough hours staring at those walls. They had a plastic sheen, likely for easier cleanup and sanitizing, but with a nubby texture to them that was faintly visible in the close-up.

At night, I used to lie on my cot and put my feet up on the wall to experience the texture (everything else in my cell was relentlessly smooth). I would pretend I was Outside and it was grass.

In fact, if I squinted hard enough at the image on screen, I felt I could almost see the slightly darker spots on the wall where I'd put my feet, night after night.

Quinn was in my cell at GTX.

And Dr. Jacobs wanted me to know it.

I closed my eyes, my breath slipping away as my chest tightened in fear and frustration.

"Ariane?" Zane asked again, sounding more alarmed.

The wall was another message, one more subtle than the words.

I wasn't sure if it was a warning—you know how hard it is to break out of GTX, forget about breaking in—or a lure. Maybe I was supposed to pick up on that clue without realizing that they'd planted it deliberately and head in to save the day, thinking that I was pulling one over on them.

Either way, the result was the same. They'd be expecting me to try to get Quinn at GTX. The already impossible security would be double or tripled.

And yet, going to the designated meet and attempting to get Quinn without being captured would be even more difficult.

I'd been trained to assess situations like this and determine the best action to take, even when the best action was none. Especially when it was none.

Surrendering serves no purpose, my logical half pointed out.

Except to save Zane's brother!

My two sides clamored back and forth, vying for dominance.

It's bait, temptation to your weaker self. You know that. Once you give in, they will have you forever, both physically and mentally.

Which was true. If I went to GTX, I wasn't coming back out. But even that wouldn't be a guarantee of Quinn's safety or Zane's. If anything, it might only make things worse. Dr. Jacobs would turn to them every time he wanted something from me.

Once again, caring only served to hurt me and others.

But doing nothing, is that really an option?

I looked at Zane, sitting next to his mother on the bed, the strain and fear written on his handsome face. Just a couple weeks ago, he'd had a regular life, worrying about tests, lacrosse games, and college essays. I'd done this to him.

And yet when he noticed me watching him, he met my gaze with confidence and, God help me, hope.

In me.

Crap.

CHAPTER 16
Zane

QUINN AND I HADN'T GOTTEN ALONG IN A LONG TIME. Scratch that, we'd never gotten along. We are brothers, three years apart. We would have fought over who had two more inches of room in the shared misery of the backseat on family excursions, who was getting more air, anything and everything.

But that was normal sibling stuff, as far as I could tell. It had changed, turned into something worse, only when we were older. One day, it was as if he were suddenly miles ahead of me, even when we were in the same room. He was a stranger I happened to share a house and a bathroom with.

I didn't know when it started or why, but I remembered when I finally figured out that something was different and it wasn't good.

We'd been in the backyard doing throwing drills with my dad. (There was no "tossing the football around" with him.) I was nine and Quinn was twelve, and for once I must have done something right, because my dad was in Quinn's face for a change.

"Even Zane did better than that, for God's sake," my father shouted. Those words, and that tone of disgust, would be permanently carved on my heart after that.

I was drowning in fury and humiliation, and then Quinn . . . Quinn glared at me, as if I was doing something wrong.

It was in that moment when it had finally clicked for me. We weren't on the same side anymore. When we'd bickered and beat on each other before, we'd always still teamed up against our parents. To get out of trouble, to weasel another hour of television, to find our Christmas presents in the weeks before the holiday.

But in one of those quick flashes of insight, where everything else seems to stop for a second while you struggle to absorb some screamingly obvious revelation, I'd known that Quinn and I were done. We weren't brothers anymore, just two people fighting over the same resources.

Seeing him in that video, though, he'd looked so vulnerable, so broken.

I swallowed hard. That wasn't the Quinn I knew. I didn't remember the last time I'd seen him cry. Or apologize to me for anything.

He really thought he was going to die.

You okay? The memory of Quinn checking on me at that party suddenly filled my head. At the time, I'd been embarrassed and angry and just wanted to disappear, and his question had only exacerbated those feelings.

But he'd been trying to look out for me, making sure I

was all right. An overture, not of peace exactly but maybe an acknowledgement of his role and responsibilities as an older brother, something I thought I'd never see again.

I should have been more grateful for the attempt.

My eyes stung suddenly. We had to save him. We couldn't just leave him in there.

The bed beneath me shook with my mother's sobs. I tentatively put an arm around her too-thin shoulders. She didn't react to the contact, her hands covering her face as she curled into herself, elbows resting on her knees.

I glanced up at Ariane, who continued to stare down at the tablet, but with a blankness to her expression that suggested she wasn't actually watching anything but thinking instead.

"Ariane?" I asked.

Her gaze flicked up to meet mine. I thought I saw a quick flash of fear and then something, sadness, maybe, before the emotion and expression drained from her face, leaving her as unreadable and unknowable as she'd ever been.

She pushed the button at the top of the tablet, putting it to sleep with an audible click; tucked it under her arm; and stepped toward my mother with a precise economy of movement.

"What's at that exit, Mara?" Ariane asked flatly.

My mom dragged her head up from her hands to stare up at Ariane blearily. "What?"

"Exit 340 on Interstate 94. What's there?" Ariane repeated, not exactly with patience. More like a robotic evenness. You could almost see the cogs and wheels turning in her brain as her personality and emotion and humanness, for lack of a better word, took a backseat to the military-type training and alien instincts that lived within her as well. She looked . . . well, she looked more like Ford than ever in that moment. It sent a chill through me.

My mom cleared her throat and straightened up, responding unconsciously to Ariane's crisp and expectant tone. "The Cheese Palace," she said.

I frowned. The what? It took a second longer for a few vague memories to emerge. A castlelike building, a giant cheese emporium, with a huge plastic mouse statue wearing a Packers jersey and holding a beer-scented candle just inside the door. Cheese, beer, and football. Pretty much the three major exports of Wisconsin.

Concentrating on it, I had another dim recollection of Quinn and me running around the store, going long with one of those little circles of cheese in red wax as our football. Then my dad had gotten ahold of us. I could still recall the feeling of his fingers digging into my shoulder when he caught me with the "ball," doing that thing where he was red-faced and shouting but only with his eyes.

Clearly, I'd been inside the Palace at some point. Maybe a family vacation, like our one disastrous attempt at camping years ago. The memory of the Cheese Palace seemed to be tied to that of a campground swimming pool with a metal edge, superheated in the sun, that burned my palms when I tried to haul myself out.

To my surprise, Ariane nodded at my mom, as if she'd somehow been expecting this answer. "A tourist attraction, in a high-traffic area."

Glad it made sense to her. It seemed insane to me. All

those people watching, both at the Cheese Palace and in vehicles passing on the interstate. "Isn't that riskier?" I asked.

"In an isolated area, I have greater freedom to take action against them. Dr. Jacobs is worried about that. He should be." Ariane's tone darkened with something that sounded a lot like grim pleasure.

In other words, it would be a lot easier for her to use her training and abilities, go all badass assassin on them—hey, man, you reap what you sow—if she didn't have to worry about innocent humans getting in the way.

So, Jacobs had set up the meeting, intending to use families, honeymooners, and random drivers with a tiny bladder or a taste for Baby Swiss as human shields.

I grimaced.

Ariane returned her attention to my mom. "You said Quinn's roommates haven't seen him since Sunday. Do you know when on Sunday? It would be helpful if we could narrow the time window."

My mom shook her head. "I don't know. I didn't . . . I wasn't the one who talked with them."

Ariane cocked her head to one side, considering. "When did the chief receive the video message?"

"This morning. Early. He called and told me he was coming and I'd better meet him." My mom stared down at her folded hands, examining the white points of her knuckles as if they held more information.

Ariane nodded, her face a blank, but I could almost hear the wheels in her head turning.

She was gathering data, trying to put the pieces together. Why that exit had been chosen as the meeting point, how long Quinn had been gone, and when he'd likely been injured.

She was planning. Ariane was going to save Quinn. Somehow she was going to get him out of there.

A rush of relief washed over me, followed almost immediately by bile-filled frustration. She was going to risk herself to save him, and I needed her to because I couldn't fix this.

In the small world of high school, I knew my way around. I'd been bored, restless, feeling like I'd outgrown it. I was just biding my time. But that meant I'd been the expert, the one who'd guided Ariane through our elaborate scheme to get even with Rachel.

Now I was nothing. Goddamn it. I was tired of feeling useless.

I stood up and stalked past Ariane to stand in the doorway. I needed to move, to do something, anything just not to feel like a lump of clay. I didn't expect to be able to do the same things she could do, obviously, but just to have a purpose, a way to contribute to the situation.

To be fair, not many people could have done something to help in this situation. Well, not many humans, anyway.

The hybrids, though, they were a different story.

I flashed on a mental image of the four of them crowded together around a whiteboard, their pale heads tipped together as they studied a series of Xs and arrows.

Which was ridiculous. This wasn't a game, and they probably wouldn't use a whiteboard anyway. They'd communicate in that eerie silence, either through telepathy or simply by knowing one another well enough, as Ariane seemed to understand them within seconds of seeing them.

It was that sense of unity, the thread that bound them together as the only (as far as we knew) aliens on the planet, that plucked at my nerves. They *belonged* to each other, somehow. Certainly, Ford, Nixon, and Carter, but also Ariane, too. Jealousy was sort of new to me, but I was pretty sure that's what this was. I'd been jealous of Quinn for years, and the feeling was similar.

They wouldn't be helpless in this situation.

I leaned against the doorway, resisting the urge to drum my fingers nervously against the wall.

"What can you tell me about Quorosene?" Ariane asked my mom, startling me out of my thoughts.

"I don't . . . you're talking about Ford and the others?" My mom sounded confused at the transition.

"Yes," Ariane said. "What can you tell me about Quorosene?"

I shifted uneasily against the doorjamb. She wasn't seriously considering this. She couldn't be.

My mom frowned. "Not much. It's part of the hybrids' treatment plan."

"What is your security clearance?" Ariane pressed, kneeling down in front of my mother to keep her attention. "Is it sufficient to get access to the Quorosene?"

"N-no." My mother shook her head. "I don't have—"

"Can you confirm that Dr. Laughlin keeps a supply in his office?" Ariane asked.

I straightened up, my heart pounding too hard.

"It's possible. He doesn't trust many people with—"

"Ariane, can I talk to you for a second?" I asked. The words came out too harshly, all broken edges and sharp.

Ariane turned to me and gave a brief nod before standing up and heading toward me.

She had to know what I was going to say, and yet she followed me into the tiny hallway without a word of protest.

I raked my hand through my hair. "You're kidding me with this, right?" I burst out. Okay, not the best approach. I took a deep breath and tried again. "Why are you asking about that stuff now?"

Emotion flickered across her face before she contained it. "You know that even if I trade myself for Quinn, that will be no guarantee of his safety or yours. If anything, it might be worse. He knows I'll do whatever is necessary to protect you from hurt or harm, and if I refuse to cooperate with him . . ." A tiny furrow appeared in her forehead, a big expression for her when she was in this battle-ready mode. A sign of how much the idea distressed her.

"That's why I don't want you to do that." But I wanted, needed, her to do something.

She nodded, clearly picking up on what I was thinking but offering no more.

I sighed, feeling years older and weary suddenly. "So what am I missing?"

Her gaze focused on a distant point beyond me. "They're holding Quinn at GTX. In my cell, in fact. I recognized the wall behind him."

I closed my eyes, feeling that slip of gravity that always accompanied devastating, unexpected, and unwelcome news. If Quinn was at GTX, getting him out would be next to impossible. I'd only succeeded with Ariane because we'd had help and no one had been expecting it. We would not have that luck a second time.

"I don't know if Dr. Jacobs is trying to warn me away or lure me into coming after Quinn. But either way—"

I opened my eyes. "We'd be walking into a trap."

She nodded again, a slight inclination of her chin more than anything.

"So, what are you thinking?" I made myself ask, even though the tightening in my gut told me I already knew the answer to this.

Hesitation flashed across her face, her emotions breaking through. "There's only one option that makes sense," she said.

"You want to try to free the hybrids first," I said dully.

"It's more than that," she insisted. "This is our one chance to stop the trials. If we're all free, then the competition is over. And Dr. Jacobs won't have any reason to hold your brother or come after you." She moved toward me, as though she'd touch my arm.

I backed away.

She froze, her hand in midair.

"And what I think doesn't matter?" I demanded, frustrated. It seemed we were a team, but only when I agreed with her tactics.

"What other option do you suggest?" she asked calmly, which somehow made it worse.

"I don't know!" I shouted. "I'm not the master strategist here. Just a regular old human." It was a low blow and not fair but the only way I could express this growing sense of being out of my league. I was an object to be worked around, extra baggage to be shuffled.

She trusted them more than me. That's what it felt like. And why shouldn't she? On the surface, they had more in common, they were advanced in ways I'd never completely understand, let alone be able to compete with.

Ariane's eyes widened, and she opened her mouth to speak.

Never one to stop when the stopping was good, I kept going. "Even as 'limited' as I am, though, I can tell you that anything—even strolling through the front entrance at GTX—is better than walking into the trap Ford has set for you."

"Zane—"

"Mark my words, you walk in the door at Laughlin's place and they are going to make sure it swings closed after you," I said darkly. "For good."

"You don't know that. You don't know them," she said, her tone gentle.

Neither do you, I wanted to scream. But that wouldn't help my case. "Ford has more reasons to work against you than with you. And I know plenty. I saw the way she reacted to you. To us." The words escaped before I could stop them, and I grimaced.

A frown appeared on her forehead. "Is that what this is about? What she said?" She lifted her chin up, challenging me.

"No, no." I shook my head fiercely. I didn't want the conversation to take this turn. In my mind, Ford's sneering implication that Ariane was lowering herself to be with me only proved that Ford didn't respect Ariane or her decisions. But to bring that up now would seem like nothing more than insecurity on my part, and I had a valid point beyond that, which was that Ariane didn't know jack shit about these people. If they were even people. They were so distant and freaking strange.

I caught myself, but not in time. Watching Ariane, it was as if a curtain dropped across her face, wiping away all expression. "Because she's not human," she said flatly. "Or, not human enough for you, anyway."

Fuck. "I didn't say that."

"You didn't have to," she said in that same even, dead tone.

"Don't do this," I said quickly. "Ford is nothing like you. She is—"

"—exactly like me, except for the years of training myself to look and act like the full-blooded. I take it you prefer that."

I threw my hands up. "Compared to Ford? Hell, yes, but that's not my point." Absurdly, I could feel my eyes burning with tears. Where was the girl who trusted me? Who thought I was worthy? I could feel her slipping away from me, no matter how hard I tried to tighten my grip. "I like you for who you are."

She stiffened. "Good to know you like me."

And I didn't realize why she was upset until I played back my words in my head.

I'd downgraded her from love to like.

"I didn't mean . . . I wasn't taking it back." I fumbled for the right words. God, they had to be here somewhere, right? Something to convince her. "I was just trying to make a point."

She raised her eyebrows. "Point made."

I wanted to grab her arms and shake her, but I suspected that wouldn't go over so well. So I kept my hands firmly locked at my sides. "This is what she wants. Don't you see that?" I pleaded. "She's manipulating. She wants to turn you to their side."

Ariane took two quick steps toward me. "What side? Whose side?" She poked her finger at my chest. "As far as I can tell, there's only the people who want to use us, abuse us, and keep us in cages, and everyone else."

"You're lumping me in with Jacobs now?" I stared at her, aghast. "I just want you to be safe."

"So does he, I'm sure." With that, she turned and walked away, down the stairs.

Stunned, I just watched her go, words pounding on the inside of my brain, begging to be set free. But I knew already that none of them would have made a difference.

CHAPTER 17

Ariane

I STORMED THROUGH MARA'S KITCHEN AND OUT THE sliding glass door, heading toward the empty house and our van—*my* van—in the driveway.

How blind did Zane think I was? I knew that Ford made him uncomfortable. He'd practically oozed disgust earlier today.

And whether he wanted to admit it or not, she and I were cut from the same cloth. Literally, if one considered DNA as a weaving of a sort.

My eyes welled with unshed tears. How could he not see that the things he hated in Ford were in me too? And beyond that, why couldn't he trust me anyway? Hadn't I proved myself worthy of that, at least?

In that moment, I envied Ford, just a little. She wasn't alone, trying to figure all of this out. There were three of them. She would never have to choose sides between human and other because she had a side of her own with Carter and Nixon.

But that didn't mean I was foolish enough to have blind faith in her. In any of them. Getting Ford and the others away from Laughlin truly was the best strategy to save all of us, including Quinn. And yeah, working with Ford left us open to betrayal, but I already had a plan in mind to address that. A plan that I would have gladly shared with Zane if he'd bothered to hear me out.

Is it possible you're overreacting? my human side nudged. *You know he wasn't suggesting that you were less than human, just different. And Ford is a bit of a freak, if we're being honest.*

It was just that his reaction brought up this horrible, inescapable fear in me that, maybe, what Ford had said was right. Maybe I wasn't being true to myself around him; I was still hiding behind my human facade. And that, in turn, raised the ugly specter of Dr. Jacobs's and Mara's words— that I didn't belong out here. That what I wanted couldn't be mine. Because, as a freak of science or manufactured miracle of human ingenuity, whatever you want to call it, I didn't deserve it. Those dreams were reserved for "real" people.

Tears ran down my cheeks and dripped off my chin. I swiped at them angrily. I shouldn't have gotten involved with Zane. It had been a mistake. I'd been fooling myself.

We were too different. He wanted me to trust full-blooded humans. First a few reporters, and then a whole planet full of them, to keep me safe. How was that any less risky than what Ford had suggested? My track record with humans was already, forgive the pun, less than stellar.

I inhaled slowly, trying to calm myself down. All I'd wanted was a small, normal life. Something to call my own. Something real. And I'd wanted it to be with Zane. A chance to go on a date, maybe, without worrying about someone following us or abducting me out of the bathroom.

But that was not to be. Not now. Maybe not ever.

And yet, I was still here. I still had choices to make and things to do. Right now, if I wanted to beat the deadline on Quinn's video, I had about twenty-four hours to get into Laughlin Integrated, find the Quorosene, and get back out.

And that started with returning to Linwood Academy before Ford, Nixon, and Carter left for "home." I figure I had maybe forty-five minutes to make the trip, and that would be cutting it close, especially with a stop at drugstore for the supplies I needed.

I squared my shoulders as I reached the sidewalk of the house we'd been using as a home base. Zane may not have agreed with my course of action. Fine. But he wasn't here anymore. It was up to me. And there was some relief in that. I would do what I needed to do.

I ducked inside the house and found the keys where Zane had left them, upstairs in the slightly damp bathroom sink. I left as swiftly as I entered, refusing to allow myself to look on any of the dirty rooms with aching fondness or reminiscence, actively blocking all thoughts of our time together.

But when I opened the van and climbed behind the wheel, I discovered that the seat was pushed so far back that it revealed a portion of the floor mat that was the original gray, unfaded by the sun. My feet were miles away from the pedals.

A ripple slipped through my forced calm. What if that was the last time we saw each other? What if I walked away and those were my final words to him?

I didn't mean what I'd said, not entirely. I knew he wasn't the same as Dr. Jacobs. But I'd let Zane think I believed otherwise. And now, away from the heat of the moment, the memory of the hurt on his face was a knife to my heart. He'd risked so much for me, and I'd crushed him like he didn't matter.

I shook my head. No. Thinking like this wasn't productive. And I didn't have time for it. Once I was done here, once I'd succeeded in freeing Ford, Carter, and Nixon and ending the competition, thereby saving Quinn and Zane and anybody else GTX might attempt to take to try to control me, then I'd come back. Then I'd see if there was anything left between Zane and me. Assuming he would even be interested. He'd been so angry. My being right might not fix that. I'd learned that a long time ago—sometimes full-blooded humans would rather be wrong and figure it out for themselves eventually instead of having someone push them toward the correct answer.

But I didn't have that luxury.

I adjusted the seat, started the engine, and backed out of the driveway, wishing for not the first time in my life that someone had bothered to teach me the mechanics of gaming traffic signals. What good was telekinesis, if not for creating a stream of green lights when you needed it?

Regular school buses, looking shockingly out of place compared to the rest of Linwood Academy, were lined up out in front of the school along with any number of shiny cars with convoluted hood ornaments. The more complicated, the more expensive, was my observation.

But, thankfully, I didn't see a single navy-blazered student.

The space near the back of the lot where Zane and I had parked earlier was full now. And I couldn't help but notice the dark SUV with tinted windows, idling nearby.

Crap.

I drove past, hoping it looked like I was searching for a parking space. I couldn't let them see me. Which sort of ruled out sneaking in the front door again.

Thinking, I tapped my fingers on the wheel and then stopped as soon as I realized what I was doing. It was a nervous fidget I'd picked up from Zane. Even away from him, I couldn't escape his lingering effects.

With an effort, I refocused my attention on the problem at hand. The dark SUV's presence ruled out the "sneaking" part, yes. But not necessarily the "in" portion of the equation. If there was no way around them seeing me, then I'd have to do the next best thing: act like I didn't care.

I made a quick loop around the parking lot and pulled into an open space, marked reserved, right near the covered entrance.

If appearing to skulk might draw attention, then behaving like an entitled student would, especially around here, make me blend right in. Except for my distinctly nonluxury vehicle. But hopefully they'd be more focused on me and not my ride.

With shaking fingers, I tugged at the knots in the scarf around my neck until the fabric pulled free. Then I wound it around and through my ponytail, tying it off at the end.

It wasn't fashionable, but it would cover most of my distinctive hair, made even more so now by a hastily application of bleach in a CVS bathroom to eliminate my lowlights.

I was hedging that Laughlin's men weren't as well versed in female fashion as other important skills like takedowns and hand-to-hand combat.

I slung my emergency duffel bag over my shoulder and climbed down from the van, hurrying for the door.

Please, God, make me look like a student running late to something.

It might have worked, but the bell rang.

Crap.

A swarm of people dressed just like I was immediately flooded out, leaving me the sole body moving upstream.

Well, at least it would make it tougher for Laughlin's guys to find me, if they were looking.

Of course, that would also make it equally tough to find Ford before she spilled out with everyone else.

I kept my head up as best I could, looking for the bright flash of white-blond hair. But with my height disadvantage, I wasn't seeing much but blazer-clad shoulders around me. And the occasional backpack flying toward my face as someone turned to talk to someone else around them.

As I stumbled across the threshold into the entryway, the crowd broke and I nearly fell forward without the press of bodies around me to keep me upright.

A hand caught my wrist and yanked me up with less care and more impatience.

I looked up to find Ford staring down at me, her mouth a flat line of displeasure.

Without a word, Nixon and Carter stepped around me, one in front and one behind. Hiding me, I guess. It made a kind of sense—I'd sort of blend in between them and most people's glances would skim right over the top of me. Hopefully.

"Why are you here?" Ford demanded.

"You said it was up to me to figure out how to get in. I have a plan."

Her gaze searched me, as if looking for building blueprints and rappelling equipment. Then a slow smile spread over her face.

I shivered. It was disconcerting and eerie.

"You want to be me," she said. I could almost feel Nixon and Carter tense.

"No," I said with a touch too much sharpness. "I want to pretend to be you. Temporarily." I wasn't surprised that she'd figured it out. As I'd told Zane, I'd recognized my own pattern of thinking in what she'd said to us in the practice room. Her logic was cold, unfriendly, maybe, yes, but I had that same voice living in the back of my head.

"We are a unit. It is not easy for us to be separated for any length of time or distance," Carter offered, his voice softer than when he was speaking for Ford. "Until we're out of range, Ford will feel compelled to rejoin us. We've tried to . . . separate before."

The pain in his voice made me wonder what lengths they'd gone to to save themselves. Or how far Dr. Laughlin had pushed them. He couldn't send all three of them into the trials, and if they didn't function well as individuals, then he was in trouble, no matter what he'd promised Ford.

"How will you keep Ford from following us?" Carter asked.

"We'll figure that out," I promised. "I've got some ideas." After all, I didn't need her to stay away forever. Just long enough for me to get inside.

Ford gave a small sigh of exasperation, as if it wasn't even worth the air to explain how stupid I was. "Even if you can successfully imitate me long enough to gain access"—her tone indicated how unlikely she thought this feat—"you will be noticed wandering the halls alone. Alarms will be raised immediately and you will be subject to examination, if only to determine how you broke free of our bond."

Not to mention it would completely leave me vulnerable to a double-cross, should she be thinking along those lines. But I wasn't done yet. Not even close. I wasn't going to be the only one with skin in the game.

I smiled at her, letting my teeth show, and my face protested at the unnatural gesture. But it worked, as she swayed back slightly with a frown.

"That's where you come in," I said.

Ford tipped her head to one side, that evaluating look I recognized. It might have also been faint admiration; I wasn't sure. "We have only a few minutes before our security team will come looking for us," she said.

"It'll be enough," I promised. Or so I hoped.

CHAPTER 18

Zane

IT TOOK ME A FEW SECONDS AFTER ARIANE LEFT TO work out that she wasn't coming back.

She hadn't just gone downstairs to get air or away from me for a few minutes. She had walked away. To them.

After days of trusting only each other, she'd just ended it. Chosen them over me.

The sudden emptiness inside me left me feeling as though I would cave in from the edges at any second. It was, oddly, a familiar feeling of just not being enough.

I turned and walked woodenly into my mom's room, where she still sat on the edge of the bed, like a version of her former self with the batteries out.

She glanced up and then behind me. "Where is 1 . . . Where is Ariane?"

"She . . ." *She took off? She decided she could do better?* I couldn't make myself say those things out loud. "She's pursuing other options."

Darkness flashed over my mom's face. "She decided that this mission wasn't 'within scope.'"

I frowned.

"Oh, she didn't use those words, but it's the same idea." She shook her head. "I told you. They look human, but they don't have the feelings, the capacity for emotion."

"Ariane's different." The words escaped before I could stop them. God, why was I still defending her?

My mom gave me a pitying look and stood with an effort to continue her ineffective struggles with the suitcase zipper. "Even her own mother wouldn't . . ." She snapped her mouth shut.

I stared at her. "What?

"Nothing."

"No, it's not nothing. You were talking about Ariane's mother. Do you know who she is?"

She shook her head. "Of course not. I didn't have that level of clearance." But she wouldn't meet my gaze.

"Mom—"

She held up her hand to stop me. "All I was trying to say was that the hybrids aren't meant for life out here. Expecting more from her or any of them is, at best, setting yourself up for hurt. At worst, it's dangerous."

I stiffened. "Did you say that to her?"

"Zane . . . honey." She turned and reached for me, her cold fingers brushing my face before I stepped away.

"Did you say that to Ariane?" I repeated.

"She didn't argue with me. She knows what she is—"

"Who she is, Mom. Who. And she knows who she is. She was trying to help you. She was asking questions," I argued.

My mom sighed. "I'm not saying that she wouldn't have helped if it benefited her."

"No, she's more than that." I knew that to my core. The girl I knew, the one who'd stood up for Jenna Mayborne, who'd taken on Rachel Jacobs and her grandfather, that was not someone who calculated the angles and acted only on those that helped her. If she hadn't stood up for Jenna, she would never have been in this mess to begin with.

"Then where is she?" my mom asked simply.

I grimaced. "She's trying to help Quinn. In her own way." But I sounded defensive, unsure, even to my own ears. I was certain she would try to save Quinn, but Ford, Nixon, and Carter . . . they would come first. She'd admitted as much.

My mom gave me a knowing look. "If she'd been willing to intervene directly on Quinn's behalf, I would have accepted her help. They are very good at what they do. But honey, you can't get attached. To begin thinking about her as more than what . . . who she is. Trust me, I made the same mistake, but once you see what they can do . . ." She shuddered.

"What, Mom, what horrible thing did she do?" I asked, getting very tired of all this paranoia without proof. She'd been against Ariane since the second we'd arrived. Well, as soon as she'd figured out Ariane wasn't Ford.

"She killed an animal because Dr. Jacobs told her to. Just stopped its heart."

I frowned. That didn't sound like Ariane at all. "Because he told her to," I said slowly. "What does that mean?"

"I mean he ordered her to do it and she did." My mom hauled the suitcase off the bed and, seemingly as an afterthought, scooped up the butcher's knife, tucking it the suitcase's outer pocket.

"Right then, without argument?" I asked. I couldn't even picture that in my head. Ford, yes. Ariane, no way.

She made an exasperated noise. "She couldn't really argue and she tried to resist for a while, but—"

"How many days, Mom? How long did she resist?" A new idea struck and my stomach turned, but I made myself ask. "What did he do to her when she did?" I didn't know everything about Ariane's lab days, but I knew enough to guess that any form of rebellion had been met with swift and severe punishment.

"It doesn't matter," she snapped. And I saw the genuine fear in her eyes. She'd gotten pulled in over her head and stayed too long. Her world would never be safe now that she knew about the existence of the hybrids and their alien progenitors. "She did it, Zane. That's the point. And she can do it to any of us."

"Yeah, but that doesn't mean she will," I said. Just because someone could do something didn't mean they would. We were all capable of horrible violence and cruelty, but that capacity didn't turn us all into abusers and serial killers. "I saw her save someone by refusing to do that same thing." Rachel Jacobs was alive today only because Ariane had refused to kill her, even though she'd been cruel to Ariane and it would have benefited Ariane to end her life.

That was who she was.

And instead of trusting that person, I'd let her walk out. Worse, I hadn't even tried to hear her out about the hybrids. Instead, I'd let my own fears get in the way.

That realization struck with such force that it made me

take a step back. She hadn't given up on me; she'd turned away when I'd stopped believing in her.

How could I blame her for that?

The urge to find her, to help protect her from the risk she was taking, overwhelmed me. I turned and headed for the door, desperation moving my limbs before conscious thought kicked in.

"Zane, where are you going?" My mom sounded alarmed. "If you come with me to meet Dr. Jacobs, maybe we can—"

I didn't stop. "I promise, I will find a way to get Quinn out of there." But first, I had to catch up with Ariane before she took a chance she couldn't untake.

The van that had been our home base since the start of all of this was parked at the front of the school, and just the sight of it sent a sweet rush of relief over me, leaving me to sag back in the cramped driver's seat of my mom's Mazda.

I wasn't too late. She was here somewhere.

The rest of the parking lot was empty but for a handful of cars. Including a black SUV gliding to a stop in front of the main entrance.

Shit. I pulled into the nearest parking space, shoved the gearshift into park, and ducked down, hiding as best as I could across the seats. Were they here for Ariane? Or just picking up Ford and the others for the day?

After a long moment, when there were no shouts or pounding footsteps in my direction, I peered cautiously over the edge of dashboard. And got my answer. From my angle, I had an unobstructed view of the doors, so I saw when Ford, flanked by Nixon and Carter, marched out.

I searched her face for signs that Ariane had found her,

but I couldn't read her any better than Ariane. She could have been pissed, bored, or her version of ecstatic. It was impossible to tell.

One of Laughlin's hired men got out and opened the SUV's back door for them. Carter climbed in, but Ford hesitated for a second.

My gaze shifted to the van automatically, looking for whatever had distracted Ford. I half-expected Ariane to burst out, shouting for Ford and throwing the guards around.

But nothing happened. Ford got into the vehicle, followed by Nixon, both of them moving as if this was routine.

The SUV pulled away a few seconds later with a squeal of tires on the new asphalt.

I let out a slow breath of relief. Well, if Ford and the others were gone, but Ariane's van was still here, then that meant she was still here somewhere, right? If I caught up with her now, before she had time to implement whatever plan she'd cooked up with Ford—assuming she'd had a chance to talk to Ford and Ford had agreed to participate—then Ariane would be safe.

The tight knot in my stomach eased slightly. I'd have a chance to talk to her, to apologize, to try to figure out another option or, hell, even help with whatever she had cooked up.

All I had to do was find her.

Filled with renewed determination, I charged out of the car and headed for the van. That would be the easiest place for her to await Ford without detection, but if that was the case, then she'd just missed her chance.

The van was seemingly unoccupied. The doors were locked, so I couldn't check the secret compartment, but I felt fairly certain that if she'd come this far, she wouldn't be hiding in there.

"Ariane?" I whispered against the passenger-side window, just in case. My breath fogged the glass, but nothing moved on the inside. I could see the map we'd used, neatly folded up and tucked into a cup holder. Napkins from one of our Culver's visits overflowed from the glove box, where I'd stuffed them. The hotel key card Ariane had kept was resting on the shelf beneath the speedometer and other gauges. The dairy fairy—a mini stuffed cow with pink gauze wings and a tiny wand in one hoof—that I'd bought for Ariane at the convenience store where we'd gotten our Illinois map dangled from the rearview mirror.

I backed away from the van, a little unnerved at seeing it empty, almost abandoned looking. It was a capsule of our time together since leaving Wingate, which was kind of awesome. But seeing the van like this, without either of us in it or preparing to get in it, it felt more like a sealed exhibit, as if the life had been drained out of it. Now it was one of those dinner scenes you see in pictures from Pompeii. The plates were still on the table, chairs pushed back. But the people were just gone.

I shook my head against the tide of superstitious and stupid thoughts. She wasn't gone. She just wasn't here.

Inside the school, then. That was the next logical choice. I headed toward the door, fists at my side, determined to fight my way in if necessary.

But unlike earlier, nobody seemed to notice my presence or care. I crossed the threshold, watching the office warily, now that I knew where it was. Postschool, it held quite the collection of teachers, chatting and laughing. I could hear the hum and thump of a photocopier, and the phone was ringing.

After hours, none of them seemed to be concerned about someone walking in. The few students I saw passing through the hall ahead of me moved with purpose, to practices, rehearsal, or tutoring, presumably.

I headed off down the hall, following the same route Ariane and I had taken before. There were dozens of rooms and an unknown number of closets and hidey-holes in this place where she might have taken refuge to avoid being seen. *Ariane?* I focused on her name and imagined projecting it throughout the school, bouncing off the walls like a sound wave.

No response. Because she didn't "hear" me or because she didn't want to?

I grimaced. She might be angry enough at me to stay away.

ARIANE! I tried again, even louder, imagining myself shouting. *I'M HERE. I'M SORRY! CAN WE TALK? PLEASE?*

Still silence. No movement.

The doors were open to most of the classrooms, as they were now empty except for teachers hunched over laptops or wiping whiteboards clean, which made searching a little easier. But no more successful.

I opened the few closed doors I could find, and in the process I discovered the practice room we'd used for our conversation with Ford. The same kid we'd scared off earlier sitting at the piano, glumly picking out notes.

He looked up at me and froze.

"Sorry," I said hastily, and backed out.

I continued down the hall, checking rooms and nodding to the few people I passed as if I belonged. When I reached a dead end, I retraced my steps and found a different branch to check.

But the school wasn't *that* big, and once I found my way to an auditorium with actual velvet chairs, like in one of those old-time movie theaters, I was running out of obvious places to check.

I returned to the hall, near the atrium, which seemed to be the approximate center of the building, all the hallways spiderwebbing around it. An atrium in northern Illinois? Why? So they could stare at snow for half the year? These people had more money than sense.

"Ariane?" I called. "Are you here? I just want to talk."

Now the quiet was taking on a punishing quality. Or maybe that was just my guilt talking.

"Ariane."

"Ariane!"

A couple heads poked out in the hall to stare at me, but I glared and they retreated. One advantage of my height is that people rarely want to challenge it.

"Ariane!" I bellowed again.

Then a door somewhere nearby banged open, and I started in the direction of the noise.

I rounded the corner and saw a door shuddering from its impact with the wall. One of the bathroom doors with the fancy clouded glass in the upper half.

A paper sign flapped on the outside of the door.

IN DISREPAIR. DO NOT USE.

I rolled my eyes at yet another instance of the Linwood Academy putting on airs. Because "broken" just wasn't good enough for them.

I felt myself pulled toward the door. Not drawn in the sense of intrigued or curious, but physically *pulled*.

My shoes slipped on the wood floor as I automatically leaned away from the force.

Only there wasn't much room for leverage. The force around me held fast, dragging me forward and squeezing maybe just a little too tight.

I stumbled into the bathroom, my shoes catching on the threshold as the power around me dissipated. And then the door banged shut after me, almost smacking into my back.

Ariane stepped out from one of the stalls, and my immediate rush of relief vanished when she opened her mouth. "You are determined to be a menace, aren't you?" Her voice was cold and harsh.

I gaped at her. No matter how upset she'd been with me before, she'd never looked at me like that. Not since the first day we'd talked and even then . . .

As she tipped her head, seemingly waiting for a response, I saw the vertical line carved into her cheek. And those eyes, dark and bottomless, as if they were void of all feeling.

Not Ariane. *Ford.*

I shook my head, my thoughts in a nauseating whirl as I struggled to catch. If Ford was here, that meant Ariane was . . . not.

A horrible feeling rose up in me as my brain replayed the scene I'd witnessed, in sharp HD quality. The trio of hybrids climbing into their big, black, Laughlin-provided SUV. And that strange momentary hesitation from Ford before she'd climbed in.

Ariane's plan was simple and brilliant . . . but incredibly risky.

And I was too late to stop her.

CHAPTER 19

||■■ || | | || ■■| |■|| |■|■|■|| |

Ariane

THE DARK INTERIOR OF THE SUV REEKED OF NEW leather and too much men's cologne, a mixture that would now forever be associated in my mind with blinding terror.

I was in the middle seat, close enough to see the precise line of the haircut on the driver's neck, smell that he was the source of the offending musky odor, and notice the plastic communication bud in his ear when he turned to check traffic before pulling out.

So close. Agent Blonde, as I nicknamed him, was so very close. And though I hadn't had the chance to confirm it, I suspected he, too, was carrying concealed under his jacket. I'd seen a gun on Lando, the other guard, when he'd held the SUV door open for us. (I named him after the *Star Wars* character he vaguely resembled. I may have been slightly punchy with panic.)

That gun—and Agent Blonde's presumably as well—was the real thing, not the kind with tranquilizer darts like I'd seen on Dr. Jacobs's retrieval teams.

Theoretically, these men and their weapons were here to protect the hybrids (a.k.a. Laughlin's investment), but I was willing to bet they'd been trained with scenarios that would involve turning those weapons on their charges.

Carter's shoulder pressed against mine on one side. Nixon was folded up on the other side of me.

I imitated their position. Staring straight ahead, hands resting neatly, palms down, on their knees. Three little statues in a row.

But on the inside, I was screaming.

I'd messed up. Years of training for covert operations—not exactly like this one but similar enough that it shouldn't have been an issue—and I'd hesitated.

In that last moment before climbing into the vehicle, I'd frozen. Just for a millisecond. Long enough for a deeply buried survival instinct to rise up and shout, "Are you freaking kidding me with this?"

It was only human. At a time when I could least afford to appear so.

That would never have happened to Ford.

I could feel sweat forming under my arms, at the base of my spine and in little pockets where my hands rested against my knees. God, what if a trickle ran down somewhere visible, like down my cheek or neck? What if they noticed I was sweating when I got out of the car? Who knew what they'd been told to watch for and report?

I could hear my breathing picking up pace and falling out of sync with the others.

Next to me, a tremor ran through Carter and his hands squeezed into fists. He kept his expression steady, though he seemed to grow paler.

On my other side, Nixon's leg began to jounce, as though he were trying to run in place.

They were feeling the effects of separation. Suddenly, my worries about my mistake seemed insignificant. If they couldn't keep it together in the car, we were so very dead. Or caught. Either way, the same thing.

Keeping my gaze fixed straight ahead and my hand low, I reached over and clamped down on Nixon's hand, pressing down to stop his leg from moving.

To my surprise, he flipped his hand up, catching my palm in his and squeezing tightly. His expression never changed—never had, in all the time I'd been watching him—but there was someone in there. Nixon was very much at home. Not the empty shell he appeared to be.

Carter edged closer until he was pressed against me in a solid line. Then his hand wiggled under my elbow until his fingers latched hard around my arm.

They were using me as a touchstone, maybe. A weight to keep them from drifting back to Ford.

I watched both of them as carefully as I could without looking at them, sick with dread that one of them would reach for the door handle and throw himself out to return to Ford. I might be able to hold them in place with my ability, but for how long, especially with two of them struggling against one of me?

"Everything okay today, kids?" Lando asked casually, lifting his gaze to the rearview mirror.

Was I, as Ford, expected to answer as leader? Or would Ford's disdain for humans keep her silent, ignoring the question? I didn't know. This wasn't one of the scenarios I'd covered with Ford during our brief consultation.

I couldn't breathe; all I could do was sit there, my heart beating so hard I shook with it.

The silence in the backseat dragged on and on. Maybe five seconds, but it felt like centuries. And it was too long.

Lando frowned—I could see the wrinkle in his forehead in the mirror—and started to turn around.

Then Carter rallied. "The day was within acceptable parameters, thank you," he said. He might have been a little more breathless than I'd ever heard before—and his fingers were tight enough on my arm to cut off circulation—but Lando didn't seem to notice.

Lando nodded, those piercing eyes now fixed on me.

I did my best to look like Ford. Bored, impatient, tired of these humans.

After a long moment, Lando's gaze flickered and then dropped away.

And it took everything I had not to sag back in relief. I'd been worried about dying inside Laughlin Integrated; now I was wondering if we'd survive the trip there.

Forcing myself to concentrate, I listened to the roar of the tires on the road until my breathing slowed. I stared through the windshield, unfocusing my eyes until the trees all rolled together in a green blur, broken only by bright sparks of light—sunshine reflecting off passing cars.

I wasn't connected to Carter's and Nixon's minds, and they'd never given any sign of hearing my thoughts, but if anxiety was contagious, so was relaxation. They'd pick up on it through my body language, if nothing else. I wasn't Ford, but I could still try to lead. They were trusting me.

By the time the SUV approached Laughlin Integrated Enterprises—a glass and concrete tower with shiny, reflective windows that made it look like a bit of hardened sky—and rolled down a ramp and past security gates into an interior garage, Nixon's grip on my hand had eased, and Carter was breathing easier. And my panicked sweating had mostly stopped, leaving me damp and uncomfortable against the leather seat but far more in control. Yay.

Agent Blonde opened the door this time, and Carter exited first. I stepped out onto an immaculate concrete floor, double glass doors just ahead and to the right.

All kinds of security blinked and flashed next to those doors: key card slots, palm scanners, intercoms, and a free-standing device with a various mechanical arms—some of which had pointy ends—and a metal cuff to hold an arm in place. Blood test, maybe? Scary.

But according to Ford, I wouldn't need to worry about any of those.

Head straight for the doors, then right, right, and left until you reach the end, she'd said.

The end of what? I'd asked.

But she'd waved my concern away. You'll know.

Nixon got out and, after a brief hesitation that almost stopped my heart dead, led the way to the entrance. I followed, hoping Carter was paying attention behind me. Looking back wasn't an option, obviously, unless I wanted to announce in not so many words that I wasn't who I was supposed to be.

Pretending to be linked to Nixon and Carter was a hell of a lot harder than I'd ever imagined.

It wasn't just knowing someone well enough that you could predict what they would say or do, it was literally becoming a part of them. One organism with many limbs. You didn't have to think or hesitate or confer any more than I had to look at my arm and tell it to move.

I watched Nixon ahead of me, listened to the sound of Carter's footsteps behind me, and tried to adjust accordingly, but the echoes off the concrete walls made it almost impossible.

Fortunately, Agent Blonde and Lando, their transportation/ guard duties complete, were seemingly absorbed in the discussion of a game from television the night before and the possibility that the referees had been bribed.

Nixon didn't hesitate on approaching the doors, and neither did I, determined not to make the same mistake twice. As if sensing that, the doors slid apart while he was several feet away, granting us immediate access. I didn't even have to slow down.

Someone was on the ball with the button pushing somewhere. I wanted to look around for the camera but didn't dare.

The doors whooshed closed behind me, presumably once Carter had cleared the threshold, and we were in a small entryway with another set of closed glass doors ahead of us.

A cool rush of medicinal-smelling air surrounded me, lodging an immediate and familiar throb of dread in my stomach. I knew that smell. Sure, here there was dark gray carpeting and ash-colored walls instead of Dr. Jacobs's all-white, all-the-time theme, but it was still a lab. It still held the scent of antiseptic, overheated plastic from the computers, and a hint of formaldehyde (a.k.a. failure).

I kept moving behind Nixon, and the second set of doors opened, just like the first.

Past those doors, the air warmed slightly and potted plastic plants and trees appeared along the walls at a regular basis, between closed office doors, along with a sanitized version of corporate art. Nothing like the luxury Dr. Jacobs had surrounded himself with.

I'd accompanied my father to the dentist once for a procedure that inhibited his ability to drive. It reminded me of this. Impersonal but worse for the attempt to make it seem like something else. The plastic plants and "art" only called attention to what they were trying to hide. The sterile confines of GTX had, at least, been honest in their nature.

I made the turns as instructed by Ford, and the slight slant to the floor told me we were wending our way onto lower levels. Interesting. No stairs or elevators. That meant fewer ways in or out. So maybe Laughlin wasn't as confident in his hold on his hybrids as he appeared to be. Or perhaps he simply thought of them as more disposable. I shuddered and then caught myself, hopefully before any of the surely numerous cameras picked up on it.

As we rounded the final corner, I noticed a sign hung flush against the wall, just above my line of sight.

GALLERY

SERIES 7.11.19

The tidy white font on the black background reminded me of the signs I'd seen for museum exhibits on television and in movies. (I'd never been to one in real life; there'd been an eighth grade field trip to the Field Museum, but I hadn't gone of course. I had asked, though, because I'd thought it might be allowed under my directive of "know the humans so you can better imitate one." Now I had to wonder how much of my father's refusal had to do with the perennial obligation of being unnoticed and how much to do with the fact that the museum was, perhaps, a little too near Laughlin's territory.)

Honestly, I expected nothing more from the gallery than a collection of the same drab photographs and prints that had decorated the previous corridors.

So I didn't understand what I was looking at, at first. The initial display appeared to be some kind of modern art statement piece, a glass box—seemingly empty but for a tiny dot in the center of it—set into the wall with a small black-and-white sign beneath it.

It wasn't until after three or four identical displays that the object in the box became large enough for me to recognize familiar features, for me to understand what I was looking at.

Large, dark eyes set behind translucent lids in a pale, delicate head. Tiny hands that looked more like flippers. A body no larger than my fist, curled in on itself, floating in an eternal sea of preservative.

And beneath it, on that neat black-and-white sign, a name: QUINCY ADAMS.

The name of a former president. These were Nixon, Ford, and Carter's predecessors on display.

My stomach revolted, and I gagged.

Carter stepped on my heels before I realized I'd slowed down to stare. "You can't stop. We can't stop," he hissed in my ear.

Oh God. He was right. Ford wouldn't stop. Because she was steeled against this horrific display; she'd have to be. She'd seen it every day for years.

I forced my sluggish legs to move, commanded my knees to bend and lift my feet. I'm sure if anyone were watching closely enough, they would have seen Ford moving as though there were strings attached to her arms and legs. Jerky, puppet-like. But I was moving. And that was the best I could do.

Especially as the "gallery" only got worse.

As the series progressed, as the names grew closer to the living Laughlin hybrids I knew, the specimens appeared to grow, in a mockery of the development of the living beings they'd once been. Signs of "progress" in Laughlin's process, obviously.

Until, finally, I was looking at full-fledged children. Not infants who might have perished before birth from some unspecified developmental flaw. No, these were boys and girls, some taller than others, some thinner and less human looking. All them, though, had the same pale and fine hair I struggled with on a daily basis. Short, long, wavy, straight, and every state in between, it hung in clouds around their heads, above their sightless eyes, floating gently like seaweed on the current. Probably thanks to the filtration system that kept them preserved and on display.

It was horrific. The exact fate I'd feared for the source of the alien DNA we all shared, the one who'd crash-landed here on Earth in 1947. I'd never dreamed . . . I'd never imagined someone would do this to us. I felt a kinship to these silent and lost souls just as much as their living counterparts. Yes, some of them, had they survived, might have wanted me dead (as Ford might still); some might have even tried to kill me during the trials. But that didn't change what we were to each other.

In the displays that contained the more advanced hybrids, metal tools lined the inside of the tank and a see-through plastic flap covered a drawer beneath, where scientists could presumably reach through and collect their bits and pieces of flesh.

My vulnerable siblings, half brothers and sisters, had no peace even in death. They would be stared at, studied, and sampled.

One of the Roosevelts, the first one, T. Roosevelt, looked like a tiny, perfect doll. Five or six years old. The same age I'd been when I'd "escaped" with my father. Even in just the quick glimpse I had of her, she reminded me of me. And the daughter I would never have. (I wasn't sure it was even possible, and even if it was, who knew what the genetic tinkering they'd done on me would result in?)

I wondered if they'd called her "T" or "Roosevelt" or nothing at all.

It was a waste. Such a waste.

Despite my extensive education in world religions and the various wars and conflict they were supposedly responsible for launching, I'd never reached a conclusion on my own opinion about souls or an afterlife. But I figured this display said more about the postdeath fate of those who'd created it rather than those who were in it. I prayed my fellow hybrids were long gone and, at the very least, feeling nothing at all anymore.

I opened my eyes wide to hold in the tears that threatened to spill down my cheeks.

Far be it from me to be thankful to Dr. Jacobs for anything, including my existence, but at least I wasn't part of something like this grotesque collection.

Then again, for all I knew maybe Jacobs had a gallery somewhere in GTX that I had just never seen. But I doubted it. This wasn't his style. He was determined, vicious, and uncaring in his pursuit of his goals. Cruel, oh yes. But with purpose. Not that that made it better, but somehow cruelty without purpose, like creating this gallery, like making the surviving hybrids pass it daily, seemed worse.

This reeked of arrogance, self-indulgence, and a twisted mind.

As the wall curved ahead of us, I could see the final displays. Thank God. Although I had to wonder if something worse lay ahead, since no one, not even Carter, had mentioned this monstrous memorial to me in preparation for this trip.

The last hybrid name I recognized, not just from human history but from Ford herself.

Johnson had been a girl, taller and stockier than Ford and me. Unlike the others, she appeared to be staring somewhere off to the left. Her neck was twisted at a strange angle that someone had tried to correct, not quite successfully.

According to the tiny plaques beneath the boxes, all of those prior to Johnson had died of "system failure." Multiple organs giving up at once, for no known reason. In my research back in Wingate, I'd learned that genetic hybrids and animal clones created in human laboratories often suffered this fate.

But Johnson had been "eliminated" when she couldn't fit in with Mara's cultural indoctrination suggestions. Dr.

Laughlin had taken away her dose of Quorosene, and she'd died. Slowly, horribly, according to Ford and the others.

Looking at Johnson's obviously broken neck, though, I wondered if someone had stepped up and put her out of the misery in the end. Killing her even though they'd all feel that death. Someone more than a sister, an extension of themselves.

Ford. I'd have bet money on it.

I couldn't imagine doing that.

Johnson had once been part of Ford, Carter, and Nixon's minds, and she part of theirs. She was represented by the line on Ford's face. On my face now, too—a temporary mark, thanks to Ford's adept hand with a pen.

Except, after having seen all of them, from Washington on, I knew the line on my face stood for every last one of them.

I wanted to stop, to tell Johnson I was sorry, and I was going to *end* this.

But hesitating again might only make it impossible for me to do that. I had to keep going, pretending to be unaffected. I could do it. If not for myself, Ford, Nixon, and Carter, then all the ones who'd come before us. Including the 106 who'd lived, however briefly, at GTX before me.

But even with that edict in mind, the very last display case caused me to stumble. There was a long stretch of unbroken wall ahead of it, so I almost missed it, thinking the gallery had (finally) ended. But there was one last tank. Empty, but that didn't matter. It was the sign beneath it that caught my attention.

"Ford," it read in that mesmerizingly bright white text.

The birth date was filled in with an ominous hyphen pointing the way to her unknown-for-the-moment death date. Ford. Not Carter, not Nixon.

Carter reached out and tugged me along as he passed.

Keep going, keep going, was the unspoken message. Of course, he couldn't say that to me. The real Ford would have understood him in her mind, no words needed.

Ahead of us, Nixon sped up, like a lost dog that finally recognizes home, and I realized we'd reached the end of our journey. The gray hallway dead-ended into a final set of glass doors. They opened into a large room with dark green walls and faux skylights—revealing an artificial night-time sky, complete with fake constellations—set into a high ceiling. An oversize structure dominated the back wall. It looked like a cross-section of a beehive but without the natural irregularity found there. This was made of plastic and precise. Four large tubes enclosed in a larger plastic box. Like the bottom side of a giant LEGO piece.

Each tube was big enough to crawl inside, and watching Nixon, I saw that was exactly what he did. He took the lower opening, leaving three cubbies open. Upon closer inspection, I saw bedding and clothing in several of them. One of them—Carter's, I'd bet—had been papered with clippings from magazines and catalogues. A white iPad charger dangled from the opening.

That was evidently where they slept and spent time when they were at "home." The only bit of seclusion they seemed to have. In the corner was a bathroom area: toilet, shower, sink. But there was no curtain, no door, no illusion of privacy whatsoever.

And with cameras likely tracking our every move, no place for a private conversation and the questions now burning a hole in my brain. Why did Ford have a tank and not Nixon? If the tanks were prepped in advance, which would make sort of a sick sense, then why weren't there three empty ones waiting? Or, at least two, designated for the ones who were not going to the trials. Instead, it was just Ford's. Which would imply that Laughlin had no intention of sending her to the trials.

I glared at Carter, who either in genuine ignorance or deliberate misunderstanding, nodded toward the upper tube on the left side, diagonal from Nixon.

Yeah, I was asking which cubby was supposed to be mine/Ford's. That's what I wanted to know at this exact moment. Right.

He raised an eyebrow in an *Are you stupid?* look he could have only learned from Ford.

With an effort, I hauled myself into the tiny bed tube/room that belonged to Ford, worrying a little about how strange it would look for me to struggle at this when Ford obviously managed it nightly.

Ford's chamber was nearly as stark as Nixon's. I crawled past a pile of clothes near the opening. At the far end, I found bedding wound in a heap with a pillow. When I moved the pillow and sheets, feeling too warm and closed in, paper rasped. Upon closer inspection, I found two small pages glued or somehow stuck to the bottom of the tube. One appeared to be some kind of diagram of a portion of the night sky, with the stars named. Someone, Ford, presumably, had circled a few of them in red. The other was a glossy page that appeared to have been torn out of a larger work, like a travel guide. It was a picture of purplish mountains surrounding a lake so blue it had to be Photoshopped. I didn't recognize the location, but—

A faint tapping sounded to my right suddenly, startling me. I sat back and listened for a moment before picking out the pattern. Morse code? Really? Well, better than attempting a conversation that would be picked up by the cameras. I doubted that Carter and Ford ever talked aloud here. Why would they when they can communicate telepathically and not risk being overheard? "Change now for training." *That* was Carter's message?

"Why didn't she tell me?" I tapped in a manner that, I hoped, conveyed my pissed-off-ness. I'd been led to believe that Ford was the one chosen for the trials. The empty tank said otherwise. "Why didn't you?"

The long delay before his response seemed to indicate a level of discomfort or perhaps, oh, God, uncertainty. "Laughlin does not understand us. He is reminding Ford that she is not irreplaceable, and that if she's gone, there will be no one to protect Nixon and me. That's all."

Except it was more than a threat.

Clambering around in the tube so I was facing out again, I could see the empty display with Ford's name. It was set apart from the others, an expanse of unbroken wall between it and Johnson's tank. Why? Perhaps to leave room for Nixon, or to make sure that Ford saw it every morning when she sat up.

That? That was a promise.

And it was proof of a lie. A lie that Ford had told.

According to that gallery and the last display, Nixon and Carter weren't in danger of being "discontinued" in advance of the trials, as Ford had implied; she was.

I'd been counting on her loyalty to Nixon and Carter to keep me safe while I was in here and to make her play her part in this scheme.

But how could I know for sure what was going on in her head? Could even Carter and Nixon know for certain? They clearly believed that she wouldn't abandon them, or else they would have spoken up. Right?

Plus, leaving now didn't even make sense. If Ford took off, that would only guarantee her a slow and painful death from a lack of Quorosene. Unless she had some kind of workaround for that. Maybe she'd weaned herself without the others knowing.

I glanced down at the picture on the bottom of her cubby again, the mountains, the lake, the trees. It looked peaceful, safe, and a little lonely. Like an end.

That was another possibility: maybe Ford didn't care. Maybe she'd had enough of trying to take care of the others. And maybe the chance to die on her own terms was worth more to her than living on someone else's. I wouldn't put it past her. Stubbornness was strong in both sides of our heritage.

And I'd just given her the opportunity and the ability to walk away from her fate, from that box with her name on it, for good.

CHAPTER 20

|||||■■ || | ||||■■| |■|| |■|■■| ||

Zane

Ford raised her eyebrows, surprised, evidently, that I'd figured out her identity so quickly. It wasn't that hard, if you knew there were two of them and what to watch for.

No matter how similar they looked, Ford had a harshness about her that Ariane did not. It just took an extra second or two of observation to see it. Ford's hair was lighter too, if you were looking for it.

"Perhaps you are not nearly as intellectually deficient as I originally thought," Ford said. "Congratulations."

For someone not particularly fluent in human, Ford certainly had a fine grasp on sarcasm. Or maybe she was being sincere. Either was possible.

"Though," she continued, rubbing her wrists, which were strangely red and raw-looking beneath the cuffs of her shirt, "running through the halls and attracting attention to yourself by shouting for someone who isn't even a student here might contradict that idea. I rescind my congratulations."

"You sent her in there, alone," I accused.

"I could hardly go with her," she pointed out.

"She's taking all the risk, while, what, you just hide out here and wait?" I asked, outraged.

Ford regarded me with a frown, then her mouth curved into a sneer. "She didn't tell you about this. Good for her. For that, at least, I can respect her. You are not worthy. I am relieved that she's finally seen the evidence for herself."

Leave it to Ford not to mince any words. And I hated how close to the truth she was, whether she realized it or not. And damn it, she probably did.

I gritted my teeth. "Look, it was my fault she left, and she would have told me the plan, but—"

Apparently bored already, Ford turned away from me, heading toward the handicapped stall she'd emerged from. I tensed, unwilling to trust her out of my sight.

When I ventured forward and peeked around the edge of the metal wall, she was standing on the toilet, her hand raised in front of the air vent. The screws were slowly removing themselves from each corner of the vent cover.

Then I noticed a familiar scarf, hanging from wheelchair-assistance bar by the toilet. Ariane's scarf. The one she'd purchased as part of her uniform here. It had been torn in half and twisted into two loops and tied to the bar, like restraints.

With a chill, I recalled the red and abraded skin around Ford's wrists. Ariane had bound Ford to keep her here, and now Ford was free. A knot of dread developed in my stomach.

The vent cover flew over my head, narrowly missing me, and I ducked reflexively.

"What the hell . . ." I stopped, the words drying up in

my throat, as Ford hauled a very familiar duffel bag from its hiding place in the air vent. Ariane's emergency supplies, everything she owned in the world. Her money, her memories of her father, her identity.

Ford should not have that. Ford could not be allowed to have that.

Under the guidance of Ford's power, it landed lightly on the floor, just a few feet away from me.

Acting on instinct rather than reason, I lunged for the duffel.

"No," Ford said casually, shoving me away with her mind, which, coincidentally, felt pretty much like being punched in the gut with a giant fist.

I doubled over instantly, choking on my own air and the urge to vomit.

"You . . . sent her in . . . and you're leaving," I croaked, when I could manage it. Which meant Ariane would be stuck playing Ford forever, or until Laughlin figured it out. I knew her. She wouldn't be willing to abandon Carter and Nixon to their fates.

This was not exactly the trap I'd feared, but only because I'd been too stupid to see it. I'd been so worried about Ford lying to win the competition or luring Ariane to her side, to them, away from me, I'd failed to see that there was another possibility.

That Ford was a self-involved and deranged sociopath who cared only about herself even at the expense of those she claimed to care for.

Ford hopped off the toilet and scooped up the bag as I coughed and wheezed, trying to catch my breath.

"It is not, I suppose, your fault that you are so short-sighted and dim," she said, as if attempting to be generous but not quite finding it within herself. "But my sister"—her tongue curled around the word, imbuing it with a bitterness that I could almost taste—"should know—"

She paused, her attention turning inward, her head tilting to one side as if she were hearing something I could not. "No, no," she muttered.

Seconds later, footsteps sounded in the hall outside the door. "I heard shouting," a confused male voice said nearby. "It was just a few minutes ago." An adult definitely. A teacher or staff person, probably.

If I yell for help . . . The thought flickered like lightning, there and gone almost instantly, but it was enough.

Ford glared at me and the weight of her power slammed down over my body, like being encased in a wet concrete cast, only one that poured down my throat into my lungs and through my skin into my veins. I couldn't move, couldn't speak, couldn't breathe. Sweat broke out at the back of my neck as I struggled to pull in air even though none of my muscles would cooperate.

Shadows moved outside the frosted glass window and a rustling sound followed. Someone examining the sign on the door. "Do you know anything about this?" a woman asked, a frown in her voice.

"No," the guy said. The doorknob rattled. "It's locked."

"I don't have a key for this section," the woman said with a sigh. "You know how Betty is. She who has the most keys wins." She gave a derisive snort.

"Jamie's still here. We can borrow his keys," the guy said,

sounding worried. "Just check it out to be sure."

White sparkles floated across my darkening field of vision. If they didn't leave soon, I was going to pass out or die. I suspected that Ford would have preferred the latter, even if that would give her the added chore of disposing of a body. I doubted it was anything she'd find too difficult, if not something in which she was already well versed.

The woman sighed again, but her response was unintelligible as they walked away, their steps growing fainter.

My knees gave, and Ford, sensing the change, allowed me to fall but did not release me. She knelt down next to me, rummaging in Ariane's bag until she pulled something free. My phone. The old one from Wingate.

"I do hope you said good-bye," she said conversationally, as she snapped the battery into place. "I understand that provides closure for your kind. You don't understand this now, but let me assure you that, no matter what her fate, she is better off without you. For whatever few years we have left, anyway."

Few years? What? I wanted to ask, but that would have required the ability to breathe. And right now the struggle to get oxygen was taking nearly all of my attention.

She slung the bag over her arm, tucked the phone up inside her opposite sleeve, and exited the stall with a sharp turn toward the door, her skirt flipping after her.

The click of the door closing sounded loud in the silence, but that was nothing compared to the moment when Ford's grip on me slacked. I sucked in a huge breath, sounding like a drowning man, and promptly coughed all the air out again.

My vision throbbed in time with my head, and fireworks went off in the blackness behind my eyelids.

Don't pass out. Don't pass out. That was all I could think. That and: *Breathe. Breathe. Breathe.*

As soon as I could, I hauled myself up to my feet and lurched after her, swaying sideways drunkenly as dizziness swirled over me.

I managed to get the door open only to run smack into someone. A man with round glasses wearing a sweater-vest.

He stumbled back and threw up his hands to protect himself or in anticipation of me falling. I wasn't sure. "What's going on here?"

It was the same voice I'd heard before outside the door. The teacher who'd heard shouting and wanted to check the bathroom.

"I was . . ." My brain stuttered to a halt before a spark lit up in a distant region and connected two pieces of information. "I thought I heard shouting. I was going for help." I sounded ridiculously hoarse, and my eyes were watering like I'd inhaled a noseful of pepper.

He squinted at me suspiciously, a thick ring of keys still in his hand despite our collision. "How did you get in?"

On firmer ground now but fighting the urge to collapse, I shook my head and tried to feign confusion. "It was unlocked."

"Is there anyone else in there?" he demanded.

"I . . ." Was it better to say yes, so he'd go in and I could leave? Or better to say no, so he wouldn't suspect anything? But he already suspected something.

My mind bumbled through these machinations far, far too slowly.

His mouth pinched in. "Stay here," he ordered as he pushed past me into the bathroom.

Yeah, right.

Struggling not to feel like I was dying, I limped and coughed my way toward the nearest exit and found myself on the side of the building.

No sign of Ford.

I jogged, or as close to it as I could come, to the front of the building, expecting to see the taillights of the van pulling away with Ford at the wheel.

But the van, weirdly enough, was still there. I hurried over, not sure what I'd actually do if I caught up with her—other than, you know, die—but the van was as empty and abandoned looking as it had been when I'd checked before.

I sagged back against the sun-warmed metal, my legs shaky. I suppose Ford could have just taken another vehicle—lack of keys wasn't exactly an obstacle for her—but the parking lot was dead. No cars coming or going at the moment. So where had she gone?

It was as if she'd vanished into thin air. But that wasn't possible. As far as I knew.

Lowering myself to the ground, I tried to think, so much harder now than ever before. Not just because of my oxygen deprivation but because I felt like I was playing at a level way above my head.

Ford was gone. And Ariane was trapped at Laughlin's facility, even if she didn't realize it yet. And Quinn, I couldn't forget about him, being tortured at GTX. What would Dr. Jacobs do with him if Ariane wasn't at the meeting point? I had no idea, and I didn't want to find out.

So . . . what the hell was I supposed to do now?

Assaulting Laughlin's stronghold was out of the question, and so was just walking in, obviously.

My brain spun through various scenarios, each as improbable and fantastic as the last.

I pounded my fist into my leg. I'd tried to warn Ariane. But she'd wanted to believe them so badly.

And sitting here now, the perfectly paved asphalt burning through the fabric of my pants to my skin, I could think of only one thing to do. A single action that might stop Ford and save Ariane.

Maybe.

But Ariane . . . oh God, Ariane would never, ever forgive me, and that was if it even worked.

I pulled my phone, the anonymous one Ariane and I had bought together, from my pocket. The sunlight reflecting off the screen slashed at my eyes.

If I did this, Ariane might never be free again. And I would have to live with that. Live with never seeing her again. Live with knowing that she hated me.

But I could feel the seconds ticking away even as I wrestled with the idea. The longer I waited, the farther away Ford got and the less likely Ariane would ever make it out of Laughlin's alive.

The memory of Quinn screaming in the video resurfaced in my mind, only to be replaced by an image of Ariane, held down and screaming, while scientists in white coats and surgical masks cut away pieces of her flesh.

I couldn't . . . I just couldn't.

With fingers fumbling and numb despite the heat, I pulled up the browser on my phone and typed in what I was looking for.

The phone number popped up instantly. All innocent, blue on the white background, just like if I'd been searching for a pizza place or dentist. Rather than the person who would determine the fate of the girl I loved.

I took a deep breath, pressed the link, and then lifted the phone to my ear with a shaking hand.

Oh God, Ariane, I'm sorry.

"Good afternoon, this is GenTex Labs. How may I direct your call?" a perky-sounding woman chirped almost instantly.

For one crazy second, I thought about saying, "Connect me to the secret lab in the basement. You know, the one with all the alien experiments."

What would the cheery and completely unaware receptionist say to that?

But there was no point in stirring up that kind of trouble and no time to waste. "Dr. Arthur Jacobs, please," I said, and because I was suddenly so weary of fighting, I added, "Tell him it's Zane Bradshaw calling." That, if nothing else, might get his attention.

The sharp intake of breath on the other end of the phone told me that the receptionist was, perhaps, not as ignorant as I'd assumed. Someone had told her I might be calling. I wondered if Ariane's name was on the list. Or my mom's.

My mom. Had she felt this torn and sickened when she'd realized what Dr. Jacobs was really up to at GTX? When she'd seen Ariane huddled in her cell and made the choice to keep working there, in the hope that something good would come out of it?

Suddenly, I could see new shades of gray in her decision, ones I'd been blind to before.

"Uh, just a moment, please," the GTX receptionist said with barely repressed excitement.

I hated her for a second then, that anonymous voice on the other end of the phone.

While I waited, hold music played. And then ads for GTX Community Outreach, their community service division. *Serving Wingate; it's our hometown too.*

It made me want to throw up.

"The youngest Mr. Bradshaw," Dr. Jacobs said, after a few moments, in a fake hearty tone. "To what do I owe the—"

"Stop. Just stop." Resisting the urge to hurl the phone away from me, I clenched it so hard in my fist that the plastic cover cracked. "We both know exactly what's going on here." I paused. "Actually, that's not true. I know what's going on. You don't."

There was a significant pause on Jacobs's end. "What can I do for you, Zane?" His tone was cool, curious, but not unduly so. As if that would fool me anymore.

I leaned my head against my knees. "I think Ariane's in trouble."

"What happened?" he asked sharply, all pretense of casualness gone.

And with bile rising in my throat, I told him everything, finding my mom, how she'd been tricked into working for Laughlin, and meeting the hybrids. How they were supposedly controlled, Ariane's plan to free them—or as much of it as I knew—and how Ford had broken loose, which meant Ariane was stuck pretending to be Ford.

"So, she's in Laughlin's facility now, you say," Dr. Jacobs said. His voice had taken on a peculiar echo. He'd probably put me on speakerphone so someone else could hear.

I didn't care. Now that I'd done it, now that I'd crossed

this line, I wanted him to do whatever needed to be done to get Ariane out of there.

"Pretending to be Ford, yes," I said.

"And the other one," he said with disdain, "this Ford—"

"She was here at Linwood Academy, but she's gone now."

"Where?" This was an unfamiliar male voice. One of the spectators in Dr. Jacobs's office. Perhaps the new head of security now that Mark Tucker was no longer around.

"I don't know," I admitted.

"Zane—" Dr. Jacobs began.

I cut him off before he could give me whatever litany of excuses he had prepared. "She has my old phone," I said. "She put the battery in. She's going to make a call, if she hasn't already." I had no idea who Ford would be calling, but regardless, it was a stupid move, using my phone. Unless, of course, she wanted people (GTX, Laughlin, God only knew who else) to chase after her. But I couldn't figure out why that would be.

There was a flurry of unidentifiable activity on the other end. I pictured black-clad GTX retrieval teams loading up with weapons and pouring out the door.

"So, if we can track her down, you're suggesting we attempt a trade?" Dr. Jacobs asked.

"No," I snapped. "I'm suggesting a hostage exchange, since neither one of them has any choice in the matter, thanks to you and your douche bag friends."

I grimaced, remembering belatedly that I was, in fact, sort of, in a twisted way, asking him for a favor. "And my brother, you'll let him go too," I added, though it lacked the force and conviction of my earlier outburst.

Another long pause. "I'm not sure what you're talking about," Dr. Jacobs said carefully. "But if there's a situation involving Quinn, I'd be happy to look into it."

Bastard.

Someone in the background murmured then, and there was a loud rustling noise. Covering the speaker so I couldn't hear, perhaps?

"Stay where you are, Zane," he said a moment later, his voice sharp with tension and more than a hint of eagerness. "We'll have someone there in forty-five minutes. Less, perhaps."

Greasy relief welled up at his reassurance, and I hated myself even more.

"Or my betrayal is free?" I laughed bitterly.

"You're doing the right thing," Dr. Jacobs said with a calm certainty. "She doesn't belong out there in the world. It's too dangerous."

"For you or for her?" I asked wearily. I wanted to cry, but everything in me felt dried up and empty.

"I know you think I'm a cruel man," he said, "but I'm just trying to protect—"

I hung up before I could hear the end of that lie. It was the same one I was telling myself.

Ariane would rather die than go back to GTX. I knew that. She'd told me as much.

But I couldn't just let that happen. Alive and in a cage was better than dead. To me, at least.

So because of my weakness, I'd taken away her choice, making me no better than Dr. Jacobs.

Just as she'd said.

CHAPTER 21

|||■■ || | | | |■■| |■|| |■ |■■| |

Ariane

Under other circumstances, I might have been fascinated—and horrified—by the differences in life at Laughlin's facility. I'd never imagined that anything could make me look upon my experiences at GTX with something that vaguely resembled fondness.

From what I could tell, Ford and the others had very little by way of possessions, beyond strategy manuals, weapon instructions, and books like *The Art of War*. There was a stack of magazines on a table to the side of their cubbies, but they all seemed to date from the last year, starting probably right around the time Dr. Laughlin had decided they needed to be "humanized." Maybe Carter's iPad served the purpose of additional entertainment/acclimation to human culture, but I was willing to bet that he'd acquired that technology only upon starting at Linwood. And neither Ford nor Nixon seemed to have one—by their choice or Laughlin's, I wasn't sure.

And to make it worse, where I'd been left to my own devices except when being tested, creating an illusion of free will, their schedule was strictly regimented.

Exactly ten minutes after our return from school, Nixon and Carter had begun to change clothes, and I had to scramble to follow suit, careful to keep my back—and the GTX tattoo on it—against the wall. There was no privacy. And no room allowed for my hesitation. Clearly, this was their usual postschool routine.

For precisely one hour, Nixon, Carter, and I ran on treadmills in a smaller room down the hall. Then there was another hour of battle simulation in a different room, one equipped with a large projector and screen, technology that was evidently intended to allow us to run through "real" scenarios. It mostly involved ducking and covering behind simulated corners and using our abilities to strip mock humans of weapons before they could fire on us. Once I got the hang of it, I did well enough to keep up, but I had no idea how Ford normally fared. I hoped that, if she was the reigning champ, anyone monitoring would think Ford was just having an off day.

After that, three-minute showers in the completely exposed bathroom unit in their quarters. (I'd kept my gaze glued to the tile wall to avoid seeing Carter and Nixon, and I'd worn my workout T-shirt in to keep my GTX mark covered. It didn't matter if Ford didn't usually do that; I'd had no choice.)

It was now 5:47 P.M., and we were sitting down at the small table in their room with meal trays filled with some unidentifiable paste, brought in during our absence.

I was exhausted but jittery with adrenaline. Because this was it, the moment of—well, not truth, but massive deception. According to Ford, Dr. David Laughlin visited during their dinner every night. At 5:45. Knowledge of that visit and its timing was integral to our plan.

Which was actually very simple. Laughlin and Jacobs—and maybe Emerson St. John too, though who knew?—were all so busy trying to eavesdrop on one another and plant spies in the other organizations, we were going to use that against them.

I was here as Ford. And Ford, as me, would use Zane's phone to make a call. It didn't matter to whom. Just so the call registered with whatever cell tower was nearby. Dr. Jacobs was surely monitoring the phone and would mobilize to track "me" down. But Laughlin, with his informants in place within GTX, would also likely hear about the call almost immediately afterward. And he'd be unable to resist the temptation—or so I hoped—to gather up his men and snatch "me" out from his careless competitor's nose, especially since "I" was so close, practically in his backyard. Thus providing a substantial distraction that would focus everyone's attention elsewhere and allow me enough time/freedom to get into Laughlin's office and back out, undetected.

There were only two tricky parts to this equation. Ford had to lead them on a merry chase but not actually get caught. If she did, this would likely end in a stalemate, which would not help us. Plus, I needed Ford to be back at the school by tomorrow morning so I could hand off the Quorosene and we could switch back, without anyone the wiser. Then they could disappear at the first opportunity available for the three of them and I could vanish with Zane. At least until we knew for sure that the trials had been canceled.

All of that meant the timing for our distraction—the phone call that would lead them to pursue Ford as me—was crucial. Ford had suggested, then, that it needed to be the end of the day, when there were fewer people on staff, and after Dr. Laughlin's daily check in with his own hybrids. We couldn't risk him coming back unexpectedly.

But Dr. Laughlin was now two minutes late.

It took everything I had to keep my leg from jouncing beneath the table. I wanted to ask Carter if it was normal for him to be late, but I couldn't, of course.

It didn't matter, though. Given what I'd seen of their clockwork schedule, I suspected a two-minute discrepancy was significant. In the back of my head, a voice screamed, "CAUGHT!" over and over again.

Had Ford accidentally started her distraction too soon? The timing on this plan had to be precise, a fact I'd emphasized repeatedly, much to her annoyance. But she'd seemed to understand. Or so I'd thought.

Against my will, I glanced up at the case in the hall bearing her name. Who knew what she was thinking or what she would do with that kind of threat hanging over her head? The niggling possibility that she'd simply walked away, taking my money and ID, wouldn't leave me alone. Although that wouldn't explain Dr. Laughlin's tardiness.

I shifted restlessly in my seat before I could stop myself.

Carter, catching my gaze, shook his head. I wasn't sure if he was trying to tell me to hold still or not to worry. Either way, it wasn't helping. I felt like a mouse with my teeth sunk into a suspiciously convenient piece of cheese, waiting only for the sudden rush of air and the crack of a metal bar on my neck.

A dull ache in my stomach started, and I was pretty sure it was only partially due to the protein paste I was forcing myself to choke down.

When Dr. Laughlin finally bustled through the open doorway, his lab coat flapping behind him, it startled me. I'd already grown used to looking up to find the hallway empty.

David Laughlin was, I realized with distaste, both younger and more attractive than the grainy photographs Zane and I had found online. His cheekbones had hollows beneath them in that fashionable manner, and his hair was highlighted with auburn streaks that were not the work of nature. Beneath his lab coat, which looked more like a fashion accessory, he wore an expensive-looking shirt with heavy cuff links and suit pants with a precise crease down the front. He was every bit the public persona he'd presented to the newspapers and other media organizations.

Two assistants—beautiful women in dark, tailored suits—trailed after him, tablet computers in hand, as if he might drop a word here or there and they would need to record it to ensure that it wasn't lost to history.

It took everything I had to maintain what I hoped to be a relaxed but attentive expression. It would have been no problem for me to pretend in GTX with Dr. Jacobs. I was used to that. But here, in unfamiliar surroundings with unpredictable strangers, I could feel myself tensing up.

"Good evening, children!" he said, in a cultured British accent. I'd known he wasn't American, but it was still startling to hear him. It reminded me, once again, how big this conspiracy was, how many people were involved. It wasn't just my small hometown in Wisconsin.

He clapped his hands together with a sound like a shot. "How was your day?"

Carter, the designated spokesperson, gave the same answer before. "Within acceptable parameters, sir."

Without warning or even so much as a response to Carter, Laughlin turned to me.

"I understand you made a new friend at school today. A human. Would you care to explain that to me?" he inquired, the casual lift of his brow making it seem as though this was a matter of simple curiosity rather than the start of my undoing.

My breath caught in my chest. *Crap.* The nosy teacher who'd caught Zane and me sneaking in. Ford hanging out with a regular student, without Nixon or Carter in sight, would definitely have struck him as strange, and he must have reported me to someone here. Probably as ordered.

I waited, praying for one of the bookend assistants to look up wide-eyed from her tablet and tug at Dr. Laughlin's sleeve, or for lights to flash and alarms to sound. Something to indicate that Ford was following through on her part of our arrangement.

But nothing happened. And the seconds ticking by between Laughlin's question and my lack of an answer were creating a gap that would soon be impossible to cross.

Across the table, Carter's knuckles went white where he clutched his spoon, and even Nixon's posture seemed stiffer than usual.

I needed to do something right now.

I took a breath and did my best to channel Ford. "You know the teachers there. Always eager to create reports on us that will generate your favor. And your money." The heavy disdain in my voice, I realized, was probably a little more Rachel Jacobs than Ford's more flat affect, but here was hoping Laughlin wouldn't notice.

A troubled frown creased Dr. Laughlin's otherwise unlined forehead.

No, no, no. Don't frown. Don't question. I am Ford, who else would I be? I sent the thoughts at Laughlin, though I knew he couldn't hear me.

"Of course. I suspected as much. That is unfortunate, though. I was hoping that Mara's immersion therapy was beginning to work. Carter here is looking like a better and better choice for the trials." He tilted his head sideways, watching for my reaction.

I stared at him, much as I imagined Ford would have, letting the unexpressed hate shine through my eyes behind the otherwise impassive mask of my face. That wasn't hard for me.

Laughlin nodded appreciatively. "That will serve you well, assuming I allow you to live."

He wasn't worried or fearful. Nor did he seem to have any doubt in his control over us. Say what you will, Dr. Jacobs had always had a cautious and healthy respect for what I was capable of.

By contrast, Laughlin was so certain that their need for the Quorosene protected him, he took chances that were foolish to say the least. Then again, he had no way of knowing

that one of his hybrids had been replaced by an undomesti-
cated substitute. Killing him now would mean blowing my
cover—probably trapping the three of us in here forever or
getting us "eliminated"—so it was a no-go.

But still . . .

I watched as he seated himself on the table, dipped his
finger in Nixon's remaining protein paste, and placed it in
his mouth, making a face at the taste.

"That is bloody awful, isn't it?" he said with laugh, wiping his hand on Nixon's sleeve. The assistants gave a polite
titter, Laughlin's devoted audience. "Have to try it every once
in a while to remind myself."

Nixon, for his part, was unmoved and unreadable as ever.
But he was in there, in his head. He wasn't an empty vessel.
He'd squeezed my hand in the car.

The arrogance of that man. Beneath the table, I curled my
hands into fists, feeling my fingernails bite into my palms. I
wanted badly to show Laughlin exactly how weak and break-
able he really was.

But that wouldn't solve our problem. Not yet, anyway.

Dr. Laughlin stayed for several more minutes, asking
Carter questions and pointedly ignoring me. I suspected that
tactic was designed to make me, Ford, worry about my fate.
But instead, it simply pissed me off. Made me even more
determined to see him fall.

His whole visit lasted less than ten minutes. Then he left,
as suddenly as he'd arrived, his coat flapping behind him and
the two assistants trailing.

Watching him walk away, I felt hope draining out of me,
like a cup with a leak. He'd arrived late, but he'd arrived,

with seemingly no agitation or concern at events that might have occurred just before his visit. And while he'd been here, there'd been no sign whatsoever of Ford's planned distraction.

I swallowed hard, my mouth gritty with paste and panic. Zane had been right.

Now what?

Now what? Now what? Now what? The phrase pounded in my head like a drumbeat as Nixon, Carter, and I pushed away from the table and returned to our bunks.

Carter attempted to make contact in Morse code again.

"She's loyal. We are one. She would no more betray us than she would cut off her own arm. . . ."

Maybe it was just me, but his tapping sounded more desperate than before. And I couldn't help thinking again about a mouse caught in a trap. Some of them were known to chew off limbs to escape.

I tuned out the rest of whatever Carter was saying. I needed to think.

My heart was a panicked animal trapped behind my ribs, trying to beat its way free.

Don't panic. Breathe. Staring up at the smooth green plastic over my head, I concentrated on my inhales and exhales until a measure of calm descended.

I had two choices. One, if I could pass the night without being detected as a counterfeit, I could get back to Linwood tomorrow and sneak out. Through the bathroom window, perhaps. It would be more difficult without Ford to take her place again and with the guards watching.

But what good would that do? Ford might be gone, but the competition was still on. Laughlin would simply send

Carter in her place. And God only knew what he would do to Nixon as punishment.

Dr. Jacobs would still be looking for me. And Dr. Laughlin would have a serious grudge, once he figured out what we'd done. Or rather, what we'd attempted before Ford broke ranks.

What hope did I have of avoiding them both forever? I was willing to bet that even if GTX had to forfeit the trials to Laughlin Integrated—no, especially if they had to forfeit—Dr. Jacobs would continue to look for me.

My second option, my only true choice, was to get the trials canceled, as planned.

I felt my heart flutter with anxiety again, but I ignored it, forcing myself to calculate.

My biggest advantage: I was inside Laughlin's facility, undetected. For the moment. It was, as I'd told Zane, a one-time opportunity.

Ford's distraction had been intended only to cause confusion and pull focus away from Nixon, Carter, and me long enough for me to slip deeper into the facility.

I didn't have that luxury anymore. But maybe I didn't need it. I knew from Mara that Ford and the others had previously used loopholes in Laughlin's commands to slip outside the facility and stalk Mara. For example, Laughlin may have told Ford to go to her quarters, but he didn't say stay. Or how long to stay, even. She just couldn't leave permanently. And rather than punishing her for finding these gaps, he'd seemed amused by them, if Mara's telling of it was in any way accurate. He'd altered their orders at some point, obviously, because the stalking had stopped.

But how many people here knew that? Would someone watching question my wandering the halls, especially if I didn't try to leave the facility? The distraction had been intended to address this concern, but maybe I could do it without that.

Laughlin was so certain of his control, so sure that Ford and the others wouldn't challenge him because they needed what he had. Did others have the same faith in his power?

I'd seen no signs otherwise.

I bit my lip and immediately released it, figuring that would not be a Ford move.

The final and largest issue was simply, was it worth the risk to try?

No! My human side shrieked. *Just stay here and hope for the best.*

But that nonhuman part of me had run the odds and gave the equivalent of a shrug. *It depends on what you value more: the slim possibility of permanent freedom or the certainty of a few final days.*

You'd get a chance to find Zane to apologize, to tell him you were wrong. To spend those hours together.

True. But what good were those hours when we both knew the end was coming and it would be ugly? Jacobs would find me, and any chance of a life would be gone. Then I would have to do anything and everything he said, just to keep him from using Zane as "motivation."

The certainty of that impending doom would color my last encounters with Zane, assuming he would even accept my apology and want to spend time with me. It would be misery with every breath counted, every second ticking away on a clock neither of us could see. And when fate caught up with us in the form of a GTX retrieval team, who knew what would happen? I couldn't guarantee Zane's safety unless I surrendered willingly, which went against every unnaturally fragile bone in my body.

I looked to my right and the curved wall only inches from my face.

Carter had given up trying to signal a few minutes ago, after my lack of response.

I could only imagine what he was feeling, abandoned by Ford and ignored by me. He and Nixon had both taken a chance, and neither one of them had done anything to deserve this result.

I turned on my side and started tapping out my new plan, quickly and quietly.

You'd think with all the experience I'd had blending in, pretending to belong, that wandering the halls as Ford would have been easy.

After all, I didn't even have to pretend to be human this time.

But my whole body was shaking, particularly as I passed through the gallery. It took every bit of self-control I had to keep from stopping to stare and mourn.

I stuffed down the human emotions rioting in my head—
Look, do you see what's going to become of you? Why couldn't you just wait? You would have been free tomorrow—and kept moving, the clear and analytical voice of my alien side a welcoming presence.

According to Carter, the Quorosene was kept locked in

a safe in Laughlin's office, both of which they were strictly forbidden to approach unaccompanied. From the layout Ford had quickly described at the school, Laughlin's office was aboveground, on the fourth floor. I had to find my way out of the maze and to an elevator that was somewhere near the doors to the parking garage.

So the security team monitors would, most likely, be expecting me to slip outside to further torture Mara or whatever other nefarious errands Ford had devised on her various field trips before Laughlin restricted them to the facility. (Speaking of which, how exactly had she managed all of that? Had she stolen a car? Managed to get Carter and Nixon on a bus? I had no idea, and all of the possibilities seemed equally unfathomable.) They would not be expecting me to approach his office. Which, I hoped, meant it would catch them off-guard and scrambling.

Or it might mean that they'd jump all over the panic button the second I headed for the elevator.

The cameras above my head, scanning the hallway with a faint mechanized whir, felt like living, breathing beings, watching over my shoulder and tracking my every move.

The good news was that, as Ford had predicted, after Laughlin's evening visit almost everyone had left. I passed two white coats who were too busy arguing over something to even give me more than a glance. I suppose that, unlike GTX, the sight of Ford and the others moving through the halls wasn't uncommon. The door on their room didn't even lock.

Still, moving quickly as I could, without looking suspicious, was imperative. I didn't want to get caught in the middle of a security shift change or something. Ford had said this time of evening was best for the attempt to reach Laughlin's office. With no other information to go on, I had to trust that she was right in that, at least. But the sooner I was back in the hybrid room, the better.

Finally, dozens of bad paintings and fake trees later, I found myself at the double doors to the garage.

I didn't so much as pause, passing the doors and then making a sharp left when the hallway ended. To hesitate in this instance might truly mean death. Anyone watching had to believe I was acting under orders.

The elevators were where Ford had indicated they would be.

I pressed the button, UP my only option, my finger slippery on the plastic, and it lit up immediately.

Watching the numbers glow above the metal doors in descending order, I was reminded of the last time I'd been waiting on an elevator and trembling with nerves.

It had only been a few days, but it felt like years ago that Zane, Rachel, and I sneaked out of GTX. Well, sneaked out of the lab part. We'd most assuredly gotten caught before crossing the threshold outside.

Maybe it was the memory of that moment, but when the bell chimed gently, signaling the elevator's arrival, I stepped to one side.

The doors rolled open, but no one burst out. No demands for me to "Hold still and do not resist" emerged.

When I peeked around the corner, the space was empty except for a brightly colored poster on the wall advocating the necessity of a flu shot, and quiet but for the buzzing of the fluorescent bulbs overhead.

I stepped in and pressed 4. No special key or key card required, which was good because Ford hadn't prepped me for that.

Then again, perhaps security would be that much tighter on the actual floor.

I braced myself, preparing to fight. Even if I was confronted, I might have a chance if they weren't ready for me. Uncontrolled, unconnected me. Ford, Carter, and Nixon were so interconnected that that had to work against them in situations like this. I wanted to save Carter and Nixon, yes, but I didn't know what it was to *feel* someone else die. That fear had to slow their responses. There were three of them, which made them three times as vulnerable. I was risking only myself. As much as I'd hated being alone—one of a kind, lonely and isolated—it was a saving grace in this situation. The more people to whom you were attached, the greater your exposure.

I thought briefly of Zane and then pushed him from my head, the ache in my chest too distracting right now.

The doors rolled back, revealing nothing more sinister than a swath of pristine white carpet. A few feet beyond that, the main part of the floor was open in the center, making it like a balcony that overlooked the floor below. A glass half wall encircled the opening to the lower level.

I stepped out cautiously and looked down. A few people still scurried among the cubicles, not even stopping to chat. Of course, it must have felt like the boss was standing over them, watching.

And, in effect, he was. Directly across from me was a giant glass box filled with black leather and steel furniture. Laughlin's office. Had to be.

And it was empty. Even the two desks in front of the door—belonging to the twin assistants who'd been following him around, probably—had been abandoned. The chairs were pushed in, the computers dark.

Closing my eyes, I focused, listening for thoughts and emotions near me. But with all the people a level below, it was difficult to hear anything.

The elevator doors closed behind me with a thunk that sounded horribly loud. No one appeared to be on this floor right now, but it would take only one person on the third floor looking up at just the wrong moment. Ford hadn't mentioned that part of this gig. Then again, it occurred to me right now that perhaps she'd never actually been in Laughlin's office. That all of her information had been gleaned secondhand, from the minds of humans around her or even schematics pulled from somewhere.

Great.

Wishing I'd found a lab coat lying around to throw over my distinctly nonoffice clothes, I inched forward, keeping away from the glass half wall and moving as smoothly as possible.

Running would draw attention. And so would looking sneaky.

Head up, shoulders straight. Don't look down. Funny that the instructions sounded pretty much like I was crossing a rope bridge over a bottomless gorge. Felt that way too. One wrong move and the end would rush up quickly.

I'd never seen the inside of Dr. Jacobs's office, but Laughlin's screamed arrogant male. Everything was stark contrasts and sharp lines.

Choking on the overwhelming scent of new leather,

something I'd associated with positive things—new shoes, bags, and car interiors—until today, I pushed forward into the office.

I was halfway into the room before I realized the obvious problem, something I should have picked up on much faster.

Glass walls. On all four sides. No wall safe. It wasn't possible.

My stomach sinking, I turned in a small circle, checking for other obvious options. A floor safe was always a possibility, I supposed. Or maybe something built into the desk.

I skirted the chrome and leather sofa that looked more like Mars landing equipment than someplace to sit, and stepped behind the desk.

In the second drawer, I scored. The drawer was a front that pulled away revealing a safe. Digital code with thumbprint authorization.

Uh-oh. Nobody'd mentioned that. Not that it was a problem. I could get through both of them, but it would take more time.

Unless . . . if the thumbprint scanner was a redundant system, more like a secondary lock than an alarm, then maybe I could bypass it.

I focused on the tumblers I knew had to be within the door. I hadn't ever seen this model of safe, so I had to hope that the ones I'd practiced on during my years with my father would be close enough. (Apparently cat burglar was a backup career plan if "normal human" didn't work out.)

After several long sweaty moments on my part, the tumblers clicked into place.

Success!

I pulled the heavy safe door open hurriedly, the hinges moving without so much as a squeak.

There was a sudden blur of motion and what felt like a bite on my skin.

I fumbled, lifting a rapidly numbing arm, to find something sticking out of my neck. Something I recognized by feel, if nothing else.

With shaking fingers, I pulled the dart out.

I twisted around to look for a guard, even as my already slowing thought process reminded me the dart had come from the front.

My center of gravity shifted abruptly, and I fell sideways with no ability to stop myself. It was like being trapped in an oversize bag of sand, my body the sand and my consciousness a speck within it.

As I toppled, I caught a glimpse of the safe's interior. No bottles or packets of pills. The safe was, in fact, empty but for a device similar to the tranquilizer guns I'd seen Dr. Jacobs's security team use.

It was a trap. Laughlin had somehow known I was coming. The desertion of this floor and no one challenging my approach had not just been luck.

Ford. I felt a hot spark of fury and fought to hold on to it, to breathe life into it, but it slipped away from me, growing dimmer under the onslaught of the drugs.

Seconds later—or perhaps minutes, it was hard to tell—I heard the soft shush of footsteps on the carpet.

Laughlin stood over me. His sharply angled face, upside down, appeared an odd collection of parts, triangles, lines, and squares rather than a whole.

"I thought one of them would figure out a way to try for it someday," he mused, as if this was an academic dilemma finally resolved. "Of course, I wasn't expecting it be *you*, 107. That's what they call you, isn't it?" He leaned down closer to me, his gaze cold and calculating.

"When the school called earlier, I wasn't sure. It did strike me as a large coincidence that my Ford would begin associating with humans on the same day we learned you were missing, but unlike the others, Ford can be . . . unpredictable. One of her finer qualities, actually. I wanted to see what she was up to."

He reached down and tapped the end of my nose in what would have been an affectionate gesture from almost anyone else but instead felt like a creepy signal of ownership, a dismissal of my right to exist as an independent entity. "But you, my darling, made a mistake," he said in a gentle scolding tone. "I could, perhaps, believe that Ford had chosen this point to make her final stand against me. I might even have been willing to believe that she'd found a way to fracture the bond with the others that she seems to hold so dear. But Ford knows there's only one way this can end. And she wouldn't have bothered with coming here for the Quorosene in that case. She would have simply destroyed herself and the others. The ultimate power play." He shook his head, twisted affection and reluctant admiration playing across his handsome face.

"But don't worry," he added, patting my shoulder. "Operations are already under way to recover Ford from whatever hole she's scampered into."

So Ford *had* betrayed us? Or . . . had I simply messed

up and revealed myself? I couldn't tell for sure from what Laughlin had said, and, frankly, at the moment I didn't actually care.

I wanted to scream, to choke Laughlin, to stop his heart. For the first time in my life, I was certain I could have killed without regret. But I couldn't gather the focus; it was like falling downhill. I couldn't stop the momentum of the drugs or their effects.

White sparkles mixed with dark spots in my vision. I was disappearing down a long, dark tunnel.

But I wasn't so far gone that I missed the slow smile that slid across his face. "In the meantime, you and I will have a chance to spend some quality time together," he said softly.

I would have shivered if I could.

"The pictures really don't do you justice, you know." He touched my cheek, smoothed my hair, and every nerve in my body shrieked in muted outrage. "I've wanted to do a true comparison, to really understand the differences between you and Ford. What a happy opportunity this is for me."

When my eyes finally shut and I drifted further down that tunnel, I could still feel his fingers against my skin.

CHAPTER 22

||||██ || ||||██| |█|| |█|██| |

Zane

THE PLASTIC ZIP-TIE RESTRAINTS WERE DIGGING INTO my wrists, rubbing the skin raw.

It probably would have helped if I could have stopped pacing the tiny and overly warm motel room, but sitting still was beyond my capability at the moment. At least my hands were bound in front of me instead of behind my back. Small favors.

I'd been stuck in here, pacing at the foot of the queen bed with its dingy flowered bedspread, for hours. But it felt like days.

Just as Dr. Jacobs had promised, a van carrying two members of a GTX retrieval team had rolled into the Linwood Academy parking lot promptly, less than half an hour after I called. They must have already been near the border. And speeding.

Even though I'd held my hands up and offered absolutely no resistance, the retrieval team guys had taken me down to the ground in a chest-crushing set of moves and bound my wrists together before hustling me into the van. From there, we'd gone to a cheap motel, not too different from the one Ariane and I had spent the night in. Except, of course, she wasn't here.

Ignoring the ache in my chest that was more than likely cracked ribs from my sudden collision with the asphalt, I counted off the ten steps to the edge of the chipped tile floor in the bathroom. And then the ten steps back to the mysterious red Tweety Bird–shaped stain near the bolted door to the outside.

The two retrieval team agents had taken up positions on either side of the room, one near the door and the other leaning against the wall next to the bathroom.

They didn't say it, but I knew they were blocking my escape routes.

Like I was going anywhere. I was waiting for the moment when the call would come, anticipating and dreading it.

Every time one of them so much as shifted toward the phone on his belt, my heart stopped.

I'd given up pestering them with questions about an hour ago. The two agents—a blond guy with a mustache and another dude with a graying buzz cut—just ignored me, though the older guy seemed annoyed with my restlessness.

Or maybe it was because moving around was only making it warmer in here, and they were wearing infinitely more layers with their bulletproof vests, heavy boots, and utility belts with every device known to mankind.

SWAT guys on private authority. Yeah, that wasn't terrifying. I wondered if they'd known Mark Tucker. If they knew about Ariane. If they knew what I'd done.

My stomach churned. But I kept pacing.

I had my back turned, heading my allowed ten paces to the bathroom, when I heard the rip of Velcro followed by a gruff "Yes?"

I spun around so swiftly that the blond agent lurched forward at me, his hands out as if to tackle me again.

"Understood," the older agent said into his phone, and I couldn't breathe for waiting.

But he said nothing more. Just hung up and tucked the phone into the designated pocket on his belt. Avoiding my gaze, he gave a curt nod to the blond guy next to me, who immediately reached out and grabbed my shoulders.

I had a flashback to every mob movie I'd ever seen. I did, after all, know too much. But what good would killing me do? Even if I told the world what I knew, who would believe me? I had no proof. And my story sounded plenty crazy enough to be a hoax, some kid looking for attention.

He shuffled me forward, as the older agent unbolted the door. We were leaving. To a hidden spot in the woods where some hunter would stumble over my body in a few months? Very possibly.

"Where are we going?" I asked, stumbling over the threshold as I tried to twist to look at them. "Did they find Ford? Did Dr. Jacobs talk to Laughlin?"

I got the same answers as before, which was to say, none. And their expressions, beneath the aviator sunglasses that seemed to be standard issue, were carefully blank.

I let them load me into the van again—as if I had a choice—as a sketchy-looking couple in a battered Crown Vic next to us stared.

Watching out the tinted window, it didn't take me more than ten or fifteen minutes to figure out we were heading north. Back to Wisconsin.

My stomach clenched with dread. What did that mean? Did they have Ariane already? Had they made the exchange? Or had they just given up? I didn't bother asking this time, knowing it was useless. Either they didn't know anything or they'd been instructed not to say anything.

Frustration at my powerlessness swelled inside me. Ariane would have been able to pick at their thoughts, to listen in and know something, anything.

I shifted in the seat, twisting my wrists around within the binding, trying to get the plastic away from my fraying skin. But everywhere it touched, it hurt.

My thoughts were in similar condition. No matter who I thought of—Ariane, Quinn, my mom—there was pain or shame or despair.

What if my GTX-provided babysitters were just driving me home? What if they'd received an all-clear signal and I was going to be dumped off at the foot of my driveway in Wingate, like nothing ever happened?

That was almost as bad as my death-in-the-woods scenario.

I'd wanted a moment, a few minutes with Ariane. A chance to explain, even though I knew it wouldn't make a difference.

But you didn't bargain for that, scolded an inner voice that sounded like a perfect replica of Ariane's.

Stay calm, be confident, and ask for more than what you want, she said in my memory. It was good advice. I wished I'd remembered it before now. It didn't take long, forty-five minutes or so, before I saw a sign welcoming us to Wisconsin. I didn't recognize these back roads; this was not the way Ariane and I had come.

We passed through several small towns, each nondescript in its small-townness—one gas station, an old brick courthouse, and a smattering of Victorian houses in various states of disrepair and peeling paint.

Until finally, after one last turn on another county highway, the van slowed.

A lake, complete with a parking area and picnic benches, seemed to spring up from nowhere on the right side. The sun was sinking into the tree line, turning the water into a brilliant orange slash of light that made my eyes water.

To my surprise, the lake was deserted, except for one guy in a bright yellow jacket fishing from a pier on the far side. The light turned him into little more than a shadow with rumpled hair.

Unlike the lake, the parking lot was quite full. A pair of black luxury SUVs on one side faced off against two black vans, identical to the one I was in.

I couldn't imagine what anyone driving by would think. The world's most depressing family reunion? A mob picnic? Maybe a lost Secret Service convoy.

But it wasn't, of course. It was GTX in the vans and Laughlin in the SUVs. And maybe, somewhere in one of them, Ariane.

I sat forward on the seat, as if that additional few inches would allow me to find her behind the tinted glass of one of the other vehicles.

We pulled into the lot and stopped, the agent placing our

van between the two lines of vehicles. Like someone about to step between two dueling parties. That couldn't be good.

My dad's SUV, dark blue and emblazoned with WINGATE CHIEF OF POLICE, was directly across from us. I could see my dad sitting stiffly in the driver's seat. He wasn't happy about this. Well, who the hell was?

For several long moments, nothing moved in the parking lot except a few dead leaves and a paper cup lifted by the breeze. Tension seemed to seep in through the van's air vents until I couldn't breathe.

At some signal I didn't see, the blond agent cut the engine, and the older one turned to me. "You're here to keep things calm during the exchange."

The exchange. So that meant Ariane was here. And so was Ford. It had worked. I felt an immediate thrill of triumph, followed by a wave of nausea. What I'd done—imprisoned Ariane with GTX, at best, or guaranteed her death in the trials, at worst—had worked. But she was alive for now. She wasn't being dissected and put on microscope slides somewhere. I had to feel relief about that, even if it was mixed with misery.

"Dr. Jacobs doesn't want it getting out of hand," the retrieval team agent continued.

I stiffened. By "it," did he mean Ariane or the situation? Either way, I wanted to shout at him, punch him. She was not an "it" and this was not some situation to be handled. This was life and death, the end of hope and the beginning of something far worse.

"You understand?" he pressed when I didn't respond.

"Yeah," I said tightly. "I get it."

"Good. Out." He reached behind himself and popped open the door closest to me.

I didn't move. "Where's my brother?" I said, my throat dry and tight with fear. But I wasn't going anywhere without him. I'd negotiated his freedom for my participation, and I may have done a shitty job of it, but I was going to get what I'd been promised.

As if he'd been expecting that, the gray-haired agent punched something into his phone.

And then the door on the van farthest from me opened and Quinn stumbled out into the open area between the vehicles, his pale skin shining with sickly sweat.

I let out a quiet breath of relief. His right arm was in a slightly larger makeshift sling than in the video, and he obviously still hadn't received medical attention. But he didn't seem any worse.

I scrambled out of the van, just as my dad stepped out of his SUV, opposite of me.

Quinn didn't seem to know where to look first. His gaze bobbed from me to my dad and then back again. He was dazed. "What are you doing here?" he asked, turning to me, his voice rusty from disuse or screaming.

Before I could answer, my mom emerged from the same van Quinn had come from, blinking in the light. She followed his path into the center and laid her hand gently on his uninjured shoulder. He didn't at all seem surprised to see her.

My heart stopped. She'd gone after him, turned herself in with the expectation of never returning. And that had worked about as well as I'd figured. She'd just given Jacobs one more hostage to work with.

Dr. Jacobs followed her, easing down from the van as though his joints hurt. His white hair was ruffled and uncombed and he looked older, as though he hadn't slept in days. But he was calm, revealing nothing in his expression. "I would prefer that all parties remain in place, obviously, until our . . . meeting is complete," he said.

I gritted my teeth. Meeting, yeah, right. He just wanted to make sure he had leverage over me, and therefore over Ariane, until the end.

"It will be safer for everyone," he added.

"Bullshit," I muttered, probably a little too loudly.

My dad glared at me before nodding at Dr. Jacobs.

Quinn, confused, looked to me. "Zane, what the hell is going on?" He stumbled over his own feet, trying to move toward me.

My mom moved swiftly, catching him by his good arm. "Just stay," she said, her gaze watchful on Dr. Jacobs. Her expression softened to something like regret when she looked at me.

I glanced away. I understood now better than ever why she'd done what she'd done, but I couldn't handle that right now. Not on top of everything else.

The passenger door on the farthest SUV opened, and Dr. Laughlin swung down to the ground. I recognized him from the pictures Ariane had found online. His dark suit was perfectly pressed, cuff links glinting at his wrists. He brushed his hair back with an impatient hand.

"Well?" he demanded. "Can we be about this already or what?"

"Hello, David," Dr. Jacobs said evenly.

"Arthur," Laughlin said with a sneer. Their history thickened the air between them. I didn't know what it was, but I could guarantee it was more than that of colleagues or even fierce competitors.

I waited, holding my breath against the expected sharp words that would trigger God only knew what.

But apparently, any nastiness that would have been dispensed was negated by the fact that they were both here against their will. Jacobs couldn't compete in the trials at all without Ariane, and clearly Laughlin wasn't willing to take his chances with one of his other hybrids. So neither one of them was coming out of this ahead of the other. No winner, no loser.

Behind Dr. Laughlin, Nixon and Carter climbed down from the vehicle, accompanied by a set of guards. The four of them made their way toward the front of the vehicle to join Laughlin, Nixon and Carter moving slowly and unsteadily as though they were in shock or drugged or something.

I frowned. Why had Dr. Laughlin brought them? Was he going to try some kind of power play, three hybrids against one? Or was he just rubbing it in Dr. Jacobs's face that he had more hybrids? Jacobs didn't look pleased, that was for sure.

A half-smothered cry drew my attention to the second SUV. Ariane was making her way slowly to the empty space between the vehicles. She appeared so small and defenseless, sandwiched between Laughlin's version of security and her hands bound in metal restraints. She wore part of her school uniform, but the long white sleeves of her shirt were smudged with dirt and splotches of blood.

My legs shook with relief and fury. They'd hurt her.

I took a step toward her without realizing it.

"No," one of her guards said, raising his weapon in my direction.

I stopped, fear shooting electricity through my veins and holding me in place. That was an M16, a military-grade weapon. Not one of the tranquilizer guns Jacobs used.

Ariane's gaze found me and locked on, but her head was lolling to one side slightly and her eyes seemed dim. They'd drugged her.

"I'm sorry," she mouthed slowly, whether to make certain I'd understand or because that was only what she was capable of in that condition, I didn't know.

I shook my head, blinking rapidly to keep from crying. She shouldn't apologize to me. I was the one who'd done this.

On the other side, doors on the second GTX van opened and Ford, sagging in similar restraints, was tugged out by a GTX retrieval team, with another team immediately behind them as backup.

The two groups, Ariane and Ford with their accompanying guards, inched toward each other.

It might have been fine—well, as fine as it could have been in that situation, meaning that Ariane would have been returned to GTX and Ford to Laughlin without more fuss than had already been generated. But as they drew even with each other, Ariane staring holes through Ford, blaming her without words, Ford suddenly straightened up in her restraints.

"You accuse me, but it was your human who called them on us," she hissed at Ariane, but it carried across the silent parking lot like a shout. "He told them where I was."

Ariane's gaze shot to me, hurt and shock making her eyes look even larger in her pale face.

"She was leaving," I said. "Taking your bag with her."

"Because he'd given away my hiding place, shouting for you and drawing the humans," Ford snapped. "I was meant to provide a distraction."

I stopped, my next words caught in my throat, horror washing over me. Was it possible? Had that been part of their plan?

"He sent them after me," Ford said, jerking her head toward Dr. Jacobs and the GTX vans. "They were already searching the area before I even had a chance to make the call. They tracked it and me before I could get away."

"If you were working with Ariane, then why were you tied up?" I demanded but weakly. I was so afraid she was right.

"To keep her from following," Ariane said, her words thick, and tears rolled down her cheeks, leaving shiny white tracks. "They are a unit. We couldn't risk that the network between them would pull her along."

She and Ford switched places, their security shuffling around them, and I stumbled back a step, my stomach pitching violently, hot acid rising in my throat. *I'd* done this. Oh my God. It was even worse than I'd thought.

"Yes, it is," Ford hissed. "Thank you for that, human."

"Oh, for heaven's sake," Laughlin said in exasperation, as Ford and Ariane cleared the center of the open space. "The fault lies with all of you for even trying. You should have known better."

Then, in a smooth motion that I didn't see coming, he removed the sidearm from the security member nearest him and fired it at Nixon's head.

I jerked at the noise, instinctively hunching against it.

The hybrid stiffened and fell to the ground, followed immediately by Carter and Ford.

Ariane froze, and my mom gave a barely muffled scream. Chaos erupted then, guards rushing in on all sides and everyone yelling.

"Stand back! Nobody move!" That seemed to come from one of the guards, but I couldn't tell which one, or even which side he was on.

"Welcome back, Ford," Laughlin said in a bitter but triumphant tone. But Ford, lying on the asphalt, gave no sign of consciousness, let alone hearing him, and Ariane remained locked in place, the shock holding her still.

"Is that really necessary, David?" Dr. Jacobs shouted. "We're trying not to attract attention—"

"What kind of game are you people running?" my dad demanded, his voice booming above the fray.

"Showmanship is part of it. You've never understood that," Laughlin snapped, handing the weapon back to his guard.

"—but you always have to have the big dramatic moment," Jacobs continued.

"Form a perimeter, maintain visual contact on the subjects," another security team member barked.

Ariane gave a low, keening cry, swaying where she stood.

A strange electrified feeling slid over my skin, and the hair on my arms stood on end. Then the headlights on all the assorted vehicles began to flicker.

Oh shit.

"Ariane?" I ventured, moving closer. But she didn't seem to hear me, her head cocked to one side as she took in the sight before her. I could see only bits and pieces between all the security team members as they moved.

A flash of white and blue that was Ford, still in her school uniform, on the ground. The red that was slowly spreading from around Nixon's collapsed form. Carter's pale hand flung forward, as if he'd tried to reach out for Nixon even as he fell.

"Stay back!" one of Laughlin's guards shouted at me, aiming his weapon my way.

My heart leaped into my throat, almost choking me as I raised my hands instinctively.

"Leave him alone," Ariane said, without even looking back.

A series of loud pops sounded, followed by the delicate rain of glass on the ground. All the windows breaking out.

"Zane!" my mom shrieked, and through the crowd I could see her waving me forward even as she shoved Quinn toward my dad's vehicle.

But I couldn't move, frozen in place by the sight of Ariane. Small and vulnerable, even though she was powerful beyond measure, being surrounded by the black-clad security forces from both companies.

This was it. I was going to watch Ariane die from a hundred different wounds, shot by those who were too afraid to understand. She couldn't stop all of them. There was no way.

"Wait, please," I shouted at the guards.

"Stand down," Jacobs screamed at them, his face turning a dangerous shade of reddish purple.

Just outside the circle of guards surrounding Ariane, Ford pushed herself to her feet, unnoticed by everyone but me, it seemed. They were all too busy focusing on Ariane.

I held my breath, not sure whether to shout a warning or to keep my mouth shut.

Ford reached out with her bound hands and flicked the closest clump of guards away from Ariane with an easy gesture. It seemed at first that she was trying to help Ariane, but as soon as she started toward Laughlin, her steps slow and shuffling at first, then growing stronger, her intent became clear.

The SUV closest to me suddenly rocked on its wheels and then flew backward, end over end into the lake, as if it had been flicked away by a giant invisible hand. I stared at the sudden waves lapping at the shore and making the fishing piers shudder, as the SUV slowly took on water.

Ford or Ariane? Which one of them was responsible? I wasn't sure. Nobody else seemed to be either, the security personnel shifting their attention back and forth between the two hybrids.

Then I watched as Ariane took a step after Ford, and a new idea occurred to me. Maybe it was both of them, working together. I couldn't see Ariane's expression with her back to me, but I recognized the stiff set of her shoulders, the tilt of her head. She'd shut out everything else, drawing deep into herself, into that distant mode where she was both more and less Ariane. She was, in that moment, exactly what they'd created her to be.

Hope flickered inside me. With the two of them together, maybe Ariane would have a chance. Maybe she could get away. . . .

"Stop her. But don't kill her," Laughlin ordered, sounding a little nervous as he backed out of sight behind the first

SUV. Like that would be any protection. It wasn't even clear who he was talking about, Ariane or Ford.

"I said, stand down," Jacobs shouted.

But one of Laughlin's jittery guards had had enough, it seemed. The one closest to Ford aimed at her, his finger on the trigger.

And then everything happened so fast, too fast.

Ford lifted her bound hands, her gaze suddenly a lot sharper, and shoved at him. His weapon arm swung wide, in my direction, and my mom screamed again.

A second shot echoed loudly, and at almost the same time I was knocked to the ground with bone-jarring force.

Ford, throwing me around again. That's what I thought at first.

I tried to sit up and found it hurt more than it should have. A white-hot pain shot up my middle. Ford had probably broken something, damn her.

Then I looked down.

Oh.

It seemed like there should have been more to say or think in that moment, a rush of curses, a wave of panic and pleading and prayer. But that was it: *Oh.* A single word in silence, like a drop of water into ocean.

There was just so much blood, more than I'd ever seen in real life, bright, slippery, and spilling warm across my hand, where I'd pressed it instinctively against my stomach. A loud buzzing started in my ears, and my lips went numb.

Whether that guard had intended to shoot Ford or not, I didn't know. Maybe when she'd used her power to shove his arm away, she'd squeezed too hard and he'd pulled the trigger inadvertently.

Or maybe Ford had done it deliberately, shifting his weapon to aim at me. The one she blamed for all of this. I couldn't argue with that. I blamed myself too.

Regardless, one thing was inescapable: all bullets, even ones released accidentally, have to go somewhere, and this one had found its final destination.

I coughed, choking on a sudden flood of liquid warmth that I suspected was more blood, more life pouring away. I'd been so worried about Ariane's survival, it had honestly never occurred to me to consider my own.

Too late now.

CHAPTER 23

‖‖■■ ‖‖ ‖‖‖■■‖ ‖■‖ ■‖■■‖ ‖‖

Ariane

ARIANE. IT STARTED OFF SMALL, A DISTANT WHISPER IN the back of my brain, a tiny flare of fear and regret. I barely registered it over the buzz and warmth of the power building up inside me and fighting against the drugs they'd pumped into me at Laughlin's facility.

But it remained, distracting me, pulling me out of the zone and the work I had yet to do.

Ariane, I'm sorry. I almost caught a rifle butt to the face that time, my attention pulled by that soft, distant voice.

So I removed the weapons from as many grasping hands as I could, snapping them together like twigs in a firewood bundle and hurling them into the water.

Next to me, Ford sent one of the Laughlin guards crashing into the remaining SUV, denting the entire side with the impact of his body. That man would not be walking away from that injury. Perhaps not ever walking again.

I felt a primitive rush of satisfaction that surprised me with its force.

344

Ariane . . .

This time, the voice penetrated, and it sounded odd, strained, frightened.

Zane. I turned to where I'd last seen him, expecting to find him watching wide-eyed and perhaps horrified by our actions. Instead, he was on the ground, a bright red stain spreading rapidly over the white of his shirt.

The sight sent a jolt through me, and I couldn't move for a second, my brain trying to piece it together, trying to make it make sense.

The second shot. The one from Ford fighting with the guard. Zane. He'd been close. But not that close. Close enough, though, apparently.

The quiet place of power inside my head devolved into a gibbering mess of panic and fear.

He's dying. Zane's dying. No one loses that much blood and survives. MOVE.

I bolted, leaving Ford to handle those who were left. Too many, I knew.

I half stumbled, half fell at Zane's side, my still-bound hands flying up to brace against the ground, his spilled blood sliding over my fingers.

"I'm sorry," he said, turning his head to look at me. He was so pale. His lips looked like gray shadows. "For calling Dr. Jacobs. I thought . . . I thought Ford . . . I saw her leaving with your bag. I thought she was betraying you." His mouth clamped shut suddenly, his teeth chattering. "You should go. Run while Ford has them distracted."

"Shut up. Just . . . don't talk." I shoved my hair out of the way so I could see, feeling the rapidly cooling blood smear across my cheek. "It's okay. You're going to be okay," I said firmly, as if it was an order that he would be required to obey.

I bit down on the inside of my cheek but couldn't stop a muted whimper from escaping as I pressed on the left side of his stomach.

He gasped, his whole body tensing before releasing. "It doesn't hurt that much. So it can't be that bad, right?" He mustered a weak and wet-sounding laugh, then moaned. His eyes closed and a shudder racked him from head to toe.

"Right," I lied, blinking back tears that blurred my vision. It would be better if it hurt. His body was in shock, protecting him from the pain. And there was so much blood, my hands and wrists were already warm with it. "You're going to be fine."

Against my will, diagrams of human anatomy—the position of major blood vessels and organs—memorized years before, flashed in my already woozy mind.

Arterial damage likely, the cool voice in my head recited. *Possibly liver and lung as well, depending on the path of the bullet once it entered his body. If it ricocheted off a rib, spraying bits of bone—*

"Help! I need some help here," I screamed over my shoulder, losing my balance as I did. "Please, someone call an ambulance." The words felt thick and woolly leaving my mouth, and I wasn't sure anyone would understand.

Not that it mattered. No one was listening. As I watched, Ford went down beneath the remaining security personnel taking advantage of her still-weakened state from the drugs and the loss of Nixon.

Dr. Laughlin and Dr. Jacobs were shouting at each other, not seemingly aware of anything else.

Mara, the lone person who seemed to recognize there was a problem, struggled against the chief, who was pulling her into his SUV, where Quinn already sat in the front passenger seat, his eyes wide with terror and confusion. "Zane's hurt!" Her panicked words were loud enough to be heard across the lot. "You have to let me go!" She shoved at her ex-husband.

But the chief didn't stop until she was in the vehicle and he climbed in after her, forcing her into the middle, while he got behind the wheel. Seconds later, the SUV roared past, the wheels chewing up the grass, as the chief drove up the park embankment to reach the road. Mara's fists against the glass were pale flashes of movement inside.

"Mom?" Zane's voice drew my attention back to him. His eyes were closed, but a faint frown creased his forehead. He must have heard her voice.

"Yep," I said. "She's coming." I choked on the lie and the lump in my throat.

Zane's eyes opened, his gaze focusing on me momentarily. He smiled at me. "Hey. You're still here." Then his face crumpled as pain struck somewhere. A tear slipped free from his eye and ran toward his hair.

"I'm so sorry," I whispered, leaning forward to press my mouth against his temple. If I could take this from him, I would, oh God, I would. "This is my fault." If I'd been less selfish, if I'd sent him home, if I'd listened to Mara and Dr. Jacobs, Zane would be safe right now. Home and bored and perfectly fine.

A faint frown creased his forehead. "No . . ." he struggled. "Not your fault. My choice." He swallowed with an effort, coughed, and then went quiet.

I lifted my hands to Zane's chest in a panic, smearing blood all over what remained of his white shirt. I was reassured to feel his chest was rising and falling, though the space between each breath was irregular and getting worse.

But even more alarming than that, when I tried to focus in on his thoughts, I couldn't hear him. Just scraps of words, random scattered images. A quick flash of a purple stuffed rabbit. The smell of a Christmas tree and the crinkle of wrapping paper. His mother, much younger than I'd ever seen her, smiling at him.

He was leaving. His body was giving up, his brain deprived of blood and oxygen, neurons giving off one last spark before they died.

And behind me, Jacobs and Laughlin continued to squabble as if nothing else was going on.

"Please!" I shouted, choking on my sobs. "Help me!" They were doctors, for God's sake—not ones I trusted, but they had to be able to do something.

Then, suddenly, as if someone had heard my entreaty and responded, a siren rose in the distance.

I sagged forward in relief, leaning closer to Zane's ear. My tears dripped onto his face, but he didn't react. "Someone's coming. Just hang in there." I'd never felt more helpless in my life.

Behind me, I sensed the sudden change in activity. Footsteps scrambling, engines revving, and doors being yanked open.

Good. I nodded to myself, trying not to see the new stillness settling over Zane, as if all the tension was draining from him. Laughlin and Jacobs were leaving, gathering up their security personnel along with Ford and Carter and Nixon's body, before the local authorities arrived. Let them go. I would wait here until help came for Zane.

"Just a few more minutes," I said to him, ignoring the slowing blood flow from his side. If they started a transfusion right away—

Hands clasped around my shoulders, and without looking I shoved with my mind, the effort draining what little strength I had left. But the satisfying thud of a body hitting the ground, followed by a grunt of pain, made it worth it.

The sirens grew louder.

"You have to come," Dr. Jacobs said from behind me, cautious but firm.

"No." I didn't bother to look at him. Dr. Jacobs wouldn't get too close. He knew better than that.

"Ariane—"

"Don't call me that," I said, shrill, hysterical. "You don't get to call me that."

"All right. 107." His agreement in that gentle tone somehow made it all so much worse. "You can't help him. You know that."

No, no, no. I turned sharply, scrambling to my feet, fury clearing my head temporarily. I would kill Dr. Jacobs for saying that, for breathing life into that reality with his words. I would stare him down and find his heart and crush it, just like he'd taught me.

But even as I moved toward him, I felt a sharp stab in my arm and recognized it with depressing familiarity. A needle, in the hand of someone less concerned with precision and more focused on just getting it done. One of the retrieval team members had snuck up behind me.

Dr. Jacobs's eyes widened in alarm, and then his face melted away in a blur of colors, cartoon style. "No, that's too much! With the other suppressant in her system already, she'll—"

I didn't get a chance to hear what I would do. A soft rushing sound rose up to greet me, sounding just like the ocean as I'd imagined it.

Everything went white, unimaginably bright, and then there was nothing.

CHAPTER 24

|||||■■ || | |||■■| |■|| |■|■■| |

Ariane

I DIDN'T REMEMBER WAKING UP. THERE WAS A BLANK space, as if the tether of my memories had been severed and I was floating, unaware and free. And then I was blinking up at a ceiling and realizing, slowly, that it was a ceiling.

A ceiling with a skylight that had a view of a fake night sky, including fake stars. The constellations were wrong.

That seemed like it should mean something. Like I should recognize it. But my head felt so heavy and full. I tried to reach up to touch it, to find out if it was actually swaddled in bandages or only felt like it, but something clanked and my arm wouldn't move.

Glancing down, I discovered my wrists were cuffed to the metal bars on either side of the bed where I was lying. It was a hospital bed. An IV was inserted in the back of my right hand, a clear line leading up to two plastic bags of fluid secured to a hook on the wall.

I reached for those bags with my mind, a half-formed

idea of reading the labels or possibly ripping them open, but nothing happened. It was like running into a wall.

And slowly I started to put the pieces together. The dull thickness coating my brain probably meant whatever was in those IVs had tamped down my ability.

"Oh, good, you're awake," a familiar voice said with some relief.

With an effort, I turned my head to the left. An observation window dominated that wall. Behind the glass was Dr. Jacobs, his hair sticking up in all directions and his lab coat torn. I'd never seen him look so out of sorts.

I frowned, trying to understand what was going on. This room wasn't familiar, but that didn't mean it wasn't part of GTX. Had I been at GTX? I struggled to pull up my last memory.

"You gave us quite a scare," Dr. Jacobs said jovially, but his smile didn't extend to his eyes.

"Where am I?" I asked, my tongue unwieldy and less than cooperative. "What happened?"

"You had an adverse reaction to the additional sedatives. Your heart slowed, almost stopped. Dr. Laughlin offered his facility, as it was closer. You would have died if we'd tried to wait." He grimaced, as if my near demise had been such an inconvenience. Which, to him, it probably had been. Only the imminent prospect of my death, and therefore his automatic disqualification from the trials, would have forced him to accept his competitor's hospitality. And Laughlin was, no doubt, gloating about it already.

The memories I'd been searching for suddenly flooded into place. The parking lot. Ford. The exchange. Nixon dying. A second shot. Blood.

I sat up, or tried; the metal restraints screeched against the bars on the side of the bed. "Zane?"

Dr. Jacobs's mouth tightened, and the silence that ensued was answer enough.

My mouth opened in a silent cry of anguish before I could stop it. "What happened? Did you just leave him there?" My imagination supplied an image of Zane lying on the ground, dying alone with no one to at least hold his hand, as black SUVs and vans rushed past.

"I tried to warn you," Dr. Jacobs said sadly. "You aren't meant for life outside."

I wanted to hate him, to seethe and scream at him. But when I looked down at myself, still dressed in my filthy clothes and Zane's blood coating my hands, how could I argue?

I had Zane's blood on my hands, literally and figuratively. Even if it was Dr. Jacobs's fault, I was the one who'd led Zane into it, who hadn't sent him home when I should have, who kept him for myself when I knew what that would likely mean for him.

Dr. Jacobs was still talking in that mournful tone that also managed to be condescending, but I tuned him out, lifting my hand to stare at the blood dried in the lines of my palm and in the edges of my fingernails. It was as if the blood had tried to find a way into a living body and failed, instead pressing itself against my skin as closely possible.

Above that, several dingy square bandages covered the inside of my arm. Laughlin's sample sites. I hadn't noticed them before, at the meet up. But he wouldn't have missed that opportunity. I lamented that none of them were close enough to where Zane's blood might have found entry. Where he might live on in me, in some small way.

I turned away from the observation window as best as I could, hot tears rolling down my cheeks and onto the pillow, dampening it beneath my face. A huge emptiness swelled inside me and I just wanted it to swallow me whole. To take me in so I could get lost inside of it. Just be gone, so I wouldn't have to feel anymore.

But, of course, that didn't happen. I was still stuck here, trapped in this facility, in this bed, in this life that I didn't choose for myself.

"How is our patient?" I recognized Dr. Laughlin's voice. He must have joined Dr. Jacobs behind the observation window.

"She's awake, responsive," Dr. Jacobs said grudgingly.

"Excellent! So happy we could be of service to you," Laughlin said.

"It wouldn't have been necessary if your man hadn't over-reacted and given her too much—"

"He was responding to a threat with nonlethal force, as you requested. Clearly, your system of control is less than reliable. Then again, if you had more than one product to rely upon—"

They sniped back and forth, taking swipes at each other's methodology and "products," and then it got personal.

"You were always a poor student," Dr. Jacobs snapped. "Too eager to advance, never taking the time to think things through."

"Says the jealous old man," Laughlin retorted. "Left behind the times with his old ideas and his backward philosophies."

I closed my hands into fists, feeling Zane's blood sticky between my fingers. This was a game to them. A competition.

One-upmanship. This had nothing to do with me. Or Ford. Or Zane.

They just wanted to win. To beat the other guy. And neither one of them cared what they did to us in the process.

Something inside me shifted, and a hard, cold piece that had formerly bumped and rubbed, never quite fitting in, clicked into place.

End them. That cool inhuman voice inside of me spoke up, and the pain in my heart eased slightly. Fury and hurt converting to something icy, clinical, and more manageable than all these feelings. All this overwhelming humanness.

You can do it, the voice said, getting stronger. My alien side was taking over, and I welcomed it. *But first you have to win.*

I'd been so focused on escaping the trials, I'd never considered another option. They'd taken escape away from me, killed my hope. But that didn't mean they'd beaten me. Far from it.

If I cooperated now, if I worked to win the trials, I would gain some measure of trust. Perhaps even a portion of freedom, having proven myself. And then I would use that freedom to destroy them all. Dr. Jacobs, Dr. Laughlin, Ford, Carter, myself. The entire program.

That was the only way to end this, the only way any of us would ever truly be free. They'd never let us go. Ever. And if we could never truly have lives, if we were only ever to be symbols of their ego, pawns on their board, then what was the point of pretending? Pretending only brought more pain.

A quick flash of Zane's smile, his gray-blue eyes regarding me with warmth, slipped across my mind.

Pretending had brought me to Zane, and my pretending

that we could be together in any real way had taken him away from me.

No. I shook my head, the pillow crinkling beneath me. I was done with pretending.

I'd failed Zane, but I wouldn't fail in this. And I wouldn't die trying, either.

A slow smile spread across my face, autonomic almost, painless and joy free. I would die succeeding, in this one thing at least.

CHAPTER 25
Zane

"CAN YOU HEAR ME?" A WARM HAND SQUEEZED MY shoulder hard, bringing me to awareness with a jolt of pain.

We were somewhere loud, people shouting, an intercom paging a Dr. Johnson to the OR. There was beeping, at regular intervals.

My eyes drifted open. A familiar outline, tall with rumpled hair, loomed over me. Memories fell into place. The man watching my mom's house as Ariane and I watched him. Ariane's flat declaration that he was not with GTX.

The same man at the lake. In the yellow rain jacket.

Who was he? Why was he here? Where was here, anyway?

I tried to ask, but I couldn't make the words come out.

"No, you can't talk. There's a tube in your throat." He looked over his shoulder at something I couldn't see. I wished he would go away. I just wanted to close my eyes again. "We have only a few minutes. My name is Emerson St. John."

Reluctant recognition tugged at me, but I couldn't place

his name. I'd heard it recently, but where? I couldn't concentrate. My body ached everywhere, especially my side where it felt like liquid fire, and yet I felt lighter than I should have, like being drunk but without that lumbering weighty feeling that accompanied it.

Where was my mom? Where was Ariane?

Ariane.

I had a last memory of her worried face over mine, blood smeared on her cheek. Her dark eyes flooded with tears for me. Because I'd betrayed her.

"You're dying." The annoying man interrupted my thoughts again.

I waited but felt no surprise at this revelation.

"They've stabilized you temporarily, but your injuries are too severe. If the shock doesn't end you, an infection will."

Again, this wasn't news to me, even though I still wasn't clear on how I knew what I knew.

"I have one question for you. Do you want a second chance? No matter what the cost?"

Did I? I struggled to think. Of course I wanted to live. I wanted to tell Ariane how sorry I was and—

"Good enough," he muttered.

What?

He patted me on the shoulder, more gently this time. "When you wake, you'll be a whole new man. Hopefully." He sounded pleased.

A little too pleased, actually. If I'd been more coherent, I might have been alarmed.

But I was drifting again, away from the pain, away from the man. Emerson St. John.

There was a loud pop near my ear, then the sound of liquid dripping.

Cold flooded my veins, and the darkness behind my eyelids exploded into stars.

Acknowledgments

THIS BOOK IS BROUGHT TO YOU BY GRANDE TOFFEE NUT hot chocolates, Maui sea glass, my regular seat at Starbucks, a family emergency that ended miraculously well, and many wonderful people.

Christian Trimmer, I don't know what this book would be without you. You said something that really stuck with me and made everything click when I was struggling. Thank you. I'll never be able to say that enough.

Linnea Sinclair, for her endless patience with me, her wisdom, and her willingness to give me a good kick in the pants when I need it. You're my Yoda.

Kristen Tracy, who saved my sanity and *The Rules* by gently reminding me that the middle of the book is important and stuff needs to happen.

Age and Dana Tabion, for allowing me to hijack dinner conversations and turn them into plot discussions. Tornadoes and death by pool skimmer—it's going to happen. Special thanks to Dana, who keeps track of the various stages of my writing despair and reminds me that I've been there before and will be fine.

Valpo people! Ed and Debbie Brown and Becky Douthitt, for being first readers and for sticking with me for all these years. Love you guys! And Tabbi Koller, for getting me that Latin translation for *Queen of the Dead* right when I needed it.

Sue, Dale, Brian, Susan, Allison, and Nathan Klemstein, for being proud of me. That means so much.

Susan Barnes, for patiently listening to me freak out and talking me off the ledge. Michael and Jessica Barnes, for always being supportive, reading my books, and coming to my events (and bringing Grace and Josh!). My mom and dad, for Sunday phone calls and Saturday breakfasts. I love you.

And finally, you. Yes, YOU. Thank you for reading my books. I have the best job in the whole world, and it's because of you.